NO STONE LEFT UNTURNED

A Detective Honeywell Mystery

ANNETTE DASHOFY

One More Chapter
a division of HarperCollins*Publishers*
1 London Bridge Street
London SE1 9GF
www.harpercollins.co.uk
HarperCollins*Publishers*
Macken House, 39/40 Mayor Street Upper,
Dublin 1, D01 C9W8, Ireland

This paperback edition 2025

First published in Great Britain in ebook format
by HarperCollins*Publishers* 2025
Copyright © Annette Dashofy 2025
Annette Dashofy asserts the moral right to be identified
as the author of this work

A catalogue record of this book is available from the British Library

ISBN: 978-0-00-871042-2

USA Today bestseller Annette Dashofy is the author of over a dozen novels including the five-time Agatha-nominated Zoe Chambers mystery series about a paramedic-turned-coroner in rural Pennsylvania. Her standalone, *Death By Equine,* won the 2021 Dr. Tony Ryan Book Award for excellence in thoroughbred racing literature. This is the third book in her Detective Honeywell mystery series set along the shores of Lake Erie. Annette and her husband live in the United States on ten acres of what was her grandfather's Pennsylvania dairy farm with one very spoiled cat.

www.annettedashofy.com

facebook.com/Annette.Dashofy
instagram.com/annettedashofy

Also by Annette Dashofy

Zoe Chambers Mystery Series

Circle of Influence

Lost Legacy

Bridges Burned

With a Vengeance

No Way Home

Uneasy Prey

Cry Wolf

Fair Game

Under the Radar

Til Death

Fatal Reunion

Crime in the Country

Helpless

What Comes Around

Standalone titles

Death by Equine

Detective Honeywell Mystery Series

Where the Guilty Hide

Keep Your Family Close

The Devil Comes Calling

No Stone Left Unturned

To Ray, who is always there when I need him, but who also knows to go fishing when I need to write

<h1 style="text-align:center">Chapter One</h1>

Dr. Shawn Malone closed the manilla folder containing enough pages of reports to rival *War and Peace*. The veterinary version.

Mrs. Winston embraced her geriatric black and white cat and beamed, her faded eyes damp with grateful tears. "I can't thank you enough, Dr. Shawn," she said.

"You're very welcome." The cat bore the unoriginal name of Fuzzy, and Shawn had been caring for her since she was little more than a mewling handful of fluff. Now, the elderly owner brought her beloved pet into the West Erie Veterinary Clinic every month or two for various age-related maladies. This visit had him following up on Fuzzy's hyperthyroidism and delivering good news. The change in medication had resulted in improved numbers on her blood panels. Equally good was the eight ounces she'd gained. "Besides, you have yourself to thank as much as me. You're the one who's so diligent about giving Fuzzy her meds."

"She's a good girl." Mrs. Winston stroked the cat's soft fur. "More cooperative than most of the others I've owned in my life. I'm very lucky."

1

Shawn added a gentle scratch of his own to Fuzzy's chin. The cat was equally lucky to have such a devoted owner—although from his experience with felines, there was always a question of who owned whom.

Mrs. Winston bent over in her chair and gently deposited the cat into its red soft-sided carrier. She zipped the lid closed and stood, lifting her precious cargo.

"Don't hesitate to call if you have any questions or concerns," Shawn said as he followed his client into the now empty waiting room.

Robin, his receptionist, waved the elderly woman over to her computer. His office manager stepped from behind the counter, concerned lines etching her forehead.

"What's wrong, Bethany?" Shawn asked. "It's quitting time on a Friday. You should be smiling."

She met his gaze, and he knew his own hopes of getting home on time were about to be dashed. "We've got one more patient to deal with." Bethany read from the file she held. "John Boyd is bringing his dog in."

Shawn echoed the name back at her. "Have we seen them before?"

"No, but he sounded distraught on the phone. Said he's afraid to let things go over the weekend, and he can't afford an emergency vet."

Shawn sighed. All of his staff had kind hearts. He wouldn't have hired them otherwise. But Bethany had perhaps the softest touch and shared his weakness for those who struggled financially. He gestured at her to continue.

"Mr. Boyd has a thirteen-year-old shepherd mix. Says she's lethargic and not eating well."

Shawn removed his bifocals and rubbed his tired eyes. "Do you mind sticking around to help out?"

"Of course not."

He replaced his glasses on his nose. "See if one of the techs is willing to stay a little longer. I'm going to call my wife and let her know I'll be late. Give me a shout when they arrive."

"Sure thing." Bethany pivoted and bustled away.

Shawn made his way to his office, where built-in desktops lined two walls, and lowered into his chair. The other two currently empty seats were assigned to the pair of veterinarians he employed to handle the demands of his clinic. As was usually the case, he was the last of the trio to leave. It was his name on the business license and the building's lease, after all.

Besides, the others had spouses with "normal" nine-to-five jobs.

He pulled up Cassie's number and listened to the ringback tones.

"Hello, handsome," she answered.

"Hello, beautiful." They'd used this same greeting since their first date thirty-eight years ago when they'd been sophomores at Ohio State, he studying veterinary medicine, she studying criminal law.

"Let me guess," Cassie said. "You have to stay late."

"It's always either you or me."

"Or both."

"I'll be home as soon as I can. I shouldn't be too long." He hoped.

"Just remember we promised to take Alissa to Splash Lagoon tomorrow."

"Good lord, I don't plan to be here all night. And no, I haven't forgotten."

"All right then. I'll see you when I see you. Love you, babe."

"Love you more." He ended the call and turned to find Bethany in the doorway, grinning. "Are you eavesdropping?"

"Just taking notes for when I'm lucky enough to find the right guy."

"Has our new patient arrived?"

"They're in room one."

Shawn entered the exam room to find a man with a scraggly gray beard and wearing clothes that looked like they'd been slept in. At his feet lay an equally rumpled dog, mostly shepherd, some husky, maybe some standard poodle in the mix if Shawn was to guess.

The man looked up, his pale eyes appearing sharp despite his slouched posture. "Dr. Malone?" He extended a hand.

Shawn clasped it. "Yes, sir. Mr. Boyd?"

"Just John is fine."

"Dr. Shawn." He looked at the dog. "And who do we have here?"

"Daisy. She's not feeling well. Not eating. Not moving around much. I'm worried about her."

The dog didn't lift her head from her paws even at the mention of her name. Shawn lowered to the floor beside Daisy, ignoring the twinge in his left knee. He reached the back of one hand toward her, and she raised her muzzle to sniff. When her tail thumped the floor, Shawn stroked her head. The tail thumped harder.

He checked her teeth and slightly inflamed gums. The dog needed a dental but wasn't dehydrated. As Shawn continued his physical exam, he questioned the owner about Daisy's dietary habits and exercise routine. He'd almost reached the dog's tail when a loud thud, as if something had been knocked over, filtered through the closed exam room door. Then a scream.

Shawn and Daisy scrambled to their feet. The dog backpedaled toward a corner.

"Stay here," Shawn told John, who hadn't moved beyond going wide-eyed and slack-jawed.

Shawn opened the door and stepped into the waiting room.

Bethany stood behind the counter, both hands raised. He followed her gaze. And froze.

A man attired in black, including a black N95 mask like the ones everyone had worn during the pandemic, swung toward Shawn, aiming a handgun his way.

Calmly, he pulled the exam room door closed behind him. "What do you want?"

"Cash," came the gruff reply. "And drugs."

Shawn shot a glance at Bethany. He sensed she wanted to tell him something but was afraid. He gave a minute shake of his head. The last thing he wanted was to put her in more danger than they already were.

A second crash reverberated from the rear of the clinic. That's what she wanted to tell him. There was more than this one intruder.

"We'll give you what we have." Shawn kept his voice level. He'd been married to a cop for decades. He hoped some of Cassie's hostage negotiation skills had rubbed off on him. "Bethany, give him all the cash we have on hand."

The gun swung toward her. "Do it," the man in black said, his tone fierce.

She dropped her hands to the desk in front of her. Although they were hidden by the counter, Shawn knew she was opening the money drawer. He also knew she was hitting the panic button for the security system.

Another crash. Another shriek. Erin, one of Shawn's vet techs, staggered into the waiting room, arms raised. A second intruder followed, one hand aiming a revolver at her head, the other on her shoulder. He wore the same black clothing and mask as his partner.

"You get what we came for?" the first man asked.

The second jerked his head toward the back. "She unlocked the drug cabinet. He's cleaning it out."

So, there were three, Shawn thought.

Erin met his gaze. "I'm sorry."

He shook his head. "You did fine."

Bethany placed a small stack of bills on the counter, her hands trembling.

"That's all?" the first man said. "You're holding out on us."

"No," she whimpered.

"Very few of our clients pay with cash anymore," Shawn said. He felt the man's eyes on him. Debating whether to believe the vet. "It's true. Let my manager step out here and you can look for yourself." Shawn immediately winced. What if the gunman went behind the counter and spotted the panic button?

Instead, he apparently accepted Shawn at his word and nodded. "Put it in a bag," he told Bethany.

She snatched one of the plastic totes they kept on hand to hold the assorted medications and flea treatments they provided to their clientele. After stuffing the cash into the bag, she shoved it at the man, who snatched it from her.

To the first gunman, Shawn said, "We've given you everything you asked for. Take it and go."

"In a minute."

Footsteps clomped from the rear. A third man in black appeared, carrying another bag, the fingers of his other hand entwined in Robin's hair, steering her ahead of him. Shawn felt certain this bag was filled with drugs, but he was more concerned about his receptionist. And with getting the gunmen to leave. Thankfully, the man released Robin, giving her a shove toward the front desk. She stumbled, caught her balance, and staggered to Bethany's side.

The first man stalked toward Erin, grabbed her by the arm, and pushed her out of the way. He handed the money to the man who'd been holding his gun on the tech. But none of them made a move toward the door.

Instead, the first man fixed his gaze on Shawn. Between the hoodie and the mask, only a miniscule amount of skin and his eyes were visible. Light brown skin, much lighter than Shawn's. And green eyes. Cold, soulless green eyes.

"Take what you came for and go," Shawn said softly but firmly. Even as he said the words, he knew the man had no intention of complying. He watched the intruder's gun come up. He heard the blast. And felt the searing burn as the bullet pierced his chest.

Chapter Two

Detective Matthias Honeywell scanned his report one last time. Satisfied, he clicked submit before leaning back in his chair and stretching his arms over his head with a groan of relief.

Behind him, his partner, Detective Sergeant Cassie Malone, chuckled from her cubicle. "I know how you feel," she said. "If ever there was a case I'm glad to see cleared, it's this one."

They'd spent the last month investigating a series of attempted child abductions. Two men had tried to lure six different kids into a white van. Thankfully, the first attempt failed because the little girl was well schooled on stranger-danger by her parents. After that, the word was out, local children were wary, and adults were vigilant. Still, the suspects remained elusive until they almost succeeded. They grabbed a four-year-old girl who'd escaped from her mother and was running down the sidewalk, giggling. The kidnappers might have gotten away with her if it weren't for a neighbor who not only witnessed the snatch but who'd turned his Rottweiler loose. The dog, it turned out, loved kids but did not love creeps in vans. By the time the police arrived, the youngster was safe with her mom. The Rottweiler still had the pervert's arm clamped in his jaw. And the pervert was begging to be arrested as long as someone called off the dog. His partner had bailed on him, which pissed him off even more. Freed from the Rottweiler and cuffed in the back of an ambulance, he'd given Matthias and Cassie every detail on his buddy, save for his social security number, which he'd have volunteered had he known it.

Now, both were locked up and waiting to be arraigned.

Matthias pushed up from his chair and circled the partition separating his cubby from that of his partner. "Things could've gone sideways so easily," he said.

Cassie ran a hand over her short light gray hair which stood out in stark contrast to her dark skin. "I need to ask Shawn if that dog is one of his patients." She logged out of her computer. "If it is, I'm going to suggest he give it free care for the rest of its life."

Matthias chuckled. "I overheard you on the phone with him a few minutes ago. I gather your dinner plans aren't happening."

"No, but that's status quo at our house. You know that. A vet and a cop. One of us is always called away on some sort of emergency. Tomorrow, though, we're shutting off our phones. We promised Alissa a day at Splash Lagoon before school starts." Cassie looked up at him. "What about you and Emma? Plans for the weekend?"

"Yeah."

Cassie eyed him. "Not giving me any juicy details?"

"Nope." The truth was he and his girlfriend of almost three months intended to spend the entire weekend together, either relaxing at his apartment or enjoying the beach at Presque Isle State Park. No demands on their time. No watching the clock. Just chilling for the next forty-eight hours or so.

Cassie's phone vibrated on her desk.

Matthias pointed to it. "You didn't turn it off soon enough."

"It's Shawn's clinic." She picked up the device but scowled. "Odd that it's not coming from his personal number."

A knock on the Major Crimes Unit's door frame drew Matthias's attention as Cassie took the call. Lieutenant Armstrong tipped his head, signaling Matthias to follow him. As odd as it was for Cassie to get a call from the clinic rather than from her husband, it was even odder for the lieutenant to beckon Matthias out of Major Crimes. Ordinarily, he'd call if they had a case or speak to them at their desks.

Matthias joined Armstrong in the small breakroom. The lines creasing the lieutenant's face, the set of his jaw, put Matthias on alert. "What's up?"

Cassie's voice rose from behind him. "Bethany, slow down. What are you talking about?"

The lieutenant's gaze darted toward the door before coming back to Matthias. "There's been an armed robbery and a shooting at West Erie Veterinary Clinic."

"Shawn?" Matthias said, keeping his voice low.

Armstrong gave one quick nod.

"Is he...?"

"He's alive as of five minutes ago. I need you to take the lead on this one. Cassie can't be part of the investigation."

The words made sense, but Matthias knew his partner. The love of her life, her husband of more than three decades, was a victim of crime. She would demand to be involved in the case, protocol and lieutenant's orders be damned.

As if reading Matthias's mind, Armstrong said, "She needs to put her full attention on her husband and granddaughter."

"Understood."

"This is our top priority right now. I called Frazier and Roth. They'll meet you there."

Cassie, her purse slung over one shoulder, burst through the door, her dark skin uncharacteristically pale, her black eyes wide and glistening. "We have to go."

Armstrong placed a hand on her shoulder. "Listen—"

She shrugged it off. "My husband's been shot."

"I know."

She looked at Matthias. "Come on. We have to get over there."

"You're not on this case," Armstrong said in his commander's voice.

Cassie spun toward him. "I don't give a damn if I'm on the case or not. I need to see my husband."

Matthias reached toward the lieutenant. "She's right. I'll drive her to the clinic. Tell Frazier and Roth I'm on my way." Lowering his voice he added, "I've got this," his words directed equally to both of them.

Armstrong studied him. Matthias raised an eyebrow, hoping his superior officer wouldn't make Cassie drive her personal vehicle across town.

"Come on." Cassie jabbed Matthias's arm and pushed past them, heading for the stairs.

The lieutenant didn't speak but lowered his head, and Matthias strode after his partner.

"If you can't drive any faster, get out and let me behind the wheel."

Matthias ignored Cassie's griping. She hadn't argued when he'd insisted on driving. Uncharacteristic for her. Now, faced with navigating the streets of Erie during Friday night rush hour, he endured her alternately ordering him to slow down before he rear-ended the car in front of them and demanding he stop driving like an old lady. He kept silent, knowing his partner was freaking out. Also uncharacteristic for her.

The area around the vet clinic was clogged with law enforcement cruisers from various jurisdictions—Erie, Millcreek, and Pennsylvania State Police—plus an EmergyCare ambulance, which was backed up to the main entrance. Everyone around the city who owned a pet knew Dr. Shawn. And everyone in local law enforcement knew who he was married to.

Cassie unclipped her seatbelt and reached for the door handle before Matthias had pulled to a complete stop. He caught her arm. "Hold on a minute."

She swore at him, wrenched free, and leaped out as he jammed on the brake. Watching her jog toward the clinic entrance, Matthias breathed a growling sigh before maneuvering the unmarked Chevy Malibu into a spot next to one of the PSP Interceptors.

A uniformed officer with a clipboard stood at the clinic's front door. "Lyle," Matthias said in acknowledgment. "So, you got stuck with keeping out the riffraff?"

"Yeah. I suck at rock, paper, scissors." Lyle scribbled on the clipboard, adding Matthias to the list of people entering the crime scene.

"Don't suppose Frazier's here yet."

"Nope."

Matthias wasn't surprised. He didn't see Frazier's or Roth's cars among the vehicles jamming the street. Considering the other detectives had been roused from home and the traffic around town right now, Matthias figured he'd be on his own for a while. He thanked Lyle and stepped inside.

Cassie was standing next to Shawn, who lay on a stretcher with two paramedics working feverishly over him. Matthias took it as a good sign. Had Shawn been dead, there would be no need.

Matthias surveyed the scene around the patient. A young woman huddled behind a reception counter, clutching tissues to her face as she spoke with a uniformed officer. A second woman and a second patrolman conversed in a hallway that led toward the rear of the building. A third uniform stood guard at a closed door, which Matthias knew from previous visits, led to Shawn's office. A fourth blocked one of the exam rooms, his arms crossed.

A closer sweep of the scene brought Matthias's focus to a glistening crimson pool on the floor between the gurney and the fourth cop. Cassie looked up, tears gleaming, and met Matthias's gaze. He moved in her direction, careful to stay out of the way of the lifesaving efforts.

"Frazier and Roth aren't here yet," she said, her voice quivering.

"Don't get any ideas about trying to fill in."

Her gaze returned to her husband. "I'm not."

"How many people were in the building when this all went down?" Matthias mused out loud, not expecting her to know.

But of course, she did, even though she'd only been there a few minutes. "Robin the receptionist and Bethany the office manager up front. A tech in the rear. A client and his dog in there." She tipped her head toward the door being guarded by the fourth cop. "Everyone except the client witnessed the shooting."

"And me," Shawn whispered. "I witnessed it, too."

"Shush," Cassie told him. "We'll take your statement later. After they get you to the hospital."

At least he was talking, Matthias thought. Conscious and alert was always a good thing.

"Speaking of getting him to the hospital," one of the paramedics said, "we're ready to transport."

"You go with him," Matthias told Cassie. "I'll take care of the investigation."

He expected an argument. He didn't receive one. She nodded in agreement. But as the medics rolled the stretcher toward the door, Cassie caught Matthias's arm. "You find out who did this and arrest the bastard."

"Yes, ma'am," Matthias said, letting his native Oklahoman drawl briefly creep into his voice. "You have my word."

She gave another nod, released her grip, and hurried after her husband and the ambulance crew. Over her shoulder, she yelled, "Keep me posted."

Matthias watched them exit the clinic, took another look around, and contemplated the two closed doors with patrolmen standing guard. He moved toward Shawn's office. "Who's in there?" he asked the uniform.

"Woman by the name of Bethany Stone. She's the clinic's manager."

Matthias looked at the door to the exam room where, if Cassie was correct—and she was almost always correct—a man and his dog waited. Matthias decided to speak with him first out of courtesy to the ailing dog. He gave the pool of blood a wide berth as he crossed the waiting room. The forensic techs would bitch about all the first responders contaminating the crime scene. He didn't want to add to their aggravation. The officer guarding the door stepped aside, granting Matthias entry.

An older man with an unkempt beard and wearing a threadbare brown shirt, stained and wrinkled khaki pants, and a camo ball cap sat slump-shouldered in the exam room's chair. At his feet, a doleful looking dog didn't bother to raise his head when Matthias stepped inside, but its brown eyes lifted.

Matthias knelt to offer the back of his hand to the dog, who sniffed and offered a tail-wag. "Hey, buddy."

"She's a girl dog," the owner said.

"Sorry. Hi, pretty girl." Matthias stroked her head. Standing, he offered his hand to the owner and introduced himself. "Detective Honeywell, Erie City Police. And you are?"

"John Boyd. What's going on out there? Is it safe?"

"The scene's been secured." Matthias withdrew his notebook from the hip pocket of his trousers. "Mr. Boyd, can you tell me what you saw or heard?"

"Not much. The vet came in and started looking at Daisy, but then there was a ruckus." Boyd gestured at the door. "A lady screamed. The vet excused himself and closed the door behind him. Then, there was a gunshot and more screams." Boyd leaned down to pet Daisy.

"What about before that? Did you notice anyone or anything out of the ordinary while you were in the waiting room?"

"No." He straightened. "I mean, we weren't. In the waiting room, that is. We came in the side door."

"Why not the front entrance?"

"I'd told the lady on the phone how anxious Daisy gets around other animals, and her being sick already, I didn't want the added stress of having to sit around with other dogs. All I was hoping for was to bring her straight into a room, but then she mentioned bypassing the waiting room altogether. I thought that was perfect."

Matthias made a note. "Did you notice anyone else when you came in?"

Boyd appeared puzzled. "There was the woman who let me in. And another woman at the front desk. The only other person I saw was the vet."

"No other patients?"

"No." Boyd's eyes shifted in thought. "The waiting room was completely empty. I could've come in the front entrance after all."

Matthias made another note. "Did you notice anyone else in the parking lot?"

Boyd shook his head.

"Anyone waiting in a car?"

"No."

"Anyone hanging around the side entrance?"

"No. No one. Oh, wait. I did see an older woman leave as I was crossing the parking lot. She was carrying one of those pet carrier things."

"She left through the side door?"

"No. The front."

Matthias studied the man and his dog. "Are you a regular client here?"

"First time." Boyd lowered his gaze. "That poor vet. I guess it might be my last."

"Do you mind telling me what's wrong with your dog?"

"Daisy hasn't been her usual energetic self."

Matthias looked at the dog lying at her master's feet and had a hard time picturing her as energetic. No wonder Boyd was worried.

"And she's not eating well. I don't have a lot of money, and I heard this clinic is sympathetic to pet owners who can't afford expensive vet bills. I was grateful when they agreed to see her on a Friday. I was afraid to put it off until Monday." Boyd looked at his dog and sighed. "I guess I have no choice now."

Matthias thought of the other vets in the practice. Weekend or not, under the circumstances, one of them might be willing to come in and examine old Daisy. "Let me see what I can find out for you."

The older man fixed his gaze on Matthias. "That vet. Is he … okay?"

"He's being transported to the hospital." Matthias flipped a page in his notebook and held it and his pen out to Boyd. "If you wouldn't mind, write down your address and phone number in case I have any more questions for you."

The bearded man scowled at the items without reaching for them. "I'm… I don't have a regular address. Or a phone."

Matthias flashed on the homeless encampment on East 16th Street he'd had to deal with a few months back. But those folks had moved elsewhere. "Is there any way I can reach you? A shelter? Someone who takes messages for you?"

Boyd shifted in his seat. "I live in my car. Daisy and me. But there's a recycling place down on Tow Road. You know it?"

"I do."

"You can get a message to me there." He gave a weak grin. "I pick up aluminum cans around town and at the park and cash them in for spending money."

Matthias jotted down the recycling center and street name before digging out a business card and handing it to Boyd. "If you think of anything else, call me."

He stuffed it into his shirt pocket without looking at it. "Am I free to go?"

"You are but stick around for a couple of minutes." Matthias bent down to stroke the dog's head. "I'm going to find you another vet to check out Daisy."

Chapter Three

Emma Anderson stood behind the Kia Sportage ErieLIVE had assigned to her partner and dug the Nikon from her backpack, which she then slung over one shoulder. She checked the camera's settings before sliding the strap over her head. As a relatively new hire, she should feel pride in her promotion to crime beat photographer. Instead, she still struggled with the sense of intrusion. She needed to create images of people on their worst day. Grief. Terror. Guilt. Those were the emotions she attempted to capture. Some days, she wished she could go back to chasing local kids around a soccer field or basketball court, snapping pictures of joy and determination. Even the sorrow of defeat was better than the sorrow of real loss.

Today was one of those days.

The police scanner at the news outlet's office had reported a shooting at the West Erie Veterinary Clinic. Emma had only lived in this northern Pennsylvania city since February, but she knew the clinic. She knew Dr. Shawn Malone. She knew his wife, Cassie.

Emma was dating—was falling in love with—Cassie's partner.

Preston Guilfoyle, the reporter Emma was assigned to, joined her at the rear of the car, his phone pressed to his ear. "Thanks," he said to the person on the other end of his call. "I appreciate the info."

"What'd you find out?" she asked as he pocketed his cell.

"Shooting victim was Dr. Shawn." Preston's tone was sullen.

Dr. Shawn had helped Preston adopt his cat. This one was personal for both of them. "How is he?" she asked.

"My source wouldn't say. Either he doesn't know, or they just aren't releasing information yet."

She lifted the Nikon to her eye and scanned the lot. Police cars from various jurisdictions. An unmarked car. She wondered if it was Matthias's. Would he be here? Surely Cassie wasn't. She'd be at the hospital with her husband.

Emma *hoped* Shawn was at the hospital. She didn't want to think about the alternative.

Preston caught her arm, and she lowered the camera. "You have a source in the department, who could give us information," he said, one hopeful eyebrow hiked.

They'd been through this before. Ever since her relationship with the detective had become public knowledge, Preston and other reporters at ErieLIVE would prod her to get them a scoop. Unless all they wanted was an answer to some minor question, she steadfastly refused. A journalist—even a photojournalist—in a relationship with a cop was a recipe for strife. Conflicts of interest abounded.

This time, though, she was tempted to fire off a text, ask Matthias if the vet was okay. If Cassie was okay. Hell, Emma and Matthias had been over to the Malones' home for a picnic last weekend. The sound of Shawn's raucous laughter echoed in her memory. A text wouldn't be a conflict. It would be a show of concern for one of their friends.

Except Preston was the one wanting answers and not simply because he'd adopted his kitty from the vet.

"No," Emma said.

The reporter looked crestfallen. "Come on, Em. Matthias will tell you what's going on in there. You know he will."

"It's an active investigation," she said, using Matthias's routine response to the press.

"Whose side are you on? We're trying to get a story. You have a source. As a member of the press, you're obligated to use whatever methods you have available."

Emma stepped back and eyed Preston. "*You* are trying to get a story. I'm here to get photographs. Don't make me choose between this job and my relationship with Matthias. It won't go the way you want." Even as she spoke the words, she wondered if she sounded as convincing as she intended. The truth was her "relationship" was nowhere near the commitment stage. If she was faced with the choice between the job or the man, she'd be foolish to give up a solid income for a cop who admitted to a lousy track record with women. Still, she didn't want to give up either, especially for the sole purpose of providing Preston with a scoop.

"That's not what I'm doing." The reporter crossed his arms. "I know you think I'm nothing more than a newshound—"

"Not true." Emma had seen the more human side of the man.

He shrugged. "I honestly like Dr. Shawn. I'd like to know if he's okay. Can't you text Matthias off the record?"

With Preston and most reporters, there was no such thing as off the record. She waved an arm around at the police officers manning the crime scene taped perimeter, keeping curious pedestrians away from the clinic. "Do your job. Ask questions. I'll do mine and take pictures. Maybe there will be an official statement made soon." She pivoted and strode away.

"If not, then will you text him?" Preston called after her.

She pretended to not hear, lifted the Nikon, and began snapping images of the clinic, the crowd, and the police vehicles.

Once she'd put enough time and distance between her and her partner, she cast a look around. Preston had found a woman at the edge of the police tape to interview. Emma pulled out her phone and touched the text icon. She tapped out the start of a message, asking Matthias if Shawn was okay. Then she pressed the backspace button and watched as the words vanished.

Matthias approached the front desk and the wide-eyed young woman sitting behind the counter. She introduced herself as Robin, one of the clinic's receptionists.

He gestured over his shoulder toward the exam room. "The man in there ... is there any chance you can call in one of the clinic's other vets to take a look at his dog?"

The woman caught her lip in her teeth and looked in that direction. No, Matthias thought, not in the direction of the exam room but at the pool of Shawn's blood in front of it.

"Not here," Matthias said, understanding her trepidation. "The clinic is a crime scene for the next day or so."

"We have a vet truck parked out back," she offered. "We usually use it for mobile spay-and-neuter events in surrounding communities. I can try to get someone to come in. He could see the patient out there."

Matthias thanked her. "I'll be back to talk with you once you're done."

"I already answered that other police officer's questions."

"I realize that." He gave her a practiced smile meant to put civilians at ease. Cassie always told him it failed. "I'll need you to answer a few more questions for me."

She studied him and returned the smile, hers showing more than a hint of flirtatiousness. "Okay. I'll be here."

Maybe this time it worked *too* well.

He turned in time to see Detectives Brad Frazier and Vince Roth trailing the crime scene techs through the front door.

Frazier spotted Matthias and said something to Roth. They veered in his direction. "How's Cassie?" Frazier asked.

"She's at the hospital with her husband and trusts us to handle this case."

"In other words, she's a wreck."

"Pretty much."

Roth took in the scene. "What do we know so far?"

Matthias updated them on his talk with the pet owner. "Uniforms have interviewed the receptionist behind the counter and the tech over there, who also witnessed the shooting." He tipped his head toward the hallway where the vet tech was now seated in a chair someone must've dragged from an exam room. "The third witness, the clinic's manager, is waiting in the office."

"What's the plan, Stan?" Frazier asked. As usual, his sense of humor fell flat.

"Divide and conquer. I'll take the manager." He looked at Frazier. "You reinterview the receptionist." Matthias turned to Roth. "You talk to the tech. Then compare notes with the officers who took their original statements."

"Do you suspect one of them is involved?"

"I suspect everyone. This is Cassie's husband we're talking about."

Frazier nodded. "No stone unturned."

"We'll compare notes after I hear what the manager has to say, then check security footage."

"On it," both detectives said in unison and strode off toward their assignments.

Matthias noted the receptionist was still on the phone, tracking down a vet for Daisy. She held up a wait-a-minute finger at Frazier.

Matthias crossed the waiting room and rapped lightly on the office door. A faint voice called out, "Come in."

He entered to find a young woman with short brown hair and red-rimmed hazel eyes. She sat stiffly in one of the swivel chairs, clutching a tissue in one hand and a bottle of water in the other.

She looked at Matthias, her anxiety evident. "Dr. Shawn. Is he…?"

"He's alive and"—Matthias checked his watch—"should be at the hospital by now."

"Oh." She breathed a heavy exhalation. "Good. I was so scared."

Matthias rolled another chair over to her and introduced himself.

She set the water on the desk and shook his hand. Hers was cool and damp from the condensation on the bottle. "I'm Bethany Stone, the clinic's office manager."

"Sorry to meet you under these circumstances." He tried to be discreet as he wiped his now wet hand on his trousers.

Her apologetic wince told him she'd noticed.

"I understand you witnessed what happened."

"I did." Her voice was barely a whisper.

"I know it's hard, but I'd like you to tell me about it."

She drew a breath. Blew it out. "We shouldn't have even been here."

"What do you mean?"

"Most of the staff had left already. Dr. Shawn was in with our last scheduled client."

"John Boyd and Daisy," Matthias said.

"No. Mrs. Winston and her cat, Fuzzy. Mr. Boyd was a last-minute emergency case. I took his call, while Dr. Shawn was finishing up with Fuzzy."

"Tell me about that call."

"The poor man was distraught about his dog. He said she was

lethargic and wasn't eating. He was afraid to let it go on any longer and said he couldn't afford an emergency vet on the weekend. I got the impression he couldn't afford a normal vet bill regardless, but it's our business model to work with low-income pet owners." Bethany took a sip from her water bottle. "He was also concerned about stressing Daisy out more than she already was. She gets nervous around other animals."

"What happened next?"

"When Dr. Shawn was done with Fuzzy, I told him about the new patient. He came in here to call his wife."

Matthias remembered Cassie taking the call.

"Mr. Boyd and Daisy arrived while he was on the phone, and I put them in Exam Room One."

"Did he come in through the front door?" Matthias already knew the answer.

"No. Like I said, he was worried about Daisy being stressed, so I directed him to come in through the side door."

"Is that common?"

Bethany considered the question. "It's not *un*common. We use that entrance to bring in emergency cases, hyper or aggressive animals, or large incapacitated pets. Anytime the owner wishes to bypass the waiting room, or we feel it's better for all involved."

He made a note. "Go on. You said you put Mr. Boyd in the exam room."

"Once Dr. Shawn was done with his phone call, he went in to see the patient." The water bottle in Bethany's hand quivered. "I was at the front desk with Robin, working on getting everything shut down for the weekend, when they just appeared out of nowhere."

"Who?"

She stared at her lap. "Three men with guns. I heard a crash and looked up to see one of them had knocked over a display shelf. Robin screamed. It's like they were just ... *there*."

"What happened next?" He had more questions for Bethany, but he wanted to hear the entire story from her first.

"One of the men ... he seemed to be the leader ... ordered Robin to take the other two into the back. He said, 'You know what we're here for.' Then he asked me who all was still in the building. I don't even remember if I answered, but I saw Dr. Shawn come out of the exam room. The man saw him, too, and aimed the gun at him. After that, everything happened so fast, it's a blur. I think Dr. Shawn asked what he wanted. One of the other men reappeared with Erin. Then they ordered me to give them all our cash. It wasn't much. Most of our clients pay with credit cards these days, and Dr. Shawn told them so. I gave him what little we had. That's when the third man came back and had Robin by her hair. He carried a bag, which I assume was filled with drugs. He pushed her and she almost fell but managed to get away from him. They could've just left at that point. They had what they came for." Bethany pressed her tissue to her nose.

"What happened?" Matthias asked softly.

"He shot him. The man aimed his gun at Dr. Shawn and—" She hiccupped a sob, shaking her head.

Matthias gave her a moment to regroup. At the same time, he studied his notes and his questions. After Bethany blew her nose, he asked, "Can you give me a description of the men?"

"They were all dressed alike. Black hoodies, black pants, black gloves, and black masks."

"Ski masks?" It was a sultry eighty-degree day outside. They likely removed the face coverings as soon as they left. Local security footage might've caught something.

"No. N95s."

"Is there anything you noticed from what little you could see? Skin color? Eye or hair color? Scars?" He touched his own, just above his left eyebrow.

She pursed her lips, thinking. "Two of them were White. The

man who—" Her voice cracked. "The man who shot Dr. Shawn was a lighter-skinned Black man, I think. I couldn't tell you eye color. All I was looking at were their guns. They had hoodies pulled over their hair, so I don't know about that either." She lowered her face. "I'm sorry."

"Don't be. You might remember more as time goes on. And we might catch something on your security footage."

Bethany looked skeptical.

"You mentioned they just appeared out of nowhere while you were at the front desk. Could they have slipped in through the main entrance unnoticed?"

"No way. We were going over the day's records, but neither of us was so engrossed that we'd have missed them."

"What other access points do you have?"

"There's a door in the rear that we use for deliveries, but it's alarmed and shrieks loud enough to break your eardrums when someone opens it."

"Unless someone disabled the alarm."

From her expression, she hadn't considered that option.

Matthias made a note to himself to check the rear entry alarm. "What about the side door? The one Mr. Boyd used? Is it alarmed, too?"

"No one can open it from the outside. Only the inside. And we don't activate the alarm system on it until the last person leaves."

"So, you let Mr. Boyd in?"

"That's correct."

"Are you sure it latched when you closed it after him?"

Her lips parted as if to answer, but she closed them and scowled. "I'm certain it closed." Her tone contradicted her words.

Matthias leaned toward her, bracing his elbows on his knees. "Which exit did the assailants use when they left?"

She swallowed hard. "The side door," she said, barely audible.

Matthias had one more question for her, one that had nagged

him since he'd spoken to John Boyd. "You had Mr. Boyd bring his dog through that side door because he told you Daisy was nervous being around other animals."

"That's right."

"You also said Mrs. Winston's cat was the last appointment of the day."

"Yes."

"If the waiting room was empty, why make Boyd and Daisy come through the side entrance?"

Bethany gaped at him. The only sound in the office was the crackle of the plastic water bottle clutched in her hands. After several long moments, she shook her head. "I don't know."

Chapter Four

While Preston interviewed a businessman who worked across the street from the vet clinic, Emma wandered the outer perimeter of the crime scene tape, capturing photos of the building, the police presence, the crowd of onlookers.

When she'd first taken over as crime beat photographer, she'd harbored a few dreams of standing beside Matthias as he did his cop thing. If she used her head instead of her heart, she knew it was a fantasy. Law enforcement and the news media rarely coexisted harmoniously. Still, she imagined she'd be able to stand back and see him at work. That was perk enough. She smiled at her mental image of Matthias, dark hair, incredible blue eyes, a physique sculpted in a weight room. Even the pair of scars on his face and a nose that had been broken more than once couldn't detract from his appeal.

She realized she was smiling and forced her mind back to the reality of her job. Long hours of waiting for something to happen. Seeking shade to avoid heat stroke. Matthias and the investigation going on inside while she stood outside with the rest of the local media. At least when she'd been photographing sporting events, she was constantly in motion, constantly snapping action pictures.

A trickle of sweat slid down her spine. She pinched the fabric of her T-shirt and pulled it away from her back, flapping it to create air movement against her damp skin. From the shade of a mature maple tree, she surveyed the parking lot filled with police vehicles. West Erie Veterinary Clinic sat on a corner lot with parking in the front and around one side. The front lot currently held only emergency vehicles and the unmarked Malibus she knew city detectives drove. If it wasn't for law enforcement, the lot would be empty.

She pulled out her phone and sent Preston a text.

Going in search of photos. Text if you need me.

Pocketing the device, Emma wandered along the sidewalk to the corner and turned, strolling toward the rear of the building and a large boxy truck parked in the back corner of the lot. *West Erie Veterinary Clinic* was emblazoned across the side with graphics of happy dogs and cats splashed above and below the name. In smaller print, *Mobile Vet Hospital*. The door on its side stood open, and soft, muffled voices drifted through the screen. Nothing she could make out. She contemplated sneaking under the crime scene tape in order to eavesdrop but reconsidered.

A wide strip of pavement stretched around the bland rear of the clinic with signs stating AUTHORIZED PERSONNEL ONLY, DO NOT ENTER, and DELIVERIES ONLY posted in clear view. Emma lifted her Nikon and snapped another picture, then let her camera drop to hang from the strap around her neck. With nothing else to photograph, she retraced her steps along the sidewalk, head lowered, thinking about Shawn and Cassie, wondering if he was all right. Wondering how Cassie was holding up.

Wondering who would do such a thing. And why?

Her phone vibrated in her pocket. She retrieved her cell, hoping to see Matthias's name and face on her caller ID. Instead, it was Eric Baker, her friend from back home in Washington County, a hundred and fifty miles to the south.

"You busy?" he asked when she answered the call.

She debated her reply. "I'm at a crime scene waiting for something worth photographing to happen."

"If this is a bad time, you can call me back later."

Emma wandered toward the street in front of the clinic, scanning the thinning crowd for Preston. She spotted him talking to a uniformed officer. "I have a few minutes. I'll let you know if I have to cut you off."

"Fair enough." Instead of launching into his reason for calling, Eric fell silent.

"What's up?" she asked.

"Have you given any thought to what you're going to do with your family's property?"

Not the topic she'd anticipated. She'd inherited over a hundred acres of what had been first her grandparents' then her parents' farm when they'd died in a car crash four years ago. More correctly, Emma and her younger sister, Nell, had inherited them. More recently, both houses on the property had been burned to the ground thanks to Emma's ex-boyfriend, who still sent an Arctic chill through her soul, even though he would never again harm either her or Nell. But Emma hadn't been able to face the prospect of doing anything with the farm. "Why? Do you want to buy it?" she asked with a healthy dose of sarcasm. She knew he didn't.

"Not me. Remember Sonny Jones?"

It took a moment for the name to register. "*Greyson* Jones?"

"Yeah. He never did like his first name."

"That's too bad." She'd always thought the name Greyson was cool, but that was back when they'd gone to grade school, and she'd had a crush on him. They'd been nine years old. "What about him?"

"He's one of my real estate clients. He bought out North Star Developing and is looking for land."

"And he wants mine?"

"Yeah."

"It's not for sale. You know that."

A raspy exhale filtered through the phone.

"Eric? Are you all right?"

"I'm fine. How are things with your brutish but hot cop?"

The change in direction brought Emma to a stop. "Matthias is good. We're good," she said, recognizing the lack of confidence in her voice. She didn't want to jinx anything.

"Are you cohabitating yet?"

The erratic conversation started to wear on her. "Quit dancing around and tell me what's going on."

"Can't a fellow ask about his bestie's romantic life?"

"Sure." Two could play this game. "Are you and Caleb still seeing each other?"

"Actually, no. Okay, forget the hot cop. Summer will be over soon. You can't stay in your sardine can of a trailer through an Erie winter. What are your plans after the campground closes?"

She was living in a seventeen-foot camper at Sara's Campground and had been since early spring. The place closed for the season in October, less than two months from now. Her future living arrangements were something she'd actively avoided thinking about. "I don't know."

Eric's exasperated sigh was so loud, she thought she'd have heard it even without the phone. "I can't be the only one thinking about your future. You need to contribute. Sonny Jones knows I've been overseeing your interests here, so he reached out to me and made an offer on your farm. I told him you were considering moving back and rebuilding."

Emma had been. It's what Nell had wanted. But that was before Matthias became more than a friend. "What kind of offer?"

"A very good one."

"What's 'very good'?"

"Six hundred grand."

She choked.

"And I think he threw that number out as a starting bid."

"Why?"

"I told you. He bought North Star Developing. He plans to develop."

Her knees rubbery, Emma managed to stagger to the shade of a maple tree and lean against its trunk. Eric's jumbled line of questioning began to make sense. He wanted to know if she planned to stay in Erie, with or without Matthias. If she was, she'd be foolish to turn down an offer of over a half a million dollars for land she had no intention of returning to.

It was a big if.

But the decision to sell wasn't hers alone. "Eric, you know I can't even think about selling right now."

His voice dropped to a near whisper. "Nell."

Emma didn't feel the need to confirm what he knew.

"She's part of the reason we need to deal with this situation. Emma, you need to come back—"

"Why?" she interrupted.

"Just listen to me. I don't mean you need to move back if you don't want to, but there are *things* going on here that require your presence."

"What kind of things?"

"I don't want to get into it over the phone. Please. Take a few days off and come home."

"What kind of things?" she repeated firmer this time. But the line went dead.

Matthias, Frazier, and Roth converged in a small room not much bigger than a storage closet. In fact, Matthias suspected that's exactly what it had been prior to its conversion to the clinic's security hub. Bethany had given them access to view the CCTV recordings from the last few days. Matthias hoped they would only need the last few hours.

He clicked through the different angles available—exterior and interior, parking lot, main entrance, rear entrance, and side entrance. But when he pulled up the frame for the side exterior, the screen went black. "What the hell?" he muttered.

Roth moved to the door. "I'll go outside and check the camera."

Matthias kept his focus on the monitor, running the recording in reverse. The screen remained black all day and into Friday's early morning hours, when suddenly a grainy, shadowy image of the side parking lot became visible. Matthias tapped the keys to select play at normal speed. Lit only by a few dusk-to-dawn lights on poles, there wasn't much to see until a shadowy figure appeared. He—or she—Matthias couldn't tell which—approached the camera. A hand came up, at which point the screen went black.

"What time is that?" Frazier asked.

"Timestamp says three-eighteen."

"These guys had a plan." Frazier fingered his mustache. "They didn't just decide over afternoon coffee, 'Hey, let's go rob a vet clinic.'"

Matthias had reached that conclusion when he heard the trio were all in black, masked and gloved.

Roth reappeared in the doorway. "Looks like someone spray-painted the camera lens."

"Not very original," Frazier said, "but effective."

And thorough, Matthias thought. He copied the footage onto a flash drive and shut down the computer. "We need to get this back to the office and start going through it frame by frame until we find something." One of the recordings Matthias wanted to view personally was the moments surrounding Bethany Stone bringing John Boyd and his dog inside. She claimed she couldn't remember checking the door afterwards. Nor could she explain why she'd let them in that way instead of through the vacant waiting room.

"What do we do next?" Frazier heaved a frustrated sigh. "How can three men with guns walk into this place in broad daylight and no one's able to give us a description?"

Matthias glanced at him. "You're surprised? These days, I'm shocked when we do get a cooperative witness and a good description." As he said it, he knew he wasn't being fair. Shawn's staff had willingly given statements. But none of them agreed on what these guys looked like except for their black attire and their "big" guns. "As for what do we do? What we always do. Work the case. Talk to anyone in the area who might've had eyes on these assholes. They didn't just walk down the street in broad daylight wearing those masks and gloves and carrying bags of cash and drugs. Check the security cameras on neighboring businesses from midnight on. I want the Drug and Vice unit involved. Were these guys planning to use the drugs themselves or sell them? Either way, I want to know who's doing what in the narcotics scene."

"On it." Roth clapped Frazier on the back. "Let's hit the streets."

Matthias slipped the flash drive into an evidence bag, labeled it, and tucked it in his pocket. Back in the waiting room, the forensics team was still at work. Matthias started for the entrance, then stopped, pivoted, and strode down the hallway leading to the side door.

A security alarm keypad was secured to the wall next to it. The frame showed no evidence of scrapes or dents. No obvious attempt to force it. He wasn't surprised. That would've happened from the outside. He slipped on a pair of Nitrile gloves and hit the push bar. A wave of mid-August heat rolled in as the steel door swung outward into the side parking lot. The same one that had shown up on the grainy CCTV footage he'd just watched. He looked back into the clinic and spotted a familiar face. "Hey, Kollman," he called to the uniformed officer.

He headed toward Matthias. "What do you need?"

"I want to make sure this thing can't be opened from outside. Stand here and let me back in when I knock."

"Got it." Kollman crossed his arms and broadened his stance as if daring anyone to get past him.

Matthias stepped out and allowed the door to swing closed. The latch engaged with a metallic snick. He grasped the handle and thumbed the release, which didn't give. Locked, just as Bethany had said. He gave it a hard tug, but it held firm.

He bent down to examine the jamb around the lock. No signs of tampering, same as inside. The door hadn't been forced, and was solid enough that without power tools, attempts would've been futile.

"Excuse me."

Matthias turned to find a haggard-looking man in scrubs heading his way. Beyond, the mobile vet clinic was parked at the back edge of the lot. John Boyd and Daisy shambled away from it.

The man in scrubs held a small plastic box in one hand and extended the other. "I'm Dr. Nathaniel Campbell, one of Dr. Malone's colleagues." He held up the box. "When can I get inside to use our lab? I have bloodwork I need to run."

Matthias shook the vet's hand. "Let me find out." He pounded on the door.

Kollman shoved it open. "Guess it was locked all right."

"Yep." Matthias gestured toward the waiting room. "Ask the

forensics techs if they've finished in the back. I have a vet here who needs to use the lab."

"Be right back."

Matthias braced the door open with his boot and watched as Boyd and his dog turned the corner on their way … where? "How's Daisy?"

Campbell followed Matthias's gaze. "Not well, I'm afraid. She's elderly and suffers from a lot of the afflictions older dogs are known for. Especially large breed dogs. Hip dysplasia for starters, and she needs a good dental, which requires anesthesia. I drew blood, but I have a feeling the results aren't going to be great. Makes it a bit risky to put the old girl under."

Matthias thought of his conversation with Boyd. "Not to mention costly."

Campbell gave a tired smile. "If the procedure is warranted, we'll work something out with the owner. In the meantime, I put her on antibiotics and an anti-inflammatory. She'll be more comfortable, at least."

Footsteps drew Matthias's attention back inside as Kollman trudged toward them.

"They're done with everything except the lobby." The officer looked at the vet. "But you can't come through this way."

Dr. Campbell nodded. "That's fine. I have a key. I can use the rear door." He thanked them both and ambled away.

A key.

Matthias looked at the lever handle on the outside of the steel door. The one that wouldn't turn when locked. He ran his thumb over the slot and wondered who all had keys to this entrance.

And if all those keys were accounted for.

The shadows outside the veterinary clinic grew long but did little to break the heat as Matthias left through the front exit. He spotted Emma at the edge of the parking lot, beyond the crime scene tape. The crowds of onlookers had dwindled from earlier, but he would've zeroed in on her in an instant, no matter how jammed the perimeter might've been.

She was looking at him, too, and he knew she was dying to talk to him. The feeling was mutual.

But he did *not* want to speak with Preston Guilfoyle or any of the other newshounds eyeing him the way he eyed a juicy steak. Thankfully, Matthias had just ended a phone call with the lieutenant. He approached the local and regional media, who began firing questions, asking for details he had no intention of sharing. He raised a hand, silencing only a few.

"There will be a press conference in the city council chambers at eight-thirty this evening," he shouted.

En masse, they checked their phones or watches for the time and realized they only had fifteen minutes to race downtown, park, and jockey for a position. A couple of impatient reporters continued to shout questions. The rest retreated to their vehicles.

Guilfoyle caught Emma's arm. "Let's go."

She continued to hold Matthias's gaze, not budging. He did the same, drinking in her Caribbean blue-green eyes, her short unruly red hair that she was growing out and constantly fussing over, her girl-next-door good looks. Her slender figure with curves in all the right places. Places he'd planned to explore in great detail this evening.

That wasn't happening now.

Guilfoyle tugged harder. "Come on."

Emma remained still as a statue. "I'll catch up to you in a minute."

"We don't have a minute."

"You go," Matthias told him. "I'll drop her off."

Guilfoyle swore and stomped away, muttering something about needing to get a different photographer.

Matthias ducked under the crime scene tape and slipped an arm around Emma's waist. Together, they made their way to his car. Once settled in the passenger seat, she clicked the seatbelt and faced him. "How's Shawn?"

"After I deposit you at the press conference, I'm heading to Hamot to find out."

Her sigh was audible. "I wish I could go with you."

"I do, too." He started the Malibu and eased out of the parking spot. As he maneuvered through the remaining police vehicles, he glanced at her. "I don't suppose you've heard anything at all about his condition?" More than once, Emma's journalist contacts had provided faster answers than he could access through police channels.

"The hospital isn't releasing information."

"If it's any comfort, I'd have been notified if Shawn had..." He let his voice trail off without saying the words *if Shawn had died*.

"No news is good news," Emma said with a sarcastic laugh.

"In this case." He hoped.

They fell silent for several minutes as Matthias cruised east on West Lake Road, braking at the cross street of Peninsula Drive. As they sat, waiting for the light to turn green, he noticed Emma gazing at the Trinity Cemetery outside her window and knew what she was thinking. That's where they'd first laid eyes on each other in May. It's where he'd kissed her for the first time a month later.

His mother, had she still been alive, would say theirs was not a traditional courtship.

The light changed, and he crossed Peninsula onto West 8th. "About our plans... Raincheck?" he said.

She faced him, and he caught her smile in his peripheral vision. "Of course." She stared straight ahead for several blocks before turning to him. "Cassie and Shawn..." she began, her voice uncertain. "I've come to think of them as my friends."

He wasn't sure where she was headed with this. "They think of you the same way."

"I'm just..." She squirmed. "I don't want to break some unwritten rule about cops and news photographers. Is it okay ... or appropriate ... for me to stop by the hospital after I'm done?"

Matthias chuckled. "As long as you don't take pictures to post on ErieLIVE's website, I think you're fine."

"No pictures. Promise."

Emma didn't speak for several more blocks, but Matthias sensed she wanted to. "Go ahead," he told her. "Ask."

"But—but—" she stuttered before dropping into what he assumed was supposed to be a gruff impersonation of his voice. "It's an ongoing investigation."

He crossed his arms, feigning indignance. "That's not how I sound."

She looked at him askance.

"I don't want our jobs to create a wall between us."

"I don't either," she said, "but I know there have to be lines we don't cross."

"I'll make you a deal. You can ask me anything. If I can't answer, I'll let you know. But don't ever feel you can't talk to me."

She thought about it. "Deal." Shifting in her seat, she asked, "Do you have any idea who did this awful thing or why?"

It was his turn to think about it, but she was about to attend the press conference anyway. "No. I'm hoping Shawn is conscious and able to answer some questions when I get there. As for why, they stole drugs and cash. On the surface, it appears they broke in after closing time, not expecting to encounter anyone."

"On the surface," she repeated with the same skepticism as he felt.

"There are a couple of things that bother me."

"Such as?"

This was where he should draw that line she'd mentioned, but he needed to put words to the jumbled thoughts that had been nagging him the last few hours. "If they really wanted to rob the place after hours, why not wait another thirty minutes and give the remaining staff time to clear out? Why come masked and armed?" He braked as the traffic light in front of him turned red and looked over at Emma. "And the big one. Why shoot Shawn when they already had what they came for?"

Chapter Five

After dropping Emma off at City Hall with a request to keep anything he'd told her just between them—she'd promised and sealed it with a kiss—Matthias drove north on State Street to Hamot Hospital.

The white-haired security guard at the front desk inspected his badge before directing him to the surgical waiting room. Matthias found Cassie seated in a back corner, bent over, elbows on knees, her face buried in her hands. Matthias's mind plunged into a very dark place. He crossed to her, and she lifted her head at his approach. She looked a good ten years older than she had a few hours ago.

His mouth went dry. "Is he...?"

"Still in surgery."

Matthias exhaled and sank into the chair next to hers. "What are they telling you?"

"Nothing good. In the Emergency Department, they were throwing around words like hemothorax and cardiac tamponade. Either way, he's bleeding into his chest. The bullet's still in there. Somewhere." Her voice trailed off.

Matthias scanned the waiting room, the worried faces of others whose loved ones were in surgery. "I'm surprised you're here alone."

"I called Alissa's babysitter. She's keeping her for as long as needed."

"I didn't mean your granddaughter. I meant someone from the department."

Cassie blew a puff of air from her lips. "I told them to leave. I don't need anyone to hold my hand. I need everyone on the street, finding out who did this." She glowered at him. "Have you caught the bastards?"

"Not yet."

"Have you even identified them?"

"We're working on it."

"Then I'm telling you, too. Get out of here. I don't want to see you until you've made an arrest." The moment she said it, she reached out and grabbed his arm. "Wait. What *do* you have? Update me. *Then* get out."

"You're not on this case."

"I know that. But as the wife of a shooting victim, I want to know. And don't give me any of that 'it's an ongoing investigation' crap."

Matthias chuckled. "Apparently, I throw that line around a lot."

"We all do."

He exhaled and told her what he, Frazier, and Ross had learned so far, then patted his pocket. "I have the security footage on a flash drive. As soon as I leave, I'll take it to the station and watch every second of it." Matthias shifted in the chair and took one of Cassie's hands in his. "Was Shawn able to tell you anything before he went into surgery?"

"He was struggling to breathe, let alone talk or answer questions."

"What about you? How well do you know the people he works with?"

"Very well. He handpicked everyone. The other doctors, the techs, even the receptionists."

"Has he ever mentioned having concerns about any of them?"

"Never." Cassie glared at him. "What are you getting at? You can't suspect these thugs had inside help."

Exactly what Matthias expected her to say. "You would hand me my head on a platter if I didn't investigate all possibilities."

Cassie opened her mouth and closed it. "True."

He hesitated before venturing further. "What can you tell me about Bethany Stone?"

"Shawn's office manager? She's hardworking, organized, good with people. Everything you could want in the person running your business." Cassie eyed him again. "Why?"

"Investigating all possibilities," Matthias repeated.

"Bethany isn't one of those possibilities." But as soon as she said it, her expression turned apprehensive.

"What are you thinking?" he asked.

"It's nothing, I'm sure."

"You don't sound sure. Tell me and let me decide."

Cassie gazed toward the waiting room's door, as if willing a doctor to enter with good news. In a whisper, she said, "About a year ago, Bethany got into some debt. Serious debt. From gambling. She came to Shawn and told him she felt tempted to 'borrow' from petty cash and realized she needed help. He got her into a Gamblers Anonymous group. She pulled her act together and hasn't placed a bet since."

Except maybe she had. "I'll look into it."

Cassie brought her gaze back to him. "Be discreet. Please. I trust this woman. More importantly, Shawn trusts her. He kept her gambling addiction quiet. No one else at the clinic knows. Keep it that way."

He squeezed her hand. "I will do my best."

She placed her other hand over his, patting it. "Thank you." Her gaze returned to the door. "I wish like hell they'd come out and tell me something."

"They're doing their job." Matthias bumped her shoulder with his. "You're giving me grief for being here instead of out there. Don't you want the doctors in there working on him instead of out here giving you updates?"

"I hate it when you're right."

"I know."

"I don't understand it. Shawn's a good man. Everyone loves him. His patients adore him. He'd give up his right arm to save an animal. Why couldn't these thugs just take the money, the drugs, and go? Why did they have to shoot my husband?" Her voice broke.

Matthias waited for her to take a few deep breaths and regroup. "I've wondered the same thing," he said, keeping his voice low. "I hate to ask but can you think of anyone who might want to harm Shawn? Beyond the money and drugs, I mean."

Her dark eyes locked onto his, realization dawning in them. "You're implying the real motive was the shooting, not the robbery."

He shrugged. "Investigating all possibilities," he said yet again.

Cassie shook her head emphatically. "No. Not Shawn. I told you. Everyone adores him." She snorted a humorless laugh. "Now if it had been me? Hell, yeah. You know as well as I do how many criminals out there would love to take us out. You and me. Not Shawn."

A tall, blond young man wearing fresh scrubs appeared in the doorway Cassie had been watching. The head of every other person in the room looked his way, hope and fear on their faces. "Shawn Malone's family?" he called out.

She launched to her feet. "That's me."

The others returned to their conversations, books, and phones.

The doctor, who looked barely old enough to be a freshman in college, made his way around the various seating arrangements to them and extended a hand, which Cassie clasped.

"I'm Dr. Tharp."

"Cassie. I'm Shawn's wife."

The doctor's gaze slid down her Erie Bureau of Police standard-issue detective's polo shirt to her tactical slacks darkened with Shawn's blood. Shifting his focus to Matthias, he took in the matching attire.

"How's my husband?" Cassie's tone was sharp, drawing the doctor's attention back on task.

"He made it through surgery." Tharp gestured toward the seats Cassie and Matthias had vacated and dragged another chair over to face them. "The bullet entered the left upper chest, transected his left lung, and lodged against the anterior aspect of his scapula. Shoulder blade," he added.

"We've attended more autopsies than you've done surgeries," Cassie snapped. "We know what a scapula is."

Matthias closed his fingers around one of her hands and squeezed. "Let him talk."

Tharp gave him a nod of appreciation. "The damage to the lung resulted in a hemothorax." He raised a questioning eyebrow at Matthias.

They understood that meant bleeding into the lung, compromising Shawn's ability to oxygenate his blood. Matthias tipped his head.

"That and the blood loss in general was our primary concern. We've stemmed the bleeding and reinflated the lung, so for the moment, he's stable, but the next twenty-four to forty-eight hours are critical."

"He's not out of the woods," Cassie said softly.

"He's not. But he's strong. And I have to tell you, the bullet's path tracked within a millimeter of his aorta." Tharp leaned toward Cassie, fixing her with a deadly serious stare. "This could've gone so much worse."

Matthias watched her react, the earlier snippiness draining away.

Keeping his voice low, he asked, "Were you able to retrieve the bullet?"

The doctor leaned back. "No. As I said, stopping the blood loss was our priority. And make no mistake, Shawn lost a considerable amount. I determined removing the bullet at this time wasn't worth the risk to his life."

"Will you go back in to get it at another time?" Cassie's tone was all worried wife, not police detective wanting to get her hands on a vital piece of evidence.

"Let's wait and see what happens, shall we?" He rose and pushed his chair back where he'd found it.

Cassie stood as well. "Can I see him?"

"He's still in recovery. From there, he'll be going to ICU. We'll keep you apprised and let you know when he can have a visitor."

She reached out to him. "I need to see him."

Tharp's smile was tired. "I'll have someone bring you back as soon as possible." He lowered his head, turned, and retreated.

Matthias stood next to his partner, watching her. He'd never seen her look so lost. So vulnerable. "You better sit down," he said.

She acted as if she didn't hear. "If anything happens to him, I don't know what I'll do."

"He's going to be fine. You heard the doctor. He's strong."

Cassie shook her head and fumbled to remove her phone from the pocket on her right thigh. "Excuse me. I have to get word to my daughter." She took a couple of steps and turned back to him. "You. Get back out there and find out who did this. Don't come back until you've made an arrest." Then she continued toward the door and the hallway, clutching her cell.

He watched her go and almost smiled. Almost. At least the kick-ass Detective Sergeant Cassie Malone he knew and loved was still in there.

Emma made quick work of sorting her photos, selecting a few that best illustrated the shooting's aftermath and the intensity of the press conference. She edited and uploaded them to post along with Preston's story. Before anyone could stop her, she ducked out of the ErieLIVE offices, found her Subaru Forester where she'd parked it ages ago, and drove north on State Street to the hospital.

Tracking Cassie down proved to be a challenge. Shawn was out of surgery but not yet in a room. Emma followed directions and the signage in the hallways to the surgical waiting room. She scanned faces, none of which belonged to Cassie or Matthias. Emma returned to the hall and dug out her phone to find Cassie's number. The call went directly to voicemail. At the tone, Emma said, "I'm at the hospital trying to find you and see how Shawn's doing, but you don't need to call me back. I'll talk to you later." She figured Cassie had her hands full. Emma could get her answers from Matthias.

Who was also busy, trying to catch the man who'd done this.

"Emma."

She turned toward her name. Cassie strode in her direction. "I just left you a message," Emma said.

"I silenced my phone while I was in with my husband." Cassie reached her and pulled her into her arms.

The action startled Emma. Cassie had never been huggy or touchy-feely with her. Or anyone except her granddaughter and Shawn. Still, Emma returned the hug. "How is he?"

Cassie released her and exhaled. "Alive."

Emma studied Matthias's partner. She looked exhausted.

"Do you have time to sit with me for a few minutes?" Cassie asked.

"That's why I'm here." Emma gave her a smile and followed her into the waiting room and a pair of chairs situated away from the other groups of family and friends awaiting news of their loved ones.

"Matthias told me you were at the press conference. What did they say?"

Emma eyed her. "No one from the department has been in touch?"

Cassie waved a hand as if shooing a fly. "The lieutenant and the chief came by earlier. Matthias, too, as I'm sure you know. I ran them off. I don't need them holding my hand as much as I need them out there, catching the man who shot my husband. Oh, they've called me but not with any real news." Her dark eyes laser-focused on Emma. "Tell me what you know."

"Not a lot." She shared what she'd heard at the conference. Three armed assailants. The theft. "The staff at the clinic took an inventory, so they know exactly what drugs were stolen. Tramadol, hydrocodone, trazodone, and ketamine."

"The usual," Cassie said. "What else?"

Emma relayed information she was certain Cassie knew. The timing of the robbery. Entrance and exit via a side door. The request for help from the public.

The muscles in Cassie's forearms, resting on her chair's wooden armrest, bunched into knots as she clenched her fists. "In other words, they have nothing. My fellow officers and detectives have no clue who did this." Frustration overpowered the anger in her voice.

Emma wished she had words of comfort to share. Wished she'd known Cassie longer and could provide reassurance by her mere presence. Instead, Emma said the first thing that came to her. "Matthias won't rest until he puts these guys behind bars."

Cassie looked at her, those fierce eyes penetrating into Emma's soul. But Emma held firm. She meant what she said. She knew Matthias. Had seen him search to the ends of the earth to find and bring in a criminal even when the effort nearly got him killed.

Cassie's gaze and posture softened. "You're right. Matthias is a damned good detective." A grin flitted across her lips as she gently elbowed Emma. "After all, I taught him everything he knows."

Chapter Six

Matthias detoured to his apartment to shower and change and made it back to his desk before sunrise on Saturday. He'd put in a long night, working with Frazier and Roth and the entire Erie Bureau of Police, reaching out to surrounding jurisdictions regarding robberies with similar M.O.s. So far, nothing came close. The Drug and Vice unit's detectives were on alert for the stolen drugs to hit the streets.

Shortly before midnight, one of the patrols searching the area had discovered a garbage bag stuffed in a trash can three blocks southwest of the clinic. The bag contained three black hoodies but no guns, gloves, or N95 masks. Matthias woke his friend from the lab and asked him to put a rush on it.

Uniforms continued to canvass the neighborhoods around the vet clinic, hoping to find a witness who'd seen something.

With the sky starting to lighten outside the windows, he settled at his computer and pulled up the footage from the West Erie Veterinary Clinic's security cameras. While the one outside the side entrance had been put out of commission, the others worked fine. This morning, Matthias focused on the same entrance but from the inside view.

He started at the eight-a.m. timestamp Friday when Bethany Stone entered. He made a note. Obviously, she had a key. As he watched, she turned to face the door, her back to the camera, and reached up to finger the ledge at the top of the door frame. She then brought that hand down to the push bar. Matthias couldn't see what she was doing, but he assumed she was unlocking the device, allowing the door to open only from the inside. Bethany reached up again, replacing whatever she'd taken from the ledge.

From there, he fast-forwarded through the events of the day, slowing the film when someone came into the frame. Employees and the veterinarians all used the side door to enter and exit, although he noted some had to be let in. He needed to get a list of how many keys were floating around out there.

He also noted several clients and their pets being escorted inside through that door, confirming what Bethany Stone had told him.

As the day wore on, some of the staff started to leave, again through the side door. Matthias clicked his keyboard to play the footage at normal speed and leaned back until the time reached four-thirty.

Bethany appeared on the screen, and Matthias came forward.

"How's it going?" Frazier appeared at his side, coffee and doughnut in hand.

Matthias hit pause and swiveled to face him. "You tell me. Anything new to report?"

"We've been out all night, questioning anyone we saw out on the streets, but most of the businesses in that area were closed."

Roth arrived, also clutching a cup of coffee and a pastry. "The clinic isn't in the kind of neighborhood where folks prowl the streets at two in the morning. Even on a Friday night."

"What we do have," Frazier said, "are warrants for those

businesses in the general vicinity who have exterior cameras that might've caught the assailants approaching or fleeing the scene."

Roth sipped his coffee. "We'll start making the rounds as soon as they open."

Frazier pointed at Matthias's computer. "Find anything yet?"

Matthias swiveled back to the screen. "I'm just now getting to the interesting part."

With the two other detectives crowding behind him, Matthias clicked play.

Bethany reached the side door, pushed it open, and stepped back, partially blocking their view. An old man—Matthias knew it was John Boyd—shuffled in, slump-shouldered. Daisy appeared in the doorway, but stopped, resistant to entering. Boyd stopped as well and backed into the doorway, looking at the shaggy dog. He appeared to say something to Bethany before leaning down to pet Daisy's head. Still, she refused to move. Boyd and Bethany both bent over, Boyd looping an arm around the dog's girth, Bethany giving a nudge from behind, finally getting Daisy over the threshold and inside the building.

Matthias leaned even closer, hoping to see Bethany somehow block the door open, but she merely brought up the rear, following the man and dog out of the frame. Matthias paused the footage and zoomed in. The door was closed. Or appeared to be.

He returned the view to normal and again clicked play. Minutes passed. Two more staff members wearing scrubs exited through the door. A few minutes later, the door opened. Three men in black stormed in.

"That's them," Frazier echoed what Matthias already knew.

How did a locked door suddenly become unlocked?

He reversed the video to the staff members who'd left moments earlier. "I want to know who they are," he said, pointing. "And I want to talk to them."

"On it," Frazier said.

Rather than switch to a different camera and stay with the intruders, Matthias advanced the video through several minutes of nothing. Then the three men in black reappeared, their backs to the camera. One hit the push bar, flinging the door open. The first two rushed out. The third man stopped, a hand on the threshold as he half turned to look back toward the waiting room. Had someone called out to him? Or was he making sure no one was following? Either way, he only paused for a fleeting moment before following his cohorts out and letting the door close. But Matthias caught sight of what might be their first chance to identify at least that last man. He hit pause and rewind before freezing the image the moment the third man touched the threshold.

"Do you see that?" Matthias zoomed in on the man's hand.

"He took off his gloves," Roth said.

Matthias pointed at the image. "And very likely left fingerprints."

Roth clapped him on the shoulder. "I'm on it." He charged out of Major Crimes.

There was no further action on the video until the police arrived. Matthias rewound to the same spot as before, where the man stopped and turned toward the camera. Matthias hit pause and zoomed in, this time on his face. What little he could see of it.

Which was damned little.

"Does he look at all familiar to you?" he asked Frazier.

The detective moved closer and squinted. "Hell if I know. He could be my own brother, and I wouldn't be able to ID him." He shook his head. "Maybe there's a better shot on another camera."

"Let's hope."

Matthias stayed focused on the story playing out on the various cameras inside the clinic.

Within fifteen minutes, Roth returned and announced that he'd spoken with the guys in the fingerprint lab. "They said there were a lot of prints and smudges lifted from that part of the door frame. I told them to get back to us the minute they find something useful."

He joined Frazier, viewing the few bits of neighborhood security cam footage they had. At nine, the pair headed out to visit the businesses near West Erie Vet Clinic that'd been closed the previous evening, leaving Matthias alone at Major Crimes.

Watching Shawn's shooting from three different camera angles was one of the hardest tasks Matthias had tackled in recent memory. He played, rewound, and replayed the moment over and over, making sure he didn't miss a thing.

And he was grateful it was him, not Cassie, handling the job.

The witnesses had been right. The gunmen had what they came for. Shawn's hands were raised and open, non-threatening. He made no move toward them, wasn't playing hero. Yet one of the men—the apparent leader—raised his weapon and fired.

For no reason.

At least, none that Matthias could see.

Different angles revealed no additional explanation, but he did have a chance to watch the two other men in action. They'd taken the receptionist with them to the rear of the clinic. At gunpoint, they forced Erin, the tech, to open the drug cabinets. One produced a cloth bag from his pocket and dropped the bottles and vials into it. Matthias noted the guy appeared to pick and choose which medications he took.

By noon, Matthias's eyes ached. He leaned back in his chair and scoured his face with his hands. Lack of sleep and too many hours staring at a computer screen had given him a fogged and aching head. He rose and stepped into the breakroom to pour a cup of coffee from the urn. One sip made him question how long the sludge had been sitting there. But fresh coffee or better yet, a cup from his favorite coffee shop, was too far down on his current priority list.

Maybe moving around got the blood flowing to his brain, or maybe it was the bitter caffeine, but a thought crept into his consciousness. A thought he should have addressed hours ago. A thought that chilled him to the bone.

He thumped the cup down on the table and jogged out of the breakroom and down the hall to Lieutenant Armstrong's corner office. The lieutenant was on his phone and raised one finger at Matthias.

"Thanks so much," Armstrong told whoever was on the other end of the call. "I'll wait to hear from you." He hung up and faced Matthias. "You found something?"

"No. Yes." Matthias winced. "Everyone I talked to at the clinic said there hadn't been a reason for the assailant to shoot. The crew had what they came for. I've been watching the video of Shawn's shooting, and the witnesses were right. He wasn't threatening them in any way, yet the gunman looked right at him and pulled the trigger."

"You're thinking the robbery may have been a cover, and shooting Shawn was part of the plan all along?"

"Cassie and I even briefly discussed the possibility yesterday. But, Lieutenant, if that's truly the case, they failed." Matthias emphasized the last two words.

Armstrong swore. He picked up his phone and punched a number. To Matthias, he asked, "Have you spoken to Cassie yet this morning?"

"No. I was hoping to have some news about the case for her." If he called just to check in, she'd probably hang up on him.

The call connected and Armstrong identified himself. "Get a pair of officers over to Hamot. I want a round-the-clock protection detail on Shawn Malone." When he hung up, he looked at Matthias. "I want you to go over there, too. Show Cassie the best image you have of the gunman. She might recognize him. With any luck, Shawn will regain consciousness soon. Find out if he can ID the guy."

"On it." Matthias pivoted to leave.

"And, Honeywell?"

He pivoted back.

"Find out who is so pissed off at Shawn that they wanted him dead."

"Count on it."

Matthias located Officer Kollman standing alone outside the intensive care unit. Kollman tipped his head toward the closed doors. "This is as close as they'll allow us."

"Us?" Matthias looked around.

"There's one other entrance. Supposed to be for staff only, but we're taking no chances. Lyle's over there."

"Good." Matthias nodded his approval. "Where's Cassie?"

"Haven't seen her. I assume she's in the waiting room." Kollman pointed back the way Matthias had come.

He thanked the officer and retraced his steps as far as the ICU waiting room. The layout was much the same as the surgical one, except these inhabitants appeared to be in it for the long haul. Pillows and blankets provided resting areas. Tables were covered in food wrappers. A coffee and snack bar occupied an alcove in one corner.

Matthias scanned the occupants and spotted Cassie in the far corner, legs extended and crossed at the ankles, arms folded in front of her, head resting back, eyes closed. To anyone else, she would appear to be asleep. Matthias knew better.

He wasn't halfway across the room before her eyes opened and her head came up. By the time he reached her, she was sitting upright and alert.

"What've you found out?" she asked.

He ignored the question and took a seat beside her. "How's Shawn?"

Cassie exhaled loudly. "Stable." She bit off the word. "Whatever the hell that means."

"Is he conscious?"

"Not really. I mean, he's not in a coma, but they have him so drugged up with painkillers, he doesn't even know what planet he's on."

"But stable's good, right? All things considered?"

"I don't want stable. I want him fussing to get out of bed and ordering me to take him home."

Matthias tried picturing Shawn as a bad patient and couldn't see it. Cassie? Yeah. She'd be the one ripping out her IVs and ordering the nurses to hand over her clothes lest she walk out naked.

"I've answered your questions," she said. "You answer mine. Where are we with the investigation?"

"First off, 'we' are not involved in the investigation. I am."

She eyed him. "We're in a hospital. If you don't tell me something damn quick, you're gonna need to share a room with my husband."

"Before Shawn got to the point of not being able to talk, did he tell you anything about the men who did this?"

"I already told you. Yes. Three men in black, wearing masks."

"Did he mention recognizing any of them?"

"No." Cassie pointed at her face. "Masks, remember?"

"Right." Matthias told her about the security footage he'd been watching. "Shawn wasn't acting threatening. They already had the drugs and cash. There was no reason for them to shoot him. Unless…"

"Unless that was part of the plan."

"Exactly. I know we already talked about this last night, but has he mentioned having trouble with anyone at work? Or anywhere, for that matter?"

"And I already told you. No."

Matthias dug out his phone, pulled up the still he'd captured of the shooter's face, and handed the device over to her.

Cassie studied the image. She touched the screen to enlarge the man's face. "This is the man who tried to kill my husband?"

Matthias gave her one quick nod. "Look familiar?"

She squinted at it with an intensity he'd rarely seen in his partner. "No. And you know how good I am with faces." She lowered the phone and scowled.

Matthias could tell she was thinking. "What?"

Cassie exhaled a frustrated breath. "I've been considering the possibility that this asshole gunned down my husband to get back at me."

"And?"

She shot him the side eye. "You know how many criminals I've put away over all the years I've been a cop? Hundreds. Hell, the number who've outright threatened to kill me is right up there, too."

Matthias made a mental note to check on convicts from Cassie's cases who may have been released from prison recently. "Anyone stand out?"

She fingered her short hair, thinking. "There are a few. That child pornography case from a couple of years ago … the one where the pervert lost his high-paying job at the university, his wife and kids, and virtually every friend he'd ever had."

"Dr. Oswald Greene." Matthias remembered the case and the evidence, which still curdled his stomach.

"Except that asshole wouldn't have the guts to take on an adult," Cassie said.

"True."

"There was a case from five years ago. Before we were partners."

"The car chase that went sideways?" Although Matthias hadn't been involved in it, the entire department had grieved the subsequent fiery crash that claimed the maniac behind the wheel as well as two innocent passengers. "O'Donovan?"

"Waylon O'Donovan." Then she shook her head. "But he had no family left. Besides, that was too long ago."

"How about the child abduction case we just cleared?"

"Again, assholes who prey on kids don't have the balls to go against a grown man or woman." She returned Matthias's phone. "Besides, we both know their faces, their families' faces, their attorneys' faces. I've never seen this guy before. Even with a mask, I know that much."

Matthias wagged his finger. "There are shots of the other men, too. I threw in pictures of John Boyd, the man with the dog, who was in the exam room when this all went down. And Mrs. Winston, who left just before."

"Mrs. Winston, I've met. Sweet old lady." Cassie scrolled and treated each photo as she had the first. "No," she finally said and returned the phone. "I've never seen any of them. Never investigated them. Never arrested them. And for as long as I've been working this job, that says a lot."

"Which means Shawn was likely the target." Matthias held her gaze and watched her face shift through a range of emotions as she absorbed the possibility.

"Thank God they screwed up," she said with a grim laugh. Then her dark eyes widened. "They must know it by now. What if they try again?"

Matthias placed a hand over hers. "Kollman and Lyle are right outside the ICU, one at each entrance. The lieutenant has ordered a round-the-clock security detail until we catch these guys. Shawn will be fine."

Before Cassie could react, a smiling nurse entered the room and strode their way. "Mrs. Malone," she said, "your husband is awake and asking for you."

Matthias and Cassie came to their feet in unison, but the nurse flashed a palm at him. "Family members only in ICU."

Matthias gave her a grin. "Don't suppose you'd believe that I'm his brother?"

"Sorry." The nurse returned the grin. "I don't see any resemblance."

Matthias shrugged and faced Cassie, shoving his phone into her hands. "If he's up to it, show him the photos. See if he recognizes any of them."

Cassie slipped the phone into her purse as she hurried after the nurse and called back to him, "I know how to do my job."

Chapter Seven

"Missed you at yoga class this morning." Kira Petersen slid into a chair across from Emma and set the tray holding her lunch on the café's table.

Emma drizzled vinaigrette from a clear plastic cup onto her Greek salad. "I had photos to catalogue, but I should've taken the time for class." She shrugged one tense shoulder and felt the pop. "I'm glad you could meet me for lunch."

Kira wore one of her gauzy floral drapes over her standard curve-hugging unitard in a vibrant pink that matched her current hair color. In addition to being her yoga instructor, Kira had become Emma's closest friend in Erie.

"I'm afraid I don't have long. I have a private session to get ready for." Kira lifted her grilled vegetable sandwich to her lips but paused without taking a bite. "Care to tell me what's wrong?"

Emma met her gaze, surprised. "Can't two friends simply get together? What makes you think something's wrong?"

Kira gave her an exaggerated eye roll. "In case you haven't noticed, I'm observant."

Emma couldn't argue the point. "Nothing's really 'wrong.' I was just hoping you could give me some advice."

"I absolutely can." Kira's grin was devious. "I can't promise it'll be *good* advice."

Emma stabbed a forkful of lettuce and cucumbers and stuffed it into her mouth, taking the time to contemplate what she wanted to say.

Kira bit into her sandwich, her focus on Emma.

After chewing, swallowing, and pressing a paper napkin to her lips, Emma lowered the fork. "You remember Eric?"

"Your handsome friend from back home. Of course, I remember."

Her handsome *gay* friend, but Kira knew that. Matthias hadn't at first, which created quite a bit of tension at the time, a memory that amused Emma. She told Kira about the phone call and Sonny Jones's offer on her Washington County farmland.

Kira took another bite, her eyes narrowed in thought. "That's quite a chunk of change."

"No kidding. And Eric seems to think Sonny's willing to go higher."

"Nice." Kira grinned wickedly. "I could use some repairs at the studio. Care to float a gal a loan?"

"You think I should sell." Emma didn't pose it as a question. She'd anticipated this reaction from her freewheeling friend.

"Are you going to give me a loan?" Kira asked with a twinkle in her eyes.

"Maybe. How much?"

Kira waved a hand, and her grin faded. "I'm just kidding. Seriously, why would you want to sell?"

Not the question Emma had expected. "Six hundred thousand dollars is a pretty good reason."

"Money isn't everything."

Also not what Emma had expected.

Kira lifted the top slice of grainy bread from her sandwich and picked off a slice of eggplant, depositing it on the plate. She licked her fingers and replaced the bread. "You're asking for my advice, right?"

"Yes."

"Don't rush into a decision. The farm's been in your family for generations. Once it's gone, it's gone."

A fact that Emma had been thinking about since the moment Eric told her about the offer. "Legally, I can't sell it right now anyway. The deed is in both Nell's and my names."

"Do you know where Nell is?"

"No."

"Do you know if she's still alive?"

The question drove a spike through Emma's heart. Her younger sister was an addict. She'd been homeless, then clean and sober, then believed to be dead, then not. The last Emma had seen of her, she'd been hospitalized before disappearing with her recovering addict boyfriend. There'd been no communication since then. "No."

Kira rested her elbows on either side of her tray and leaned over it, keeping her voice barely above a whisper. "I'm sorry."

"I am, too."

"How do you plan to find her?"

Again, Emma thought. The last time she'd searched for her sister, she at least knew Nell was somewhere here in Erie. Now? "I don't even know where to start. But without Nell, any legal matters involving the two of us are on hold. Indefinitely. So, 'rushing into a decision,'" Emma said, making air quotes, "is something I have no choice about."

"Good."

They fell silent, eating their lunches. Emma's mind plunged into memories of her troubled sister. Memories of mourning her supposed death. Celebrating her return. Losing her again. How many times could Emma's heart break and still keep beating?

Kira finished her sandwich and pushed the tray to one side. "There's something else you need to take into consideration where the sale of your farm is concerned. Or, I should say someone else."

"Matthias."

"You're in love with him."

Emma didn't argue.

"And he's in love with you." Kira shifted in her chair and leaned one elbow on the table. "For now."

The two words hit like a sucker punch.

Kira raised a hand to silence Emma before she had a chance to form a rebuttal. "Matthias is hot. I've said that all along."

She had. Especially when she'd been sleeping with him before he and Emma hooked up.

"But," Kira continued, "he's a long way from being ready to make a commitment. You know his history with women as well as I do."

Better, Emma thought. She'd spoken with the woman who'd shattered him. Kira hadn't.

"The fact that you've been dating for a couple of months now says a lot. But my mother would label him as 'not the marrying type.'"

Emma started to argue that marriage wasn't on her radar right now either.

Kira stopped her with a raised finger. "You asked for my advice. Hear me out."

Annoyed, Emma pressed her lips closed.

"If things don't work out between the two of you, would you really want to stay in Erie? You came here because of Nell. You're staying because of Matthias." Kira spread her arms wide. "While I'd love to think me and my yoga classes would be enough to keep you in town, I suspect the siren song of home would be the stronger draw."

Emma pondered her friend's words.

"I'm right and you know it."

"You're the one who kept pushing me and Matthias together," Emma protested. "Now what? You're telling me he isn't all that into me?"

"I'm telling you to keep your options open." Kira pushed her chair back and stood, taking her tray with her. "Besides." She smiled, a devilish gleam in her eyes. "You have two months to make up your mind."

"Two months?" It took a few seconds for the time limit to register.

"Sara's Campground closes for the season in October." Kira cocked her head. "By then, Matthias will either have moved on, or he'll ask you to move in with him. That would be a big step toward knowing whether or not you need the farm anymore." She fluttered her fingers at Emma. "Sorry, I can't stay. We'll talk again soon."

Emma watched Kira pivot, deposit the tray in the receptacle, and sashay toward the door. Kira might have a point. But even if Matthias was to offer, Emma wasn't sure it was a good idea for her to accept.

Matthias moved to a quiet corner of the waiting room to call Lieutenant Armstrong with an update, including the conversation with Cassie. Armstrong remained quiet for a few moments after Matthias finished speaking.

"While I would never doubt Cassie's opinion on potential suspects," the lieutenant said, measuring his words, "she may not be thinking as clearly as normal. I'm going to put some men on digging into anyone who might have a beef with her."

Matthias agreed. "Good. Cover all bases."

After ending the call, he crossed the room to gaze out a waiting room window. The only view it offered was a brick wall. No one came to this spot for the scenery. Behind him, a television with the volume set low droned on. Equally muted conversations drifted throughout the space. Here, everyone's lives hung suspended, uncertain, awaiting news of whether their futures would go on as planned or veer in a totally different direction. Would Shawn fully recover? Matthias wasn't one for prayer, but had he been, he'd be saying one now. For Cassie's sake.

Rapid footsteps drew his attention from the lousy view. Cassie approached, Matthias's phone in hand, her expression unreadable.

"Well?" he asked.

She returned the phone. "He didn't need the photos. Said he'd never forget their eyes, which is all he saw."

"He remembers the shooting?" Matthias asked. Victims often didn't remember the immediate moments of a traumatic event.

"He does." Cassie leaned a shoulder against the window frame. "The shooter was a light-skinned Black man with green eyes. The other two were White. One with brown eyes, one with blue. Shawn's quite certain he'd never seen any of them before."

Matthias knew there was more and stayed still.

She turned a thoughtful gaze through the window. "He's also positive the gunman fully intended to shoot him all along."

"Did he say why?"

Cassie kept looking out at the brick wall. "I asked. He said he has seen that look in men's eyes before. Cold. Soulless. Spiteful."

The last word caught Matthias by surprise. "Spiteful? He thinks this guy was out to get him?"

Cassie brought her focus back to Matthias. "Some people are out to get us, no matter what."

Matthias took a moment to digest her emphasis on *us*. "You think Shawn was shot because he's Black?"

She didn't reply other than hiking one eyebrow. *Duh.*

"But Shawn said the shooter was another Black man."

"How long have we been partners? And you're still thinking like a White boy."

The way she said it set Matthias's teeth on edge, but he bit back a denial.

"Have you never heard of Black-on-Black violence?"

His statement had been stupid. He knew it the moment the words left his lips. "You know I have." He lowered his voice. "I'm sorry."

Cassie's sharp glare eased. "Apology accepted."

"I just don't want to limit our investigation by assuming the shooter's motivation was racial or political. You taught me that."

"That's right. I did. But I don't want you to limit the investigation by ruling it out either."

Matthias held out an open hand. "Deal."

She looked at his palm for a few long beats before placing her hand in his.

And holding on.

Her eyes shifted. Matthias had seen that look before. "What is it?" he asked.

The lines in her forehead deepened. "I keep thinking we're missing something obvious. Something that's staring us in the face, yet we can't see it."

"Not we. Not us. Me. You're not working this case, remember?"

She finally released his hand. "How can I forget? But be serious. I'm only allowed back there to see him for a few minutes each hour. The rest of the time, I sit here and think horrible thoughts. What if he never comes home?"

"Stop," Matthias growled. "Shawn's awake. Alert. He's strong. He's going to pull through this and be fine."

"I've been married to the man for over thirty years. I know how strong he is. I've also been around long enough to know they don't keep you in ICU for the pleasure of your company." She shook her head. "The only way I can keep the fear at bay is to think like a cop. And thinking is all I can do."

Matthias folded his arms. "Okay. What have you come up with?"

"Not a whole helluva lot. But something Emma said has been bothering me."

"Emma?"

"None of you guys will update me, so she did. She mentioned they entered and exited through the clinic's side door."

"That's right."

"How did they get in that way? It's locked."

"We're trying to figure that out."

"You've watched the security video?"

"You know we have."

"And?"

Matthias's phone vibrated in his hip pocket. "Hang on," he told his partner as he retrieved the device. Roth's name and number filled the screen. Matthias showed Cassie and answered the call.

"We've got one of them," Roth said.

"Under arrest?"

"No. But we got a match on one of the sets of fingerprints from that side door frame. A guy by the name of Kirk Zimmerman. Has a rap sheet three miles long. Possession. DUI. Was just released from Albion after serving time for aggravated assault." Roth listed an address on Cascade as Zimmerman's last known residence.

Matthias cupped his hand around the mic and looked at Cassie. "Does the name Kirk Zimmerman mean anything to you?"

Her eyes shifted. "No." She wagged a finger at the phone. When Matthias uncovered the mic, she asked, "Do you have a photo?"

Matthias brought the phone to his ear as Roth replied, "I'm sending you the mugshot now."

"We need to get a warrant," Matthias said, "and pay Mr. Zimmerman a visit."

"I've already written the affidavit. Waiting for the judge to sign off on it."

"Good." The phone vibrated with the incoming text. "Hold on a second." He pulled up the photo attachment and showed it to Cassie.

She studied it with a laser-sharp intensity before shaking her head. "Never saw him before."

Matthias reclaimed the phone and told Roth, "Cassie doesn't recognize him. I'm heading to Cascade now."

"Meet you there."

Matthias ended the call and met Cassie's fierce gaze. "Send that photo to my phone," she said. "I'll show it to Shawn the next time I'm allowed in."

"Will do."

"Now get outta here and arrest that bastard. Beat him bloody if that's what it takes to get the names of his pals."

Matthias rested a hand lightly on her arm. "Armstrong wouldn't approve."

"The lieutenant's wife isn't fighting for her life in the ICU. If she was, he'd tell you the same thing I did."

"We'll get them." Matthias turned to leave.

Her words trailed after him. "You damned well better."

Chapter Eight

Wearing his ballistic vest over his polo shirt, Matthias sat behind the wheel of his unmarked Malibu and watched the front of the narrow, beige-sided house from half a block away. An oak tree partially blocked his view, but he dared not edge closer and risk alerting their man. The house had two doors facing the street. One on the front. Another in a small add-on toward the rear of the structure, probably a separate entrance to the second-floor apartment.

A sharp rap on the passenger side window made him flinch. "Dammit," he muttered as Roth opened the door and slid into the seat.

He patted his windbreaker's pocket. "Got the warrants, no problem."

"Do we know if Zimmerman lives on the first floor or the second?"

"His address of record lists Unit B."

Upstairs, Matthias thought.

"We've got two uniforms watching the rear in case he rabbits. He doesn't own a car, so if he takes off, it'll be on foot."

"Not owning a car doesn't mean he doesn't have access to one."

"True." Roth shrugged. "Frazier and two more uniforms are down the street, ready to go when you give the word." Roth pointed north, on the opposite side of the house in question.

Matthias reached for the door handle. "Let's do this."

Roth gave the order through his handheld and stepped out of the car. He may have Matthias beat in height, but Matthias outpaced him and reached the address first. Frazier and two officers in uniforms, all wearing ballistic vests, jogged toward them from the opposite direction. Matthias hoped this went down easy. Hoped Zimmerman opened the door, raised his hands, and allowed them to take him into custody without a struggle. An optimistic outcome that Matthias didn't believe would happen.

The door closest to the street had a letter A tacked above a brass knocker. They approached the second one, which was labeled as B. Matthias pressed his shoulder against the jamb on one side. Roth, the other. Frazier positioned himself against the side of the house. All three of them kept one hand on their sidearms as Matthias raised his fist and pounded.

No sound came from inside. No footsteps. No voices. No background noise from a television.

Matthias pounded again. "Kirk Zimmerman?" he shouted. "Erie City Police. Open the door and keep your hands where we can see them."

Still nothing from inside.

But the crack of a fallen twig swung Matthias and his partners to face the street. A young woman with a blond ponytail, long tan legs, and terrified wide brown eyes stood at the front corner and stiffened, her empty hands held away from her sides.

"Don't shoot," she squeaked in a little-girl voice.

"Miss, you need to go home, get back inside, and stay there," Matthias ordered.

She aimed a thumb at the door with the A on it. "But this is my house."

"Do you know the man who lives here?" Matthias gestured at Unit B.

"Zim? Yeah. He's my boyfriend. What's he done?"

"Is he in there?"

"Yes." Her gaze darted to the door. "Why do you want him?"

Matthias debated repeating his order for her to go inside and lock her doors. He opted to enlist her help. "What's your name?"

"Misti with an i," she said, her tone hesitant. "Misti Dunlevy."

"You say Kirk Zimmerman is your boyfriend?"

"Yes." Her answer sounded more like a question.

"Could you do us a favor and call him? Tell him we need to talk to him."

"Okay." Again, it sounded like a question.

She retrieved a sparkly blue phone from the hip pocket of her cut-off jeans and thumbed the screen. Not enough to text a warning, for which Matthias was grateful. This kid looked too young and innocent to be dragged down by the likes of Zimmerman. Matthias would hate to haul her cute ass off to jail.

Misti with an i pressed the phone to her ear and waited. After several long seconds she shook her head. "That's not right. He always answers when I call him." Without asking permission, she pushed her way through them to the door and knocked. "Zim?" she called. "Open up. It's me."

She didn't receive a response either.

"Something's wrong." Her hand was on the doorknob before Matthias could stop her.

It clicked open. He grabbed her wrist, stopping her from swinging the door inward. "That's enough." He kept his voice barely above a whisper, hoping against hope that Zimmerman wasn't on the other side. "Go back into your apartment and lock the door."

She shook her head, her ponytail swinging. "No. You don't understand. Something's wrong. I know he's in there, and he never leaves the door unlocked."

Unless he was expecting company and wanted them to walk into an ambush.

Matthias took her by her shoulders and turned her toward Frazier. They exchanged a look, and he nodded, understanding. Matthias turned her over to him, and Frazier escorted a protesting Misti to the front of the house.

Matthias locked gazes with Roth, an unspoken question in his eyes. *Ready?* Roth tipped his head once. Matthias slammed the door open and stormed inside, bellowing, "Police!"

Emma cruised down West 12th Street, heading home. Traffic was heavy along the stretch of road with restaurants and businesses lining both sides. Somehow, she was managing to hit every traffic light red. Each stop gave her time to scan her surroundings. And to think.

At lunch, Kira hadn't been helpful in the least. Or to be more precise, she hadn't offered the advice Emma had expected. Especially where Matthias was concerned. Granted, Emma knew part of the reason she'd earned his respect was the fact she appreciated his devotion to his job and didn't complain when work called him away from their plans. This weekend for example. She didn't make demands. Wasn't clingy or needy.

She didn't expect him to invite her to move in once the campground closed for the season and was afraid if he did—and she agreed—the constant togetherness would drive a wedge between them. Whether or not Kira was right about Matthias not being the marrying type, Emma wasn't going to pressure him.

But two of Kira's words kept echoing in her brain.

For now.

Matthias was in love with Emma.

For now.

She realized she hadn't considered him dumping her anytime soon. She'd only imagined the two of them, relaxed, taking their time, enjoying each other's company with no ties.

The one green light she hit was at the intersection with Peninsula Drive where she made the turn downhill toward Presque Isle State Park and—just before the park entrance—Sara's Campground.

Emma made another right, this one as the descent leveled off, pulling through the parking lots of a Thai restaurant and a shop selling beachy trinkets to tourists and bait to fishermen. Ahead of her, Sara's Restaurant, the fifties-style diner fronting the campground with the same name, boasted a long drive-through line, making her glad her stomach was still full.

She powered down her window and eased through the open gate, adhering to the five-mile-an-hour speed limit along the trailer- and tree-lined blacktop road. A few of the other residents were outside and waved as she passed. She waved back.

Beyond the block building housing the showers, Emma made one more right turn, up the final grade to home, a seventeen-foot camper with a covered deck that nearly doubled her living space. She nosed her Subaru in toward the trailer's hitch and stepped out. The empty lot between hers and the next site remained vacant despite rumors that it had been leased, for which she was grateful.

Until this past February, she'd lived most of her life on the farm property Sonny Jones now wanted to buy, with the nearest neighbor nearly a quarter mile away. While she'd come to love this place, the lack of privacy still bothered her. The space between campers was limited to a matter of feet. Her door and covered deck faced downhill. The older man who leased the lower site only showed up a few days a month, and then spent the bulk of his time out on his boat, returning to camp after dusk to sleep.

Her previous uphill neighbor had become a friend before a tragedy took his life a few months ago. Since then, Emma had become accustomed to the empty spot—a buffer zone—between her kitchen window and the next guy up the hill, who was notorious for overindulging in alcohol and playing his radio too loud. Which was exactly what he was doing at the moment. The man was nowhere to be seen, but his music blasted at full volume.

Inside, she drew the blinds over the kitchen sink, washed her hands, and splashed cold water on her face before reaching into her fridge for a soda. She slid into the bench seat at the kitchen table, which doubled as her home office, computers taking up all the surface space. Closing her eyes, she let the hum of the ceiling-mounted air conditioner drown out all but the bass beat.

However, the rumble did nothing to drown the ringtones of her phone. She opened her eyes and dug it from her pocket, hoping to see Matthias's name and face on the screen. Instead, the caller ID informed her Preston was on the other end of the line.

"What's up?" she asked.

"Something's going down with Dr. Shawn's case." Preston sounded breathless.

She sat up taller. "What do you mean? Is he okay?"

"I said with the case. Not with him. Are you telling me your cop boyfriend hasn't let you know?"

Evidently not. "Know what?"

"According to my source, police have responded to a residence on Cascade Street where a suspect in the shooting is holed up."

The words settled like a block of lead on Emma's heart. *Matthias* was responding, not the generic police that Preston had reported. The imagined scene flashed through her mind. Matthias trying to take down the crazed gunman who'd shot Shawn

Malone. Guns blazing. Matthias being struck. Lying in the street, bleeding.

"You still there?" Preston's words cut through her mental nightmare.

"I'm here."

"Where's 'here?' Do you need me to pick you up on the way?"

"I'll meet you there. Text me the address."

With his sidearm in hand, Matthias led the way up the narrow staircase, the words *kill zone* bouncing inside his head. If Zimmerman appeared at the top of the steps with a gun, there was no place to take cover. Matthias pounded to the top, Roth and the uniforms on his heels.

No Zimmerman.

Matthias hesitated only long enough for the others to join him before swinging to the left. Roth went right without being told. The pair of officers split off as well. The dark hardwood floors felt tacky beneath Matthias's boots.

The upstairs apartment was sparsely furnished with what looked like thrift store purchases. A drab brown sofa faced a wall holding the one newish looking piece—a huge television. Keeping his Glock ready, Matthias picked his way through the empty pizza and takeout boxes that overflowed from a coffee table covered in stains from spilled food and beverages. The place stunk like rotting trash.

From behind him, Roth called out, "Clear."

Beyond the meager living room, an open door revealed an equally meager kitchen. Matthias eased to the threshold, alert to any hint of movement, any minute creak of floorboards. As he stepped through, he saw he needn't have worried. "Got a body," he called to the others.

A male lay crumpled face up between a vintage table and a wall of builder's grade cabinets. Matthias stepped to his side and knelt, feeling for a pulse. Finding none.

"Is it our guy?" Roth asked from behind him.

Matthias opened the picture of Zimmerman's mugshot on his phone. Comparing the image to the pale face of the decedent on the floor, Matthias exhaled. "Yep."

So much for getting any answers from this guy.

He gave the body a long look without touching it. No blood. No obvious wounds.

At Matthias's shoulder, Roth echoed his assessment. "Doesn't look like he was shot. I wonder what happened."

Matthias waved the others back. "That's for Hamilton to determine. Let's clear the area and secure the scene until he gets here."

Chapter Nine

Cascade was already barricaded by police vehicles when Emma arrived, forcing her to park on the next street. She grabbed her backpack, slung her press pass around her neck, locked the Subaru, and darted across traffic.

Matthias hadn't responded to her text. She told herself it was because he had his hands full, not because he'd been gunned down. As she made the turn onto Cascade and jogged toward the house in question, she spotted the coroner's van parked in the street and picked up her pace. Yellow crime scene tape was strung across the sidewalk a few hundred feet away from the address. A uniformed cop stood guard with his arms crossed as if daring her to try anything.

She held up the laminated press ID and offered a weak smile. "What happened?"

He barely glanced at the pass. "You'll have to talk to the deputy chief."

"I don't need a statement." That was Preston's job. "I have friends in the department. Were any officers hurt?" Her voice cracked on that last word.

Before the cop had a chance to reply or refuse to, Emma spotted Matthias, looking very much alive and unharmed, standing in front of the house at the center of all the activity. He was talking to a young woman, who was doubled over, her hands covering her face.

"You made better time than I did," Preston said from behind Emma.

She glanced back at the reporter. Worrying about the man she loved may have led her to push the speed limit and accelerate through a yellow light or two.

"What's going on?" Preston asked.

"I just got here." She pointed at the cop. "He told me to talk to the deputy chief."

Preston made an annoyed face. "Go take pictures. I've got this."

Emma caught a glimpse of a raised eyebrow and the hint of a bemused grin on the cop's face as she crossed the street and followed the crime scene tape's perimeter down the sidewalk. Matthias didn't look up when she found a spot in the overgrown front yard directly across from the address. She lifted her Nikon and grabbed photos of the coroner's van, the house, and the distraught young woman, careful to crop Matthias from the image. He didn't want his face posted online, and she didn't want to put him in danger should he need to go undercover.

Pivoting, she snapped photos of the gathering bystanders, an audience running the gamut from older folks to several people who'd brought their dogs, to parents with younger children.

When she focused her attention back to the house, Matthias was striding her way, his expression dark. "We have to stop meeting this way," she quipped.

He didn't smile.

"Is there anything you can tell me?" she asked.

He remained stone-faced, as she'd expected. After a quick look around, he asked, "Where's Guilfoyle?"

"Doing his thing. Asking questions of anyone who'll answer." Which would not be Matthias, she thought.

"Tell him there'll be a press conference in city council chambers at eight o'clock."

"I will. Thanks."

His lips pressed tightly closed but twitched. She knew he wanted to say more.

"It's an active investigation. I get it," she said.

"I know you do. It's just..." He inhaled and shot a glance at the coroner's van. "This isn't how I planned for us to spend the weekend."

"I know. I doubt it's how Cassie and Shawn planned to spend their weekend either."

He huffed a humorless laugh.

"Any word on him? Is he doing any better?"

"I was with Cassie when I got the call about ... this." He gestured over his shoulder at the house being swarmed by law enforcement. "He's still in ICU but is conscious. Cassie was able to show him some security stills from the robbery."

"Did he identify anyone?"

He fixed her with his stern cop expression again.

Emma raised both hands. "Sorry. Being a worried friend sometimes crosses the active investigation border."

Matthias's face softened. He leaned closer and whispered, "Shawn didn't recognize anyone in the photos. Neither did Cassie. But he gave us as much of a description of the shooter as he was able to." Matthias pulled back. "That's all I can tell you. They may say more at the press conference."

"Got it. Thanks."

"That stuff about Shawn and Cassie not recognizing anyone?

Keep it between us. I'm not sure how the higher-ups are going to play this."

Emma understood without being told. The cops may decide to let the public—and the suspects—believe they knew more or less than they did to throw the assailants off guard.

Matthias's phone buzzed. He checked it, stuffed it back in his pocket, and met her gaze. "I have to talk to the coroner." He touched her arm with his fingertips. "Can I call you later?"

"I'd like that. I'll be home if you can get away." She let the statement hang, tipping her head flirtatiously.

He winced. "I wish. This will be another all-nighter." He lowered his voice. "These guys tried to take out Cassie's husband. One of our own. We'll keep on this case until we drop."

Emma watched him stride away, admiring the breadth of his shoulders, the way his tactical trousers fit his backside, and imagined what was beneath the cop attire. She sighed. The promise of a phone call would have to suffice for now.

Blinking away her X-rated fantasies, she lifted her Nikon and once more focused on the people gathering outside the crime scene tape.

Matthias returned to the kitchen where Erie County Coroner Felix Hamilton, whose sun-bleached hair and youthful tanned face made him look like he'd spent the day surfing in the Pacific, was standing over the decedent as his deputies unfolded the body bag next to it.

"Got anything for us yet?" Matthias asked.

Hamilton turned to him, his expression determined. "Nothing official until I get him to the morgue."

"Unofficially then."

Hamilton tipped his head toward an unoccupied corner of the

room. Matthias followed him there. "Unofficially, he was strangled."

"With what?"

"I wish I could tell you. The details will have to wait. Both officially and unofficially."

"You pulled me over here just for that?"

"No. I have a few observations. There's no ID on the body."

"Not surprising. He's at home. No need to keep his wallet in his pants."

"Just saying you and your people need to look for it."

Matthias gave him a snide grin. "You telling me how to do my job, Ham?"

"Yep." The coroner lowered his voice. "And I'm going to tell you some more. I'm not a cop, but it looks to me like someone cleaned up the scene."

Matthias looked toward the decedent being zipped into the body bag and noted the pristine kitchen was a stark contrast to the pizza boxes and takeout containers in the next room.

"This isn't a huge space," Hamilton said. "It seems to me that if someone was trying to strangle him, he'd put up a fight."

"And in the process, stuff would get knocked over."

"Exactly." Hamilton ran a hand through his disheveled hair. "Have you talked to Cassie?"

"Right before I responded to this."

"Shawn?"

"Improving but still in the ICU."

Hamilton nodded. "Give her my best. And tell her I'm glad I didn't have to do a postmortem on her husband."

"Sure. I'll tell her," Matthias said, knowing there was no way in hell he was going to relay the last part of that message.

The meeting room at the Erie City Hall was packed with reporters from local, state, and national news outlets. Emma and Preston edged along the wall to get a spot as close to the podium as possible, which wasn't all that close. The reporters, photographers, and videographers talked amongst themselves, voices rising to be heard over the din. Emma silently observed.

Preston leaned toward her, his mouth nearly touching her ear. "What did your cop tell you?"

"Nothing."

Preston smirked at her. They both knew she was lying.

The room fell quiet when a man Emma recognized as the police chief entered through a door near the podium. Square jawed and wearing a gray buzzcut, the man's eagle-like gaze swept the room, commanding as much respect from the journalists as from his officers. She brought her camera to her eye and tripped the shutter.

Preston clicked on his phone's recorder and aimed the mic at the speaker.

"Good evening. I have a brief update on the shooting of Dr. Shawn Malone after which I'll take questions."

Preston leaned over to whisper in Emma's ear. "But he won't answer them."

She shushed him.

"Police responded to the believed residence of one of the suspects in the shooting, at which time they found the body of one Kirk Zimmerman. The investigation into Mr. Zimmerman's death is ongoing. I'll release further information as it becomes available. We've obtained a description of a second man involved in Dr. Malone's shooting and would like the public's assistance in locating him. He's described as a light-skinned Black man, approximately six feet tall with green eyes. He's believed to be armed and dangerous. If anyone thinks they know the identity or location of this man, do not approach, but call 9-1-1 immediately."

"Not much of a description," Preston whispered. "I hope their call center is well staffed tonight."

Emma elbowed him. "Shut up." But she needn't have bothered to silence him. The chief opened the room to questions.

As Preston had predicted, most of the responses were vague or a repeat of what he'd already said.

Or what Emma already knew.

The chief refused to release additional information on Shawn's condition or details about the dead suspect. Or how they'd tracked him down. Or who gave them the description—such as it was—of the man they were looking for.

As the questions dwindled, Preston raised his hand. When the chief pointed to him, he asked, "Has there been any progress in locating the drugs that were stolen from the veterinary hospital?"

"We're continuing to investigate," the chief said before turning from the podium and disappearing through the door.

"In other words, no," Preston muttered.

Under her breath, Emma said, "Not necessarily."

He turned to look at her. "Are you holding out on me again?"

"No," she replied. Not this time.

Chapter Ten

Sunday morning, Matthias nursed a cup of coffee laden with two extra shots of espresso as he, Roth, and Frazier walked the two and a half blocks to the morgue. The phone call he'd hoped to make to Emma last night had turned into a quick text —*Sleep well*—just before midnight. By the time the crime scene techs finished processing the house on Cascade and he and his fellow detectives had questioned the hysterical girlfriend and neighbors, it was close to dawn. Exhausted, Matthias slipped out to his Jeep parked across the street from the police station and caught almost an hour of sleep in his front seat. Far from refreshed, he headed back inside where he showered and changed into a clean polo shirt and pair of tactical trousers. As ready for a new day as possible under the circumstances.

Felix Hamilton, a pair of autopsy techs, and Dr. Alexandra Browning, the forensic pathologist, were about to start the autopsy on Zimmerman when Matthias, Roth, and Frazier took up their usual positions—close enough to observe but far enough back to stay out of the way.

Matthias knew attendance at autopsies was part of his job, but he often showed up late intentionally, leaving Cassie to handle all but the final collection of evidence. Today, Cassie was otherwise occupied, and if Zimmerman was part of the crew who'd robbed and shot Shawn, Matthias wasn't about to miss even a minute.

Dr. Browning, a fifty-something woman with gray hair perennially secured in a bun, recorded her observations of the postmortem, starting with the victim's height as five foot eleven. His weight was one hundred and eighty-two pounds, general physical condition was well muscled and fit. Browning noted petechial hemorrhages in the decedent's eyes and some irritation on his hands.

"What would cause the irritation?" Matthias asked.

"I'm taking skin scrapings to confirm, but my educated guess? Allergies."

Matthias thought of the security footage and Zimmerman stripping off his gloves before exiting the vet clinic. "Like a latex allergy?"

"Exactly like that."

As the autopsy proceeded, the only obvious injuries were ligature marks around Zimmerman's neck. Once the body was opened, the pathologist reported a crushed larynx and trachea. Cause of death was noted as asphyxia. Browning also pointed out the presence of defensive wounds on the man's fingers. Matthias imagined having a rope around his own neck, struggling to get free. He had studied martial arts and self-defense and knew more effective escape techniques than merely clawing at the rope, but Zimmerman probably lacked those skills.

"Can you tell what the killer used to strangle him?" Matthias asked.

The pathologist's dark gaze slid to Matthias. "You expect me to do your job, Detective?"

He raised both hands in surrender. "Just looking for whatever help you can give me."

She returned her attention to the body and bent over, studying his neck. "The indentations on the decedent's neck are an inch wide and appear flat rather than concave."

Matthias considered her words. "You're saying strapping of some sort rather than a rope or a wire."

"I'm not saying anything. I'm only telling you my observations."

Matthias caught a glimpse of Hamilton rolling his eyes behind the pathologist's back.

"But," she continued, "a strap would be consistent with my findings."

"What kind of strap?" Frazier asked. "The kind used to keep packages together for shipping?"

Before Dr. Browning could snap a noncommittal response, Hamilton said, "Possibly." He gazed at the body on the stainless-steel table. "But wider than what you're talking about. To me, it looks more like what's used on backpacks."

"Or the handles of reusable shopping totes?" Roth asked. "My mother has a whole car trunk full."

"More like those, yes," Hamilton said with a nod. He gestured toward several evidence bags piled on a nearby stainless-steel shelf. "We've collected trace fibers from the decedent's neck. The lab should be able to give you a clearer idea of what you're looking for once they have a chance to examine them."

"What kind of fibers?" Matthias asked.

Dr. Browning shot an annoyed look his way, but Hamilton again cut her off. "Like I said, the lab will give you a better idea than I can."

"What about drugs?" Frazier glanced at Matthias. "We still haven't determined if the stolen pharmaceuticals were intended for personal use or to be sold."

"You know the routine, Detective," Hamilton replied. "I'll let you know as soon as we get the results back from toxicology."

"I *can* tell you this much," Dr. Browning added. "I see no indication of the kind of organ damage that I'd expect in a habitual user."

Matthias sent Roth and a handful of uniformed officers back out to Cascade Street to recanvass the neighborhood in the hopes of finding anyone they'd missed last night. The residents they'd already spoken with denied having seen an unknown vehicle parked in the vicinity or anyone unusual coming or going from the house. They'd also determined that no one within three blocks of Zimmerman's house owned a security camera, but Matthias ordered Roth to expand the search in all directions, hoping to catch a glimpse of the perpetrator. Matthias and Frazier returned to Major Crimes for a deep dive into Zimmerman's history.

Seated at his desk, Matthias was painfully aware of the vacancy behind him. He'd texted Cassie earlier and learned that Shawn was steadily improving and might be moved from ICU to a regular room later today. Matthias planned to swing by Hamot for a visit when he had a chance. He hoped like hell he'd have progress to share with his partner. If he didn't, Cassie would have his head. Even worse, she'd insist on working the case herself.

Leaving the social media side of Zimmerman's life to Frazier, Matthias searched every criminal database he had access to. As Roth had told him yesterday, Zimmerman had a long and colorful rap sheet going back to a drunk and disorderly on his eighteenth birthday. From there, he'd had multiple drug arrests for possession and possession with intent to sell as well as a smattering of simple assault and reckless endangerment charges. Matthias became convinced the guy'd had a hell of an attorney, who'd likely pled him down from more serious charges in order for Zimmerman to have spent only minimal time behind bars. His luck ran out when he'd been convicted of involuntary manslaughter and sentenced to five years, of which he served three.

Matthias wondered if even that was a lesser charge than what Zimmerman had in fact committed. Further digging into old news reports revealed Matthias was right. Zimmerman had originally been charged with third degree murder when he'd struck and killed a thirteen-year-old bicyclist while fleeing police in a stolen vehicle.

Matthias found and printed out a list of Zimmerman's known associates and scanned the names. He recognized a few low-level thugs he'd encountered while investigating other crimes, including a few he'd help put away. None of the names leaped out at him as potential partners in the vet clinic robbery nor as suspects in Zimmerman's murder. Nevertheless, it was a start.

From the cubby on the other side of Cassie's vacant one, Frazier called out. "Find anything?"

"A list of Zimmerman's known associates. What about you?"

Frazier appeared next to Matthias. "Not much. He has a Facebook account that he hasn't posted to in over a year. I searched his friends list, looking for some connection to Shawn and came up empty. Zimmerman has a stronger presence on X, though." Frazier shouldered the edge of the cubicle and crossed his arms. "He's basically an ass. Spouts a lot of paranoid accusations and open hatred of anyone and everyone who isn't White and male. No mention of Shawn or anyone else I recognize. No rumblings of his criminal activity either. At least he's smart enough to not brag about his ill-gotten gains online."

Matthias handed him a copy of the known associates list. "Check to see if any of these folks are connected to his social media accounts."

Frazier studied the names. "On it." He turned away, hesitated, and came back. "Why do you think someone would want this guy dead?"

Matthias eyed Frazier. "Seriously? No one on that list is a fine, upstanding citizen."

"I know that." He fluttered the paper. "But what if his killer isn't on here? He was just part of an armed robbery turned homicide. Maybe one of the other two who held up Shawn didn't want to share the bounty."

Matthias had been thinking along those same lines. "Or they found out we'd identified him, were close to an arrest, and were afraid he'd rat them out to save his own ass."

Frazier nodded thoughtfully. "Or it might have nothing to do with the robbery at all. Maybe he pissed off his girlfriend."

Matthias pictured Misti with an i and couldn't see it. "Zimmerman wasn't exactly a body builder, but his girlfriend is maybe a hundred pounds soaking wet. If she'd caught him off guard and wrapped her purse strap around his neck, he could've thrown her off like a flea."

Frazier looked at him askance. "You ever try to de-flea a dog? It takes some heavy-duty chemicals and a good bath."

"That's for a flea infestation. One flea? You pick it off and..." Matthias mimed pinging something from his thumb with a forefinger.

"True." Frazier's eyes narrowed. "But who's to say little Misti didn't have help?"

Frazier had a point. Matthias leaned back and scrubbed his face and his tired eyes. "Okay. You take that angle. Dig into Misti Dunlevy." He rose from his chair and moved to the breakroom to pour a cup of coffee.

Frazier followed him. "What are you going to do?"

Matthias took a sip and instantly regretted it. "First, I'm dumping this and making a fresh pot." He pulled the plug, but before he could move the urn to the sink, a thought stopped him.

They'd been digging into Zimmerman's past, his life, his social media. What they had not dug into was Shawn Malone's.

Matthias abandoned the coffee maker, pivoted slowly, and stalked past a puzzled Frazier and back to his desk. Investigating Shawn felt like an invasion of Cassie's privacy—because it was—but he also felt remiss for not having gone there.

"What the hell are you doing?" Frazier asked.

With a heavy sigh, Matthias dropped into his chair. "I'm looking at a different angle." Then he typed *Shawn Malone* into the search bar.

Emma left the campground early Sunday morning and drove to the hospital. The security guard posted at the entrance took her driver's license and made a phone call. After clearing her, he said, "Dr. Malone has been transferred to a private room." He gave her the number and handed her a peel-and-stick visitor's pass.

As Emma took the elevator, she battled memories. The last time she'd seen her younger sister was a couple of months ago in this part of the hospital.

The doors opened with a soft chime. Emma shook off the memories and stepped out.

Voices and laughter floated out of the room as Emma approached. She recognized Officer Kollman seated in the hallway. He gave her a grin and gestured for her to go in.

She stopped in the doorway and enjoyed the sight. Shawn was sitting up in the bed, a broad smile on his handsome face. Cassie stood over him looking relaxed and relieved. Alissa, their eight-year-old granddaughter, perched next to her grandfather on the bed, showing him sheets of paper and giggling at the overjoyed look on his face.

He caught a glimpse of Emma and waved. "Don't just stand

there," he told her, his voice raspy, yet surprisingly strong for having been shot in the chest only thirty-six hours ago.

Cassie came to her feet. "Emma. Come in." Pointing at her husband, she said, "Doesn't he look good?"

"He does. If I didn't know, I would never have guessed he was a shooting victim."

Shawn made a pained face and pulled the neck of his hospital gown down to reveal the top edge of a white bandage. "Trust me. I am."

"How are you feeling?" Emma dragged a chair closer to the bed.

He touched the nasal cannula nestled beneath his nose. "Better. Breathing is easier." He pointed to an I.V. stand next to the bed. "They've got me on morphine for the pain."

"Better living through chemistry," Cassie quipped.

Shawn's attention returned to his granddaughter. "And I have this little princess to cheer me up."

Alissa shifted to face Emma and held up a sheet of paper on which she'd sketched remarkably recognizable images of Shawn and Cassie with a big heart framing them. "See what I drew."

"That's amazing," Emma said. She looked at Cassie. "Seriously. At her age I was drawing stick figures. You may have a budding artist on your hands."

Cassie beamed. "Her mother's quite a talented artist, too. You've been to our house. Have you ever noticed the landscape over our mantle?"

"I have." Emma had more than noticed it. Every time she looked at the landscape of a lake surrounded by trees in autumnal shades reflected in the water, she felt envious, uncertain if even her camera could capture the scene as well as the artist had. "Your daughter did that?"

Cassie tipped her head. "Indeed, she did."

Which triggered another question. "Does she know what happened?"

Shawn shot a scowl at Cassie and grunted. "Her mama called her Friday night. Now she's on her way back here."

"Denene would be furious if I kept her in the dark," Cassie said to him. She met Emma's gaze. "She's been granted compassionate leave."

Alissa clapped her hands. "Mommy's coming home."

"Just for a visit," Shawn told her.

Cassie leaned down to plant a kiss on the little girl's head. "She needs to see for herself that her father's not on death's doorstep."

Shawn's expression held less enthusiasm, but Emma sensed he chose to keep his thoughts to himself in front of Alissa, so she didn't ask.

Cassie pulled a large sketch pad from a tote on the floor and flipped the cover open to reveal a blank page. "Alissa, why don't you draw something for Emma?"

"Okay." Alissa cast large dark eyes at her. "What do you want me to draw?"

Emma paused to think, but Cassie replied, "She used to have horses. Right?" Cassie lifted a questioning eyebrow at Emma.

"I did."

Alissa clapped. "I love horses. What color?"

"Reddish-brown," Emma replied, not sure if Cassie's granddaughter knew the terminology.

"Chestnut?" Alissa asked. "Or bay?"

Emma should've known. Little girls and horses. Alissa might not own one, but she'd probably read every book on their care and feeding available. Emma remembered having done the same thing. "Light chestnut," she said, then added, "Sorrel. With a star and stripe." She placed a finger on her forehead.

Alissa gave a quick nod and slid down from the bed to dig a pack of markers from the tote. Cassie settled her in a chair with the tablet and left her to sketch. With Alissa intent on her art, Cassie caught Emma's gaze and tipped her head to the opposite side of Shawn's bed. Emma followed her there.

In a low voice, Cassie asked, "Is there any news about the incident?" Despite Alissa's focus, Cassie still shot a glance to make sure the little girl wasn't eavesdropping.

"Hasn't Matthias updated you?"

"No." Cassie exhaled. "I think he's scared to admit they haven't made any progress."

Emma hated being in this position. Maybe Matthias didn't want Cassie and Shawn to know about Zimmerman yet, although she couldn't imagine why.

"You do know something." Cassie pointed a finger at her. "I can see you're thinking how much to tell me."

No wonder Matthias was avoiding Cassie. "Have you heard about the homicide last night?" Emma asked.

"What homicide?"

Shawn reached for his bed rail and the button to turn on the TV, but Cassie held out a hand to stop him. Lowering her voice even further, she said, "We've intentionally kept the television off." Tilting her head toward the young artist, Cassie said, "We've finally gotten her calmed down about all this. I don't want her seeing news reports about Shawn and getting freaked out all over again."

"I understand." Matching their whispered tones, Emma shared what she knew about Kirk Zimmerman. "They identified him as being one of the men who held you up," she said to Shawn. "When they got to his house, he was already dead."

"Shot?" Cassie asked.

"I don't know. There's supposed to be another press conference later today, but as of last night, the chief was giving the usual non-answers. He did give a description of one of the others. Light-skinned Black man with green eyes."

Shawn made a face. "They got that from me. He's the one who pulled the trigger."

A movement from the chair across the bed drew their attention as Alissa lifted her face to scowl at them. "Is Mommy all right?" she asked.

"Your mommy's fine, baby," Cassie said. Turning to Emma, she added softly, "Alissa is scared to death her mother's going to get shot over there. Certain words trigger her. Like 'trigger.'"

The irony struck Emma. Alissa's mother served in the Army. Her grandmother was a cop. And yet it was her veterinarian grandfather who took a bullet.

A knock at the door drew Emma's attention. Matthias stood in the threshold, his face unreadable as he took in the scene before him.

"Uncle Matthias!" Alissa squealed and slid from the chair, dropping her marker and tablet. She dashed to him, arms outstretched.

He scooped her up with a big grin. "Hey, Peanut. Why aren't you in school?"

"It's Sunday," she replied, sounding as if it was the stupidest question ever.

He chuckled and shifted his gaze briefly to Emma before settling on Shawn. "Good to see you, man."

"It's good to be seen."

Emma shot a glance at Cassie and could tell she wanted nothing more than to grill her partner about the case, but Alissa provided a shield. Emma was pretty sure Matthias knew it and was making no move to set the little girl down.

Cassie cleared her throat. "Emma, would you do me a big favor and take Alissa down to the snack bar for some ice cream."

Alissa's eyes brightened. "Ice cream!"

Cassie reached for her handbag, but Matthias interrupted. "Cassie, you should take her. You could use a break."

Emma looked from Matthias to Cassie, whose expression turned dark. "I'm fine," she said, her words clipped. She pulled out her wallet. "Emma, get yourself something, too."

Still carrying Alissa, Matthias stalked toward Cassie without looking at Emma. "All three of you should go." His voice was low and filled with gravel.

Emma had heard that tone plenty of times and it was never a good sign. He wanted to talk to Shawn alone. If Emma could tell that much, surely Cassie could as well.

"I'm not going anywhere." Cassie's tone matched his.

Part of Emma was glad to be left out of Matthias's line of fire. Another part was curious as hell.

The two detectives stared each other down. Alissa started to squirm in his arms.

"Oh, for crissakes, Cassie," Shawn muttered. "Take Alissa and Emma and go get something to eat. We all know Matthias wants to talk to me about the case."

Cassie whirled on her husband, her mouth open.

Shawn raised a hand and shushed her. "You aren't part of the investigation, remember?"

"But—"

He shushed her again.

A dark shade of red rose in Cassie's cheeks. Emma half expected smoke to hiss from her ears.

"Fine," Cassie said through tight lips. "I'll take Alissa." Her eyes met Emma's. "You stay."

Emma didn't need to ask why. Cassie expected her to report back every detail of the conversation between the two men.

Matthias handed Alissa to her grandmother. "No. All three of you go."

Emma wanted to argue but didn't. She appreciated Cassie's trust in her. She also did not want to be placed in the position of spy, taking sides against Matthias.

Cassie settled Alissa on one hip while continuing to scowl at her partner. "We will talk later," she said to him.

Matthias didn't blink.

She shot a threatening glare at Shawn before heading for the door. "Let's go," she called over her shoulder to Emma.

Matthias met Emma's gaze. "Close the door on your way out," he said with less of the gravel.

She did as she was asked, but as the door drifted shut, she overheard Shawn say, "I guess you have a few questions for me."

Chapter Eleven

atthias had more than a "few" questions for Cassie's husband. Pulling out his notebook, Matthias asked, "Have you remembered anything more about Friday night?"

Shawn shook his head. "It isn't a matter of not remembering. I replay the whole damn incident in my mind every time I close my eyes."

"But you don't know any of the men who robbed your clinic?"

"I don't believe so. With the masks and hoodies, it was impossible to tell for sure. Except for the man who looked me square in the eyes and shot me." A muscle popped in Shawn's jaw. "I'm absolutely certain I've never met him before, but I'm equally sure I'd recognize him if I saw him again."

Matthias went back over old territory, asking him about the day leading up to the break-in. Most of Shawn's answers confirmed his staff's accounts. "Do you have any idea how they gained entry?"

Shawn appeared startled by the question. "I was with a patient. I assumed they'd come through the front doors."

Matthias jotted a note.

"Didn't they?" Shawn asked.

"According to security footage, they entered through the side door."

Shawn scowled. "That can't be right. We keep that door locked from the outside. We can get out, but unless you have a key, you can't get in."

"Who all has keys?"

"I do, naturally, and so do each of the other doctors. Bethany Stone, my office manager." Shawn's gaze shifted as he thought. "Robin Tucker…"

"The receptionist?" The *flirty* receptionist, Matthias thought.

"Yes. And Sharon Long."

Matthias thumbed back through his notes.

"Sharon's my senior vet tech. She had family plans and left before everything went down."

Matthias found the name in the list of other clinic employees and made a note to make sure she'd been questioned. "All told, how many keys are there?"

Shawn shook his head. "You'll have to ask Bethany. She keeps on top of that sort of thing better than I do."

"I will." The mention of Bethany gave Matthias an easy segue to his next questions. "How long has Bethany been working for you?"

Shawn pushed himself up in the bed with a groan. Once settled, he heaved a sigh. "Bethany has worked for me longer than any of the others. I'd have to check to be exact, but about twenty-five years or so."

"And you trust her?"

For the first time since Matthias had entered the room, Shawn's expression turned hard. "With my life."

Matthias didn't point out that Shawn had very nearly lost that life. "Cassie mentioned Bethany'd had some issues with gambling."

"Cassie shouldn't have said anything."

"I'm investigating a shooting. *Your* shooting. Cassie wants answers more than anyone else does."

Shawn's gaze shifted to the window before coming back to Matthias. "Bethany had some gambling issues, as you put it. She's been in Gamblers Anonymous ever since."

"You caught her stealing from petty cash."

"No, I did not. She came to me because she felt the temptation becoming too strong. Ratted herself out, so to speak. I directed her to Gamblers Anonymous and that was the end of it. Do me a favor and leave it be."

Matthias lowered his face and his voice. "I wish I could." He met Shawn's eyes. "I was digging through social media sites earlier today, trying to find anything that might point to who would want to harm you."

Shawn's mouth twitched.

"There was nothing on your personal page."

"I hate social media. I'm only on it for the business."

"I gathered that, so I scrolled through the clinic's page. Bethany is a regular poster there."

"It's part of her job."

"I clicked over to her page."

Shawn's expression softened from tense to curious.

Matthias used his phone to open the website he'd viewed an hour ago. He tapped on a photo before turning it toward Shawn.

He took the phone and squinted at the image of Bethany Stone.

She hadn't posted it. A friend had tagged her in it. The photo showed Bethany and two other women mugging for a selfie. Behind them, through a wall of glass, the shot looked down at a racetrack with horses streaking by. The location was tagged as Presque Isle Downs and Casino.

Shawn touched the screen, zooming in on the same thing that

had caught Matthias's attention—Bethany's hand clutching betting slips.

"This has to be an old picture," Shawn said, his voice ragged.

"It's dated two weeks ago." Matthias held out his hand, knowing there were more photos, but Shawn didn't need to see the ones of Bethany making an exaggerated pouty face and tearing the losing stubs in half. "I have the lab guys checking to make sure, though."

Shawn returned the phone, and his chin dropped to his chest. "I can't believe it."

"I know you wanted to keep her gambling addiction quiet, but you realize I have to question her about it."

Shawn's eyes came up. "She didn't have anything to do with this." His fingers lightly brushed his chest.

Matthias wasn't so sure. He forced a grin. "Do you want to be the one to tell your wife that I'm not going to follow a potential lead? Because I sure as hell don't."

The attempt at humor didn't put a crack in Shawn's dour expression. "You do what you have to do. But I'm telling you, she had nothing to do with the robbery or the shooting."

The door swung open, and Alissa galloped into the room clutching a small teddy bear. "Look what I got you, Pappy," she chirped.

Matthias bent down to lift her onto Shawn's bedside while catching a glimpse of Cassie's face. Shawn cooed over the little girl and her gift. Cassie stormed toward them, and Matthias wondered if Shawn's full attention on Alissa was his defense mechanism against Cassie's rage. If so, Matthias wished Alissa had brought him a gift, too.

Cassie stood tall before Matthias, hands on hips, towering over him as though intentionally reminding him of their height difference. "Well? What'd I miss?"

"Nothing, dear," Shawn said without taking his gaze off his granddaughter. "He's just doing his job."

Matthias stuffed his notebook and phone back in his pockets. "And I have other witnesses to talk to."

"Not until you talk to me," Cassie growled.

He leaned closer and fixed her with a stern glare. "You need to focus on your family right now and trust me to handle the investigation."

She matched his angry gaze as if expecting him to back down. He didn't.

Her shoulders sagged. "Will you at least give me an update as soon as you have some news?"

"As soon as I have news, yes." Matthias looked at Shawn who was watching him from the side of his eye. "You rest and heal up."

Shawn dipped his chin ever so slightly.

Matthias turned away from the Malones and came face to face with Emma. He studied her, wishing Friday evening had gone much differently. Wishing the two of them were spending today on the beach at the state park. From the gleam in her eyes, he suspected she wished the same thing. "Walk out with me?" he asked softly.

The corners of her mouth canted upward. She looked past him and called out, "I'm glad you're feeling better. I'll talk to you later."

Behind him, Cassie cleared her throat. He caught Emma meeting her gaze and a look passed between the women. What the hell were the two of them up to?

As Matthias escorted Emma from the room, he acknowledged Kollman, who responded with a nod.

Emma walked silently beside him on the way to the elevator, but he had a strong feeling she wanted to tell him something.

Or ask him something. Had Cassie assigned her the job of wheedling information from him?

In much the same way, he knew Shawn was keeping something from him. Only in Shawn's case, it was something he did not want Matthias to know. He'd looked way too relieved when Matthias mentioned Bethany.

What else did Shawn fear Matthias would find out?

"How's the case going?" Emma asked.

He looked at her, walking at his side, and wondered if her motivation for asking came from her job, Cassie, or simple curiosity.

She must've understood his hesitance. "I know you can't tell me anything specific. I was wondering if you're making any headway." She winced and shook her head. "That still sounds like I'm digging for a story. I'm not. That's Preston's job."

Her uneasiness forced him to laugh. "You're not helping him land a scoop?"

"As much as he wants me to, no." She lowered her face, partially concealing her flushed cheeks. "My loyalties lie with you, not Preston or ErieLIVE."

"Don't let Laurie hear you say that."

"My boss would understand."

Matthias wasn't so sure.

"Cassie, though, is harder to say no to."

"Is she employing you as her informant?" He tried to keep his tone light.

"As a matter of fact, yeah. Kinda."

"I hope she's paying you well."

Emma lowered her gaze. "She's not paying me. And I made no promises."

"I know how persuasive Cassie can be. Just try to avoid giving her any insider information that might entice her to jump into the investigation herself. She needs to sit this one out."

"Got it."

"As for the case, it's a cluster," he told her. "The one suspect we've identified was dead before we got there."

"Zimmerman."

"Yeah." They reached the elevator, and Matthias pressed the down button.

"What about the shooter? The chief mentioned him at the press conference last night. Shawn admitted to me that he's the one who gave them the description, but it's pretty vague."

Two women and a man, all in brightly colored scrubs, joined them in waiting for the elevator.

"His description is all we've got," Matthias said to Emma before falling quiet.

With a ping, the doors swished open, and they filed in. The others chatted in soft voices about an incident in the staff lounge involving a shaken can of Pepsi and the resulting fizz explosion. Matthias sneaked a look at Emma's profile, her short, unruly red hair, the smattering of freckles across her nose and cheeks. She started to turn her head, and he snapped his gaze back to the closed doors before him, pretending he hadn't been wishing they were alone. Not here, in an elevator car, but at his apartment mere blocks to the south.

The bell chimed again. The doors opened on the ground level, and they all stepped out. The hospital employees strode off, leaving Matthias and Emma standing there, hardly alone in a lobby filled with visitors and staff coming and going.

He noticed a troubled crease above her brows. "Are you okay?"

She opened her mouth only to close it again. "I'm just bummed that our plans fell through. I understand," she added quickly, "but I'm still bummed."

He had a feeling their canceled plans weren't the real reason for the lines on her forehead. "How about coming over to my place this evening?"

The creases disappeared from her brow and gathered next to her lips instead. "I thought you were tied up with this investigation."

"I am. I'm also exhausted. I probably won't be much company, and I might fall asleep on you. But I think a few hours of shuteye might help me see clearer." He tipped his head toward her. "And having you by my side couldn't hurt either."

She flushed again. "What time?"

––––––––

Emma left the hospital parking garage and drove south along State Street, past the police station, to the offices of ErieLIVE. Traffic was light, and she had no problem finding a parking space.

As she rode the elevator up to the newsroom, memories of her conversation with Cassie roared in her head. While Alissa perused the gift shop's offerings, Cassie had drawn Emma aside. Someone tried to kill Shawn. It looked like the shooting was the real purpose of the break-in. Cassie understood, or so she claimed, that she couldn't actively work the case, but she was pissed off about being kept in the dark. Her fellow detectives, Matthias included, didn't seem to trust her with information.

"I don't have to be on the street to be valuable in this investigation," Cassie had said. "But I need something to do besides sitting and watching Shawn sleep."

Emma knew better than to argue, but Cassie had made it clear she expected Emma to keep her in the loop.

The elevator doors opened to a quiet newsroom. A few reporters sat hunched over their computers, the clickety-clack of keyboards softer than during regular business hours. Preston, however, wasn't one of them, for which Emma was grateful.

She often pointed out to him that she wasn't a reporter. That was his job. This afternoon, she wished she'd paid more attention to how he did it. Not questioning victims or witnesses or family, but research.

She crossed the room to her desk and booted up the computer she normally only used to edit photos. Today, she had other plans.

Cassie wanted answers and expected Emma to get them from Matthias, much like Preston did. But Emma didn't want to add to the stress between her and Matthias. Kira's words kept haunting her.

He's in love with you. For now.

If their relationship was doomed to crash and burn, Emma didn't want to rush the inevitable failure.

Which meant that Emma had to get Cassie's answers on her own.

When the computer was ready to go, Emma clicked on the icon for the archives, not sure what she'd be able to find.

A search of Shawn's name pulled up an overload of articles about the clinic and all the volunteer work he and his staff did for low-income pet owners, their vaccine and spay-and-neutering clinics, as well as various community accolades. The most recent stories were Preston's posts about the shooting and contained nothing Emma didn't already know.

Matthias's frustrated comments stirred in her mind. He'd called the case a cluster, and she knew he meant the street slang version. It was a muddled mess. The investigation was going nowhere.

"Looking for something?"

She spun to find Preston looking over her shoulder. "Where'd you come from?" She hadn't heard the elevator's bell.

"What do you mean? I work here."

"But you weren't here a minute ago. I didn't hear the elevator. Did you climb in through a window?"

He snorted a laugh. "I use the rear staircase, remember?"

She did but thought he only did that to avoid running into people in the currently empty lobby.

"You didn't answer me." Preston crossed his arms. "What are you looking for?"

She debated how much to say. Should she include him in her research efforts? Cassie hadn't forbidden it. And if Preston helped Emma uncover something that might aid the police, Cassie—and Matthias—would be happy for the assistance.

Wouldn't they?

"The one suspect the police identified in the shooting has turned up dead," Emma said. "They have a guard outside Shawn's hospital room…"

A hungry smile spread across Preston's face. "The police think the shooting was the real reason for the robbery and they're afraid he'll try again."

"That's the conclusion I came to." Emma didn't want to give up Cassie as her source. Nor did she want Preston to assume Matthias was feeding her information. "I can't imagine why, though."

"It's obvious." Preston rubbed his hands together as he strode to his own desk and computer. "Dr. Shawn has an enemy out there. And I'm going to find out who it is."

Emma abandoned her chair and scurried after him. "No. *We* are going to find out who it is."

Chapter Twelve

Matthias stepped out of his Malibu at the West Erie Veterinary Clinic just before four p.m. and admired the only other vehicle in the lot—a tricked-out white Jeep Wrangler High Tide, which he assumed belonged to Dr. Nathaniel Campbell. Matthias's personal vehicle, a red Wrangler, was older and smaller than this one. Campbell's veterinary career paid better than Matthias's law enforcement gig.

"Nice, huh?"

Matthias turned toward the voice and saw Campbell, dressed in jeans and a dark short-sleeved button-down shirt, standing in the entryway to the clinic. "Very." Matthias approached him, hand outstretched.

The vet's grip was strong but not crushing. Matthias could well imagine this guy restraining a rebellious pet with a gentle touch.

"Thanks for agreeing to come in on a Sunday," he said once they were inside.

"Anything to help catch whoever did this to Shawn. And to our clinic."

The last sentence struck Matthias as odd. "The amount of cash stolen was minimal from what I understand. Were that many drugs taken to cause your business hardship?"

"I didn't mean it that way. The theft won't impact us too badly businesswise. We have insurance." Campbell stopped in the middle of the waiting area and crossed his arms. "I meant the clinic's staff. Robin and Erin have already requested a few days off."

"What about Bethany?" Matthias had called her after speaking with Campbell, asking her to come to the clinic. She'd sounded jittery as she begged off, claiming she had a family get-together that afternoon.

Campbell gazed into the distance, thinking. "Bethany's the one I'm most concerned about. She's great under pressure. I've seen her stay cool when we had a dog crashing in the back, its owners hysterical out here, and two other dogs trying to tear into each other, all at the same time. Bethany broke up the fight, calmed the owners, and made sure we had what we needed in treatment to save the dog. She's amazing. But I talked to her yesterday, just checking in to see how she was doing..."

"And?" Matthias prompted. "How *is* she doing?"

"Not well. She won't admit it, but Friday evening shook her up badly. I told her to take a couple of weeks off. Goodness knows, she has the vacation time saved up. I also referred her to a college friend of mine who's a therapist."

"Good," Matthias said, although Bethany being on vacation didn't help him with the investigation. "I'd hoped she could join us this afternoon, but she said she had family plans."

"Oh?" Campbell's eyes shifted. "Yes, that's right. I remember she said something about a birthday party."

Matthias's internal lie detector kicked in. Campbell was covering for his employee. Matthias made a note to track Bethany down tomorrow morning in case she decided to use her vacation time to fly off to Maui.

The vet inhaled deeply and planted his hands on his hips. "My wife has plans for me later, too, so what can I help you with, Detective?"

Matthias had a long list of questions where the clinic was concerned. "Could you go through your client files and find out if you've ever had a patient by the name of Kirk Zimmerman?"

"You mean a patient's *owner* by that name," the vet corrected with a grin that quickly faded. "That's the man who was found murdered yesterday, right?"

"Right."

"And you believe he was one of the men involved in our robbery. And Shawn's shooting."

"That's correct."

Campbell wiped a hand over his mouth. "What kind of pet did he have?"

"We don't know that he did. But I need to make sure I'm not overlooking the obvious."

"Understood." Campbell pointed toward the office. "I'll start going through our records."

"While you do that, I'm going to wander around. In case we missed anything on Friday."

Campbell waved. "Go right ahead. Let me know if you need me."

Once the vet disappeared into the office, Matthias strode in the opposite direction, to the dark hallway leading to the side door. He tried one of three switches on the wall. The lights came on over the reception desk. He tried a second. The hallway to the rear of the building lit. The third switch was the one he wanted.

He approached the side entrance, searching for some tidbit he'd missed before, knowing he wouldn't find anything. He hit the push bar to open the door, but it didn't give. Remembering the security footage of Bethany early Friday morning, he reached up, feeling along the ledge above the door. He felt something and pulled down a small Allen wrench. He fit one end into the hexagonal-shaped recess in the bar. As he was about to unlock it, he spotted the keypad. Rather than set off the alarm, he replaced the Allen wrench where he'd found it.

Matthias headed for the back of the clinic—the treatment and surgical areas, the lab, the drug cabinet targeted by the crew—and the rear door. Like the side one, it was locked. He felt for another Allen wrench and found it on the ledge. Another security keypad next to the door kept him from testing the lock.

He returned to the lobby and to the office where Campbell hunched over a computer. "Are all the entry doors alarmed?" Matthias asked.

Campbell swiveled to look at him. "Of course."

"Are they armed now?"

"I disarmed the side door when I came in, as well as the front door that you used."

"What about the back door?"

"It should still be armed."

"Could you check it, please?"

He shrugged and rose. "Sure."

Matthias trailed him, retracing the steps he'd taken a moment ago. At the keypad, Campbell touched a button. *SYSTEM ARMED, REAR ENTRANCE ARMED, SIDE ENTRANCE OFF, MAIN ENTRANCE OFF* scrolled across the screen.

"Who all has the code to disarm the system?" Matthias asked.

"Everyone who works here. We used to limit it to specific staff members, but it got to be a pain when a delivery arrived and those with access were busy. Now, once a new employee passes their probationary period, they get the code. When someone leaves our employ, we change it."

"Is it the same with the keys?"

"Oh, no. First of all, there's no need. Anyone can unlock them from inside." Campbell reached up and retrieved the Allen wrench that Matthias already knew about. "Only us doctors have the key to unlock this one from the outside, and we rarely use it. For the most part, the rear door stays locked."

"What about the side one?"

"That's different. Employees use that door all the time."

"Who all has keys to it?"

Campbell replaced the Allen wrench. "You'd have to ask Bethany. Any list I'd give you wouldn't be complete. She's the one who keeps track of that sort of thing."

"Do you know how many keys there are in total?"

"Sorry, no. Again, you'll need to speak with Bethany."

Matthias decided to be on Bethany Stone's doorstep first thing tomorrow morning.

Campbell checked his watch. "Are we done back here?"

Matthias took a last look around, his gaze settling on a trio of doors along the wall closest to the front of the building and a hook on the wall with several dog leashes hanging from it. He headed toward the doors. "What are these?"

"Those access the examination rooms," the vet said. "Patients enter from the waiting area. The doctors and techs enter from back here. And they give us quick access to equipment or the lab if a pet requires bloodwork or emergency treatment."

Matthias fingered the nylon leashes, thinking about what Hamilton had said about Zimmerman's strangulation.

"Those," Campbell said without being asked, "are for clients who don't bring a lead for their pets. You'd be surprised how many don't heed the sign out front. The one that states all animals must be on a leash or in a carrier. We keep more at the front desk."

"You loan them to clients?"

Campbell gave a dismissive wave. "In theory, but we rarely get them back. Rarely as in never. Bethany orders them in bulk, so it's no big deal." He grinned. "Unless we get repeat offenders."

Campbell led the way back to the front, shutting off the lights Matthias had turned on. In the office, the vet returned to his computer.

"Find anything?" Matthias asked.

Campbell jiggled the mouse, awakening the screen. "There's only one Zimmerman in our system and she was an elderly woman with a geriatric dog. Both have passed on, I'm afraid."

Matthias asked for her name and made a note of it in case she had a grandson named Kirk. "Speaking of elderly clients, what can you tell me about Shawn's last scheduled patient on Friday? A woman by the name of Winston."

Campbell pivoted in his chair to face Matthias. "Ah. Fuzzy Winston. That's the cat, not the owner. Mrs. Winston has brought her pets to us since we first opened our doors."

"Do you have her address?"

"I do, but I know this woman. She won't answer her phone or her doorbell to anyone she doesn't know. Tell you what. I'll call her and have her contact you."

"Great. Thanks. And what about that dog? Daisy? How'd her bloodwork turn out?"

"Not half bad for an old girl. Definitely better than I expected. Mr. Boyd is supposed to come in tomorrow to get the results and discuss a treatment plan for Daisy's hip dysplasia."

Matthias pictured the old man and his frightened dog seated in the exam room on Friday, grateful that he'd pressed to have Campbell come in and finish the exam Shawn had started. "What time?"

Campbell faced his computer and clicked to another screen. "One o'clock. We don't usually schedule appointments between noon and two so staff members can grab lunch and get caught up if the morning was crazy. And Monday mornings are always crazy. This way, Mr. Boyd and Daisy shouldn't have to deal with a crowded waiting room."

And therefore could use the front door. "Good to know," Matthias said. "How about I stop in during that time? I want to talk to your employees who'd left before the robbery. Find out if they might have seen something out of the ordinary without realizing it."

"Fine by me. You can corral whoever isn't busy at that particular moment without disrupting patient appointments." Campbell reached for the computer's mouse. "Is there anything else you need from me?"

Matthias checked his notes. "Not right now. Thanks for your time."

Campbell clicked the mouse, logging out of the computer. "Whatever it takes to catch those thugs."

———

Preston had assigned Emma to search ErieLIVE's digital archives while he dug through his sources and databases. Emma grew increasingly convinced that Shawn was a saint. Each time his name popped up in an article, he was being given some accolade or award. Or he and his fellow vets at the West Erie Veterinary Clinic were participating in some volunteer endeavor to benefit the community. If ever there was a human being with no discernible enemies, it was Dr. Shawn Malone.

Emma typed his name into the search bar and only came up with more of the same. She rubbed her tired eyes and looked over at Preston. "Have you found anything?"

He leaned back in his chair and faced her. "Not a blasted thing. You?"

"No. In this day and age, I didn't think it possible for someone to be so squeaky clean."

"I know, right? He doesn't have so much as a parking ticket."

The idea struck Emma as funny. "He's married to a cop. If he did get a ticket, I bet Cassie could make it disappear."

Preston's jaw tensed, and Emma spotted a strange gleam in his eyes.

"What?" she asked.

"You're a genius."

She choked. "Uh. I don't think so."

"I do." He wheeled his chair over to her desk. "What if there really is something in his past, but we're not finding it because it's been covered up?"

"Covered up? You have to be kidding. You're thinking there's a conspiracy theory involving Shawn Malone?"

Preston shrugged. "I don't know. Maybe."

Emma didn't want to go there. Cassie wanted her husband's shooter to be found. If there was any kind of coverup to explain the crime, she'd have said something.

Although probably not to Emma. Cassie wouldn't want the press to know. But Matthias?

Emma looked at the computer screen and her search results. "Wait," she said. "I just realized something."

Preston leaned forward. "What?"

"I've been digging through every news item that mentioned Shawn. There's no wedding announcement. No birth announcement for their daughter."

Preston blew an annoyed breath. "That doesn't mean anything. These digital archives only go back a little over twenty years. How long have Dr. Shawn and Detective Malone been married?"

"Longer than that."

"There you have it."

"What happened to the archival material from earlier?"

Preston aimed a finger at the floor. "The basement. ErieLIVE used to be the *Erie Tribune* when it was a print newspaper. All the print issues from before digitalization are stored downstairs along with the antiquated printing presses. It's like a haunted museum. And it might be where the secrets are stored."

"We should check it out," Emma said, although the whole haunted museum thing did not appeal to her.

"Tomorrow. It's creepy enough downstairs during the day. You don't want to find yourself in those archives at night."

Emma grinned. "One of us can search while the other stands guard with a wooden stake and a silver bullet."

Preston swiveled to face his desk and logged out of his computer. "Wooden stakes and silver bullets might be fine for vampires or werewolves, but I doubt there are any of those around. Besides, you're talking like I'm going to help." He shook his head. "I've read enough to know there's no motive for murder in Dr. Shawn's recent past. The archives and his distant past are all yours."

Sunday night, the weekend campers had gone home. Emma took advantage of the solitude by lounging on her deck, her ankles propped up and crossed on the railing. Oldies rock and roll tunes drifted up from Sara's Restaurant below. A breeze rustled the cottonwood leaves. Emma closed her eyes and rested her head against the back of her chair.

She wasn't sure how long she'd been relaxing when her phone vibrated. The screen revealed it was after nine and the text was from Matthias.

I'm home if you feel like coming over.

She thumbed a response.

Would you like me to grab some takeout from Sara's?

A few moments passed before the phone buzzed again.

That would be great.

A half hour later, Emma used the key Matthias had given her to let herself in and climbed the stairs to his loft.

He looked up from his seat on the sofa and deposited the document he was studying onto a pile of papers spread across the coffee table. "Hey," he said, his voice thick with exhaustion.

"Hey," she said back.

He rose and waved her toward the kitchen island.

While she unpacked burgers, fries, and coleslaw, he opened his fridge and retrieved two bottles of beer. He held one up, giving her a questioning look.

She understood. He knew she rarely accepted alcohol if she planned to drive. Asking—even silently—if she wanted a drink was the same as asking if she wanted to spend the night. "Yes, please."

He uncapped both bottles and handed her one. Pointing at the two cheeseburgers, he raised an eyebrow. "Did you give up on being a pescatarian?"

"Nope." She held her arms wide, indicating the food on the counter. "This is all for you. I ate earlier."

He didn't argue and began devouring the first burger.

Emma settled onto one of the stools. "Anything new in the investigation? That you're able to talk about, I mean."

Matthias looked as though he'd lost his appetite. He dropped the burger onto the wrapping paper. "A few possible leads. Nothing promising." His gaze shifted to the windows across the room. "It's frustrating as hell. I'm missing something, but dammit, I can't figure out what."

After the afternoon and evening Emma'd had with Preston, she understood his exasperation. "Are you still operating on the belief that the shooting was the real motivation for the break-in?"

He met her gaze, his expression guarded.

She held up both hands. "I get it. Ongoing investigation."

Matthias lowered his face as if debating what to do with the dinner she'd brought. He looked utterly drained.

Softer, Emma said, "For what it's worth, you have my word anything you tell me won't leave this apartment, but I understand if you can't—"

"I don't know." He shook his head. "I can't come up with anyone with a motive to want Shawn dead."

"What about Cassie?"

Matthias met her gaze with a frown.

Emma realized how her question sounded. "I don't mean that Cassie wants Shawn dead. I mean, could Cassie be the target? Could the shooter be trying to get to her through him?"

Matthias exhaled and picked up his burger. "We considered that. It's the more logical scenario. But Cassie looked at all the photos from the security cameras. She's got a helluva memory for recalling people she's arrested, and she swears she's never seen any of them before."

"They were wearing masks."

"I know. She's still certain she doesn't know them. I trust my partner. If she says she's never seen them, she hasn't."

Emma sat in silence and watched him eat. When he was almost done with the second burger, she decided to confess. "Preston and I were trying to dig up anything from Shawn's past that might shed some light on all this."

Matthias stopped chewing. She expected him to chide her, demanding she leave it alone. Instead, he finished chewing, swallowed, and washed the last bite down with a long draw on the beer. "Did you find anything?" he finally asked.

"Not yet." She told him about all the positive stories and honors.

"Shawn's a good guy," Matthias said.

"He is. But maybe there's something from way back. Something neither of us has found yet."

"Like what?"

"I don't know, but I know where I'm going to look." She went on to explain about ErieLIVE's basement and the pre-digital archives stored there.

Matthias showed no signs of excitement about her plan to venture into the bowels of the building. "You say those archives are from over twenty years ago?"

"Yeah."

Matthias shook his head. "I appreciate you trying to help, but even if you found some old story that makes Shawn look bad, why would someone wait all this time to act on it?"

Emma didn't have an answer.

"Besides, Cassie and Shawn have been married for thirty-some years. She would know of an old motive to harm her husband, and she wouldn't keep it to herself."

Emma sighed, defeated. "You're right. I was just looking for some angle we've all missed."

Matthias gave her a tired smile and reached across the island to place one strong hand over hers. "I appreciate it."

She gathered the emptied food containers and wrapping paper and deposited it into his trash can. Together, they moved to the couch with what was left of their beers.

Emma snuggled against him and pointed at the documents spread across the coffee table. "What's all this?"

He drew her even closer, resting his cheek on her head. "Basically, my version of what you and Preston were doing."

"Have you found any more than we have?"

"Nope. And we don't have a dusty archive in the basement."

They fell silent. Matthias's breathing grew deeper, steadier, and Emma thought he'd fallen asleep.

But then he said, "Enough about what's going on with me. What's going on with you?"

"What do you mean?"

He turned his head to look at her. "You've had something on your mind since Friday. What is it?"

She realized what he was talking about and wished she hadn't. "I forgot you're telepathic."

"Just observant. It's part of the job." He again rested his cheek against her hair and waited.

Emma sighed. "I got a phone call from Eric."

"Oh?"

She poured out the gist of the conversation—the developer wanting to buy her farm, the generous offer, Eric's belief that they would go even higher. "I really don't know what to do. Even if I did decide to sell, I can't without Nell's signature. Her name's on the deed, too." Emma paused, waiting for Matthias to add his thoughts.

None came.

She turned her head toward him ever so slightly. His eyes were closed, his lips parted, his breath steady and deep. Emma sighed. Supporting his head, she slipped out of his arms and gently eased him down on the couch. He never stirred.

She lifted a blanket from the back of the sofa and opened it before draping it over him. Then she bent down and pressed a kiss to his cheek. "Get some sleep, my love."

Chapter Thirteen

Matthias jolted awake to the buzz of his vibrating phone. Disoriented, he flailed against the blanket cocooning him. Where the hell was he?

He sat upright, blinking. Ambient city light filtered through the tall windows set in the brick walls of his loft's otherwise dark living area.

He was on his couch. Not in his bed. Memories flooded in. Emma had been there. He'd fallen asleep while she was talking. About what? Eric had called. Something regarding a real estate developer and her farm. After that, Matthias remembered nothing.

The phone stopped buzzing.

He kicked free of his blanket—Emma's doing, no doubt—and checked the phone, sitting atop a haphazard pile of reports on his coffee table. He found a missed call from Frazier but no accompanying voicemail.

Matthias climbed to his feet. He made his way to the light switch and clicked it on. Two almost empty beer bottles sat on the kitchen island. He stumbled to the bedroom, hoping to find Emma. His bed was empty and showed no signs of being slept in.

Dammit.

He checked the clock on his bedside stand. Five a.m. He swore again. He'd known whatever was on Emma's mind was important, yet when he'd finally had a chance to ask her about it, he'd fallen asleep.

Cursing, he debated calling her. Or at least texting her. But at five in the fricking morning? Bad idea. He shuffled back to the couch, sat, and scoured his face with his hands, trying to clear his brain and gather his thoughts.

It was Monday. His first order of business was paying a visit to Bethany Stone before she decided to take advantage of the two weeks Dr. Campbell had bestowed upon her and head for someplace tropical and unreachable. Unless she'd already booked a pre-dawn flight, it was too early to knock on her door.

He needed a shower. A long one.

His phone vibrated. He snatched it, hoping the incoming call might be from Emma.

Caller ID identified Frazier again. Matthias answered with a too sharp, "What?"

"Sorry for waking you." Frazier's voice carried a hint of excitement. "But I thought you'd want to know."

"What've you got?"

"I just met with one of my CIs."

Confidential Informant. Matthias came fully awake. "And?"

"He told me a new dealer has elbowed into the regular drug market on the streets. Specifically, he's selling tramadol, hydrocodone, and trazodone. And ketamine."

"The haul from Shawn's clinic."

"Sounds like it. Even better, my CI gave me a name. I've just arrived at the station to dig up some background on the dealer."

"I'll be there as soon as I grab a quick shower." Not the long one he'd hoped for.

"See you in a bit."

Matthias tossed the phone down and started toward the bathroom. A glimpse of a small white sheet of paper beneath one of the beer bottles caught his attention. He detoured to the kitchen island.

Emma's loopy scrawl covered the note.

You look exhausted and need your sleep. I'm going home. We'll talk later.

Matthias exhaled. Had Emma been about to tell him she was going to sell her farm and stay in Erie? Or—more likely—was she about to tell him she missed home and was going back to Washington County? Leaving him. The thought settled like a block of lead on his gut. He couldn't breathe. Over twenty years ago, his ex-girlfriend told him his work would always come first, relationships a distant second. Last month, she'd told Emma the same thing. Had Emma reached a similar conclusion?

Even worse, here he was, about to grab a shower and head off to his job rather than touching base with her, making sure she was all right. He crossed to the coffee table and picked up his phone. Five a.m. or not, he should call her.

But he stopped. Waking her at this ungodly hour would be rude, perhaps even more so than falling asleep on her. Instead of placing the call, he made a mental note to contact her at eight, a more reasonable hour.

Then, holding onto the memory of Shawn bleeding on the clinic floor, Matthias clenched his fists and headed for the shower.

Despite there still being an hour before dawn, the air in downtown Erie was sultry. By the time Matthias jogged up the concrete stairs inside the police department, he was already sweating. He cursed himself for having chosen the shower over a call to Emma.

Most of the detectives' floor was dark, but light blazed from inside Major Crimes. Matthias found Frazier at his desk, staring intently at the computer monitor as his fingers tapped the keyboard.

"Find anything?" Matthias asked.

Frazier looked up, startled, as if he'd forgotten Matthias was on his way. He blinked and inched his chair to one side, making room. "The person in question is Henry 'Hank' Urban. And before you ask, no, he's not on the list of Zimmerman's known associates. Urban's last known address is over on Holland."

Over Frazier's shoulder, Matthias scanned the screen. "Quite the arrest record."

"He started with simple possession but worked his way up. Released a month ago after serving five years for possession of crack."

"Not a quick learner," Matthias muttered.

"No, he is not." Frazier crossed his arms. "Let's go knock on Mr. Urban's door and see if he's up for a friendly chat."

Matthias pondered the suggestion. "He's not gonna talk to us. And I'm not sure I want to tip him off about us being on to him."

"We don't have enough to make an arrest yet. No judge will grant an arrest warrant on the word of an informant."

Matthias knew Frazier was right. They needed more. But, he thought, they already had more. He leaned down and clicked on Urban's mugshot, filling the screen with his face. The dude was doing his best to look hostile. Badass. But his brown eyes were open a little too wide to carry it off. If Matthias was any judge, the man in that photo was scared shitless. "Make a print of this. Then put it side-by-side with the best image we have from the clinic's security camera."

A grin tugged at Frazier's mouth. "On it."

While the printer whirred, Matthias ducked out to the breakroom and filled a cup with the crap coffee from the urn. It wasn't as nasty as he'd anticipated. Frazier must've made a new pot before Matthias got there.

Frazier had both prints laid side-by-side on Matthias's desk when he returned. "What do you think?"

Matthias set his cup down and studied the two images. He placed a hand over the lower half of Urban's face on the mugshot. "Looks like the same guy to me."

"You think it's enough to get a warrant?"

"Maybe, but let's be sure." Matthias straightened and looked at the other detective. "Put together a photo lineup. Let's see what Shawn thinks."

———

The sky was brightening by the time Matthias and Frazier arrived at Hamot, the mostly gray clouds to the east looking as if they'd been touched with an artist's brush, shaded in pastel hues of pink and lavender. Matthias wondered if Emma would be out on the peninsula, capturing photos of the sight.

He pushed thoughts of her aside and stepped into the lobby's elevator with Frazier, who had the envelope holding six mugshots clamped against his side with an elbow.

An officer sat in the hallway outside Shawn's room. They exchanged greetings and stepped inside to find the patient sitting up in bed, scowling at the breakfast plate on his tray. He looked up at them, his expression sour.

"Good morning," Matthias said.

Shawn grumbled something he couldn't make out.

"What's wrong?"

"This slop they call breakfast is what's wrong." At least Shawn's voice sounded stronger.

"They feed you that to encourage you to get well and get the hell out of here."

Shawn grunted. "If only."

Matthias tipped his head toward the empty chair. "Where's Cassie?"

"At the cafeteria getting me something edible."

Frazier elbowed Matthias. "He's feeling better."

"I would be if they weren't planning to keep me here for the foreseeable future." Shawn fingered his chest. "They're so pleased with my recovery that they've decided to do more surgery. Go in and try to remove the bullet. You guys any closer to figuring out who put it there?"

"Possibly." Matthias looked at Frazier. "Show him."

The detective withdrew the brown envelope, approached Shawn's bedside tray, and deposited the contents next to the plate of hospital food.

"What's this?" Shawn covered the plate and pushed it aside, making more room.

Matthias moved closer. "Some photos we'd like you to look at."

Shawn spread the pictures out in two rows of three and squinted at them.

A voice in the hallway drew Matthias's attention. Cassie said hello to the guard and breezed in, a bag in one hand, a disposable coffee cup in the other. She stopped at the sight of the two detectives. "What's going on?"

"We brought some pictures to see if your husband recognizes anyone," Matthias said.

She crossed to the chair, deposited the bag and her purse on its seat, and moved to Shawn's side, tipping her head to see the photos. Matthias feared she'd add her opinion, but he needn't have worried. His partner was too professional to risk tainting an identification.

Shawn glanced around. "Where are my readers?" he asked Cassie, reaching for the coffee.

She handed him the cup and turned to pick up the eyeglasses from his nightstand. "Right where you put them."

He slid them onto his face and took another slow, thorough look at the images. After sipping his coffee, he set it down and did the same thing Matthias had. He placed a hand over the lower half of each face. After several long minutes, he pinned a finger to one picture. "Him. He's not the one who shot me, but he's the one who dragged Robin from the back of the clinic by her hair. He's the one who had the bag full of drugs."

"Who is he?" Cassie asked, her voice as cold as Matthias had ever heard it.

He picked up the photo Shawn had selected. "Henry 'Hank' Urban." Matthias handed it to her. "Know him?"

She studied the photo with even more intensity than Shawn had. Pursing her lips, she shook her head. "Never saw him before." She returned the photo to Matthias. "What do you know about him?"

He debated how much to tell her but knew if he tried to keep her in the dark, she'd only press harder. "He served time for drug offenses in the past. We have an address for him." Matthias turned to Frazier. "And now we should have enough for an arrest warrant."

He gave a quick nod. "I'll get started on the affidavit."

"I'll meet you in the car." Matthias watched him stride from the room, then faced Cassie. He wanted to ask her how she was holding up, knowing that her husband would be going under the knife yet again. But not here. Not in Shawn's presence. Instead, he asked, "Where's Alissa? Back in school?"

Cassie's smile was forced. "Denene got home late last night.

Alissa didn't want to leave her mama even though Denene needs some sleep, so last I saw, my daughter was on the couch and my granddaughter was watching cartoons."

"Denene will be in later this morning." Shawn eyed the bag on the chair, just out of his reach. "Hey, woman, you gonna let my breakfast get as cold as this one?" He tapped the lid on his hospital food.

"Sorry." Cassie spun to snatch the bag as Matthias collected the photos from the tray. She removed a pair of takeout containers and popped off the lids to reveal scrambled eggs and sausage in one and hashbrowns in the other.

Shawn beamed. "Now that's what I'm talkin' about."

As he dug in, Cassie drew Matthias aside and held out a hand. "Give me the photo of this Urban fellow."

"Why?" He studied her. "What do you plan to do?"

"Nothing," she said. "I just want to memorize that man's face. If we ever cross paths, I want to see him before he sees me."

Matthias knew damned well there was more to it. "We're going to bring him in." He fixed her with a hard gaze. "And then we're going to get him to tell us who the other man is. The one who fired the shot."

She continued to hold out her hand and wiggled her fingers.

He sighed and placed Urban's photo on her outstretched palm.

"Thank you." She tipped her head toward him, matching his fierce gaze. "Now get the hell out of here and arrest this son of a bitch."

Chapter Fourteen

The address they had for Henry Urban was one of a row of two-story apartments, all mirror images of the next. Brick on the first level, vinyl siding on the second. Solid steel doors with the units' numbers on them. Small lawns with a few shrubs served as landscaping. An older tan Ford Focus sat in front of the apartment. Not Urban's. Like Zimmerman, Urban didn't own a car.

Matthias and Frazier parked on the street in front of the address. Roth and two teams of uniformed officers had taken up positions around the corner and on the next street over and awaited orders.

"Let's go," Matthias said and climbed out of the Malibu.

Frazier keyed his handheld radio. "Moving in."

They strode up the sidewalk toward the front door. Matthias hoped he wouldn't need the warrant to get Urban's cooperation. He kept the man's mugshot in the back of his mind. At that time, Urban was trying hard to act tough but was terrified beneath the "gangsta" façade. But the photo had been taken before he'd served five years. Time in prison changed a man and not usually for the better. Not to mention, Urban likely wouldn't want to go back.

Matthias hammered on the windowless steel door. From inside came the muffled sound of movement. He sensed someone on the other side of the door peering through the tiny peephole. Matthias held up his badge and ID to whomever was looking out. "Henry Urban? Erie City Police. Open the door and keep your hands where I can see them."

A soft *snick* indicated the turning of a deadbolt. The door edged open a few inches to reveal a sliver of a face with terrified eyes. But not Urban's. A girl, no older than ten or eleven, peered out at them.

"There's no one here by that name, officer," she said, her voice quivering.

"What's your name, miss?"

"My daddy doesn't like me telling anyone my name. Says it's no one's business."

"Is your daddy here?"

She shot a glance over her shoulder, telegraphing to Matthias that he was.

But before Matthias could ask to speak with him, Frazier's walkie crackled.

"We've got a rabbit," Roth's voice shouted through the radio. "Subject just exited the backdoor. Heading east on foot. Fast."

Matthias swore.

Frazier jogged toward their car. "On our way," he yelled into the handheld.

Matthias took one step after him and changed his mind. Instead of the car, he sprinted across the front of the building to the corner where he nearly collided with a little boy on a tricycle. Matthias sidestepped to avoid bowling the kid over and mumbled, "Excuse me."

He charged around the side of the structure and into the

expanse of shared lawn the apartments used as a backyard. A figure, well ahead of him, was racing in the direction of German Street. But several obstacles stood in his way. As Matthias pounded after him, the runner vaulted a privacy fence as if he practiced parkour daily. Arms pumping, Matthias sprinted toward the fence. He was no track-and-field athlete, but he'd done his fair share of military-style obstacle courses. He measured his stride. Timed his approach. He leaped, grabbing the top of the fence with both hands. With a combined effort of legs and strong arms, he heaved himself over. Not as effortless or graceful as Urban. Matthias stumbled on the landing but didn't go down. He counted it as a successful wall jump. Urban, however, had added distance between them.

Ahead, he spotted a uniformed officer cut in from the right, joining the chase on foot. "Police! Stop!" the officer shouted.

Urban did not comply. Instead, he veered into a neighborhood church's empty parking lot. The uniform followed with Matthias careening after both.

By the time Matthias reached the paved lot, Urban was already sprinting along 16th Street toward an area that held too many memories for Matthias, including one where he'd caught a bullet.

Sirens screamed not far away. Backup was coming. Matthias was losing ground. The uniform was pulling away, but Urban was still increasing the distance between them. He loped across the street and down the sidewalk edging the abandoned warehouses.

Matthias knew where Urban was headed. Knew neither he nor the uniformed officer stood a chance in hell of catching him once he reached the narrow gap between two of the structures. Farther down 16th, a patrol cruiser screeched around a corner and barreled toward them, sirens wailing.

Their only hope of stopping Urban was if the cruiser got there first.

Urban vanished between buildings. The cruiser screeched tires, filling the air with the scent of burnt rubber. Two more officers dived out and took up pursuit on foot.

Matthias's lungs burned. His legs had lost their strength. By the time he chugged up to the gap and the crumbling sidewalk between the brick warehouses, all he could see were the receding backs of three uniforms. He stopped, braced a hand on the corner of one of the buildings, and gasped for breath. His regular runs around the peninsula clearly weren't training enough for a full-out foot chase. Beginning tomorrow, he would pick up his pace during those runs.

Or maybe the day *after* tomorrow.

As he fought to catch his breath, he watched the far end of the walkway. One officer stood in the shadows looking around. The other two must have continued after Urban. Having pursued a man down this same path not that long ago, he knew what those officers were seeing. A chain-link fence, trees, railroad tracks, and possibly some railcars. It was a perfect place for someone to disappear, as had the man Matthias once chased.

Two more Erie PD patrol cars and two unmarked ones rolled up behind Matthias. The officers acknowledged him and jogged after the other uniforms but at a slower clip. Frazier and Roth stopped next to Matthias, following his gaze.

Roth slapped Matthias's back. "What's the matter, old man? Getting out of shape?"

Matthias turned a cold glare at the younger detective—the look Cassie always said scared people. "You wanna try to take me? Name the gym." He knew his muscle mass and mixed martial arts training gave him a huge advantage over either Roth or Frazier.

"No thanks," Roth replied with a smug grin. "But if you want to try me in a foot race, I'll be there."

Matthias grunted but was saved from responding when Frazier's radio crackled with static.

"We lost him."

The same wide brown eyes peered out at Matthias through the crack in the door. "We need to speak with your father," he said, his tone making it clear he wasn't taking no for an answer.

The girl turned to look at someone out of Matthias's view. A muffled voice said something he couldn't make out.

The girl again met his gaze. "Do you have a warrant?" she asked in a timid voice.

They did, but it was for Urban's arrest. A whole team of cops including a K9 unit were scouring the area into which the suspect had disappeared. Until they found him, the warrant was worthless.

Matthias drew a breath. This was not the time for playing bad cop. He forced a smile. "All we want to do is talk to your father. He's not in any trouble." Knowing the man was listening, Matthias added, "Yet."

The girl turned toward the person—presumably her dad—inside the house. "He says—"

"I heard what he said. I'm not deaf."

Matthias raised his voice. "Sir, we need to speak with you. I'd rather do it here than downtown."

The door swung open and a massive man in a white undershirt and plaid boxers filled the doorframe, nudging the diminutive girl aside. He stepped out. Matthias and Frazier backed up, giving him space as he pulled the door shut behind him. "You ain't coming inside."

"That's fine." Matthias was aware of the neighbors in the next unit watching through their window. Farther down the row, other neighbors gathered on their lawns. He wasn't sure if they were merely curious or showing solidarity against law enforcement.

Either way, the last thing either Matthias or Frazier wanted was a public scene and a publicity nightmare for City Hall.

Showing his badge, Matthias introduced himself and Frazier. "And you are?"

The big man appeared to debate whether or not to give his name. Then he shrugged. "Isaac Cooper. Folks call me Coop."

Matthias was aware of Frazier next to him, making a note, then turning and walking away. To Coop, Matthias asked, "How well do you know Henry Urban?"

"Who?" Coop asked, a challenge in his eyes and his tone.

"The man who took off out your back door when I was here earlier."

"Don't have a clue what you're talking about."

So, this was how Coop was going to play it. "Okay," Matthias said, speaking loud enough that the folks standing nearby could hear. "Let me tell you about who you had staying with you while your daughter was in the house. Henry Urban, or you may know him as Hank, has served time for dealing and using drugs. Last week, he took part in an armed robbery that resulted in a good man ending up in the hospital with a gunshot wound."

"Hypothetically, if this Hank Urban dude had been here and assuming any of what you say is true, he had nothing to do with the shooting. Hypothetically, that is."

"Doesn't matter. He was part of the break-in and robbery. He was armed. He forced a young woman to turn over narcotics. That means he's facing charges of *at least* attempted murder regardless of whether he's the one who pulled the trigger. And the shooting victim isn't out of the woods yet."

Coop shrugged. "None of that matters to me. I don't know any Hank Urban. And if he's as bad as you claim, I sure wouldn't let him near my daughter."

Matthias kept his focus on the man in front of him, but became aware of Frazier's return, phone to his ear. "Thanks," the detective said, ending the call. To Coop, Frazier said, "You're claiming you don't know Henry Urban?"

"That's right."

Frazier crossed his arms. "That's odd. You see, I just made a phone call and guess what." He turned to Matthias. "Isaac Cooper happens to be married to Darla Urban, Henry's older sister."

"Really?" Matthias said, exaggerating his surprise. He brought his gaze back to Coop, whose staunchly defiant attitude had become less staunch.

"I mean," Frazier said, "I suppose there could be more than one Isaac Cooper married to a Darla Urban."

Matthias acted like he was considering the possibility.

"But I doubt there would be another one living at this very address."

"Doesn't seem likely, does it?" Matthias let the act drop away and fixed Coop with his darkest glare. "Let's start over. Tell us about your brother-in-law."

Coop exhaled a loud breath. "What do you want to know?"

Emma stood at her desk at ErieLIVE, her backpack on her chair and her phone, cameras, and lenses spread in front of her. She'd already cleaned the optical glass on each lens and was swapping out the batteries in the camera bodies for fully charged ones when her phone chirped.

The text from Eric read, *Sonny Jones upped offer to $650K. Wants an answer soon.*

She wished she hadn't gotten out of bed this morning. Maybe she could pretend she hadn't. She turned the phone face down on the desktop and returned to her photography equipment.

The phone chirped again.

She finished replacing her camera equipment into the backpack.

Another chirp.

"Oh, for crying out loud," she muttered and picked up the device.

Two more texts from Eric.

I know you're ignoring me. Followed by *I think he'll go higher, but we need to at least let him know you're interested.*

Emma typed in a smart-ass reply. Then deleted it. *Not ignoring you. Busy with a story.* It was a lie, but Eric didn't need to know that.

The phone rang. Not a text this time.

Emma groaned loud enough that the man at the next desk gave her a concerned look. She gave him a quick smile before swiping the green button. "What part of busy don't you understand?"

"You're not busy. You're avoiding the situation. And me." Eric sounded annoyed. "My feelings are hurt."

"Okay, maybe I am. But I can't deal with real estate right now. That's why I asked you to handle everything back there in the first place."

"Handle, yes. That's what I'm trying to do. I could give Sonny your number, and you could talk to him directly—"

"No."

"That's what I thought, so let me do my thing and start the ball rolling on this deal."

"No," she repeated.

"Why not?"

"Because I'm not ready to sell."

The line fell quiet. Emma pictured Eric on the other end, eyebrow raised, waiting.

She couldn't take the silence. "We're not talking about a piece of furniture or an old car. We're talking about a hundred and fifty acres of property that's been in my family for three generations. If I sell, it's gone. Forever."

"More like a hundred and sixty-two acres, but who's counting?" Eric sighed through the phone. When he continued to speak, his tone was more congenial. "You know I only have your best interest at heart. I'm a real estate consultant, for crying out loud. This is what I do for a living. Think about it. Do you really need all that land? I can't picture you raising cows and chickens or growing wheat and oats and mowing hay."

"No, but maybe I want to get another horse someday." She thought, but didn't add, Matthias grew up riding horses, too.

"That's fair," Eric said.

It was?

"I'm certain that Sonny would be happy to negotiate. Let you keep ten acres or so. The area where your grandparents' and parents' houses were and the surrounding property. We could insist on the same money for less ground. Or even *more* money for less ground." Eric sounded exuberant. "I like that idea."

"It's not *your* property to sell."

"I know that."

Emma spotted Preston rise from his desk and pocket his phone. If she was lucky, he had a story and needed her. Then she wouldn't be lying when she told Eric she was busy and hung up on him. As she hoped, Preston did turn toward her and start her way, but the look in his eyes wedged a lump in her throat. Whatever he'd just learned wasn't good.

"Emma? You there?" Eric asked.

"I have to go."

"Wait. Before you do, there's something you need to consider."

"I mean it, Eric. I have to—"

"Think of Nell."

Her sister's name stopped her from hitting the red button. "I don't know where she is, which is another reason I can't sell."

"Is it a reason or an excuse?"

Emma didn't have a good answer for that one.

Preston stopped in front of her, his gaze intense.

She held up a finger. "Eric, I have to—"

"You're not being fair to your sister," he said.

"What do you mean?"

"Have you ever thought that Nell might actually *want* to sell? She's trying to make a new start in life. You know that's not an easy thing. The money might be exactly what she needs right now."

Preston drummed his fingers on her desk.

"I'm serious, Eric. I have to go. Now."

"Fine. But think about what I said. I'll call you later."

The line went dead. Emma stared at her home screen, ironically a photo of the farmhouse before it had burned.

"Are you done?" Preston asked impatiently.

"Yeah. What's up?"

Chapter Fifteen

After going back inside to put on a pair of pants, Isaac Cooper joined Matthias and Frazier in the Malibu. Coop sat in the passenger seat. He didn't want to talk where either his daughter or the neighbors could hear, but he also said he didn't want to go to the station. The car was a compromise.

"All right, yes," Coop said grudgingly, "Hank is my wife's baby brother. He's a mess. Been a mess his entire life. But he never shot nobody."

In the backseat, Frazier took notes and muttered, "Double negative."

Matthias shot a look at him.

He shrugged. "Just sayin'."

Matthias ignored his temporary partner and focused on Coop. "Any idea where we can find him?"

"Nope. He and my wife grew up not far from here. Him and his buddies used to roam around those warehouses and railroad tracks all day long. If he wants to stay hid, you ain't gonna find him."

"Do you know who those friends are?"

"I'm talking about when they was kids."

"What about now? Who does he hang with these days?"

"These days? Most of his so-called friends are in jail. Least ways, the ones I know about."

"How long has Hank been living with you and your family?"

"Since he got outta prison. He needed a place to stay as terms of his parole. My wife don't approve of how he's wasted his life, but Hank's still her baby brother. She can't turn him away."

"What about you?" Matthias asked.

Coop hiked an eyebrow. "What *about* me?"

"I understand a sister wanting to take care of her brother, but how do you feel about it?"

He glowered. "Don't matter how I feel. Darla's a good woman. A good mother. A good sister. Maybe too good."

Matthias let that last statement hang.

The silence did the trick. Coop shifted in the seat. "Okay, so I'm not thrilled about a drug addict staying under my roof. Even a reformed one."

"Hank told you he was clean?"

"He did."

"And you believed him?"

"He wouldn't be in the same house as my daughter if I didn't."

"What if I told you he's been dealing?"

Coop's jaw tensed. "Hank? You sure?"

"We have a witness who saw him selling drugs—the same kind of drugs that were stolen from the vet clinic—on the street. That witness IDed Hank. That's how we ended up on your doorstep. Yours is his address of record."

Coop spit out a stream of profanities. "Darla's gonna kill him. And if she don't, I will."

"I'd prefer you didn't. I want him under arrest and alive, so he can answer some questions about the man who pulled the trigger."

"You said he's facing attempted murder charges even though it wasn't him doin' the shootin'."

"That's true. But if he cooperates, the DA might cut him some slack."

"Don't bullshit a bullshitter. Hank's spent more of his adult life locked up than walking free. The legal system is not his friend."

Matthias shifted sideways to scrutinize Coop. "You may not be aware, but the veterinarian who was shot is married to an Erie cop. Law enforcement takes that sort of thing very seriously. We want the gunman. We want him bad."

Coop appeared to digest Matthias's words. "I still can't tell you where Hank is. I don't know, and that's the truth." He held up a finger. "But I'll tell my wife what you said. She might have some way of contacting him. Now, I don't know that for sure, but she might. Even if she can't, Hank'll call her eventually. He got no one else. I'll have Darla convince him to turn himself in."

Matthias had his doubts. An ex-con with Hank Urban's history wasn't going to give himself up just because his sister said to.

Coop must've read Matthias's mind. "You don't know my wife. She can be very persuasive."

"Fair enough." Matthias pulled a business card from his pocket and held it out. "If either of you hear from him, call me. Immediately."

Coop took the card and squinted at it. "Will do." He stuffed it in his pants pocket. "We done here?"

"You're free to go."

Coop glanced at Matthias. "My neighbors," he said, gesturing at the surrounding houses, "mostly don't like you guys. Cops, I mean. Me talking to you? Well, it wouldn't look good if they thought I was cooperating. Understand?"

Matthias didn't reply.

"So don't take what I do next personally." Coop opened the door and stepped out.

"What the hell does that mean?" Frazier asked.

Coop slammed the door and thumped the car's hood with a meaty fist. "You goddamned cops think you're so high and mighty," he shouted. "Well, you can just go to hell and leave me and my family alone." He stormed away toward his apartment.

The neighbors, who were still outside, watching, glowered at the detectives. A few of the men moved toward the car.

Matthias turned the key. "Don't take it personally, he says. Meanwhile, he throws gasoline on a fire while we're sitting in the middle of it."

"Let's head over to 16th and see how the search is progressing," Frazier said from the backseat.

"Good idea." Matthias checked his watch. Urban had been missing for nearly an hour. Odds were good that he was long gone.

The last time Emma stood at this spot, there had been a homeless encampment set up mere yards away. Now, all evidence of it was gone. Just as all evidence of her sister was gone. Police vehicles, including a K9 unit, were parked up and down the barricaded street, but most of the activity was happening on the far side of the warehouse.

Preston was interviewing a man who lived across the street, but he'd denied her request to photograph him. Instead, Emma captured random shots of the vicinity. With any luck, the cops would find the missing suspect, and she could capture the moment they took him into custody.

When Preston told her the police were closing in on one of the robbery suspects and had lost him near the railroad tracks between 16th and 14th Streets, her knees had weakened. She had too many bad memories of the area, from believing her sister had died there to Matthias getting shot. He was, no doubt, part of the chase, and she wondered if he still carried the mental scars of that night to match the physical ones.

A Chevy Malibu turned a corner and crept down the street toward her. She stepped off the sidewalk for a better view of the driver, but the sun reflected from the windshield, making it impossible to see through. The car eased over to the opposite curb. The driver's door opened, and Matthias stepped out. He met her gaze, his expression unreadable. After saying something to Detective Frazier, who climbed out of the backseat, he strode toward her.

"Hey," she said. "Are you okay?"

A faint, sad smile flickered across his lips. "Yeah. How about you?"

"A little PTSD, but otherwise, I'm fine."

He nodded. "Same here."

"Is there any news about this guy?" She hiked a thumb over her shoulder. "Anything you're free to tell me, I mean."

"You probably know as much as I do."

She doubted that. "So, they haven't caught him yet?"

"Nope."

"At least Cassie will be glad you've got a name for another one of them."

"She'll be happier when we arrest the bastard."

Emma couldn't argue the point.

He glanced around and lowered his voice. "About last night. I'm sorry I fell asleep on you."

She wanted to reach up and touch his face, but there were too many bystanders to witness such an intimate gesture. "Don't apologize. You were exhausted. You needed the rest."

"You were starting to tell me something about Eric and your farm."

"It's no big deal."

His expression told her he knew she was lying.

A shout went up from the direction of the passageway between two of the warehouses. Matthias's handheld radio crackled with static followed by a clear voice. "We've got him!"

Emma heard Preston shouting her name, but she kept her gaze on Matthias.

"We'll talk later," he told her before taking off at a jog.

"Okay," she whispered to no one.

"Emma!" Preston sounded closer.

She looked around and spotted him striding in her direction. She met him halfway. "They've got him," she said.

"I heard." Preston's eyes gleamed the way they always did when he smelled a big story about to break. "I already got the suspect's name. Henry Urban. One of the police K9s located him. I posted to ErieLIVE as a breaking story with details to follow." He reached out and tapped her camera. "I need photos to go with it."

"That's what I'm here for."

His gaze locked onto hers. "I'm glad to hear it. I was afraid your only purpose was to visit your boyfriend."

Emma thanked her instincts for warning her away from touching Matthias's face. "What the hell, Preston? You're always pressing me to get information from him. Now you're pissed that I was talking to him at a crime scene? Make up your mind, for crying out loud."

"Were you asking him for some inside information on the case or just getting cozy?"

"I did ask him about the status of the case," she protested.

"What did he say?"

Emma fought to keep from sputtering. "That the suspect hadn't been caught yet. But then it came over the radio that he had."

The reply appeared to satisfy Preston. "All right. At least you tried."

His condescending tone infuriated her. "Quit being a jackass," she snapped. "You do your job, and I'll do mine, which, by the way, does not include being your informant." Before he could say anything more, Emma stormed away. She readied her camera, double-checking to make sure the shutter release mode was set for high-speed continuous shooting. As long as she kept her finger on the button, the Nikon would keep recording images.

She positioned herself in the middle of the street, out of the way of the cops, who gathered near the passageway, but with a good angle on the spot where she anticipated they'd appear with the suspect. Matthias and Frazier stood off to one side, waiting.

Everyone was waiting.

She caught snippets of radio reports. Urban was in custody. They were bringing him back to 16th Street for transport. Voices rose and activity increased. When they appeared from the shadowy gap between buildings, Emma had her camera to her eye and began capturing photos in rapid-fire succession. She didn't want to miss a moment.

Someone moved in front of her, blocking her view. Without lowering the Nikon, she sidestepped and continued recording the action.

Two officers flanked the man in custody, whose wrists were cuffed behind his back. Other officers maneuvered around them. One opened the back door of a patrol car. They directed the suspect toward it. Turned him around. An officer placed a hand on Urban's head.

A single loud *crack* reverberated through the air. The sound transported Emma back to her years on a southwestern Pennsylvania farm, during deer hunting season. The unmistakable boom of a high-powered rifle.

Chapter Sixteen

Matthias and Frazier stood in the shade of the old warehouse, observing as the officers prepared to transport, when the first shot rang out. Matthias flinched, instinctively looking for the source and not finding it.

Screams went up from the bystanders across the street.

As Matthias watched, Urban's knees buckled. The two uniforms flanking the suspect grabbed him before he could go all the way down. One spun to look in the direction they'd just come. A spot of crimson appeared on Urban's chest, blossoming from the size of a quarter to the size of a grapefruit in the few seconds it took the other officer to drag the wounded prisoner into the car.

Every cop on the street was shouting.

"Gun!"

"Everyone, get down!"

"Sniper!"

"Take cover!"

All Matthias saw, though, was Emma, frozen in place in the middle of 16th Street, clutching her camera and looking around frantically.

Civilians scurried in all directions, yet Emma didn't move.

Matthias's fellow police officers raced to their vehicles to break out long rifles and take up positions. He took a step toward Emma and shouted her name.

She pivoted in place, scanning the area.

But made no move to take cover.

Matthias swore, keeping his eyes on her.

"The warehouse," Frazier said. "They're saying the shot came from a third-floor window in the warehouse."

Matthias realized all the cops who'd taken up positions behind their vehicles, were looking up at the brick building with its boarded windows.

He brought his focus back to Emma. She remained where she'd been, but now had her camera aimed in the same direction as the police officers' rifles.

Another shot rang out followed by the plink of metal piercing metal. Matthias wheeled toward the car carrying their injured suspect. A bullet hole had pierced the steel skin of the car's now closed back door.

Matthias jogged toward the vehicle waving at the officer in the driver's seat. "*Go,*" he barked. "*Get outta here.*"

With a squeal of tires and the stench of burning rubber, the squad car peeled out.

Matthias turned once more toward Emma. She was staggering backward but not looking where she was going. Her camera to her eye, she continued to keep the Nikon raised toward the warehouse's upper windows.

The periphery of his mind registered an exchange between the other officers.

"*I have a shot!*"

"*Take it!*"

Matthias launched toward Emma just as two more loud cracks

rang out in rapid succession. One from a few yards away. The other from above.

A minute puff of gray dust exploded from the pavement at her feet.

Matthias closed the distance between them. From behind, he reached around her. Wrapped his fingers around her right hand and the barrel of the long lens she gripped. At the same time, he encircled her waist with his left arm, lifted her from the ground, and half carried, half dragged her behind a parked patrol car.

"What the hell?" he asked, breathless as they hunkered down against the vehicle's tire. "Are you trying to get yourself killed?"

"No," Emma squeaked. Her hands began to tremble, and she set the camera on the ground before it slipped from her fingers.

"Why didn't you take cover?" He heard a hint of terror in his voice and hated it.

She looked at him, her Caribbean blue-green eyes wide. "I—I didn't know which way to run. At first, I couldn't tell what direction the shot came from. Then I spotted the gun sticking out of a window and adrenalin kept me taking pictures."

"You saw the gun?"

"Yeah."

He processed the implications of this tidbit. "You took pictures of it?"

"Not very good ones."

He pointed at the Nikon. "May I?"

She picked up the camera, her fingers still trembling, and handed it to him. Around them, there was more shouting.

"*Is he hit?*"

"*I don't know. I can't tell.*"

But there were no more gunshots.

As Matthias studied the Nikon's controls, Emma pressed up to peer over the cruiser's hood.

He snatched her wrist and forced her back down to the concrete. "Just stop. Okay?"

"Sorry."

He pulled up the photos onto the camera's display screen and pressed the button to scroll through them. Emma leaned closer to watch.

"There." She pointed. "Those are the ones."

He stopped scrolling and pressed another button to enlarge the image. "I need to see these on a bigger screen."

She gave him a weak smile. "I don't have one with me at the moment."

"I'm serious. You might've captured a picture of the sniper."

"I doubt it. Not from this angle."

"We don't know that."

"I'll email them to you."

"No." He imagined a defense attorney arguing their evidence hadn't come from the original source. "I need you to come to the station. If this provides anything we can use, I'll make you a copy, but we'll need to keep the memory card."

More shouts went up. Footsteps pounded.

Something was going on. Matthias reached for the handheld he kept clipped to his belt and came up empty. "Dammit. I left my radio in the car." He set the camera down and aimed a finger at her. "Stay here. I mean it. Do not move." He climbed to his feet and jogged off to find out what the hell was going down.

Alone—at least she felt alone—Emma let out a long breath and slumped back against the tire of the car she was hiding behind. The reality of the last few minutes set in. She'd been standing in the middle of the street with a sniper firing overhead. She could easily have been shot. Matthias, too. And Preston.

Adrenalin kicked in again. Where was Preston?

She dug her phone from her pocket. No messages. She scrambled to her feet and, staying low, rose just enough to look over the car's hood.

The patrol car that Urban had been getting into when he was shot was gone. She assumed to the hospital. All the other vehicles were still there, but only a few officers remained, crouched behind cars, weapons ready, their gazes on the warehouse. She guessed everyone else had entered the structure and were searching for the sniper.

Preston was nowhere to be seen.

She sat down and typed out a text.

Where are you? Are you ok?

While she waited—prayed—for a reply, Matthias returned. He extended a hand to help her up. "We're clearing the area. You're coming with me."

"Why?"

"Because they found the sniper's nest, empty. And you might have a picture of him."

"I told you, I really doubt it. Not from this angle."

Matthias gripped her shoulders, his expression as fierce and terrifying as it had been the first time she'd seen him. "It doesn't matter. You were standing in the middle of the street with a camera aimed up at him. Whether you captured his image or not, he saw *you*."

Every ounce of strength in her body drained to her feet. "And he believes I *did* see him."

"That's a safe assumption." Matthias's eyes shifted, looking toward a spot on the concrete.

She followed his gaze and realized the spot was very near where she'd been standing when he grabbed her.

He glanced around before striding to the area in question. He stood over it, looking down, then at her. "See this?"

She moved to his side. "See what?"

He pointed at a pockmark at his feet. "This is where the sniper's third shot ricocheted off the pavement."

To Emma, it looked like any of the other cracks and divots in the street's surface.

Matthias pointed a few feet away. "*That* is where you were standing."

She vaguely recalled hearing a *tick* following the sniper's final shot and how it had registered in her mind as being close. Had it been *that* close? "How can you tell this was caused by a bullet? The rest of the pavement isn't exactly pristine."

His intensity unnerved her. "Because I saw the dirt the bullet kicked up," he said. "I was watching you. Didn't you hear me shouting for you to get down?"

She tried to reply, but the words stuck in her throat. She'd heard shouts from a dozen or more officers. In the chaos, she hadn't noticed one of those voices was his. "There was so much confusion," she said, sounding lame even to herself. The rest of it —the part he hadn't directly said—sunk in. "You think he was shooting at me?"

"I don't think. I *know*. One of our men thought he had a clear shot and took it. We think he missed, but it must've been enough to throw the sniper's aim off."

"Thank God." She swallowed hard. She'd stared death in the face before, but this felt different. Always before, she'd known the person threatening her. She'd been angry as much as or more than afraid, and the anger had carried her through. This time, her life could've been taken without her even being aware. She could be dead right now.

The vibration of her phone startled her from her nightmare.

The notification indicated a text from Preston. She exhaled another prayer of thanks and opened the message.

At hospital. Urban is dead. Interviewing staff. See you at the office.

The phone buzzed again.

Hope you got some good pix. This is a big one.

Preston had no idea how big.

"What is it?" Matthias asked. At the same moment, his phone buzzed.

She gestured at it. "That's probably the news I just got. Urban didn't make it."

Matthias read his message. "Dammit. I wanted to lean on him and find out who the third man was at the robbery. The one who shot Shawn."

Emma looked up at the window from which the gun barrel had protruded. "I'm thinking the third man didn't want you leaning on Urban any more than he wanted me to take his picture."

Matthias stuffed his phone in his pocket and placed a hand on the small of her back. "Let's get you and your camera to the station and see what's on it."

Chapter Seventeen

After leaving Roth at the scene, Matthias and Frazier followed Emma's Subaru to the station. She pulled into an empty spot along South Park Row. Matthias ordered Frazier to stop and let him out. "See you inside," Matthias said as he shut the door.

Before Emma joined him, his phone vibrated with an incoming call. Cassie's face and number appeared on his screen. Great. He wasn't ready to respond to her deluge of questions and sent the call to voicemail.

Emma locked her car and approached him, her backpack containing her camera and gear slung over one shoulder.

Without a word, he guided her around to the rear of the building and inside through the underground parking garage. Halfway up the stairs, his phone buzzed again, this time with a text. Also from Cassie.

What the hell is going on? Call me. Now.

He pocketed his phone and led the way through the breakroom and into Major Crimes.

Frazier was waiting at Matthias's desk and nodded an acknowledgment to Emma. "Thanks for coming in."

She shot a glance at Matthias. "I don't think I had a choice."

Frazier smirked. "Sure you did. You aren't in handcuffs." He winked at Matthias. "Or maybe you're saving that for later at your place."

Emma's cheeks blazed.

Matthias took a menacing step toward Frazier. "Stop being an ass."

He raised both hands in mock surrender. "I'm just kidding. Sheesh. Can't you take a joke?"

"Sure I can," Matthias growled. "But *you* aren't funny."

Frazier appeared chastened. Head lowered, he mumbled an apology to Emma before retreating to his desk.

Matthias offered his own apology. "Frazier thinks he's a comedian, but he's far from it."

A fleeting smile crossed her lips. She let the backpack slide from her shoulder onto the floor next to his cubby, unzipped the bag, pulled out the camera, and removed the memory card, which she handed to Matthias.

He inserted it into his computer. While the files loaded, he grabbed Cassie's empty chair and positioned it next to his, motioning for Emma to sit.

Matthias found the start of the photos from the 16th Street incident and whistled. "How many did you take?"

"A lot. I set the camera on continuous mode, so as long as I kept my finger on the shutter, it kept firing."

"Like a fully automatic weapon."

"Except I don't kill people."

He winced. "Sorry. Bad comparison."

"Not really. Cameras and guns use a lot of the same

terminology." She pointed at the computer monitor. "Anyway, this works a lot like the old power winders on film cameras. Only I'm not limited to thirty-six exposures on a roll of film. This is a 512-gigabyte memory card. It can easily hold thousands of photos."

Matthias clicked through dozens of pictures of bystanders, uniformed officers, some more artsy images of reflections in car windows. "Looks like you filled the whole thing."

She wrapped her arms around herself. "Not quite. At that point, we were all just waiting. I got bored. That's when I reverted to my old freelance habits."

He remembered one of their first meetings. She'd been taking pictures of debris along the shore of Lake Erie and inadvertently caught an image of a dead body. Pointing at one of the reflection photos, Matthias said, "They're good."

"But not for ErieLIVE. And they're no help to you."

He kept clicking until the first image of Urban appearing from between the two warehouses filled the screen. "I'll bet they'll be happy with that one."

"Maybe."

He noticed her gaze was laser-focused on the monitor. He slowed down, studying each photo in turn. Had he sped up, he could've made the pictures appear to be in motion. With each frame, Urban and the two officers progressed toward the waiting car. They turned him around and started to ease him down to the backseat. The next frames captured the end of Henry Urban's life. A small hole pierced his chest. His expression changed to one of surprise, then terror. Then his face went flaccid. One of the officers dived in to protect him, blocking the view.

Matthias looked at Emma. All color had drained from her face. "You okay?"

She shook her head. "When it was happening, I was so focused on what I was doing, it didn't entirely register." She met his gaze with a weak smile. "At least Preston and Laurie should be pleased."

Matthias returned to the computer. "You got your shot for ErieLIVE. Let's see if you got anything to help my investigation."

"*Our* investigation."

Matthias swiveled to find Frazier standing in the aisle, watching the slide show. Ignoring him, Matthias faced the monitor and clicked the mouse.

There were a handful of images of brick walls and boarded windows.

"Those are a waste," Emma said.

But the next photo filling his monitor was not. The weather-blackened plywood appeared to have shifted, leaving the bottom corner of the window uncovered. A rifle barrel protruded.

Behind them, Frazier swore.

Emma leaned in closer, her shoulder pressed against Matthias's. He continued clicking. Several more images of the same window and the same gun barrel appeared.

"He's waiting," Matthias said and looked at Emma. "These were taken after the first gunshot, right?"

"Yeah."

"He hit his target. The earlier pictures show that. Center mass." Matthias tapped the screen. "The man can shoot. We can't see it here, but assuming he's using a scope, he had to know he hit his target." Matthias looked at Frazier. "Why stick around? Why not pack up and leave? He had to know law enforcement would be moving in at any second."

"Insurance? He wanted to make sure his target was dead." Frazier slapped Matthias on the shoulder. "Keep going."

A few frames later, Matthias stopped at an image that revealed an almost indiscernible flash of light at the muzzle. "There's the second shot."

"The one that hit the car." Frazier nodded. "Like I said.

Insurance. Just in case the first one didn't kill Urban, he shot at him through the door."

Matthias wondered if the sniper had been able to see his target through the car's window at that angle, which raised another question. "Did the second shot hit Urban? Was he shot once? Or twice?"

"I don't know." Frazier slipped his phone from his hip pocket. "I'll text Hamilton and find out."

Matthias continued advancing through the photos. The barrel remained in sight even after the second shot. He stopped at an image that brought a gasp from Emma. Matthias saw it, too, and moved the cursor from the arrow that advanced the pictures, to the plus sign, zooming in.

Behind the gun's maw, part of a face was visible. The man holding the weapon was leaning forward, looking down at the street below. Matthias enlarged the image as much as he could, but it pixelated beyond recognition. He zoomed back out a few clicks.

The shooter wore a camouflage ball cap. Protective eyewear covered what little of his face they could see.

"What are you doing?" came Cassie's angry voice.

Matthias looked around the computer's monitor to see his partner storming into the room and toward him. He minimized the photo before she got there.

"Well?" she demanded, stopping at his cubby.

"What are *you* doing here?" he asked. "You're supposed to be with Shawn."

"Denene and Alissa are with him. I heard about one of the assholes involved in the robbery getting gunned down and dying, yet *you*"—she aimed a fierce finger at Matthias's face—"won't return my calls or texts."

"Who told you about the shooting?"

Cassie clenched both fists. "It doesn't matter. What matters is I had to hear about it from someone other than my partner."

"You're not on this case."

Frazier reached for his phone and slunk back to his cubby. Matthias wondered if the device had really vibrated or was merely his excuse to retreat. *Coward.*

"I'm the spouse of the victim. That should give me some degree of courtesy even if I'm not on the case. But if you don't read me in right this instant, I'm going to place myself on the case whether Armstrong approves or not."

Matthias knew she was just venting, but also knew her well enough to not press the issue beyond giving her a silent *you-know-better* look.

Emma started to rise. "I should leave."

He stopped her with a hand on her arm. "These are your photos. Stay." To Cassie, he said, "Grab a chair."

Some of the bluster faded. "What photos? What's going on?"

"Grab a chair and I'll 'read you in.'"

Emma slipped free and rose. "Here, take this one. It's yours anyway. I'll stand." She looked at Matthias. "I can't leave without the memory card or a receipt. Laurie would fire me." Emma's phone buzzed. She checked it. "Speaking of Laurie, she wants to know when I'd be back at the office." Emma thumbed in a reply.

With Cassie settled next to Matthias, and Emma standing behind him, he updated his partner on what had transpired since Shawn confirmed Henry Urban was one of the assailants.

"Who shot him? The same man who shot Shawn?"

"That's the most likely scenario, but I'm not ruling anything out." Matthias maximized the photo from the warehouse. "Emma caught some pictures from the scene this morning. We were just going through them when you arrived."

Cassie leaned toward the monitor, squinting. "That's the best you have?"

Matthias sensed Emma grow tense. "I don't know," he said. "We haven't viewed all of them yet."

Cassie made a looping motion with one hand. "Keep going then."

Matthias clicked to the next image. And the next. The sniper kept his head down. Most of his face was hidden below the window ledge, but from what little they could see, he appeared to be searching the street below.

"What's he looking for?" Emma asked.

Then the gunman must've spotted Emma with her camera. The face withdrew into the shadows. The muzzle aimed directly at the lens. Or so it appeared. Another flash.

There was one last blurred image, perhaps snapped as Matthias had grabbed her. "That's it," he said. "End of show."

"To answer your question," Cassie said to Emma. "What the sniper was looking for was anyone who might be able to identify him. Like you." She flopped back in her chair. "Except not a single photo can provide an ID."

But the sniper didn't know that, Matthias thought.

"I'm sorry," Emma said.

Cassie swiveled toward her. "I'm not blaming you. Hell, you stood there out in the open and kept taking photos. I'm not sure if you're brave or crazy."

"I vote for the latter." Matthias glared at Emma. "And I better never catch you doing that again."

"It's my job." She didn't sound like it was a part she enjoyed.

"They don't pay you enough to put yourself in the line of fire."

She met his gaze and held it. A faint smile crossed her face.

God, he wished he hadn't fallen asleep on his couch last night.

"Okay, you two." Cassie's tone was gently scolding. "Get a room. Later. Right now we need to figure out who this guy is and why he tried to kill my husband."

Matthias returned his attention to the computer. Cassie's words stirred the concern he'd felt earlier.

"What?" Cassie asked. "I've seen that look on your face before. What are you thinking?"

He asked himself the same question and struggled to put his uneasy gut feelings into words. "Something doesn't fit." He scrolled back through Emma's photos, stopped on the one where Urban took a bullet, and pointed. "That's a helluva shot. If he was shooting at one of our practice targets, he'd have hit a bullseye."

Behind him, Emma rested a hand on his shoulder. "It's not that exceptional. My father was a hunter. He could bag a deer at almost three hundred yards. This shot wasn't nearly that far. And Urban wasn't moving."

Cassie nodded. "She has a point."

"And I agree." Matthias swiveled to face Cassie, meeting her eyes. "Shawn wasn't moving either, and the shooter was a lot closer to him than to Urban."

"The shooter wasn't using a high-powered rifle on Friday." But Cassie's voice carried some doubt. "A handgun isn't as accurate."

"I know. But how far apart were they?"

Cassie exhaled. "Less than ten feet."

"You see my point?"

"I do." She sighed. "I don't like it, but I see it. You think we have two different shooters."

He pondered the question. "I'm not ruling it out."

"Excuse me," Emma said, "but couldn't it be the same shooter, except he's more skilled with a rifle than a handgun?"

"Which is why I'm not ruling it out."

"Something else is bothering me," Cassie said. "How did the sniper know where Urban was going to be? How did he know where to set up his nest? And how did he get in and out without being seen?"

"Good questions." Ones Matthias didn't have answers to.

He looked at Emma, holding her gaze. "None of this leaves this room. Understood? I don't want to read our speculation on ErieLIVE's website."

She plastered an exaggerated innocent look on her face. "I was never here."

Frazier reappeared from his cubicle. "I just talked to the coroner's office. Urban did suffer two gunshot wounds. Hamilton won't tell me any more until after the autopsy."

Cassie pushed away from Matthias's desk and pivoted to look at him, Frazier, and Emma. "What are your plans now?"

Matthias considered reminding her that she wasn't on this case but knew it would be a waste of his energy. He refocused on Emma. "I need to get your memory card down to the tech guys. See if they can enhance the shooter's face enough to ID him."

"I doubt it," she said.

"I do, too, but we have to try. I'd also like to see what, if anything, they can tell us about the gun."

"I'm gonna need a receipt and a copy of my photos."

"I'll make sure you get both." He swiveled to Cassie. "I'd intended to go to Bethany Stone's residence this morning and have another talk with her before she takes off for parts unknown. This incident with Henry Urban got in my way."

Cassie pulled out her phone. "Let me call Bethany and make sure she's still at home."

"Don't. I'd rather not give her any advanced warning."

"You still suspect she's involved?"

"I suspect everyone." He grinned at his partner. "You taught me that."

Cassie stuffed the phone back in her pocket. "I hate it when you throw my wisdom back in my face."

"After I visit Bethany, I'm going back to the clinic to talk with the staff members who'd left before the robbery went down on Friday."

Frazier took a step forward. "Do you want me to go with you?"

"No. I want you to go back to 16th Street. You and Roth go over the sniper's nest with a fine-toothed comb. Look for blood, too. I want to know if our guy managed to wound him."

"Isn't that what the crime scene unit's for?"

Cassie climbed from her chair and took one step toward the detective.

He raised both hands and backed away. "Just kidding."

"You're not funny," she said.

"That's what I keep telling him," Matthias said, then added, "I want to know how he knew where to position himself to take that shot, how he gained access, and how he managed to get out with law enforcement swarming the place. And while you're there, I'm curious to know if the sniper had an angle on the backseat when he fired the second shot at Urban or if he was just lucky."

"Does it matter?" Emma asked.

"Maybe. Maybe not. It makes more sense if he could see his target. Otherwise, he was shooting blind." Which didn't prove anything, except Matthias still couldn't make sense of Urban's shooting combined with Shawn's. Were there two gunmen? Two separate cases? Matthias wasn't buying it. The sniper was a good shot. No argument there. But was he a pro? If so, he should've been able to handle a pistol as well as a rifle.

And Shawn would be dead.

Chapter Eighteen

E mma found herself in the middle of a debate between Matthias and Cassie over who would escort her from the station. As fierce as Matthias could be, he was no match for his partner.

Although he lost the battle, he drew Emma aside and leaned close, his forehead touching hers. "I don't suppose I can talk you into going to my place and locking yourself in with the alarm set." The security system was a new addition after his apartment had been broken into last month.

"I'll be fine," she insisted. "He has no reason to come after me. I've already turned everything over to you."

Matthias's expression was equal parts pissed off and concerned.

She smiled at the concerned half. "I promise to be on high alert. If I see anything at all that makes me edgy, I'll call you."

He grudgingly agreed to her "terms," and on Cassie's orders, he left for Bethany Stone's residence. Frazier departed for the warehouse on 16th. And Cassie led Emma downstairs to a tiny room filled with electronics where a young man copied her memory card and printed out a receipt for the original.

"You'll get it back," Cassie told her.

"I better. Laurie's going to remind me how much that little chip cost. I just hope she doesn't take it out of my salary."

"If she does, let me know. I'll make it right."

"It'll be fine." Emma had been exaggerating. She hoped. "How long will you need it for evidence?"

"It's hard to say. Depends on if we use any of the photos when the case goes to trial. If so, we'll need the original data source."

Emma understood, but hoped cooperating with the police didn't land her among the unemployed.

The ErieLIVE's offices were only a couple of blocks south of the police station. It took her longer to find a parking spot than it did to drive there. The short trip didn't offer nearly enough time to rehearse what she would say to Laurie.

When the elevator doors opened to the newsroom, a furious Preston appeared in front of her. "Where have you been?"

She hadn't decided what to say to him either. "Is Laurie here?"

"In her office."

"Good." Emma sidestepped him and started across the room. With a glance over her shoulder, she told him, "Come on." She might as well deal with both of them at the same time.

Laurie Kassim, ErieLIVE's news manager, sat in her glass-enclosed office with the door open. Emma stopped at the threshold and rapped lightly.

Laurie looked up from her computer. "There you are." Her tone was only a notch less irritated than Preston's.

Emma entered, allowed Preston in as well, and closed the door. Ignoring the reporter, she faced her boss. "I'm sorry for being out of touch—"

Preston edged in front of her. "You have photos I need for my story. At least I hope like hell you have photos."

"I do." From her pocket, she withdrew the flash drive Cassie had given her and held it up.

"That's not your memory card," Laurie said.

"No, it's not. The police confiscated it." From her other pocket, Emma withdrew the folded receipt and placed it on the desk.

"The police?" Instead of angry, Preston sounded intrigued.

"During the shooting on 16th, the police saw that I had a good angle and may have captured an image of the sniper. They took me to the station to view the photos I took."

"Those are ErieLIVE property," Laurie said. "You should've refused."

Emma had anticipated this response. "The sniper took a shot at me. The police pulled me out of the line of fire. I felt it would be unappreciative to be noncompliant after they saved my life." An exaggeration, but she hoped it was a good enough excuse to buy her some grace.

Laurie softened. "You were shot at? Are you okay?"

"He missed. I'm fine."

"Did you get a picture of it?" Preston asked eagerly.

"*Preston,*" Laurie chastised, although from the look on her face, she wondered the same thing.

"I did." Emma waved the flash drive. "Like I said, they kept the memory card. Something about needing the original source in case they use any of the photos in court. But they made me a copy."

"They," Preston said under his breath, scoffing. "You mean Detective Honeywell."

Emma pretended not to hear him and grinned at Laurie. "Want to see them?"

"Of course, I do." She held out her hand, and Emma deposited the drive into it.

Preston crowded in behind Laurie and watched as she inserted the device into her computer and pulled up the photos.

Emma stood back, letting the two of them lean closer to the screen.

As Emma had expected, Laurie and Preston were ecstatic about the pictures of Urban being shot. Emma didn't share their enthusiasm. A man had died. Granted, he wasn't a fine, upstanding citizen, but he was a human being. He had loved ones ... at least she hoped he did ... and they would see that photo splashed across the news. All because of her.

She knew she should be beyond this by now, but she still felt sick to her stomach. Maybe getting fired over her cooperation with the police wasn't the worst thing that could happen.

Laurie didn't take as much time examining the images as Matthias had. She selected two of them—one of Urban and one of the barely visible sniper—to go along with Preston's story, and returned the flash drive to Emma.

Preston darted from the office, off to work on his report. As Emma turned to follow, Laurie stopped her. "Emma. Wait."

She faced her.

"I know you have a close relationship with a certain detective, and I appreciate that you felt grateful for the police saving you this morning, *but*—" Laurie emphasized the word. "You're a photojournalist now. There are boundaries we must keep with law enforcement in order to maintain our integrity with our reading public."

Emma fought against becoming defensive. "What would you have had me do, under the circumstances?"

"I would not have turned over the memory card unless they provided a court order."

"Even if I might have caught a picture of the killer's face?"

"The victim was already dead. The time it would take to get a warrant wouldn't change that."

"Unless the shooter left the scene and killed someone else. Identifying him quickly might've been vital to saving a life."

Laurie brushed aside her argument with the wave of a hand. "It's all a moot point. You did *not* capture an identifiable image of the sniper, and you couldn't stop him if he planned to kill anyone else." She sighed. "What's done is done. I realize you're still new here and there's a lot you don't know. Let's file this under lessons learned and move on. From now on, all photos taken for ErieLIVE are seen by me first. I will then decide if the police can access them. Understood?"

Arguing would get Emma nowhere. Laurie was right. But Emma pictured Matthias's face after he'd dragged her out of the sniper's line of fire and doubted she could side with her boss if the situation arose again. "Understood." She hoped she sounded more convincing than she felt.

From the look on Laurie's face, Emma knew she didn't. "Go," Laurie said. "You need to clean up those photo files before Preston posts them."

Emma darted from the office and dodged the other journalists on her way to her desk. As she slid into her chair, Preston appeared next to her. "I'll have these two images ready in a couple minutes," she told him.

"I'll wait." He didn't move.

She booted up her computer, inserted the flash drive, and selected the two photos Laurie had chosen. With Preston looming over her, she cropped the images and adjusted the exposure. "I can do this without you watching," she said, keeping her focus on the monitor.

"I know."

She lifted her gaze to him. "What do you want?"

"You just spent the last hour with your detective discussing this case, right?"

Emma returned to her photo editing. "The police looked through my photos to see if they could identify the sniper. That's all."

He leaned down, annoyingly close to her face. "Bullshit," he whispered harshly.

She saved the edited files, opened her email, attached them to a message to Preston, and clicked send. Facing him, she lifted her chin and said, "The photos are in your inbox. Go post the story."

"Not until you tell me what you know. Don't even try to convince me you weren't privy to any conversations regarding this shooting."

She looked at him without blinking. And without saying a word.

"Did they confirm the sniper is the same man who shot Dr. Shawn?"

"How can they confirm anything when they don't have an ID on the sniper?" she snapped.

"But that's the working theory, right? The same man who shot Dr. Shawn killed Zimmerman and now this Urban guy. That way he doesn't have to split the cash and drugs they stole, *and* it keeps his partners from ratting him out. No honor among thieves and all that."

Emma hadn't thought about Zimmerman, the man who'd been strangled. All of the discussion about handguns and rifles hadn't taken him into consideration.

"What?" Preston asked. "I can see you're thinking of something."

"It's nothing."

His eyes widened. "Wait. Did you see the shooter?"

"No. You saw the photos. The only thing visible was his hat and his shooting glasses."

"That's all that was visible in the photos. But you saw something more, didn't you?"

She eyed him. "Are you nuts? I had the viewfinder to my eye the entire time."

"But you said he took a shot at you. If he saw you, it makes sense that you saw him."

Emma folded her arms. "Give it up. I didn't see anything more than what's in the photos, and I didn't overhear any confidential information from the police investigation. Go post your story."

He must've finally believed her. Disappointed, he stood to his full height and turned away.

"Wait," she called after him. When he faced her, she motioned for him to come back. When he had, she said, "Last night you were determined to find out who wanted Shawn dead."

"I was. You were there. We didn't find anything."

"In the digital archives of your databases," Emma corrected him. "You mentioned the old stuff in the basement."

"And I told you, I'm not going down there. If you want to, go right ahead." He pointed to his desk. "I'll be over there posting my story. Let me know if you find anything."

Emma looked toward the door to the back staircase, drew a breath for courage, and started in that direction.

"Hold up," Preston said.

She pivoted to him, hoping he was about to come with her.

"Are you seriously planning to go down there by yourself?"

"I could use your help."

He shook his head. "I have stories to investigate. And you have photos to work on, I'm sure." When she continued to stare at him in silence, he added, "You've clearly never been down there. It's like the Dark Ages."

He was only strengthening her resolve.

Preston snorted. "Fine. If you're so determined to get a face full of cobwebs, go right ahead, but you need to talk to Laurie first."

"You think she'll tell me to leave it alone?"

"No. Unless she has an assignment for you, she'll probably think it's a great idea. Anything to crack a case before the cops."

Which wasn't at all what Emma planned to do. She wanted to find something to *help* the police catch a killer. "So why do I need to check with Laurie?"

"To get the key, you idiot. They don't just leave the archives unlocked so anyone can wander in and take what they like." Preston turned his back on her and returned to his desk.

Emma drew a breath. Maybe she *was* an idiot. But she needed to figure out what was going on with Shawn and the two dead thieves.

Chapter Nineteen

Matthias didn't expect an answer when he rang Bethany Stone's doorbell, but from inside, dogs began barking and yapping. He didn't have time to guess the size or number of canines. Considering how quickly Bethany responded, the vet clinic's office manager had either been waiting just inside or she desperately wanted to silence her welcoming committee.

"Quiet," she ordered. "Back."

Four dogs, four different sizes, and all looking to be of mixed heritage, stepped away from the door and dropped to their haunches without so much as a whimper.

Bethany's pale skin was devoid of makeup. Her short, messy hair and the gray shadows under her eyes indicated she hadn't slept well. Probably since Friday.

"Detective Honeywell," she said, sounding as tired as she looked. "How can I help you?"

"I was hoping we could talk for a few minutes."

After a long pause, she stepped back. "Come in. Don't mind the dogs."

"They're well trained," he said.

She offered a weak smile. "Thank you."

With the dogs trailing, nails clicking on the tile floor, Matthias followed Bethany down a center hallway to a kitchen that hadn't seen a remodel in decades but was spotless and bright. Pots of herbs sat on the windowsills and a faint scent of garlic permeated the air.

Bethany offered him a seat at a small, round table. "Can I get you some coffee?"

"No, thank you." He dug out his notebook and placed it and his phone in front of him.

The dogs apparently felt their duties were complete and disappeared into another room. Bethany slid into a chair across from Matthias and waited.

"How was the anniversary party yesterday afternoon?" he asked. Dr. Campbell had said she had a birthday party, which was why she couldn't join them at the clinic. Matthias hadn't believed him.

Bethany looked puzzled. "Anniversary party? Who told you that?"

Matthias acted contrite. "I'm sorry. I meant birthday party."

She shook her head. "No. You must have me confused with someone else. I was here all day. I took a Benadryl to help me sleep and could hardly get off the couch."

He believed her, although she appeared to need more sleep than she'd gotten. "You're right. I must have you mixed up with someone else. Have you heard from Dr. Malone?" Matthias asked, redirecting the conversation. Plus, he was curious.

"I called him this morning." Her eyes brightened. "He sounds good. A little raspy, but that's to be expected. He told me they're going in after the bullet tomorrow." She lowered her gaze, sadness evident in her creased forehead. "I'm as scared about this surgery as I was when he first got shot."

Matthias was worried, too, but didn't admit it. "I heard you were taking some time off. I thought you might be on your way out of town."

"Oh, no. I mean, yes, I'm taking vacation time. Dr. Nathaniel was kind enough to suggest it. But I'm not going anywhere. Not with Dr. Shawn still in the hospital."

Matthias considered nudging her down on the suspect list. If she'd been involved, the smart move would've been to head for parts unknown. He picked up his pen. "Now that you've had a few days to think about what happened, can you remember anything more than you already told me? Even something you think is insignificant?"

She chewed her lower lip, thinking. Then shook her head. "I'm afraid not."

"Let's run through Friday's events again. Maybe talking about it will jar a memory loose."

Her expression soured, but she agreed.

"Let's begin with the final patient of the day," he said. "The older woman with the cat."

"Mrs. Winston and Fuzzy." Bethany retold the same story as she had on Friday. The call from a man with Daisy, an old dog that wasn't doing well. He couldn't afford an emergency clinic and was afraid to wait until Monday. She brought him in by the side door to avoid other clients when Dr. Shawn was on the phone to Cassie. While the doctor was in with Daisy, Bethany and Robin were working at the front desk. The three intruders appeared in the lobby, armed and dressed all in black. Two went to the rear of the clinic. The third stayed in the lobby. Dr. Shawn came out and calmly encouraged them to take what they came for and leave. Instead, one of them shot him before all three escaped through the side entrance.

Matthias studied his notes and pressed the tip of his pen to one sentence. "Why did you bring Mr. Boyd and Daisy in through the side entrance?" He'd asked her on Friday, but Bethany hadn't given him an answer.

"Because the dog would be stressed around other animals. It's not something we do all the time, but it isn't unusual either."

"But Mrs. Winston's cat was the last patient of the day, correct?"

"Yes."

"And she had left, meaning there were no other animals in the waiting area."

Bethany exhaled a loud sigh. "That's true. I wasn't thinking clearly. The poor man sounded so distraught on the phone. Mrs. Winston was still in with the doctor when I spoke with Mr. Boyd. As I said, we do use the side entrance with pets that are skittish or disruptive around other animals, so I automatically directed him there."

It was more of an answer than she'd given Matthias before, but he still wasn't satisfied. Everyone had told him how efficient Bethany Stone was. "Why weren't you thinking clearly?"

She stared at him. "I..." She licked her lips. "I don't know. I guess I was thinking about the weekend. It'd been a long day."

Matthias suspected why she wasn't thinking clearly and jotted a note. He'd get back to that in a minute. "The side door. You keep it locked from the outside, correct?"

"Yes. Always."

"But during business hours, you can open it from the inside."

"Yes."

"Is there any way to open that door from the outside?"

"Not unless you have a key."

Which was where Matthias was headed with this line of questions. "How many keys are there, and who all has one?"

Her brow creased. "Let me think. The doctors all have one. That's three. I have one. Robin Tucker, our receptionist has another. And Sharon Long has one. She's the senior vet tech." Bethany rubbed her neck. "Six."

"Are there any spares floating around?"

"No."

"Do you have yours here?"

"My key? No."

This piqued Matthias's interest. "Where is it?"

"I gave it to Dr. Nathaniel when he told me to take time off. As I said, we don't have spares. I'm sure he'll pass it along to whoever fills in for me."

"Who would that be?"

"I don't know. You'll have to ask Dr. Nathaniel."

"And no one else has a key?"

"They shouldn't."

Shouldn't and didn't, Matthias thought, were two different things. Time to circle back to the topic he really wanted to address. He leaned back and intentionally struck a casual pose with an ankle crossed over a knee. "I hate to bring this up, but I have to ask. Tell me about your gambling problem."

Any blood remaining in her pale cheeks drained. "Who told you?"

He shrugged, keeping his expression neutral. This was the kind of thing that Cassie handled better, but he could pull off the easygoing act when needed. "Does it matter? I didn't realize it was a secret." A lie.

Bethany fought to regain her composure and failed. After a few stuttering starts, she ran her tongue over her lips. "I'm in Gamblers Anonymous. Yes, I have a problem. But I went to Dr. Shawn about it. He was very kind. He's the reason I'm in GA now."

Matthias picked up his phone. "How long have you been with the program?"

"It'll be a year next month."

"Have you ever slipped?"

"Slipped?"

"You know. Placed a bet?"

Bethany rubbed a spot on her neck. "No." She looked as if she was about to say more but reconsidered.

Matthias nodded. He opened his phone to the social media page he'd saved and selected the image of Bethany at Presque Isle Downs. "Are you sure about that?" He turned the screen to show her.

Her sharp intake of breath was audible. She didn't say anything for several long seconds, her gaze never leaving the photo. When she did speak, her voice was strained. "That's an old picture."

"Are you sure about that?" Matthias asked again, this time losing the congenial tone.

Tears brimming, her eyes shifted from his phone to him. Then any remaining composure dissolved. She lowered her face into her hands. "Oh, God," she choked.

Matthias set his phone on the table and let her sob for well over a minute. Eventually, she uncovered her face and dug a tissue from her pocket. Still, she kept her head lowered until she'd mopped her tears, and her shoulders no longer spasmed.

After a deep breath, she met his gaze. "You caught me. All right. I went to the track with some friends. I made a few wagers."

He thought of the picture he hadn't shown her—the one of her tearing up her betting stubs. "How much did you lose?" he asked, keeping any accusatory tones from his voice.

She looked at the table's surface. "Two thousand four hundred and ninety-three dollars."

Not twenty-five hundred, he noted. Maybe that was the limit she'd given herself. "Ouch," he said. "That had to hurt."

"It did." She lifted her face, her chin jutted. "But not the dollar amount. I had enough to cover my losses. What hurt was knowing how I'd let my sponsor down."

"Did you tell your sponsor what you'd done?"

"I did. The next day I went to a meeting and confessed."

"But you didn't confess to Dr. Malone."

The glimmer of tears returned. "No, I did not. I couldn't stand to disappoint him again. Not when he'd put so much trust in me." Bethany came forward, reached over the table, and clamped a hand over Matthias's. "Please. He doesn't have to know, does he?"

Matthias wasn't that good a poker player.

She released his hand. "Oh, God. You already told him."

Instead of replying, Matthias asked, "Did you have anything to do with the robbery on Friday?"

She gasped. "No."

"You didn't unlock the side door to allow access? Maybe for a cut of the take?"

"No." Bethany clenched both fists. "I would never do something like that. Not to Dr. Shawn of all people."

Matthias studied her. "All right." He scooped up his notebook, pen, and phone. "All right," he said again and rose.

"You believe me." Not a question.

"For now. Unless I find something else that you're not telling me." He tipped his head. "And I will find out anything you aren't telling me."

"There's nothing else to tell."

He thanked her for her time and showed himself out. As he walked to his car, he replayed the conversation in his head. He believed her. At least the part about not doing anything to harm Shawn.

Because he was now absolutely certain of one thing.

Bethany Stone was in love with Cassie's husband.

Preston hadn't been kidding when he told Emma the basement was like a haunted museum. She stood just inside the door, clutching the key Laurie had provided, and stared into the gloom and cobwebs, debating how far she really wanted to go to find what in Shawn's past might have prompted a homicide attempt in the present.

Emma found the light switches next to the door and flipped one at a time. Overhead fluorescent lights flickered on. A few continued to strobe and buzz. With her imagination running wild, she turned back to the door and pictured it slamming shut, locking her in. She retreated into the stairwell, searched the ground, and found a rubber wedge. She opened the door wide and kicked the wedge under it, securing it from closing. Then she stuffed the key deep in her pocket for safe keeping. She checked her phone for a signal. The ErieLIVE Wi-Fi remained connected even down here.

Mildly confident that she would not be trapped and die, leaving her rotting bones to be found by the next curious researcher, she eased her way into the musty room.

The right half of the mammoth space appeared to be reserved as storage for old dust-covered linotype machines and printing presses—museum pieces in this digital age. The left half made her think of a police evidence room that had been hit by a tornado. Rows of metal shelving held dusty boxes, some of which had been pulled out, set on the floor, and never replaced. Four heavy wooden tables filled the space between the two sides. More boxes sat on them. Emma pictured reporters digging for old information down here and not wanting to spend the extra few minutes to replace the research material where they found it.

Treading carefully, she made her way along the first row, checking the markings on the boxes. Some had dates scrawled on them. A few were labeled with bigger news stories. Curious, she pulled out one of the boxes from May 1985 for no reason other than wanting to see what was inside. She placed the box on the floor and knelt next to it to lift the lid. Whatever she'd hoped for, this wasn't it. Yellowed clippings had been tossed on top of brittle-looking folded newspapers. She was afraid to even touch them for fear they'd disintegrate into dust.

Emma swore. Everything appeared to be filed by date. She didn't know what she was looking for and definitely didn't know what time span to search. How could she possibly locate anything specific to Shawn?

Unlike others, Emma replaced the lid and slid the box back into its slot. Then she slowly weaved her way through the rows, scanning the markings. Maybe something would jump out at her. Did she really expect to find one labeled SHAWN MALONE'S PAST?

Once she reached the far end of the space without any such discovery, she found a door open to a second room. She reached inside the jamb, found a light switch, and flipped it. More fluorescent lights flickered to life, illuminating a wall of file cabinets. Tarps covered what appeared to be two large pieces of equipment. She approached them and wrestled the covering aside, revealing a pair of microfilm readers. For the first time since she'd stepped into the basement, she felt hope.

She selected a random drawer and discovered it was packed with small boxes, each labeled with a range of dates. Carefully, she opened one of the boxes and deposited a spool of microfilm into her palm. At least it and the boxes were in better condition than the newspapers and clippings. The reader machines seemed in good shape as well.

But one problem remained. Unless she planned to spend the next year of her life scanning through every edition, she needed to narrow her search by date. The even bigger problem was she didn't even know whether there was anything to find, dated or not.

She returned the spool to the box and the box to the drawer. If she was going to track down a reason for someone wanting Shawn dead, it wasn't going to happen here. Not without a lot more information.

Chapter Twenty

M atthias sat in his car outside the West Erie Veterinary Clinic, listening to Roth over his speaker phone.

"The crime scene techs have finished with the sniper's nest. No blood, so it seems our guy missed. I doubt they've come up with anything else useful either. The shooter wasn't the only one using that room. From the look and smell of the place, vagrants have been taking up residence, junkies have shot up there, and all sorts of vermin call it home. If the scat's any indication, there are some hellaciously big rats in here."

"What about shell casings?"

"Nothing. He policed his brass."

Matthias pinched the bridge of his nose. "Is there anything at all that might help us ID this guy?"

"The techs collected a shitload of fibers and trace evidence. It's going to take them a while to go through all of it, but, hey, we might get lucky."

"Why start now?" Matthias grumbled under his breath.

"I didn't catch that. What'd you say?"

"How's the view? Would the shooter have been able to see Urban through the cruiser's window?"

"Hang on." Matthias heard shuffling and a thunk before Roth said, "I'm at the window now." A pause. "It's hard to tell. Maybe. Do you want me to get one of the uniforms to park his vehicle at the spot where Urban was shot?"

Matthias considered whether they would learn anything truly useful from the experiment. Probably not. Still, he didn't want to miss anything. "Yeah. Do that. And get a photo."

"Should I call in your girlfriend?"

Matthias could hear the snark in Roth's voice. "Let me know when you're done."

"Wait. There are a couple more things you'll find interesting. We were wondering how the shooter knew exactly where Urban would be—how he knew where to set up to take the shot."

Among other things. "Yeah."

"Turns out he didn't need to be too precise. He'd loosened the plywood covering every window up here. The room is huge. Wide open front to back. One of the windows facing the railyard had the plywood unfastened, same as the one he actually shot from."

"He had a view from both north and south," Matthias mused.

"That's right. Maybe he couldn't get a good angle when Urban was captured and being brought back to 16th Street. All he had to do was cross to the south side of the building and wait for an opportunity. And we were wondering how the sniper got in and out without being seen? We found an old tunnel in the basement that connects this warehouse to the next one. It'd been blocked off, but someone reopened it at some point."

Matthias hadn't been aware of the tunnel, but from previous cases, he knew the structure was a labyrinth of passageways with stairwells leading down into a catacomb-like basement. With some knowledge of the maze, the shooter could easily manage to slip in and out without being noticed. "But how the hell had he known Urban would go to that exact area at that exact time?"

Roth fell silent, probably pondering the question before coming up with a theory. "Between the time Urban gave us the slip and we got the search organized, the K9s here, it was—what? Almost two hours by the time he was captured?"

"About that."

"If the sniper had a police scanner and knew where we were looking for Urban, he'd have plenty of time to get here and set up shop."

"It's a reasonable supposition," Matthias said. More reasonable than any other theory they'd come up with. "Keep me posted."

"Will do."

Matthias ended the call and stuffed the phone in his pocket.

Inside the clinic, he didn't recognize either of the women behind the registration desk. Only one gray-haired man sat in the waiting area with a small pet carrier on the chair beside him.

Matthias approached the desk with a smile. "Slow day," he commented.

One of the women returned the smile. "Hardly. We just don't schedule appointments during lunch. Can I help you?"

He showed his badge and identified himself.

Her mouth formed an O. "You're the detective investigating the shooting and robbery. Cassie's partner."

"That's right."

She extended her hand, which he shook. "I'm Sharon Long."

The name was on his list. "You were here on Friday but left prior to the incident," he said.

"Yes." She shook her head. "It may sound horrible, but I've never been so glad to have cut out of work early."

Matthias opened his notebook. "I understand Robin and Erin aren't in today?"

"They asked for a couple of days off, and Dr. Nathaniel granted the request."

"Is he here?"

She tipped her head toward the closed office door. "He's eating lunch."

Matthias referred to his notes, although he didn't need to. "I understand you're one of the staff members who has a key to the side door."

She blinked. "Yes?"

"Do you happen to have it on you?"

"Yes. I always do."

"May I see it?"

"It's on my key ring in my purse." When he didn't comment, she pointed toward the hallway and added, "In the back."

"I'll wait."

Sharon scowled. To the other woman at the desk, she said, "Excuse me a minute."

While she was gone, Matthias chatted with the receptionist, whose name badge labeled her as Fran, and learned she normally only worked part-time. "I'm filling in while they're shorthanded," she said.

"Are you specifically filling in for Bethany Stone?"

"I am. Why?"

"Do you have a key for the side door?"

"Not usually, but Dr. Nathaniel gave me one to use while Bethany's on vacation. Do you want to see it?"

"Were you here on Friday?"

"No." Her startled expression told Matthias she understood where he was going and volunteered her alibi. "Since I'm only part-time, I have another job." She named a chain restaurant near the mall. "I was there from noon until nine."

He made a note. "Yes, I would like to see your key if it's not too much trouble."

While he was examining it, Sharon Long appeared from the hallway, strode toward him, and held out a ring with at least a dozen keys on it. She selected one and held it up. "Do you need me to remove it from the ring?"

"Not necessary." He took it and compared it to Fran's. They matched.

"What are you looking for?" Sharon asked.

"I'm not sure." But he'd know it if or when he saw it. He returned both keys. "I want to touch base with Dr. Nathaniel." To Sharon, he asked, "Would you be willing to sit down and talk once I'm done?"

She gave him a deer-in-headlights look. "I guess so. Sure. I'll either be here or in the back."

Matthias gave her a smile meant to put her at ease. While she looked terrified at the prospect of being questioned by a cop, he'd seen hundreds of innocent eyewitnesses with that same expression. It was the ones who acted cocky and cool that were the most concerning. "I won't keep you long. I promise."

Leaving the two women to their work, he crossed to the office door and knocked.

"Come in," a muffled voice called.

Matthias entered to find two men in white lab coats, one of whom was Dr. Nathaniel Campbell with a sandwich in hand and a full mouth. Seeing Matthias, the vet waved and pointed to the empty chair.

The second vet introduced himself and shook Matthias's hand. "I was out of town at a symposium in Harrisburg last week," he said. "Didn't get home until late Saturday. I was shocked when Nathaniel called and told me what happened."

Matthias asked him the name and location of the symposium and made a note to confirm the alibi. He followed with the usual questions and received the same answers as he'd gotten from everyone else. No, he didn't know of anyone who might want to harm Shawn. No, he wasn't aware of any disgruntled pet parents. No, he hadn't seen any suspicious characters around the clinic in the days and weeks leading up to the incident.

The veterinarian excused himself and left Matthias and Campbell alone.

Campbell placed what was left of his sandwich on the paper wrapping and swiveled to face him. "Any news on the shooting?"

Instead of answering, Matthias pointed at the computer. "Yesterday, I asked you whether you had a client by the name of Zimmerman."

"We don't."

"How about Henry Urban?"

"Doesn't sound familiar." Campbell turned to his keyboard and typed in the name. After a few seconds, he shook his head. "No one in our client database has the last name Urban. Sorry." He looked at Matthias. "Who is he?"

"He was one of our suspects for the robbery."

"Was?"

"He's in the morgue right now."

Campbell scowled. "Is he the one who shot Shawn?"

"He doesn't match the description Shawn gave us."

The vet looked like he wanted to say something but didn't.

"I'm going back over everything that happened here on Friday," Matthias said. "I still haven't heard from the cat lady, Mrs. Winston."

Campbell gave a short laugh. "I tried calling her. Didn't get an answer. Let me try again." He typed the name into the computer to bring up the client's file before picking up the desk phone's receiver and punching in a number. After a few seconds, he met Matthias's gaze and nodded. "Hello, Mrs. Winston. This is Dr. Nathaniel from the West Erie Veterinary Clinic. How's Fuzzy doing?"

Matthias could hear what sounded like an elderly feminine

voice coming through the phone but couldn't make out her words, although she seemed enthusiastic. And very chatty.

Campbell managed to break in. "I'm glad to hear it, Mrs. Winston. The reason I'm calling… I don't suppose you heard the news about Dr. Shawn?"

There was another long reply.

"I will pass along your well wishes. I was wondering if you'd be willing to speak with a police detective who's investigating the case. His name's Detective Honeywell, and he's sitting right here, if you have the time." After another long commentary from the cat lady, Campbell thanked her and handed the phone to Matthias. "She's happy to help."

He took the receiver and introduced himself.

"Dr. Nathaniel told me you're trying to find those awful people who hurt Dr. Shawn," Mrs. Winston said, "and I sure hope you do. How horrible. Dr. Shawn is such a lovely man. All of the doctors there are. They've saved my precious Fuzzy's life more times than I can count. And the fact that I had just left? Well, that terrifies me. Fuzzy and I could've been there. She might've been hurt. I can't even imagine—"

"Yes, ma'am," Matthias broke in. "I'm very glad that didn't happen. Could you answer a few questions for me about Friday afternoon?"

"I will if I can, but I'd already left, as I said. I don't know what I could possibly tell you that would be of any help."

"Did you notice anyone in the parking lot when you were leaving?"

"No. Mine was the last car. There wasn't anyone else around."

"You didn't see anyone on foot near the clinic? Specifically, anyone dressed all in black?"

"In black? My heavens, it's been so hot out. Way too hot to wear black. I most certainly would've noticed anyone dressed like that."

The rest of the conversation was more of the same. Long, rambling replies. No helpful information.

A knock came at the door as Matthias managed to end the call with a thank you.

"Come in," Campbell called out. To Matthias, he said, "Sorry. I should've warned you. Mrs. Winston lives alone with only Fuzzy to talk to. Once she gets a human ear, she doesn't like to let go."

Sharon Long opened the door and poked her head in. "I apologize for disturbing you, Dr. Nathaniel, but John Boyd and Daisy are here for their follow-up. They're in room one."

Perfect timing. Matthias waited until the vet thanked Sharon and she retreated from the office before saying, "I'd like a few minutes of Mr. Boyd's time, too."

"That's up to him. Let me have my consultation with him first. Then I'll encourage him to stick around."

"Appreciate it." Matthias followed Campbell out of the office and watched as he disappeared into the first exam room. Sharon was alone behind the desk, her head down, studying some patient files. Matthias noted the elderly man with the pet carrier was no longer waiting and crossed to the senior vet tech. "While Dr. Campbell is in with his patient, do you mind if we talk?"

"I guess now's as good a time as any." She gathered the papers, tapped them on the desk to even the edges, slid them into a folder, and placed it in a slot of an upright file sorter. "We have the afternoon patients coming in soon, though."

"I promise I won't interfere with business."

"All right then. How can I help?"

Matthias skimmed through the same questions he'd asked everyone else and received similar answers. If he didn't personally know Shawn, he'd be sorely tempted to think the man was too good to be true. No human could be so well thought of. No man could have made it to his age without ruffling some feathers.

Then again, maybe Cassie ruffled enough for both of them.

"What can you tell me about Bethany Stone?" Matthias asked.

Sharon reacted. An expression Matthias translated as, *oh shit*, flitted across her eyes before she recovered, trying too hard to act impassive. "What about her?"

He didn't want to feed office gossip. Not yet. Not until he had a better grip on the situation. "I asked first," he said with a practiced grin.

"She's hard working. It feels strange, her not being here. She's *always* here. First to arrive. Last to leave."

"How long has she worked for the clinic?"

"Longer than I have, which is saying something."

"Does she get along with everyone?"

"Oh, yes. The clients love her. All the pets adore her." Sharon relaxed enough to snicker. "Then again, why wouldn't they? She works here at the front desk and hands out treats. *I'm* the one who pokes them with needles."

"Doesn't seem fair, does it?"

Sharon shrugged. "Frankly, I'm happier working hands-on with the animals than dealing with employee schedules and billing. A few bites and scratches don't amount to anything when you save a pet's life. It's the best feeling in the world to see an animal that came in on the verge of death, return to its human all wagging tails and snuggles."

Her tone was so genuine that Matthias hoped like hell Sharon wasn't somehow involved. "You mention billing. Is that part of Ms. Stone's duties?"

Sharon tensed again, and Matthias knew. This woman was well aware of Bethany's money troubles. "Yes, it is," Sharon said.

Matthias folded his arms and rested his elbows on the counter as he took a quick scan of the room. They were alone. "You know about Ms. Stone's gambling addiction."

"No. I don't. I mean, what gambling addiction? I'm sure

Bethany would never." Her voice trailed off as if she realized she was babbling.

Matthias stayed silent and motionless, watching Sharon squirm beneath his steady gaze.

Finally, she exhaled and glanced at the doors and hallway entrances. They were still alone, but she leaned toward him and lowered her voice to a whisper. "No one else here knows. Please keep it that way."

"Dr. Malone knows."

Sharon waved a hand. "Well, obviously. He's the one who got her into Gamblers Anonymous. But no one else."

"*You* know," Matthias pointed out.

"Because she and I are friends."

"The kind of friends who share everything." He posed it as a statement, not a question.

"Yes. Exactly."

Not everything, Matthias noted. Sharon Long was not one of the women in the Presque Isle Downs photos. Unless she'd been the one taking them. "So, you're aware she recently spent an afternoon at the racetrack, betting on the ponies."

Sharon's lips parted in shock. No, she hadn't been the one taking the pictures. "That can't be right. She wouldn't."

Matthias reached into his pocket, pulled out his phone, and opened the page with the images of Bethany before handing it to Sharon.

She studied the social media posts, enlarging the photos for a closer look. Her shoulders sagged as she returned the phone. "I can't believe it." Meeting Matthias's gaze, she asked, "Does Dr. Shawn know?"

"I'm afraid so."

Sharon touched her lower lip with trembling fingers. "Does *she* know that he knows?"

The way she asked it made Matthias think this was an even

bigger faux pas than the act itself. And the pain in Sharon's voice further solidified another of his presumptions. "She knows," he said.

Sharon winced and lowered her face.

He decided to go for it. "How long have you been aware that Bethany's in love with him?"

Chapter Twenty-One

Emma crossed the newsroom and stopped in front of Preston's desk. "I need a date."

He didn't look up from whatever he was typing. "Isn't that what your cop is for?"

It took a moment for his wisecrack to sink in. "Not that kind of date, you idiot."

Preston chuckled. "Now you're starting to sound like me." He finally looked up at her and wrinkled his nose. "What the hell did you get into?" he asked, wagging a finger at his own hair.

She ran her fingers through her short tresses and immediately encountered a slightly sticky and highly tenacious spider web. Having grown up around old barns and farm buildings, she was no stranger to getting tangled in the things, but this brought back the old familiar fear.

Was the web old and abandoned? Or was a spider still residing in it?

Preston chuckled as she batted at her head to knock off any hitchhiking arachnids.

"Shut up and just tell me if you see any spiders on me."

He stood and rounded to her side of his desk. "Stop." He took both her wrists and lowered them to her sides, then grasped her shoulders and turned her in a circle. "Nope. No spiders," he said once she again faced him. "Just a bunch of webs." He brushed her cheek. "And dirt. You need to go to the washroom and clean up."

"In a minute." Emma didn't want to lose her train of thought.

Preston returned to his chair and dropped into it. "You've been exploring the haunted museum in the basement."

"I have. How does anyone find anything down there?"

"I warned you. The only guy I know who was able to navigate those archives was an old dude, and he retired two years ago. Right before he left, I was doing a piece on historic Erie. Couldn't find a damn thing on my own, but he came up with a bunch of old photos and clippings for me."

"Think you could call him in to help me out?"

"I doubt it. Last I heard, he moved to Oregon."

Emma grunted. "Could he get any farther from Erie without leaving the country?"

Preston shrugged. "Hawaii. Alaska."

She shook her head. This wasn't getting her anywhere. "You didn't mention the room with the microfilm. It seems to be in better shape than the rest of the files."

"Not everything has been converted to microfilm. Whoever was in charge of the conversion stopped once we went digital and switched to doing the rest of it that way."

Emma had already searched the digital files and come up empty. "The stuff that *is* on microfilm, though. It's all sorted by month and year, which is what I meant when I said I needed a date."

"What date?"

"That's the problem. I don't know. If there's something in

Shawn's past that has come back to bite him in the butt now, I can't find it unless I have a date. Or a range of dates."

Preston rocked back in his chair. "Are you listening to yourself? *If* something in his past is the reason for him getting shot. You don't know that. It was a supposition when we first talked about it, and I quickly realized there was no way for us to dig that deeply. You need to focus on the present rather than searching the past. With or without a date." He came forward and brought his attention back to his computer. "Now go get cleaned up before Laurie sees you."

Emma dug into her desk drawer, pulled out her comb, and headed for the restroom, fretting over what Preston had said. He was right, darn it. For all she knew, she was looking for something that never happened. The shooting might've been random. A drug addict with a gun in the middle of a robbery didn't need a motive for attempted murder. She'd seen how far being under the influence had driven her sister. The need to score the next hit could be reason enough for some addict to pull the trigger and nearly end the life of a decent man.

At the sink, she dug her comb from her handbag and worked it through her hair, picking out what remained of the cobwebs. Satisfied she'd gotten them all, she turned on the water and splashed her face to wash away the dirty smudges. Staring into the mirror at the damp hair edging her face and the water droplets glistening on her lashes, she continued to roll Preston's words through her mind. He was probably right. Probably. Either way, she was at a dead end.

She smiled. Preston *was* right about one thing. If she wanted a date, she needed Matthias.

All color drained from Sharon Long's face. Her lips opened, closed, opened, and closed again.

Matthias had hoped like hell she would double over in laughter at such a preposterous claim. *Bethany? In love with Dr. Shawn? You must be kidding.* Instead, she looked like she wanted the earth to open up and swallow her.

Without saying a word, Sharon had answered his question and unleashed a thousand more.

They were still alone, but more than ever, he didn't want to risk being overheard. He moved around the counter and stepped through the gate bearing an AUTHORIZED PERSONNEL ONLY sign to stand inches from the tech. He almost choked on his first question—the one that meant the most to everyone involved. Especially Cassie. "Is the attraction mutual?"

Sharon lowered her face. "No."

Matthias exhaled a sigh, his knees weak with relief. "Are you sure?"

"Absolutely." She lifted her chin to meet his gaze. "Dr. Shawn is the best man I know. He loves his wife and his family. That's part of the attraction, I suppose. Bethany's been in some bad relationships. Seeing how much he cares for his wife, how steadfast he is, Bethany couldn't help but fall for him." Sharon huffed a short laugh. "Heck, I think all the women here are a little in love with him. Maybe a couple of the men, too."

As long as Shawn wasn't stepping out on Cassie, Matthias didn't give a damn about his staff having a crush on their boss. However, another unlikely but feasible motive came to mind. "Are any of those women—or men, who are a little in love with Shawn—married or in a serious relationship?"

Sharon looked at him, the puzzlement on her face morphing into shock. "You think one of our staff's spouses might be so jealous as to shoot—" Her voice rose to a squeak before breaking.

"I don't think anything except that I can't ignore an obvious possibility."

She considered his words. "I understand what you're saying, but I can't think of anyone who would do that. Besides, Dr. Shawn saw the man who shot him. Wouldn't he have recognized him? I mean, we have family picnics and get-togethers. He's met all the spouses, partners, and significant others."

From across the waiting room, a door clicked open, and Dr. Campbell appeared. His gaze landed on Matthias and Sharon. "Detective, if you would like to speak with Mr. Boyd, he's agreed to talk to you." Campbell hiked a thumb over his shoulder. "You can use the exam room. We still have roughly thirty minutes before our regular appointments begin."

Matthias thanked him, refocused on Sharon, and dropped his voice. "I'd appreciate it if you could give me a list of employees' spouses or partners."

"*All* of them?"

"Please. That way I won't overlook someone." He gave her a comforting smile. "And you don't have to decide which of your friends' and colleagues' husbands or wives warrant investigation."

"Wives, too?"

"Wives, too."

John Boyd, attired in the same rumpled brown shirt, khakis, and ball cap as three days ago, sat slump-shouldered in one of the chairs, a red leash coiled in his hand. Daisy lay on the floor next to him, her chin on her front legs. Only her eyes moved, shifting to Matthias as he entered.

He approached the dog first, squatting to pet her. "Hey, girl. How you doin'?" She lifted her head, thumped her tail, and gave him a doggy smile. Matthias looked at Boyd. "I'm no vet, but she looks better to me."

"I think so, too." Boyd managed a fleeting grin. "She's eating better. I can't really say if she's any more energetic, but she's old. Like me." The faint smile disappeared. "And Dr. Campbell didn't give me a lot of hope."

"Oh?" Matthias took a seat in the second chair. "I was under the impression that her bloodwork came back better than he'd expected."

Boyd raised an eyebrow. "You and the doctor discussed my dog?"

The question drew Matthias up short. Were there HIPAA privacy laws where veterinarians were concerned? He didn't think so. "She's a sweet girl. I admit I've been worried about her."

Boyd seemed appeased. "She is a sweet girl. And yes, the doctor says her bloodwork was good enough to have the surgery. But I can't afford the kind of money they're talking about. Sure, Dr. Campbell has offered a darned good deal. Better than I'd get anywhere else." He sighed. "But I still have to figure out how to come up with the cash."

Matthias pictured the pair. Homeless. Scrounging to get by. Looking at Daisy, he considered offering to help with the cost but reminded himself why he was here. "I wanted to touch base to find out if you'd remembered anything from Friday. Even something insignificant."

Boyd thought about it, then shook his head. "Like I told you before, I didn't see anything. I heard a lady scream after the vet left me alone in here. And I heard a gunshot. I'm too much of a coward to stick my head out when there's shooting going on." He bent down to stroke Daisy's head. "And I sure didn't want to put my dog in harm's way."

"I don't blame you. What about before you came into the

clinic? Did you see anyone outside? On the street? Or lurking nearby?"

"No one who stands out."

Matthias guessed that ruled out three men dressed head-to-toe in black. His gaze returned to the dog. He bent down to stroke the top of her head, and her tail again drummed the floor. "How long have you and Daisy been together?" he asked.

"I've had her since she was a pup," Boyd said with a sad smile. "Been a long time. It's hard to see her get old. Be in pain."

Matthias again thought of how he could help. He straightened and met Boyd's gaze. "You make the arrangements with Dr. Campbell to get Daisy's surgery done. I'll see that the bill's paid."

Boyd blinked. "Are you serious?"

"I am."

The old man looked down at his dog. "You hear that, girl? You're gonna get your hip all fixed up." Then he extended a hand to Matthias. "Thank you, sir."

After a relatively quiet but sweaty afternoon spent with Preston, covering vandalism at McClelland Park, Emma clocked out and returned to the campground. Being Monday, and a sultry day at that, most residents were either holed up in their trailers or had headed home for the work week.

Once inside her camper, she locked her door, turned on the AC unit, and kept the blinds drawn against the sun. She grabbed a bottle of water from her refrigerator and took a long draw, relishing the cold liquid. Before she could replace the lid, her phone buzzed. Matthias's face lit the screen.

"Hey," she answered. "How's Shawn?"

"I just talked to Cassie. He's doing well, all things considered.

I'm heading to the hospital to visit him and wondered if you'd like to come along."

Emma peeled her shirt fabric away from her sweat-dampened skin. "Only if you give me time to grab a shower. I've been outside all afternoon." She didn't mention the hours in the cobwebby basement of ErieLIVE.

"Are you at the campground?"

"Yep. Just got here."

"Go get showered. I'll pick you up there." He ended the call before she could respond.

Chapter Twenty-Two

Clouds over Lake Erie hinted at rain, which would either cool things down or create steam if the sun came back out before dusk. For now, Matthias kept his windows closed and the AC cranked as he maneuvered his Jeep through Monday evening traffic and listened to Emma share her day.

"So basically," she said after telling him about what she called "the haunted museum" in ErieLIVE's basement, "without a date or at least a date range, it would take months to find anything. If there's even anything to find."

"There may not be," he told her.

Emma shifted in her seat to face him. "I thought you believed the shooting was the real reason for the robbery. That Shawn had been targeted. Have you changed your mind?" In Matthias's peripheral vision, he noticed she made a face. "I'm sorry. You probably aren't free to discuss the case with me."

He battled a smile. "You're right. I'm not. So, I better not read anything I tell you on ErieLIVE's website."

"Promise. Cone of Silence."

"Seriously?" Matthias lost his battle. "You're quoting *Get Smart*?"

"It's a classic." She grinned back at him. "But I'm trying to help you figure out why this happened. I am *not* assisting Preston. And for what it's worth, Laurie gave me hell for turning over that memory card. If it happens again, I might be out of a job."

"She must understand why we need it, though. I've known Laurie Kassim for years. She's always supported law enforcement."

"Her main concern was the lack of a court order. She says in the future, all photos are to be seen by her before you get your hands on them."

Matthias wasn't going to make any such promise, and he didn't believe Emma expected him to. He braked at a red light. "Anyhow, getting back to Shawn's case." He shot a look at her. "Yes, the Cone of Silence is in place."

"Got it."

"I have severe doubts that what happened Friday night has anything to do with what happened in the distant past."

"Oh?"

He pondered how much to say, regardless of Emma's promise to keep it between them. Right now, his suspicions about Bethany Stone were only that. Suspicions. The woman had problems. But were money and unrequited love motives enough for her to help a trio of gunmen gain entry to her place of employment? In the back of his mind, he heard Cassie saying, "*Love and money are two of the strongest and oldest motives for murder*." But if Bethany wanted Shawn to herself, why kill him? Cassie perhaps, but the object of her obsession?

"I get it," Emma said, interrupting his internal conversation. "The Cone of Silence only goes so far."

"For now. I'm still sorting it out."

"Good," Emma said.

"Good?"

"Yeah. If you believe what happened doesn't involve the past, I don't have to go back into the archives and get coated in spiderwebs again."

As Emma and Matthias approached Shawn's hospital room, raucous laughter rolled out into the hallway. The cop guarding the entrance was standing in the doorway rather than seated in the hall and appeared to be enjoying whatever was going on.

Matthias greeted the cop, who stepped out of their way, and led Emma into the room. She took in the scene before her. Shawn was sitting up in his bed, still anchored to an IV drip and oxygen tubing. Alissa perched at his feet, a sketchpad on her lap. A Black woman who looked a lot like Cassie, only a good twenty-five or thirty years younger, stood beside the bed, arms crossed and a clearly mock scowl on her face. Denene, Emma guessed. Shawn and Cassie's daughter and Alissa's mom.

Cassie stood back from the others, wearing a broad grin. She spotted Emma and Matthias and waved them in. "Welcome to the Malone family zoo," she said.

"What's going on?" Matthias asked. "Did they decide to discharge you?"

Denene placed an index finger on her chest. "Do you mean me from the Army or Dad from this luxury resort?"

Cassie snorted.

"Either."

"No such luck," Shawn said. "They're just demonstrating how surrounded I am by crazy women."

"Three generations," Denene said, her chin jutting. "Look how lucky you are."

Shawn gave an exaggerated eye roll. "Is that what you call it? Lucky?"

Cassie moved to her daughter's side. "That's exactly what you are. Lucky and blessed to have three gorgeous and brilliant women fawning over you."

Emma thought she noticed Matthias wince, but he covered the reaction so quickly, she wasn't sure.

If Cassie had detected it, she didn't react. Instead, she introduced Emma to Staff Sergeant Denene Malone with a distinct note of pride in her voice. Greetings completed, Cassie gave her daughter's shoulders a squeeze and said, "You girls stay here and keep an eye on our patient. I have some business to discuss with our visitors."

Emma looked at her, surprised. Visitors. Plural. Cassie was including her?

Cassie must've read her face and gave a quick nod. "Yes, you, too." She again looked at her family. "I'm taking orders. What do you want from the snack bar?"

"Ice cream," Alissa chirped.

"You've had enough of that today," Denene said. "Chocolate milk for the artist and a black coffee for me, thanks."

"Do they have Jack Daniels?" Shawn asked.

Cassie scoffed. "It'll be green Jell-o for you."

All three responded with "*Eeew!*" and Alissa punctuated it with, "Yuck."

Chuckling, Cassie herded Emma and Matthias out of the room and toward the elevator. As they waited for the car to arrive, Cassie looked back and forth at them. "Okay. Spill. What's new with the case?" She pointed a finger at Matthias. "And do not tell me 'nothing.'"

With a ping, the doors swished open, revealing a half dozen occupants. Emma squeezed in along with Matthias and Cassie.

She had a feeling he was grateful for the delay in having to answer.

But the delay ended once they found a secluded table in the cafeteria and sat with cups of coffee in front of them. Cassie locked eyes with Matthias and crossed her arms. "What's new with the Urban homicide?"

"His autopsy is scheduled for tomorrow morning." Matthias sipped his coffee and recoiled.

"Oh, stop with the coffee snobbery."

"This is awful. Even the stuff in the breakroom is better."

"Try being stuck here for four days and counting. It grows on you."

"Like fungus." He pushed the cup away. "The crime scene techs have gone over the sniper's nest, but the lab will have a helluva time discerning evidence from trash."

Cassie turned her attention to Emma. "How much trouble did you get into regarding the camera's memory card?"

"Enough." Emma added more sugar to her coffee. Matthias was right. It was nasty. "I got a pass because I'm new to the job, but that won't work next time."

"What makes you think there'll be a next time?" Cassie shot a knowing grin and a wink at Matthias before turning serious again. "How did your talk go with Bethany?"

Emma spotted the same wince as earlier when Cassie mentioned the three Malone women fawning over Shawn.

Again, Matthias recovered quickly. "She tried to deny her day at the races until I showed her the pictures on social media. She admitted falling off the wagon. Says she contacted her sponsor at Gamblers Anonymous and went to a meeting."

Emma leaned back in her chair. This was what Matthias was still sorting through. Or part of it, at least.

"She seemed more upset to learn I'd told Shawn about it than anything else."

Cassie nodded, thinking. "I'm sure." She looked at Emma. "What about you? Have you learned anything from your colleagues at ErieLIVE?"

That's why Cassie had included her in the trip to the snack bar. "Not yet." Emma debated how much to share, but Cassie's intense stare helped her decide. "I've been trying to come up with a motive for the shooting, since the assumption is the robbery was secondary. But your husband seems to be loved by all."

That same expression flashed across Matthias's face a third time. He covered by taking a long sip from his coffee, which only deepened the pained grimace.

"I've been talking to Shawn about it," Cassie said. "Neither of us can come up with a reason someone would want him dead." She shifted her attention to Matthias, but neither spoke.

Emma suddenly felt very much like a fifth wheel. "Since I have nothing to add, why don't I get Alissa's chocolate milk and Denene's coffee and head back to the room."

Cassie opened her purse and placed a twenty-dollar bill on the table. "Don't forget Shawn's green Jell-o."

As soon as Emma left the snack bar, Cassie reached over and grasped Matthias's arm. Hard. "Now tell me the rest," she said.

He pried free of her talon-like grip and swore. "The rest of what? We're not going to have anything solid until tomorrow's autopsy, if then."

"That's not what I mean. I saw the look on your face. Back in the room when the girls and I were joking around and again when I asked you about Bethany. What aren't you telling me?"

Dammit. He'd hoped to avoid sharing this part of his suspicions, especially after talking to Sharon Long, but Cassie wasn't going to let it go. "Are you aware that Bethany is in love with Shawn?"

The hand Cassie had used to nearly raise bruises on his arm now slid to her lap. After a few beats, she replied, "No."

He wasn't sure if she meant she wasn't aware or didn't believe him.

She sat in stunned silence. Matthias wished he knew what was going on behind her dark eyes.

Finally, she said, "Why do you think that? Did she say something?"

"Not directly. But her expression when she found out that I'd told Shawn about the gambling ... her reaction when she denied helping the assailants gain access to the clinic ... she said she'd never do anything like that to Dr. Shawn."

"And I believe her. She wouldn't."

Matthias raised an eyebrow at her. "There was more to it than disappointing her boss." He put a hand around his coffee cup but didn't lift it from the table. "I asked Sharon Long when I spoke to her. She confirmed it."

Cassie choked.

He raised a hand to silence her. "Sharon also confirmed that Bethany's feelings were not reciprocated. In fact, she said just about everyone who worked there was a little in love with your husband."

Which brought a short laugh. "Now *that* I believe. So, what you're calling Bethany 'being in love' is just a crush."

Matthias wasn't so sure.

Cassie's expression turned solemn. Matthias could see her trying to digest the revelation. Then she shook her head. "Assuming Bethany is 'in love' with Shawn, if anything, it removes her from the suspect list."

"I've been thinking the same thing, except..."

"Except what?"

"Remember the movie *Fatal Attraction*?"

Cassie shot him the side eye. "Seriously? We're using old movies in our investigations now?"

"I'm just saying. A woman going after a lover who jilted her is not unheard of."

Cassie's expression grew fierce. "Shawn is not Bethany's lover."

"I know that." Matthias came forward and rested his forearms on the table. "Look, I admit, I'm far from convinced she's involved, but she's the last one who opened that side door before the suspects gained access through it. I wouldn't be doing my job if I ruled her out without digging deeper."

Cassie opened her mouth but closed it again before leaning back in her chair and falling into a thoughtful silence.

He studied her without saying more. This wasn't something Cassie would come to terms with over a cup of bad coffee. And with Shawn going into surgery tomorrow morning, Matthias hated that he'd added to her worries.

Chapter Twenty-Three

Matthias caught about two hours of sleep Monday night after dropping Emma off at the campground and returning to his apartment. The glorified nap didn't rejuvenate him, but it helped clear some of the mental fog. He was back at his desk well before dawn and dove into Urban's background.

Roth shuffled in around five-thirty, carrying a cup of coffee from the all-night convenience store a couple of blocks away. "Any word on Shawn?" he asked.

"He looked good when I saw him last night." Matthias glanced at Roth before refocusing on his computer. "They have him scheduled for surgery to remove the bullet this morning."

"That's good, right? They wouldn't go back in so soon if he wasn't doing well."

"Yeah," Matthias said, skimming the list of Urban's known associates he'd compiled. He half expected to find Bethany Stone's name on it but was relieved when he didn't.

"What've you got?" Roth asked.

"A whole lot of nothing," Matthias grumbled.

Roth shambled past Matthias's desk on his way to his own.

219

"Frazier and I made another round of the area pawnshops overnight."

"And?"

"No guns turned in."

More nothing, Matthias thought. He rocked back in his chair, replaying the slim developments of the last few days. They'd started with three perpetrators, all armed. They'd found the discarded hoodies in the trash and were still waiting on the lab for any information the clothing might provide. Now two of the three were dead. A search of Zimmerman's apartment had turned up nothing useful. Not even a wallet.

Matthias thought of the messy living room compared with the nearly pristine kitchen where they found the body. Had there been any evidence from the robbery, someone had removed it.

"Did you take a look into Misti Dunlevy?" Matthias called out to Roth.

"Frazier's on it," he replied.

"On what?" Frazier entered, carrying a paper bag and coffee from a fast-food drive-through.

"Misti Dunlevy." Matthias rolled his chair into the aisle, blocking Frazier's passage. "Whatever's in there, you better have brought enough to share."

"Of course." Frazier opened the bag and held it out. "Egg and sausage breakfast sandwiches for all."

Matthias reached in, withdrew a hot paper-wrapped bundle, and rolled out of the way. "I'll talk to the lieutenant about giving you a promotion."

Frazier smirked. "Right." He continued past Matthias to Roth. "As for Misti Dunlevy, she looks clean. A couple of parking tickets. Paid, but late. Otherwise, nothing in the system. She's attending Mercyhurst's School of Health Professions, about to start their graduate program in nursing. I'm still waiting on her financials and expect to find student debt. The question remains, is it enough for her to get involved in a robbery?"

Matthias thought of the look on her face, how she'd taken on a greenish pallor when she'd learned Zimmerman was dead. If she was involved, and Matthias had his doubts, he didn't believe for a minute that she had anything to do with her boyfriend's death.

"Also, we expanded our perimeter to the blocks surrounding Cascade and found a half dozen exterior security cams. Two of them were businesses who voluntarily turned over the footage. The others demanded warrants, which we're waiting on."

"What about Urban's shooting?" Matthias asked. "Anything new on the sniper's nest?"

"Check your inbox," Roth said. "I just sent you the photos you wanted."

Matthias opened his email, clicked on the message from Roth, and then on the images, all shot from the window, looking down on a police unit parked on the street in the exact spot where Urban was gunned down. Sniper's-eye-view. Matthias put himself behind the killer's eyes, imagining the street as it had been yesterday. The first shot, with Urban handcuffed and backed against the car's backdoor, had been a gift. Unobstructed, easy view of center mass. But the second shot? The officers had dragged the mortally wounded suspect into the car. Had closed the door. Matthias zoomed in on the image until it pixelated into hazy blocks of color and shadow, but he didn't care about the poor quality. He wasn't trying to identify anyone or anything. He wanted to imagine the sniper's line of sight through the cruiser's window.

"What do you think?" Roth stood at Matthias's shoulder.

He zoomed out again. "I think I want to hear what Hamilton and Dr. Browning have to say."

"What time is the autopsy?" Roth asked.

"Eight a.m." Matthias checked his watch. Still a couple hours away. "Until then, let's dig deeper. We have an armed robbery with attempted murder and two homicides. Only one of the assailants from the first crime is left standing. Roth, you take Zimmerman. Frazier, you take Urban. I want to know every last detail about their lives, their families, their friends. I want to know where they went to grade school. Hell, I want to know where they were born. There's a connection somewhere that ties them together and links them to someone else. I want to know who or what that is."

"On it." Roth started to turn away, then came back. "Who are you going to focus on?"

Matthias let out a breath. They were missing something. He thought about checking in with the lieutenant, but he wouldn't be at his desk this early. "Shawn," he replied to Roth. "And everyone else who works at his clinic."

"We've already gone over them," Roth said.

Matthias eyed him. "That's right. We have. And I'm going over them again."

Less than two hours later, Matthias left Roth and Frazier at Major Crimes and walked to the county courthouse and the morgue. He hoped like hell that Urban's postmortem revealed something, anything, to give him direction. So far, the veterinary clinic's staff was coming up squeaky clean. The third vet's alibi checked out. He was indeed at a symposium in Harrisburg, roughly three hundred miles away. None of the spouses or partners of the employees had more than a parking ticket in their records. And no one appeared to have a connection with Zimmerman or Urban.

Then there was Bethany Stone. Beyond her recent slip-up at the racetrack, though, Matthias hadn't found anything that pointed to her as a potential accomplice in the robbery.

He arrived at the morgue just before eight and paused outside the door to the autopsy suite. The sign on the glass read NO GUTS, NO GLORY and had been there for years. It was the only part of this building that ever brought a smile. Days like this ... weeks like this ... he needed whatever bit of humor he could find, even if it was morgue humor.

Hamilton looked up as Matthias punched through the door. "Good to see you, Detective." He gave a nod to Dr. Browning and the techs. "The band's all here. Let's get started."

Emma stepped off the elevator into ErieLIVE's newsroom to see Preston storming her way. The crazed look in his eyes made her consider retreating into the elevator car, but the doors whooshed closed behind her, blocking her escape.

"What's going on?" she asked, afraid of his answer.

"I had dinner with my grandparents last night."

Hardly a reason for concern, except she knew there was more.

"My granddad and I were sitting on the back porch after we ate, and he was asking me about my work." Preston paused as if expecting her to say something.

"And?"

"And I mentioned Dr. Shawn and the robbery and how you think the shooting might have to do with his past." Another pause.

"And?"

"And Granddad remembered something from years ago. Something about Dr. Shawn being in trouble with the law. Big trouble."

"What kind of trouble?" she asked, not at all sure she wanted to know.

"He couldn't recall."

Emma exhaled. "Well, that's not helpful."

Preston grinned. "It wouldn't be, except he remembered when it happened."

"How can he not remember *what* but can remember *when*?"

"Because it happened about the same time my dad got arrested."

"Your dad got arrested?"

"He was being stupid after his high school graduation party. One of his buddies got a case of beer. They got drunk. Dad got behind the wheel, and he wrecked the car."

Emma had seen Preston drunk. Maybe he'd inherited the propensity from his father.

"No one got hurt," Preston continued. "Well, except for the thrashing Granddad gave him afterward. I don't think Dad's had a drink since."

While glad the story had a reasonably happy ending—or at least no one was injured in the crash—Emma's mind was racing ahead. "This happened during your father's graduation party, so we know the year."

"And the month. June. Thirty-eight years ago. That's the same time Dr. Shawn was in trouble."

"I need to get down to the archives," Emma said.

Preston held up a key. "I'm already ahead of you. Let's go explore the haunted basement." He pivoted and strode away toward the rear staircase.

Emma jogged to keep up, happy to let him lead the way down the steps to the archives and clear away any spiderwebs reconstructed since her last visit.

He stopped at the door and took in the room as the fluorescent lights flickered. "Wow. It's even worse than I remember."

She gripped his arm and pointed to the far end of the space. "The microfilm room is back there."

"All right. I'll take that. You check out here."

He took off before she had a chance to complain. Of course, he would take the easier, more organized option.

She made her way down the rows of shelving, from the very earliest editions of the *Erie Tribune* dating back to the mid-1800s, to the early 1900s, through the 1950s. She slowed her progress once she reached boxes dated in the 1980s. Finally, she found what she wanted.

Emma dragged the box from its shelf and carried it to one of the dust-covered tables near the center of the massive room. She gently placed it on the wooden surface and lifted the lid. The stench of mold and rot slapped her in the face.

She wasn't sure what she hoped to find, but it wasn't shredded paper bunched into what she knew was a mouse's nest. The contents that hadn't been gnawed into paper fluff were dotted with dark brown specks and stained with yellow blotches.

From the microfilm room, Preston called out, "Did you find anything?"

"A mouse's bed and bathroom," she replied, replacing the lid.

"Then you better come here."

She looked over to find him in the doorway, grinning. "I think I found what we're looking for," he said and waved her in his direction.

Emma swiped her hands together to brush off the dust and whatever else she'd picked up handling the rodent motel and hurried toward Preston, who disappeared into the room. Inside, he'd taken a seat in front of one of the microfilm readers. A page of newsprint filled the screen. Not a front page, she noted. "What is it?" she asked, leaning over his shoulder to view the monitor.

He tapped a headline halfway down the page—*below the fold* in newspaper-speak—and glanced back at her. "Read for yourself."

She leaned closer.

ERIE TEENS FACE CHARGES

Erie County District Attorney Byron Lydell announced he is charging two area teens as adults in the vehicular homicide of Justin Wheeler last month. Wheeler was killed when a pickup truck driven by Shawn Malone, 17, crashed into Wheeler's Datsun 310. Wheeler was declared dead at the scene by the county coroner. Tests revealed Malone and another passenger in the pickup, Jerry Bain, age 18, were above the legal blood-alcohol limit. Vehicular homicide will be added to underage drinking charges already filed with the magistrate.

Emma shivered against a sudden chill. She straightened and met Preston's gaze. "Holy crap," she said.

"Yeah."

She stared at the article, her mind clicking ahead. "Wait. If Shawn was charged as an adult, Matthias should've been able to find a record of this. He couldn't."

Preston rubbed the stubble on his jaw. "Huh. That's weird."

"Unless the DA changed his mind. Shawn was seventeen. He was a juvenile. If it turned out he wasn't charged as an adult, this would be in his juvie records."

"And sealed," Preston said.

"Exactly. Which would explain why Matthias couldn't access them."

Preston looked at her, a spark in his eyes. "We need to keep digging."

For the next three hours, Matthias stood well clear of the postmortem, arms crossed, watching every move, every cut, listening to every snippet of conversation. By the time the pathologist and the coroner completed the autopsy, several of

Matthias's questions had been answered. Both of the sniper's shots had been hits. Dr. Browning pronounced the first one, which struck Urban nearly dead center of his chest, as the kill shot, piercing the heart. He'd bled out within minutes. The second bullet hit lower, in the upper left quadrant of his abdomen.

"Are you sure of the order?" Matthias asked, although from what he'd witnessed, he believed the pathologist's initial assessment.

"It matches the police report," Hamilton said. "The trajectories of the gunshot wounds indicate different angles. The victim was shot from above, correct?"

Matthias nodded. "The shooter was on the third floor of an abandoned warehouse."

"The trajectory of the bullet that struck the victim in the chest is at a downward angle. He was standing when hit. The abdominal GSW is at a slight upward angle. He was already on his back." Hamilton mimed the bullets' paths over Urban's body on the table.

"So, the sniper was hedging his bets by making the second shot," Matthias said.

Hamilton shrugged. "It's my job to give you the evidence. It's your job to determine how it fits into the case."

Chapter Twenty-Four

By the time Matthias stepped outside, the sky had turned an ominous gray. The air was still thick with humidity, but a breeze ruffled the flags in front of the courthouse and thunder rumbled in the distance.

On his way back to the police station, he pulled out his phone to call Cassie but reconsidered. Shawn should be in surgery by now. Cassie would be on edge, wanting a progress report. All Matthias had was confirmation of what he'd already suspected regarding Urban's death.

As he crossed Peach Street, the first fat raindrops splattered the pavement and struck his head and shoulders. He broke into a jog but was soaked before he made it to the underground parking lot. His damp clothes had felt good against the heat outside, but once he reached the air-conditioned interior, he shivered. Still, he didn't want to take the time to stop in the locker room and change. He charged up the stairs, bypassed Major Crimes, and strode down the hall to Lieutenant Armstrong's office.

The lieutenant looked up from his computer. "How'd the autopsy go?"

Matthias gave him a quick summary.

Armstrong scowled. "So, nothing useful."

"Have you had any luck looking into Cassie's past arrests?"

Armstrong shook his head. "I know you're looking for another angle since the one we're working on doesn't appear to be going anywhere, but I've had a team of six officers looking into every one of Cassie's cases. Every threat against her, every convict who's recently been released. They've followed up on those that seemed plausible, but—" He shook his head. "Nothing. I fear we've exhausted that route."

Frustrated, Matthias thanked him and trudged back to Major Crimes.

Both Frazier and Roth wore smiles reminiscent of the Cheshire Cat. "What do you have?" Matthias asked.

Instead of answering, Frazier asked, "Did you learn anything from the autopsy?"

"Urban's dead of a gunshot wound," Matthias replied flatly. "What did you find out while I was gone?"

"We got the lab report on the black hoodies we found in the trash," Roth replied, forcing the smile from his face. "They were all the same off brand. Made in China. Available in every big box store in the area, not to mention Amazon. They got hair and epithelials from each of them, so we have DNA."

Except running DNA took time they didn't have.

Matthias studied the two detectives, who both looked on the verge of bursting. "You found something," he said. "What?"

From behind his back, Frazier produced a sheet of paper, which he placed on Matthias's desk. "Check it out."

He dropped into his chair and scanned the printout. Two columns. Zimmerman topped one, Urban the other. Beneath the names were two lists of more names. He recognized some of the ones below Zimmerman. "Known associates," Matthias said.

"Yep." Frazier bent over his shoulder and used a red pen to

circle one name in the first row. Then he circled a name in the second.

The same name.

Matthias looked closer. "Grady Elkins."

Roth moved to Frazier's side, another printout in hand, and read, "Grady Elkins, age 45, black hair, green eyes. Race: African American. Served in the Army. Dishonorable discharge. His rap sheet includes auto theft, carjacking, armed robbery, and assault with a deadly weapon. Each time, his lawyer made some sort of plea deal—except for the last one. It looked like he was finally going to be put away on the assault charge, but the case was dismissed due to the judge throwing out evidence on a technicality."

Green eyes, Matthias thought. African American. Shawn had stated the man who pulled the trigger was a light-skinned Black man with green eyes. "Grady Elkins is our shooter."

"That's our take on it, too," Roth said.

"Address?"

"West 7th Street."

"Get a warrant," Matthias growled.

Roth's smile broadened. "Already got one. We were just waiting on you."

Emma sat at Preston's side as he scanned back through earlier editions of the *Erie Tribune*. They found the initial report on the traffic accident followed by Justin Wheeler's obituary. At 35, he'd been married with two young children, a boy and a girl. He'd been a volunteer firefighter in addition to his career as a mechanical engineer.

And Shawn Malone had been responsible for his death. Not intentionally, of that Emma was certain. He'd been a stupid kid doing stupid shit with his buddy. He'd made a stupid choice to drink and drive.

She couldn't even fathom how that had eaten at the kid who became the kind-hearted man she knew.

Preston started advancing the roll of microfilm in the other direction, skimming articles in the days following the original piece they'd read. Over an hour later, he flopped back in the chair and covered his face with his hands. "I'm toast," he said. "My eyes are burning, and my fingers are cramped."

Emma looked at her watch. "And I'm starved. No wonder. It's almost one."

He let his hands drop. "What do you think? Have we hit a dead end?"

She knew what he was really asking. Should they keep looking or give up? "The legal system grinds slowly. There has to be something here. Even a short article stating the charges were dropped."

"Maybe we missed it."

Emma didn't think so.

Preston stood and stretched. "I say we give up. All this happened decades ago. It can't possibly have anything to do with what happened last week."

Except it could. "If you want to call it quits, go right ahead." She slid from her chair to his. "I'll keep searching."

Preston's annoyed exhalation filled the room. "Tell you what. I'll grab us both some lunch and come back. That will give my eyes and hands a break."

Emma smiled to herself. He was afraid she'd find something he'd missed. "That'll work," she said and then called after him, "Don't forget. I don't eat meat."

He waved over his shoulder. "But you do eat fish. I remember."

The storm had passed, and patches of blue showed between the thinning gray clouds. Matthias sat in his car outside a painted brick house on Erie's West 7th Street, although "painted" might be an exaggeration. The red paint had largely peeled off, revealing red bricks beneath. Why, he wondered, would a person apply the same color over perfectly fine bricks? But whoever had done the job clearly lacked remodeling skills. The porch roof had been removed, leaving only the pillars with nothing to support. Weather-blackened wooden two-by-sixes framed out the top of the pillars to stabilize everything, but the work appeared to have been done ages ago and never completed.

His radio crackled. Roth's voice came over the speaker. "In position."

The plan was to avoid a repeat of what had happened with Urban. They'd doubled the number of uniforms parked out of sight in the alley directly behind the house and on foot throughout the neighborhood. If Elkins tried to rabbit, they weren't about to let him get away.

Attired in his ballistic vest, Matthias climbed from his car. Two uniforms stepped from the vehicle behind his. Together, they approached the roofless front porch. Matthias knocked, his heart pounding a beat against his sternum. Elkins was a bad dude. The ways in which this could end poorly were innumerable.

A short Black woman with white hair, thick glasses, and a cane opened the door and squinted up at them. "What's going on?"

Matthias showed his badge and identified himself. "Ma'am, we're looking for Grady Elkins. Is he here?"

The woman curled a lip. "No, he is not."

"We have this as his address."

"His mail comes here," she said, still sneering, "and he's

supposed to help me out with chores and driving me to my doctor's appointments and such in exchange for room and board."

Matthias's tension ratcheted down. "And you are?"

"Olivia Elkins."

Elkins? "You're Grady's..." Matthias let the question hang, unwilling to fill in the blank incorrectly.

"Grady's daddy was my son. He died a violent death when the boy was only two. As much as I tried to keep my grandson on the straight and narrow, the apple didn't fall far from the tree, if you get my meaning."

"Do you have any idea where he might be?"

"No, I do not. If I did, I'd go there myself and drag him home by his ear."

Matthias had little doubt she would, too. He pulled a sheaf of paper from his hip pocket and held it out to her. "Ma'am, we have a warrant to search your house."

She straightened, adding a couple of inches to her diminutive height, and glared up at him. "Search for what? I already told you Grady isn't here."

"Yes, but he may have been involved in illegal activity on Friday. We're searching for evidence."

"You're on a fishing expedition."

"We're doing our job."

Olivia stood her ground and didn't appear to have any intention of stepping aside. Matthias really didn't want to have her physically removed from her home. She unfolded the warrant and lowered her gaze to it. Matthias waited as she read and watched her expression shift from determined to concerned.

"Am I reading this right?" she asked, still focused on the document. "You believe he had something to do with the shooting of that animal doctor?"

"Yes, ma'am. I'm afraid it looks that way."

She continued to read the warrant with the thoroughness of a lawyer studying a contract. With a nod, she stepped back and to one side. "Do what you have to do."

Inside, the home wasn't fancy, but it was tidy. Carved wood-framed chairs were covered in what looked like needlepoint and a sofa with a gracefully curved back and equally graceful wooden claw feet was upholstered in floral fabric. Matthias wondered if they were family heirlooms or purchases from a thrift shop. He suspected the former.

Roth and Frazier arrived, since there was no one to chase, and joined Matthias and the uniformed officers. Matthias fixed them with a stern scowl. "Be respectful," he told them in a low but firm voice.

Leaving them to the search, he directed Olivia onto the roofless porch. "I was wondering if you could help me out." Matthias withdrew his phone and pulled up Zimmerman's mugshot. Turning it toward her, Matthias asked, "Do you recognize this man?"

She adjusted her glasses and squinted. "That's one of Grady's no-good friends. Don't know what his real name is. Grady only ever called him Zem or Zim or some such thing."

Matthias reached over and slid a finger on the screen while letting her continue to hold the phone. Urban's mugshot replaced Zimmerman's. "What about him?"

Olivia grunted. "He's another of his friends. Hank, I think, is what Grady called him. Good for nothin' low-lifes, the both of 'em." Her gaze lifted to Matthias's. "Are they in on the animal doctor's shooting, too?"

"We're still investigating."

She nodded. "In other words, yes."

He didn't contradict her but held out his hand for his phone.

She placed it on his palm. "Which one of 'em was the shooter?" Her tone was matter of fact, as if asking what brand of bread he wanted at the store.

Matthias pocketed his phone without answering.

Olivia heaved a sigh. "It was Grady, wasn't it?"

"Why would you think that?"

"Because I seen him with a gun."

"When was that?"

"About a week ago. He had it stuffed down the back of his pants like they do on TV. I told him nothin' good never came from carryin' a gun. But he gave me lip. Told me to mind my own business." Her eyes suddenly welled. "What that boy never could understand"—her voice broke—"is that he *is* my business. He's all the kin I got left in the world."

Matthias waited for her to regain her composure before saying, "Dr. Shawn Malone. The veterinarian who was shot. Do you or your grandson know him? Have any business with him?"

"No," she said, sounding like it was the stupidest question ever. "We got no pets. No reason to have no business with someone like that." But her eyes shifted. Her brow creased.

"What is it?"

"Well, there is one reason Grady might have business with him."

"What's that?"

Her dark, rheumy eyes came up. "Drugs," she said, her voice almost too soft to hear.

"Did Grady do drugs?"

She swallowed and looked away. "I better not say any more. I probably already said too much." She shook her head and turned her back to him. "I'm done."

Emma wasn't sure how long Preston had been gone when she found what they were looking for. "Oh, my God," she whispered as she scanned the article.

"What?" came Preston's voice from the doorway. "Did you find something?"

She spun to find him standing there holding a takeout bag from a brew pub around the corner. The smell wafting from it reminded her how famished she was. "I think so." She pointed at the bag. "Let's eat first."

He shook his head. "Let me see what you found. Then we eat." He set their lunch on a file cabinet next to the door and moved to her side. "What is it?"

Emma vacated the chair and let him take a seat.

The article she found was dated over a year after the story about the car crash. She leaned over Preston's shoulder to reread it.

VEHICULAR HOMICIDE CASE GOES TO TRIAL

Jury selection begins tomorrow in the vehicular homicide trial of Jerry Bain, who was 18 when a pickup truck he was driving while intoxicated struck and killed Justin Wheeler.

The rest of the article rehashed the information from the previous one, except for the final sentence.

An unnamed teen was a passenger in the pickup truck.

Preston looked up at Emma, stunned. "Unnamed teen was a *passenger*?"

"That's what it says. I almost skimmed past it because Shawn isn't named."

"I'm surprised you spotted it. I don't think I would've." Preston again faced the screen. "And this says the other kid was the driver. What the hell?"

"Somewhere between here and the first article, someone changed their story."

"But which one is right?"

Emma wished she knew. "Seems to me there must be an article we missed that explains what happened."

"I agree. And now we know we're looking for Justin Wheeler or Jerry Bain instead of Shawn Malone."

Emma's stomach rumbled. "Can we eat before I pass out from starvation?"

Preston didn't budge. "You go ahead and wimp out if you want. We're on to something here. I'm not quitting until I find it."

She sighed. No way did she want to spend the rest of her career at ErieLIVE listening to Preston calling her a wimp. "What did you get me for lunch?"

"A chopped salad, hold the bacon."

"Dressing on the side?"

"Yep."

At least it wouldn't wilt too badly. And it wasn't fish. She couldn't stomach cold fish. "Fine. We'll eat after we find the connecting article."

Chapter Twenty-Five

Matthias left Olivia Elkins alone on her roofless porch and went inside to check on his men. Roth clomped down the staircase, a brown paper evidence bag in hand.

"What'd you find?" Matthias asked.

"A man definitely lives here along with the old lady. Lots of male toiletries in the downstairs bathroom." He aimed a thumb toward another room. "Only women's stuff in the one upstairs. Two bedrooms up there. One for grandma, the other with the usual trappings of a dude trying to look like a *gangsta*."

Matthias pointed at the bag. "What's in there?"

Roth looked smug. "Opioids. Same varieties as what was stolen during the robbery. All packaged nice and neat for distribution. Found them in the back of the closet."

"What about black gloves, masks, pants?" Matthias paused. "Firearms?"

"No gloves or masks. Lots of black pants. Can't tell if they were worn at the clinic. We're bagging them in case the lab rats can pull trace from any of them." Roth mirrored Matthias's pause. "No firearms. No weapons of any kind."

Of course, it couldn't be that easy.

"Are you sure?" came Olivia's voice.

Matthias turned and saw her peering at them through the screen door. "Excuse me, ma'am?"

"Didn't I hear you say you didn't find any firearms?" She held up the warrant. "I see you have handguns and rifles listed here."

Matthias suspected where she was going with her question. "You said he had a gun he wore in his pants. He probably still has it on him."

She stepped inside and let the screen door swing shut with a creak and a slam. "Yes, yes. I figured that. But what about the rifle?"

Matthias exchanged a look with Roth, who gave a quick headshake "What rifle?" Matthias asked.

"It was my late husband's hunting rifle. Grady kept it in his closet."

"Did your grandson ever use it?"

Olivia shrugged. "He's never been interested in hunting. Too much being out in the woods. Grady's into concrete instead of grass and trees. But lately, he's shown more of an interest in the rifle. He's taken it out a few times. Said a buddy and him was going to a shooting range to target practice."

The hairs on Matthias's neck prickled. "Do you know which buddy?"

"He never said."

Matthias turned to Roth but didn't need to say anything. "I'll tell the men to look again," Roth said and walked away.

Matthias came back to Olivia. "Our records don't show a car registered in your grandson's name."

Olivia looked like she'd gotten a whiff of sour milk. "That's 'cause he don't own one. He drives mine." She flipped her wrist toward the door. "That's another thing. That boy went and left me here with no way of getting around. Thank goodness for my neighbor lady. She drove me to my doctor's appointment yesterday."

"When was the last time you saw him?"

"Saturday afternoon. Hasn't so much as checked in with me. I could be dead for all that boy knows."

"What kind of car do you own?"

She jutted her chin toward a beige handbag on a chair next to the door. "May I?"

Matthias gave her an easy smile. "You don't have a gun in there, do you?"

"I do not. But you so all fired worried, go ahead. Look for yourself. I got nothin' to hide. The car's registration's in my wallet."

He picked up the handbag, surprised at how heavy it was. Maybe she did have a gun in it. He opened it and removed a leather wallet while taking a look at what else was inside. Tissues. Hand sanitizer. A romance novel.

No gun.

The wallet, however, seemed to be the source of all the weight. She must have twenty dollars' worth of coins in there. He handed it to her.

Olivia unsnapped the flap to open it wide and withdrew a folded piece of paper, which she handed to Matthias.

"This is the car Grady was in the last time you saw him?"

"It is."

Matthias unfolded the paper and pulled out his phone to call the station. "This is Detective Matthias Honeywell," he said. "I need you to put out a BOLO on a silver 2018 Hyundai Accent."

Emma was happy to find a full paper towel dispenser in the basement restroom. She ran a handful under the tap and used them to wipe down one of the tables. At least enough of the surface for her and Preston to eat while they reviewed their findings.

He'd finally tracked down a third article about the wreck and resulting homicide charges. This one had been buried. Not merely below the fold, but deep within the pages.

CHARGES DROPPED ON ONE TEEN, TO BE FILED ON ANOTHER

New information came to light at yesterday's preliminary hearing in the vehicular homicide death of Justin Wheeler, 35, of McLean. The 17-year-old, who originally claimed to be the driver of the pickup truck that struck and killed Mr. Wheeler, recanted his statement. The Pennsylvania State Police investigators are now convinced the driver was actually 18-year-old Jerry Bain.

The DA states new charges will be filed against Bain later this week.

Both Preston and Emma had written down all three stories word-for-word in their notebooks. "What do you think?" he asked her as they ate their lunch.

She speared a forkful of field greens, cucumber, and pepper rings. She'd been pondering the turn of events since she'd read the third of the articles—the second one they found. "Shawn is only mentioned by name in the first article. The one where he's listed as the driver. The other kid, Jerry Bain, is eighteen. Or was at the time."

"Shawn was only seventeen," Preston said. "A minor."

Emma studied the vegetables on her fork. "Maybe Shawn offered to say he was driving to save his buddy. Maybe he thought since he was underage, he'd get off with a slap on the wrist."

Preston took a bite of his turkey sandwich and scowled in thought.

"But," Emma continued, letting her thoughts spill out into words, "when the DA planned to charge Shawn as an adult, he got cold feet and told the truth."

They ate in silence for several minutes before Preston set down his sandwich and wiped his fingers with a paper napkin. "Or they made a deal."

"They?" she asked around a mouthful of lettuce.

"Shawn and Jerry. Shawn really was the driver, but his parents paid off the Bain kid. Bribed him to take the fall."

She swallowed. "That's pretty lame, don't you think? I mean, why would Jerry Bain agree to that?"

Preston rubbed his thumb against his index and middle fingers, the universal gesture meaning money.

Emma shook her head. "I don't buy it."

"Does Shawn come from a well-to-do family?"

"I don't know," she admitted.

"It's something to look into." Preston gazed into the distance. "Might not have been money. Might have been some other kind of deal."

Emma shook her head.

"Hear me out. They make a deal. Bain takes the rap. Goes to prison for vehicular homicide. Underage drinking. Whatever else."

"We don't know any of that. He might've gotten off. The latest article we found is about jury selection."

"We need to keep looking. But I'm spitballing here. Bain spends time in prison for something he didn't do. Years later, he gets out. Like maybe recently."

Emma wanted to point out they didn't know that either but kept quiet.

"Bain's upset. Whatever deal they'd struck never happened and he wasted years in prison for something he didn't do. Now he wants revenge. Shawn's a veterinarian making good money.

Bain's an ex-con with friends in the criminal world." Preston met Emma's gaze, smiling triumphantly. "They plan to rob and kill Shawn as payback."

"Except two of the three men involved are dead. Neither of them is named Jerry Bain. And Shawn saw the third man. The one who shot him. If it was his old pal, wouldn't he have recognized him?"

"Would you be able to recognize someone you knew from high school if you could only see this much of his face?" Preston covered his nose and mouth with one hand, his forehead with the other.

Emma thought about it. She hadn't been out of high school as long as Shawn, yet she'd already been unable to recognize a couple of her male classmates when she ran into them on the street. The women? Yes. The men? Not so much.

Preston must've read the doubt in her expression and pointed at her victoriously. "See? I'm right."

"Not so fast. If your theory is correct, this is a man who went to prison to save Shawn's ass. In that case, I'd damned sure recognize him, even just his eyes."

Preston deflated. "Point taken. Still, this has to be what's behind his shooting. It's the only blemish on Shawn's otherwise perfect record. Not to mention, it's been intentionally swept under the rug. Shawn's name was mentioned in the first article. After that, he's an unnamed teen."

Emma couldn't argue, although she certainly wanted to. Another question occurred to her ... one she wasn't going to share with Preston.

Did Cassie know about any of this?

Emma really didn't want to be the one to ask her. Nor did she want to talk directly to Shawn. What would she say? *"By the way, Shawn, did you get away with killing a man when you were seventeen by throwing your buddy to the wolves?"*

No. But there was someone who needed to know what she and Preston had found. The man investigating Shawn's shooting.

Matthias.

Preston popped the last of his sandwich in his mouth and crumpled the wrapper. He pointed at her half-eaten salad. "Finish up. We need to get back to the microfilm. I want to know how the case played out."

She snapped the lid closed over the remnants of her lunch. "You don't need me down here."

He studied her dubiously. Then his eyes brightened. "You're going to talk to your cop boyfriend."

Emma struggled to come up with an excuse that didn't involve Matthias and couldn't come up with one fast enough.

"Don't try to deny it." Preston stood and stuffed the balled wrapping into the takeout bag. "I think it's a great idea. Just be sure and let me know what he says."

No way, she thought. "Sure," she said.

Preston pointed an accusing finger at her. "I mean it. You're giving the police a name and a possible motive. It's a two-way street. They get something from us, we get something from them. Your detective's been around long enough to know how this game is played." He pivoted and strode back into the microfilm room as if the subject was closed.

Emma inhaled a deep breath. Blew it out. As much as she hated admitting it, Preston was right. Matthias had been around long enough to know the game. That was part of what she feared would eventually tear them apart.

She looked at the salad, no longer hungry, and added the remains to the takeout bag. After studying a trash can next to the door, she wondered how often the janitorial service came down here. Rather than provide additional lure for the basement rodent population, she took their lunch remnants with her and headed for the exit.

A phone call to Cassie let Matthias know Shawn was still in surgery. Cassie sounded on the verge of a meltdown, whether from the length of the operation or being sidelined in the investigation.

"Tell me you've found something," she said.

"We've found something," Matthias replied. "I'm on my way to the hospital to catch you up." He ended the call before she had a chance to demand answers over the phone.

He found her pacing in the surgical waiting room. Denene and Alissa were seated in the far corner, working on coloring books. Everyone in the place looked up when he entered. All but the three Malone women lost interest when they realized he wasn't a doctor bringing news of a loved one's procedure.

Cassie met him midway to the mom and daughter artists. "What did you find?" she asked *sotto voce*.

He matched her low volume. "We have an ID on the third man."

"The one who sh—" She broke off before saying "shot" and looked around. The room wasn't packed, but it wasn't sparsely occupied either.

While no one was looking directly at them, the fact Matthias was dressed in his detective's duds and had his service weapon on his hip made him quite sure a few of them were listening intently. Cops drew attention—good or bad—wherever they went.

Cassie clearly thought the same thing. She caught his arm and guided him to a pair of chairs near Denene and Alissa. She gestured for him to sit while she spoke to her daughter and granddaughter. "I know you two have to be exhausted. Denene, why don't you take her outside for a bit. Get some fresh air." She held up her phone. "I'll call you the second I hear anything."

Denene glanced knowingly at Matthias. She'd been a cop's

daughter all her life and knew when her mother didn't want business to interfere with family. Or in this case, didn't want Alissa to overhear gruesome details. "Sure," Denene said to her mother. To Alissa, she asked, "Do you want to go for a walk?"

"I'm hungry," the girl replied. "I want tacos."

Denene winked at Cassie. "And there happens to be a Mexican restaurant less than two blocks away." She gathered the coloring books and crayons into a neat pile and stood. "Can I bring you something, Mom?"

"I'm not hungry."

Denene looked at Matthias. "How about you?"

He smiled. "No, thanks."

Once the younger Malones had disappeared through the doors, Cassie dropped into the chair next to him. "Now. Out with it."

"Does the name Grady Elkins mean anything to you?"

She thought for a moment. "No. Do you have a picture?"

Matthias produced his phone and Grady's mugshot.

"Matches Shawn's description. You think he's the one?"

"I more than 'think.'" Matthias shared the details he'd learned about Grady's ties to Zimmerman and Urban. About the interview with Elkins's grandmother, the gun he'd been carrying in his pants, the hunting rifle that was missing from his grandmother's house. About the drugs found in his closet.

"Do you have any idea where he is?" Cassie asked, her voice as tight as a coiled spring.

"Not yet." Matthias rested a hand on her arm. "But we have an ID. We have a plate number and a description of his car. And we have a BOLO out on him. It's only a matter of time."

Cassie pressed a palm to her forehead as if keeping her brain from exploding. "I hope like hell we can bring him in alive. I want to look him in the face and ask why he did this."

Matthias's phone buzzed with an incoming text. "It's Emma,"

he said and was about to ignore it for now. Then he spotted the first line of the text following her name.

May have found info about Shawn...

Matthias opened the text.

May have found info about Shawn that might pertain to his shooting. Old news article about him being involved in a traffic fatality when he was underage. Call me when you can.

Matthias reread the message, trying to make sense of it.

"What is it?" Cassie asked. "From the look on your face, it's a dear John text, but Emma wouldn't do that."

He closed the text before Cassie could lean closer for a look. "No. Just questions about a story she's working on." Before he could pocket the phone, it vibrated in his hand. For a second, he thought Emma was too impatient to wait for him to respond, but the lieutenant's name filled the screen. "It's Armstrong," he told Cassie and answered the call. "Honeywell here."

"Are you with Cassie?" His voice was stretched thin with tension.

"Yes." Matthias didn't look at her.

"At Hamot?"

"Yes."

"Good. I just got a call from emergency operations. There was a hit-and-run, vehicle versus pedestrians, at the corner of 3rd and State."

That was just outside the hospital. Matthias's shoulders knotted.

"The pedestrians are injured but alive."

He knew before the lieutenant spoke the names.

"Denene and Alissa Malone."

Matthias swallowed, keeping his eyes lowered, refusing to look at Cassie.

From across the room, a voice called out, "Shawn Malone family?"

"That's Shawn's surgeon," Cassie said and raised a hand to him.

Matthias couldn't breathe. He gave her a nod, still not looking her in the eye, and stepped away.

"What's going on?" Armstrong asked.

"Shawn's surgeon just came in to talk to Cassie." God, Matthias hoped it was good news.

"Roger that. Denene and Alissa are being transported to the Emergency Department there. I'm on my way. But, Honeywell, there's something else."

Matthias waited, holding his breath.

"According to witnesses, the car that hit them was a silver Hyundai Accent."

Chapter Twenty-Six

E mma fidgeted at her desk in the newsroom. She wanted Matthias to call. *Now.* Had she not made it clear how urgent this was?

Or was it? Maybe he already knew about Jerry Bain. Maybe he'd already determined that Shawn's youthful indiscretions had nothing to do with the current case. After all, Matthias had told her as much yesterday, sharing his suspicion that the shooter's motivations weren't connected to the past. If that was the case, why didn't he just text back and let her know she was chasing mist?

Laurie appeared in the doorway to her glass-enclosed office and looked around. Her gaze settled on Emma, and she strode in her direction, phone in hand. "Where's Preston?" Laurie demanded.

"In the archives." Emma could feel the energy vibrating from ErieLIVE's office manager, which could only mean one thing. There was a story breaking. A big story. "What's going on?"

Laurie didn't reply but pounded on her phone's screen, then held it on the flat of her palm.

"What's up boss?" Preston's voice came over the speaker.

"Get over to Hamot. Two pedestrians were run down while crossing the street at the corner of 3rd and State. They're being taken to the Emergency Department."

Emma turned away. If the patients were on their way to the hospital—or more than likely already there, considering the close proximity—her photography skills weren't needed.

But Laurie reached out to her while still talking to Preston. "Take Emma with you."

There was silence on the line. He probably wondered the same thing she did. Why? Only he was too savvy to question his boss's choices. "Is she in the newsroom?"

"Yep. I'll have her meet you at the car."

The call ended, and Laurie's gaze burned into Emma's soul.

Emma felt the breath leave her body. The look on Laurie's face meant one thing. This was personal. Oh, dear God. Matthias?

Laurie lowered her voice and gave Emma the victims' names.

Matthias had never seen Cassie collapse before.

The news from the surgeon wasn't great. There had been a bleed. Shawn lost a lot of blood on the heels of having already lost so much four days ago. They'd managed to retrieve the bullet. But they'd had to use extreme measures to save him. He was alive. "He's amazingly strong," the surgeon said before adding, "The next twenty-four to forty-eight hours are critical."

Cassie stayed upright until the doctor left the waiting room. Then her knees gave out. Matthias caught her and eased her into the chair she'd refused when the doctor had told her to sit down. She sobbed against Matthias's shoulder and mumbled something about needing to tell her girls.

She must've felt him tense. She pulled away and searched his eyes. "What's going on?" Her gaze shifted. Came back. "That phone call."

He wanted so badly to lie to her. Tell her everything was fine. But they'd been partners too long, and she was too good at reading people. Especially him. He had to tell her. But the words fought him every inch of the way.

"Denene and Alissa were struck by a car at the corner of 3rd." He pictured the intersection. Hamot sat on State. To get to the Mexican restaurant, they had to cross 3rd. "They're alive. They should be downstairs in the ER by now."

He expected Cassie to crumble again. Instead, she straightened, and her face went scary still.

Matthias realized why. Shawn was Cassie's rock. She couldn't fathom going on without him. But Denene and Alissa were her babies. Cassie was morphing into warrior mode.

"What do you want me to do?" he asked. "Do you want to stay here, and I'll go—"

"No." Cassie stood and wiped a hand across her face. "I can't do anything for Shawn right now." Her voice threatened to shatter. She cleared her throat. "I need to see my girls." She met his gaze. "I need you to come with me and find out what happened."

"We already have a good idea."

Cassie drew back. "You do?"

"The car that struck them matches the one Grady Elkins has been driving."

Her face turned to ice. "Then get out there and catch that son of a bitch."

"The entire department is searching for him. We'll get him." It wasn't a hollow promise. Matthias wouldn't rest until Elkins was locked up. Neither would anyone else in the Erie PD. "I need to talk to Denene." If she was able. "Find out if she saw the driver. What exactly happened."

Cassie turned from him and headed toward the door. "I can do that."

Matthias caught up to her. "Right now, you're her mom. Not a detective."

She choked a mocking laugh. "Spoken like someone who's never had kids. Being a mom is how I've honed my lie detector skills."

"You know what I mean. Let me do my job. You take care of your girls. I'll take care of the investigation."

They had the elevator to themselves for the ride down to the Emergency Department. "What did Emma want?" Cassie asked.

"Nothing urgent. I'll talk to her later."

Cassie shot him the side eye.

He expected her to chastise him for putting work ahead of his relationship. But she didn't. Not this time.

When the doors whisked open, Cassie exited with the force of a freight train. Matthias followed in her wake, hoping no one stopped in front of her. At the security desk, Cassie placed both palms on the counter. "Detective Sergeant Cassie Malone," she said. "My daughter and granddaughter are here. Denene and Alissa Malone. Where are they?"

The guard, an older man with kind eyes but a take-no-shit stance, glanced at Matthias, his gaze resting briefly on the badge embroidered on his department polo shirt. To Cassie, he said, "I'll take you back, Sergeant."

He guided them to a cubicle in which Denene sat in bed with the head raised as a pair of nurses worked on her left arm.

She looked up when they entered. "Mom, we're okay."

Cassie looked around. "Where's Alissa?"

"Getting an X-ray. She may have a broken arm."

"Dear lord." Cassie moved to Denene's right side. "What happened?"

"It was crazy." She made a pained face at something the nurses were doing.

Matthias took a good look at her. She had a serious case of road rash showing through shredded jeans along with the arm in question, and the start of a goose egg on her head.

"We were standing at the corner, waiting for the light so we could cross. When it turned green, I looked both ways. It was clear. We started across 3rd Street, and this car came blasting through like his ass was on fire."

Matthias opened his notebook. "Came blasting through from where?"

"Across 3rd, traveling west. He blew through the red light and came right at us. No brakes. No horn."

"Did you get a look at the driver?" Matthias asked.

"No. I barely saw the car in time. Alissa and I were talking about what we were going to get at the restaurant to bring back for Mom." Denene glanced at Cassie before bringing her gaze back to Matthias. "I looked both ways. There was no one coming when we started across, and then he was just there."

Cassie closed her fingers around Denene's right hand. "He hit you?"

"No." Denene shook her head. The action drew a sharp wince.

One of the nurses pressed a gauze bandage to Denene's arm. "We're taking you for a CT scan as soon as they're ready for you." She looked at Cassie. "She may have a concussion."

Cassie's eyes welled. "But he didn't hit you. Did he—" She swallowed. "Alissa?"

"No. I saw the car out of the corner of my eye and grabbed her, pushing her out of the way. He just missed us, but I tripped and fell on top of her. If her arm's broken, it's because of me."

"She's alive because of you," Matthias said.

"I guess so." Denene lowered her head. "Anyhow, that's how I got all scraped up. I had a hold of Alissa and didn't let go to break my fall."

"You didn't see the driver. Did you notice anything about the car?" Matthias asked.

"Not really. I mean, I didn't get a plate number." She wrinkled her nose and looked at her mother. "Sorry."

"It's fine, baby."

Denene came back to Matthias. "It was gray. Or silver. And not very big." She huffed. "Thank God it wasn't an SUV or a truck."

An orderly appeared in the doorway. "CT is ready for the patient," he said.

One of the nurses ripped a piece of tape from a spool and placed it over the bandage on Denene's arm. "And the patient is ready for CT." She turned to Cassie. "You're welcome to stay here. We'll bring her back once she's done."

"What about her daughter?" Cassie asked. "Alissa?"

"She'll be coming back here, too."

Cassie nodded. "Then I'll wait."

The orderly unlocked the wheels on Denene's bed and rolled it and her toward the door.

"Wait." She reached out an arm toward Cassie. "What about Dad? Have you heard anything?"

"He's out of surgery and resting," Cassie said with a smile Matthias knew was a fraud. "So, let's focus on you and Alissa right now."

Denene bought the lie. "Okay. Back in a bit."

Once Cassie and Matthias were alone, she turned to him, her face a picture of rage. "Why the hell is Grady Elkins gunning for my family? He couldn't kill Shawn, so he's going after his girls?"

Matthias was wondering the same thing. They'd answered who. But not why. Elkins had shot Shawn. This attempt on Denene and Alissa solidified one theory. The shooting was not a knee-jerk reaction of a nervous armed robber faced with a perceived threat. Shawn was the target. The robbery was a mere cover.

With Shawn in the hospital and a guard outside his door, his child and grandchild were a relatively easy target.

But how did Elkins know about Denene and Alissa—who and where they were?

And what about Zimmerman and Urban? Had they become liabilities? Was Elkins afraid they would cave if questioned by the police? Or was there something else going on?

"You stay here and wait for the girls," Matthias told Cassie. "I'm going to check in with the lieutenant."

"You do that. Then find Grady Elkins and put him somewhere I can't reach him." Cassie's expression turned stoney. "Because heaven help the man if I get my hands on him."

Emma paced the waiting room. She'd tried to sit but couldn't stay still. Cassie's daughter and granddaughter were behind the doors leading to the treatment area.

A growing group of city police stood near the entrance, speaking in hushed tones. Their faces, though, radiated fury. Someone out there was messing with the family of one of their own.

Matthias was not part of the group. Emma imagined he was with Cassie.

Preston was speaking with Lieutenant Armstrong, also too softly for Emma to hear.

She dug in her purse and came up with a couple of dollar bills. Clutching them, she stalked off to a row of vending machines. The options weren't appealing. Salty snack foods, candy bars, cans of soda, and a coffee dispenser. Ordinarily, she'd have picked the coffee, but she was jittery enough without adding more caffeine to her bloodstream. She fed the bills into the soda machine and selected a lemon-lime beverage. After she popped the tab and sipped, she remembered why she didn't like the stuff.

Still, it gave her something to do. The hospital didn't allow photography, so she'd left her camera bag locked in the car. As she strode back to the chair she was too edgy to sit in, Preston broke away from the lieutenant and approached her.

"What's going on?" she whispered.

"They're being close-lipped," he muttered. "They aren't releasing names. Officially, a woman and her young daughter were involved in a hit-and-run incident a block from here. No word on injuries, but they did state they've put out a BOLO on a silver 2018 Hyundai Accent and asked that the public report any sightings of the car. He stressed 'report but do not approach.'"

"Meaning they know who did it and he could be armed and dangerous."

Preston shrugged. "That would be my assumption, but they aren't confirming that last part. Have you seen your boyfriend?"

"No."

"He might be with the victims."

Emma didn't reply, even though she'd been thinking the same thing. Movement near the automatic doors that led back to the exam rooms caught her attention. Matthias strode out and toward the other cops. "There he is."

"Go talk to him."

She bristled. "I'm not a reporter."

"No." Preston's tone softened. "You're his girlfriend and a friend of the family involved in the hit-and-run. Go talk to him. If you can't share what you find out, fine. But if you can…" He tipped his head at her and winked.

"Thanks." She turned to go.

Preston snatched the soda can from her hand and took a sip. "No problem. But next time, get the Coke."

"Get your own." Emma spun away and headed toward Matthias. Almost there, she reconsidered interrupting him and stopped. He was deep in the middle of an investigation. Whoever was driving the silver Hyundai likely wasn't Jerry Bain.

Matthias spotted her, meeting her gaze. He said something to the cop he was talking to, broke away, and moved toward her.

"How are Denene and Alissa?" she asked.

His mouth tightened, and she noticed his gaze slide to Preston.

"He and I have reached an understanding. He doesn't expect me to share anything I don't want to. Or you don't want me to."

Matthias's blue eyes came back to her. "Alissa may have a broken arm. She's in X-ray. Denene's pretty scraped up and may have a concussion. The car didn't make contact with either. He tried. But Denene got herself and Alissa out of the way in time."

Relieved, Emma sighed. "Any word on Shawn?"

"He's out of surgery."

She registered the tension in Matthias's voice and knew there was more. She waited, but when he didn't offer to elaborate, she changed the subject. "Did you get my text?"

"Yeah. Sorry I didn't call back." The corner of his mouth twitched. "I've been busy."

"I know. But listen. Has the name Jerry Bain come up in the investigation?"

"No."

"What about Justin Wheeler?"

"No. Why? Who are they?"

She gave him the abbreviated version of her time in the archives and the articles she and Preston had uncovered.

Matthias remained motionless, but she sensed his mind was swirling.

"Had you ever heard about any of this?" she asked.

He gave a minute headshake.

"Okay. Well, it might have nothing to do with anything, but I thought you should know."

"I appreciate it. Do me a favor?"

"Anything."

"Don't let Preston print any of this stuff. If it does turn out to have bearing on the case, I'll give him the go-ahead. If it doesn't—"

Emma lifted a hand. "He won't. We've already had this discussion. Shawn was just a kid at the time."

"Thanks." Matthias glanced at the other cops.

"I know you have to get back to work." She took one step back. "I'll talk to you later."

He reached for her, catching her wrist, his strong fingers gentle on her skin. "Wait. Do me another favor?"

"Like I said. Anything."

He tipped his head toward the doors to the exam area. "If I can get you back, would you stay with Cassie? She's trying to be tough but trust me. It's an act. She could use a friend right now."

Heat rose behind Emma's eyes. She didn't have a lot of friends in Erie, and while she liked the idea of Cassie being one of them, she hadn't truly believed the feelings were mutual. "I'd be glad to."

Chapter Twenty-Seven

The security guard didn't argue about Matthias's request and buzzed Emma through the automatic doors. Matthias gave her an appreciative smile as she disappeared behind them, then rejoined the rest of his brothers in blue. Armstrong, Roth, Frazier, several other detectives including a few from other departments, and half a dozen uniforms held court, discussing the case.

"In addition to the BOLOs on Elkins and the silver Hyundai, I've released the description of the car to the press," Armstrong said. "I stressed that the public only report sightings. Do not approach."

"What about Elkins's name and description?" Matthias asked.

"The Chief is holding a press conference this evening. He may release the suspect's information then. Until that time, keep it to yourself. This man is willing to run down a child. There's no telling what he might do if he believes some poor schmuck is trying to play hero."

Matthias's jaw ached. No telling? He knew exactly what this guy would do if he perceived a threat.

Armstrong shifted his focus to Matthias. "This has been your investigation. What do you want to add?"

"We know the car that tried to run down the Malones. We know where and when. I want to see the traffic cam footage at that intersection."

Roth raised a hand. "On it."

Matthias gave him a nod. "This all goes back to the robbery at Shawn's clinic. It's connected to Zimmerman and Urban. When can we expect anything from the lab?"

Frazier stepped forward. "I just spoke with them. They've promised to have some of the results to us first thing tomorrow morning."

"Good." Now if only those results provided a lead. Matthias held Frazier's gaze. "I want us to take another look at Bethany Stone. We need to go back through Zimmerman's, Urban's, and Elkins's known associates. See if she ties in with them somehow. And if not her, another name that connects to two or more of this crew." He thought about the names Emma had given him. She'd found information unavailable to the police. Most likely because of Shawn's age. Juvie files were sealed. Matthias wasn't discounting any of it, despite the amount of time that had passed. But he wasn't going to shine a light on Cassie's husband's youthful indiscretions. Not to Cassie's coworkers. Not now.

He was saving that part of the investigation for himself.

―――――――――

Preston hadn't offered even a hint of an argument when Emma texted him about staying with Cassie. In fact, his response had been nothing short of supportive. He would make sure her camera equipment made it safely back to the newsroom. And she should let him know if she needed anything.

He wasn't fooling her. Regardless of his earlier statement about being fine if she couldn't divulge information to him, Emma knew that's exactly what he was hoping for.

As Emma approached the cubicle to which she'd been directed, an orderly approached from the opposite direction, pushing a bed with a sorrowful-looking Alissa in it. She sported a bright pink cast on her left arm, which she cradled against herself with the right. Emma waited as the orderly steered the bed into the cubicle, then moved to watch from the doorway as he parked and locked the bed's wheels.

"There you go, Miss Alissa," he said. "Safe and sound."

He nodded to Emma as he left.

Cassie had already scooped the sobbing child into her arms by the time Emma entered the small room. "It's okay, baby," Cassie cooed. "You're safe now. No one's gonna hurt you."

Alissa's soft, plaintive wail was muffled against Cassie's chest. "Mommy." The last syllable dragged into about five more. "I want my mommy."

Emma met Cassie's gaze over the girl's head and aimed a thumb behind her. "I can leave," Emma said softly.

"No. Stay."

She moved to a corner and took a seat in a scuffed vinyl-upholstered chair.

The sobbing went on for several minutes with Cassie rocking and shushing and reassuring Alissa. Finally, the little girl quieted and eased away from her grandmother. "Where's Mommy?"

"They're taking pictures of her head," Cassie said. "Same as they took pictures of your arm."

"It's broken." Alissa fingered the cast. "I have to wear this until it heals."

"It's very pretty, though." Cassie looked at Emma. "Don't you think so?"

"Very pretty." Emma took the cue, rose, and moved to their side. "You can get all your friends to sign it."

"That's right," Cassie said. "We'll have to get you a marker to carry around with you."

"Can Mommy sign it?"

"Absolutely."

A nurse bustled in carrying a small can of ginger ale and a package of cheese crackers. "I heard you got hurt on your way to get something to eat. I thought this might hold you over until you can get some real food."

Alissa's eyes lit. "Yes, please."

With Alissa seated on the edge of her bed and her small bounty spread on a paper towel on the bedside table, Cassie drew Emma aside. "I don't want to sound ungrateful, but what are you doing here?"

"Matthias thought you could use a friend."

For a second, Emma thought Cassie was going to argue. Instead, she offered a weak smile. "He's partly right. What I really need is a clone. Shawn's upstairs in recovery. Now both of my babies are hurt, too. I want to be with each of them."

"What can I do? Do you want me to go upstairs and get an update on Shawn?"

Cassie thought about it but shook her head. "I can just as easily call, but if there was any change, I'm sure they'd contact me first."

"How is he?" Emma asked in a whisper.

The look Cassie gave her spoke volumes, none of it good. "He made it through surgery, but there were complications."

Emma waited for her to elaborate, but she didn't. "What you can do is go to the nurses' station and find out what's going on with Denene. She's supposed to be getting a CAT scan for a possible concussion, but it's been..." Cassie looked at her watch and sighed. "I guess it hasn't been as long as it seems."

"Hospital time is slower than regular time."

Cassie sneered. "You got that right."

Emma offered to check anyway, and Cassie didn't argue.

The nurse, however, had no news, which was about what Emma expected.

A half hour passed before a dark-haired woman in a lab coat bustled in clutching a computer tablet. "Mrs. Malone?"

"Detective Sergeant Malone," Cassie corrected as she came to her feet.

"Detective Sergeant." The woman extended a hand. "I'm Dr. Witherspoon. Denene Malone is your daughter?"

"Yes. How is she?"

"They'll be bringing her back here in a few minutes." She looked at the tablet. "I'm afraid your daughter has a rather significant scalp hematoma. What you would call a goose egg."

Cassie exhaled. "That's not serious, right?"

"Probably not. The CT scan didn't show any bleeding within the skull or any fractures. Nonetheless, I would feel more comfortable if we admitted her for observation overnight. The CT scan isn't infallible, and if she was to pass out or become nauseated, I wouldn't want to delay treatment."

Cassie looked down at her granddaughter. "What about Alissa?"

Dr. Witherspoon smiled at the child. "Alissa does have a break of the radius and ulna. It's a clean break and should heal nicely as long as she doesn't reinjure it. That means no acrobatics or monkey bars for at least a month, Miss Malone. Understood?"

"Yes, ma'am," Alissa said softly.

"Does that mean she can come home?" Cassie asked.

"Absolutely."

Cassie thanked the doctor. Once Witherspoon left the cubicle, Cassie again drew Emma aside. "I hate to ask you this, but…" She hesitated, glanced at Alissa, and brought her gaze back to meet Emma's. "Would you mind staying at my house with us tonight? We have a lovely guest room."

"Whatever you need," Emma replied.

"Thanks. I would feel better knowing there's someone in the house in case…"

Cassie didn't finish the statement, but Emma knew and finished for her. "In case you get a call and have to rush back here."

Cassie nodded. "Alissa's been through a lot. I'd rather not have to drag her around in the middle of the night if I don't have to."

"I'm yours for as long as you need me."

Chapter Twenty-Eight

Matthias's plan to dig into the names Emma had given him fell apart when the lieutenant ordered Frazier to go home and get some rest, leaving the deep dive into Zimmerman and Urban all on Matthias. By two a.m. Wednesday, he'd gone over every known detail of their lives and their connections to Grady Elkins or anyone else. Specifically, Bethany Stone. If any of the trio had known her outside of the robbery, they'd kept it well concealed.

Armstrong ambled into Major Crimes and stopped at Matthias's desk. "Anything?"

He didn't answer.

The lieutenant grunted. "Take a break. Go home. Get some sleep."

"No," Matthias said. "Not until—"

Armstrong showed him a raised palm. "That's an order, Honeywell. You're wiped out."

"Meaning no disrespect, sir, but so are you. So is everyone else working this case."

"You're absolutely right. Which is why I'm ordering each man to take a few hours off in shifts. When you're exhausted, you can't think straight. You might miss something that's right in front of you. Cassie and her family deserve better than that. We need to be sharp. You, Honeywell, are not sharp."

Matthias couldn't argue that point.

"Frazier should be coming back on duty any time now. It's your turn. Be back here at your desk by eight. Then it'll be Roth's turn."

"Sir, what about you? When do you get to sleep?"

Armstrong gave him a tight smile. "It's not your job to worry about me. Go home."

Matthias thought there was no way he'd be able to sleep with everything going on, but he was wrong. His alarm went off at seven-thirty and jarred him out of a nightmare in which he was fighting off dozens of civilians trampling a crime scene. A shower helped clear his head. A coffee at his favorite café, complete with two extra shots of espresso, brought him fully alert.

Both Frazier and Roth were at their desks and looked up when Matthias entered Major Crimes. "Get me caught up," he said. Pointing at Roth, he added, "Then you go home. Lieutenant's orders."

"I know," Roth replied. "I've already been given the 'we-need-to-be-sharp' speech." He picked up a sheet of paper from his desk and handed it to Matthias. "That's the best image I could pull from the traffic cameras at 3rd and State."

Matthias studied the grainy photo. A light-colored Hyundai compact—no doubt Elkins's grandmother's car—with what appeared to be a single occupant, a driver wearing a ball cap with the brim tipped low, as if shielding his eyes from the sun.

Except the afternoon sun was at his back. The only reason he'd have his hat pulled down that far would be to conceal his face.

"Not much help," Roth said, "but we already know who's behind the wheel. I checked other cameras in the area, trying to find out where Elkins went, and managed to catch him heading east on 6th, then picking up the Bayfront Parkway driving southeast." He winced. "I lost him after that."

"We need to check business security cameras in that area. Maybe one caught him turning off the Parkway."

Roth nodded and moved toward his desk. "On it."

"No. You're not. Go home. The lieutenant's right."

Once the detective grudgingly acquiesced and headed out, Matthias turned to Frazier. "Have you got anything new? What about the lab results?"

"The email just hit my inbox when you walked through the door." Frazier returned to his desk.

Matthias followed and watched as he opened the message and clicked on the attachment. Leaning over Frazier's shoulder, Matthias read along with him.

"Fibers found on Zimmerman's neck are red nylon," Frazier said. "The type used for straps."

"Or dog leashes." Matthias pictured them hanging from a hook in the vet clinic's waiting room with more in the back room.

Frazier pointed at the screen. "There were also a few dog hairs found in Zimmerman's living room."

"A few," Matthias echoed. He knew how dogs shed. Had there been a dog in the apartment, there would've been more than a few. "Transfer."

"I agree. And it doesn't tell us much. Hell, Zimmerman had been in the vet clinic during the robbery. He might have picked some up there."

"Have we gotten the results from trace on the hoodies they discarded?"

"I'll call them now." Frazier picked up his phone.

Matthias waited, listening to one side of the conversation.

When Frazier hung up, he looked at Matthias and shook his head. "No dog hairs—or any hairs—found on any of the hoodies."

Matthias grunted. "But that doesn't definitively rule out the dog hair coming from the clinic. Or from someone who works there."

Frazier smirked. "Bethany Stone."

"Yeah. Except I couldn't connect her to any of the three."

"Shawn's a vet. Anyone with a connection to him would likely have pets."

Matthias ran down his internal checklist. What were they missing? "Did you finish the background check on the rest of the veterinary clinic staff?"

Frazier swore. "I got sidetracked."

"Get on that now." Matthias turned and headed for his desk.

"What are you gonna do?"

"Look into a tip I got yesterday." It was time he focused on the names Emma had given him.

Maybe Shawn's distant past really did hold the key to the crimes of the present.

***

The bed in the Malones' guest room was infinitely bigger and more comfortable than the sleeper sofa in Emma's camper, yet slumber had eluded her for most of the night. The sound of footsteps followed by the aroma of coffee convinced her it was time to give up the effort. She slipped quietly into the bathroom across the hall, not wishing to wake Alissa, and changed out of the pajamas Cassie had loaned her and back into the same clothes as yesterday.

Emma found Cassie in the kitchen, her phone to her ear, talking in hushed tones. When she spotted Emma, she gestured toward the coffee pot.

"I'm waiting to speak with Shawn's nurse," Cassie whispered.

Emma held up a hand with crossed fingers. Cassie nodded.

The nurse came on the line while Emma poured a cup of coffee and doctored it with the creamer Cassie had set out. Cassie's side of the conversation gave little away. "Yes, this is she... Yes... Okay... Of course... When do you expect—" She stopped mid-sentence, her expression sour with annoyance. "Yes, I understand... Please do. Thank you." Cassie stabbed the phone's screen and thunked it down on the kitchen island.

"That didn't sound good," Emma said, breathing in the fragrance of the coffee.

"It's not *bad*." Cassie crossed to the refrigerator and opened the door. "It's just a lot of nothing. Shawn's stable. For now. But he's still not out of the woods. God, I hate that term. What the hell does it mean anyway? What's 'in the woods' have to do with your health?"

Emma knew Cassie was venting and didn't expect an answer.

"They can't give me any idea of how long he'll be in ICU. I swear, I felt like I had a better grasp on his condition right after he was shot than I do now."

Emma thought, *because you were at the hospital with him*, but wasn't about to say it out loud. "Any word on Denene?"

Cassie withdrew a dozen eggs from the fridge and turned to face Emma, her expression brighter. "According to her nurse, they're waiting for the doctor to make his rounds and then she should be discharged."

"That's good."

"It is." Cassie held up the egg carton. "Would you like some breakfast? I'm not as good a cook as Matthias, but it's hard to mess up scrambled eggs."

"Do you want me to do that? I'm not as good a cook as Matthias either, but..."

Cassie shook her head. "I need to keep busy, or I'll lose my mind."

"In that case, I would love some scrambled eggs."

As Cassie prepared their breakfast, Emma set her phone on the island. "I need to call Laurie and let her know I won't be in today."

"Why? Don't you feel well?"

"I'm fine, but I want to stick around and help."

Cassie wrinkled her nose. "I appreciate the offer, but I—*we* will be fine. Really." She set down the whisk she'd been using to beat the eggs. "I'm deeply grateful that you stayed last night. It was a comfort knowing you were here to stay with Alissa if I had to run to the hospital. But Denene will be released soon and can take over her mom duties while I'm with Shawn."

"You're sure?"

"Positive."

"In that case, I need to go home and change clothes before I go to the newsroom."

Cassie lit the stove, pulled out a skillet, and set it on the burner. "Not before you eat."

"No problem. I'm starved."

Cassie busied herself with popping bread into the toaster and was pouring orange juice when the doorbell chimed. "Stay there," she told Emma and strode to the front entrance.

"Detective Sergeant?" a male voice called from outside. "It's Officer Isley."

Emma watched as Cassie peered through the peephole, then relaxed, unlocked and opened the door. "Is everything okay out there?"

Isley, a young man with light hair and freckles, grinned sheepishly. "I didn't mean to scare you. Everything's fine. No signs of anyone who shouldn't be around. But if you don't mind, I need to use the facilities." He displayed a travel mug. "And possibly get a refill?"

Cassie waved him in and took the mug. "Bathroom's down the hall, second door on the left."

He thanked her and hurried off.

Cassie returned to the kitchen and the coffee pot. In a low voice, she said, "Isley is a good kid. A little green, but hardworking and a quick learner." With a chuckle she added, "I bet he's running the department by the time I retire."

While they waited for the young officer's return, Emma's mind shifted to the information she and Preston had found. Did Cassie know about her husband's past? She and Emma rarely had time alone like this.

She drew a breath. "I've been trying to find some motive for Shawn's shooting."

Cassie set the filled travel mug on the island and returned her focus on the meal prep. "We all have."

"I may have found something."

This brought her eyes up, a tense light in them. "What did you find?"

Emma decided to leave Preston's name out of it. "I was going through the microfilm archives from the old *Erie Tribune* and came across a story about a traffic fatality. A man named Justin Wheeler was killed." Emma watched for a reaction from Cassie. There was none. "There were three stories. In the first, Shawn was named as the driver. He was seventeen and had been drinking. There was a second teen in the vehicle, also intoxicated. But in the other two articles, the other teen was the one listed as the driver instead of Shawn."

Cassie remained still, her face giving nothing away. She looked like she was about to speak, but footsteps from the back of the house stopped her. Isley appeared, his phone to his ear. His smile and wave let them know the call had nothing to do with them. He continued out the front door.

Before Emma could come back to the topic of the news story about Shawn's arrest, Cassie's phone rang. She glanced at it. "It's

Denene. Excuse me a minute." She turned off the stove, grabbed the phone, and moved to the end of the kitchen.

"Grammie?" came a small voice. Alissa stood at the bottom of the staircase, rubbing her eyes with her good hand.

"I'm on the phone with your mama," Cassie called to her.

Emma circled to the other side of the island. "Can I get you some orange juice, Alissa?"

"Okay."

Before Emma could start to pour, she noticed the travel mug. "Officer Isley left without his coffee."

"Oh, good grief," Cassie muttered. She returned to the stove, the phone pinned between her ear and shoulder. "I'll get the juice. Emma, can you run that out to him. We can't have an under-caffeinated officer keeping watch over us."

Emma snickered. "Sure thing." She stopped to boost Alissa onto one of the stools at the island, snatched the mug, and headed to the front door. The doorbell chimed as she reached it. "I guess he realized what he'd forgotten," Emma said. She pulled the door open, expecting to see young Officer Isley. Instead, she came face to face with the muzzle of a gun held by a man she'd never seen before.

———

As expected, Matthias's search for Justin Wheeler brought up an old incident report about the traffic fatality. Wheeler was dead, having left behind a wife and two children who moved to Chicago following the accident. Bain had served his time but hadn't learned his lesson. He'd been in collisions twice while driving under the influence. The final time, he'd swerved off the road, rolled his vehicle, and been declared dead at the scene. There was no mention of Shawn in any of it. And the incident had happened decades ago. If a family member blamed Shawn, they weren't likely to have waited forty-some years for retribution. Another dead end.

"Anything on the clinic staff?" Matthias called to Frazier.

"Nothing of interest. The worst charges against any of them are a handful of misdemeanors. Nothing violent or recent."

More dead ends.

Matthias rose from his desk and stalked to the breakroom to refill his coffee cup. "Grady Elkins," he grumbled to himself. "Who the hell are you and why are you going after Shawn and his family?" As he brought the cup to his lips, his own words echoed back at him.

And he froze.

Shawn *and his family*.

Cassie.

Friday at the hospital, while Shawn was in surgery, Cassie had told him, "*Now if it had been me? Hell, yeah. You know as well as I do how many criminals out there would love to take us out. You and me. Not Shawn.*" And later, when presented with the photos captured from the clinic's CCTV, she'd said, "*It's crossed my mind that this asshole shot my husband to get back at me, but no.*"

"Dammit." He returned to his desk as Armstrong appeared at the door.

"Did you find something?" the lieutenant asked.

Matthias spun to face him. "No. But didn't you say you had men working on the possibility that Cassie was the true target in Shawn's shooting?"

"I did. They couldn't find anyone in Cassie's past who might be a viable suspect."

"Did they specifically investigate Elkins?"

Armstrong didn't reply but crossed his arms, his expression unreadable.

"The day Shawn was shot," Matthias said, "I considered the possibility that he wasn't the real target and dismissed it when

Cassie insisted she didn't recognize any of the assailants. What if Elkins wasn't targeting Shawn, but was trying to get to Cassie through her family?"

Matthias expected Armstrong to consider the idea. Instead, he looked pained. "The reason I'm here is I just got a phone call. I need you and Frazier to get over to that abandoned manufacturing facility on West 19th. We have another body."

Chapter Twenty-Nine

The coroner's van was backed into an open delivery bay at the front of the single-story brick and steel-paneled building. A trio of marked police cruisers sat along the street, and yellow police tape fluttered on the morning breeze. Matthias parked between two of the vehicles, and he and Frazier stepped out into the already humid air. The stench of decomp hit them even before they reached the entrance.

This wasn't their first visit to this address for a dead body. No matter how many times the owner tried to secure the building with plywood on the windows and chains on the doors, addicts managed to find a way in to shoot up or snort their way into oblivion. And sometimes they went too far and spent their final hours in this dump.

The coroner knelt next to the body and looked up at Matthias and Frazier's approach.

Matthias moved closer, trying not to breathe through his nose while getting a glimpse of the corpse. "What've you got?"

Hamilton swept an arm, indicating the area around the decedent. Used needles were scattered everywhere along with other drug paraphernalia. "At first glance, I'd say another OD. I would estimate he's been here a while."

"Define 'a while.'"

"More than a couple of days. Less than a week. It's been ridiculously hot out. Even more so in here with a metal roof and no air circulation. Speeds the rate of decomposition."

Matthias studied what he assumed was a man lying on the ground. At least what was left of him. Sneakers, faded blue jeans, a T-shirt with a rock band emblem printed on the front. The victim's face was approaching a mummified state. This dude could've been Matthias's best friend and he wouldn't be able to recognize him. "Don't suppose he had any ID on him."

"You would suppose wrong." Hamilton held up a wallet. "Found this lying beside him. No cash or plastic." A dark look crossed the coroner's beach-boy face. "Only his driver's license."

Matthias wiggled his fingers into gloves before accepting the wallet and thumbing out the license. Frazier looked over his shoulder. They both swore.

"Grady Elkins?" Matthias said. "That can't be."

Hamilton shrugged. "I mean it's possible someone planted Elkins's ID on this guy. Or..."

"Or Elkins has been dead for days," Frazier said.

"In which case, who the hell have we been chasing?" Matthias asked. "And who tried to run down Cassie's daughter and granddaughter yesterday?"

"Are you okay?" Cassie whispered.

Emma squirmed on the cargo van's floor and managed to push up to sit. No easy feat with her wrists bound behind her. "Been better."

"I told you two to shut up," snapped the man behind the wheel.

Emma pressed her lips closed. From her position, she could see the driver—the man who'd barged into Cassie's home at gunpoint. Emma still had no clue who he was. But she had a feeling Cassie did. If only they had a chance to talk. To come up with a strategy. But the man with the gun had the upper hand as long as he had Alissa.

Back at the house, he'd gained control quickly by shifting the aim of his gun to Cassie's granddaughter.

Cassie had growled at him, "Don't you touch her."

But he'd laughed. "I could just shoot her right here and now."

"It would be the last move you ever make."

"Maybe." He sneered. "But she'd still be dead. And it would be on your head."

Emma had watched Cassie's herculean effort to control her rage. The battle continued as he made them leave their cell phones behind and herded them through the garage and into the back of a van, all while keeping one hand clamped on Alissa's shoulder, the other holding the gun aimed at her temple.

He had Cassie press the button to open the garage door. In fact, Emma realized, he touched nothing in the house except Alissa and his gun. There would be no fingerprints for Matthias to find.

Once inside the van, the gunman produced a zip tie from his pocket and ordered Emma to put it on Cassie, restraining her wrists behind her back. Emma did her best to covertly leave it loose. Then he ordered Alissa into the front passenger seat while he secured Emma's hands with a piece of strap. Unfortunately, he'd been wise to Emma's efforts and had yanked the zip tie snug enough to make Cassie grunt.

Now, as they bumped along a road Emma couldn't identify from her narrow view of the windshield, she replayed the whole scene.

He hadn't planned on her. That's why he only had one zip tie. His intent was to kidnap Cassie and Alissa. The term collateral damage came to mind. Emma looked at him and noticed his eyes reflected in the rearview mirror. Watching her.

And wondering what to do with her, she suspected. At least he hadn't gunned her down back at the house.

But no. That wouldn't have been smart. Cassie would've seized his momentary shift of focus from Alissa and taken him out.

He kept Emma alive to prevent his entire scheme—whatever it was—from blowing up.

However, Cassie was now restrained, no longer a threat. He could put a bullet in Emma's head and drop her alongside a deserted road any time he wished.

Another thought followed on the heels of that one, and she knew—sort of—who this guy was.

The sniper. The man who'd shot Shawn.

Except, the driver, watching her in the mirror, was White. Not the light-skinned Black man Shawn had described.

Matthias left Frazier to oversee the investigation into the most recent homicide and drove back to the station. On the way, he tried to call Cassie to warn her. If Matthias's suspicions were correct, she was the real target. He just didn't know who was after her. He hoped she might be able to come up with some possibilities.

But the call went to voicemail. Cassie never let her calls go to voicemail. Especially with Shawn and Denene in the hospital. He left a message to call him back asap.

No sooner had he ended the call and prepared to call Emma, who, as far as he knew, was still with Cassie, than his phone vibrated in his hand. He didn't recognize the number. "Detective Honeywell."

The voice on the other end sounded anxious. "Matthias, this is Denene Malone."

"Hey, Denene. What's up?"

"I'm hoping you can tell me. I was on the phone with my mom about her coming to pick me up at the hospital when she said she had to go. She sounded strange, and I haven't been able to reach her since. Do you have any idea what's going on?"

Matthias's fingers tightened on the steering wheel. "Let me make a few calls. I'll get back to you."

Denene mumbled something as he hung up and made the call to Emma.

Voicemail again. He left another message.

He took the turn into the police station's garage way too fast, squealing tires, screeched into a parking spot, slammed the shifter into park, and cut the engine. As he loped to the stairs, he tried Emma again. Still no answer.

He fought off the memory of the last time this had happened. She'd been taken but released unharmed. He held no delusions about that happening this time.

At the top of the stairs, he passed the doorway to the breakroom and Major Crimes and continued down the hall to the lieutenant's office. Armstrong sat at his desk.

"Have you heard from Cassie?" Matthias asked.

"No. Why?" Armstrong scowled. "Should I have?"

"I called her, but she isn't answering. Her daughter can't reach her either."

Armstrong picked up his desk phone and punched one of the buttons. After a few moments, his gaze came back to Matthias. He didn't need to say anything. Matthias knew. Cassie hadn't picked up for him either.

The lieutenant hit another button. Whoever he called this time answered. He identified himself, then said, "Who do you have watching Detective Sergeant Malone's house?" A pause. "Get in touch with him and tell him she's not answering her phone. I need him to check on her. Thanks." Armstrong hung up. "We'll hear something in the next few minutes."

Matthias wanted to try Emma's number again but controlled himself. He'd left two messages for her already. She would call him back once she got them.

She would call him back once she got them. She would call him back once she got them. If he repeated it to himself enough times, he might believe it.

The phone rang. The lieutenant grabbed the receiver. "Armstrong." As he listened, his face grew darker. Finally, he said, "Keep me posted," and hung up. To Matthias, he said, "They can't raise the officer who's guarding Cassie's house. They're sending units. Get over there now."

But Matthias was already halfway down the hall, Armstrong's last few words fading behind him.

Chapter Thirty

Three marked units were parked across the street from the Malone residence when Matthias pulled in. The cruiser in the middle had its trunk open. One uniformed officer sat on the curb. Another squatted next to him.

Matthias strode toward them and heard sirens in the distance. The moment he got a clear view of the officers, he stopped cold. The kneeling one was pressing a blood-saturated gauze against the seated one's head. "What happened?"

"Someone used Isley's skull for batting practice," the one providing first aid said. "He's also one lucky son of a bitch."

Isley winced. "Not lucky enough. He blindsided me. I was coming back to my car after checking on Detective Sergeant Malone. I caught movement out of the corner of my eye but before I could react, he hit me."

"With what?" Matthias asked.

"I don't know. Baseball bat, tire iron, two-by-four? I didn't see whatever it was. Next thing I knew I was on my knees, and he put something over my head. I couldn't breathe."

The cop with the first aid kit filled in the blanks. "It was a trash bag. When we got here, I heard thumping coming from the trunk. When we popped it open, he was in there, bleeding from this gash." The second officer indicated the bloody gauze. "And there was a black trash bag near his head."

"What about Cassie?" Matthias looked toward the house, its front door hanging open.

The cop holding the bandage appeared grim. "She's gone."

The word hit Matthias hard, and his face must've shown it.

"No, I don't mean dead. I mean she's not here. The house is empty."

An EmergyCare ambulance with lights flashing rumbled around the corner and rolled their way. Matthias thanked the officers, wished the injured one well, then took off at a jog toward the house.

Three more uniforms stood inside Cassie's home, comparing notes.

"Talk to me," Matthias said.

"The front door was unlocked. We've gone through the entire house. No one's here. No sign of a struggle. But we did find these." The officer moved to a table next to the door to the garage and pointed to a travel mug and a pair of cell phones on its surface.

"Have these been photographed?" Matthias asked.

"They have."

He put on gloves, picked up the phone in the black case, and pressed a button. A lock screen with a generic factory-set photo popped up. Yep, it was Cassie's. He set it down and picked up the other. Like his partner's, he'd seen this phone often enough to know, but he still pulled up the lock screen with the photo of Emma's family farm. Feeling like he'd been punched in the gut, he placed it beside the other.

He realized they were missing one. "What about Alissa's phone?" Cassie had bought it for her last birthday. Child-safe,

Cassie had said. Alissa could play a few parent-approved games on it and could make calls, but the internet was blocked. It did, however, have a tracking app installed.

"Pink bejeweled case? We found it upstairs in a pink backpack."

Matthias swore. "What else have you got?"

"Two vehicles are in the garage. One registered to Detective Sergeant Malone. The other to Dr. Shawn Malone."

Matthias forced down the panic that threatened to derail his train of logical thought. He turned a slow pivot, taking in the house. All was as it should be. The smell of coffee, toast, and eggs drew him to the kitchen island. Two slices of browned bread peeked up from the toaster. A skillet of cooling scrambled eggs congealed on the stove, burner off. A bottle of orange juice sat on the counter along with a glass. A half-empty cup of coffee with creamer rested on the island. Another, black, and almost drained, perched next to the sink.

Two cups of coffee. Cassie took hers black. Emma preferred creamer. The juice would be for Alissa.

Cassie had been caught off guard by the intruder. In any other situation, there should have been signs of a battle. Cassie would've fought like a warrior. But no. Not if Alissa was threatened. Cassie wouldn't risk her granddaughter's safety under any circumstance.

He continued to survey the scene, buoyed by what *wasn't* present. Blood. Bodies. He allowed a modicum of hope to seep in. If this bastard wanted them dead, he'd have come in, killed them, and been gone.

Or he had plans for them that involved something worse than death.

The thought quashed the glimmer of hope. Matthias's breath became shallow. Strained. He turned, staggered to the door, and yanked it open. Gripping the jamb, he inhaled deeply, trying to calm his racing mind. Who the hell was behind this? Who had orchestrated the robbery, Shawn's shooting, the homicides of the three assailants, the hit-and-run that injured Denene and Alissa?

And now, the abduction of Cassie, Alissa, and Emma.

Denene. Dammit, he needed to call her back. He considered pawning off the task on the lieutenant, but no. He had to be the one.

She answered on the first ring. "Did you find her?"

"I'm at the house along with half the department." He told her about the police guard being attacked. About the empty house and the abandoned phones. Except for Denene's measured breaths, Matthias would've thought the call had been dropped. "I'll find them and bring them home," he told her.

"You do that." The dangerous undertone in her words reminded him of her mother.

He gave her his word and hung up.

Still standing in the doorway, he surveyed the yard and street in front of him. Uniformed officers swarmed the neighborhood. He closed his eyes and let the fresh air, humid though it was, settle his thoughts. With a loud exhale, he opened his eyes and studied the latch plate, the deadbolt, and the door frame. No signs of a forced entry. Cassie wasn't the type to open her door without confirming who was on the other side. Had she known the person?

Matthias formed a plan. With a steadier hand, he called Armstrong, who'd already been updated on what had happened. Matthias told him what he intended to do next.

"I'll call Roth and have him take over there," Armstrong said. "I'll see you back here in a few minutes."

Emma studied Cassie's face, her expression simultaneously fierce yet still. Emma remembered Matthias once calling his partner part Amazon warrior, part mother hen. Now, Emma was seeing what he meant. Cassie would remain calm in order to keep Alissa calm as well. But beneath the still surface, Cassie radiated a white-hot fury that Emma could feel from across the van. Given half a chance, Cassie could—would—kill their captor with her bare hands for threatening her granddaughter.

Emma needed to be prepared, ready to do whatever she could to help.

If only she and Cassie could communicate somehow. But the driver's eyes were always shifting. Watching the road. Watching Alissa beside him. Watching Emma.

She didn't think he could see Cassie.

He didn't need to. He knew that if Cassie made even the slightest move, Alissa would react.

Emma swore to herself. If there was one thing this guy *wasn't*, it was a fool. He'd deliberately placed Cassie where Alissa could see her. Her grandmother's presence would keep her from misbehaving. And the little girl wasn't skilled at deception, so he only needed to observe her to know if Cassie was trying anything.

Emma wondered if Cassie had figured that out yet. Probably. She was no fool either.

The van slowed. Emma shifted slightly to get a better view out the front window. The narrow two-lane road cut a course through nothing but trees. She hadn't spotted a house or building of any kind for miles.

The driver steered onto a side road. No, Emma realized, not a true road but a driveway of broken pavement with weeds growing through the cracks. Ahead, a flat-roofed red-brick structure with broken windows squatted off to the left. Beyond it, a larger yellow-brick building rose out of the weedy lot. Otherwise, nothing but grass and trees.

They hit a rut. Hard. Emma bounced and slammed back down, sending a shimmer of pain from her tailbone up her spine. From the front, Alissa whimpered.

"Shut up," the driver barked.

Which only fueled the small cry into a sob.

"I told you to shut up!" he yelled, adding a few age-inappropriate epithets.

"Grammie," Alissa squealed.

"It's okay, baby," Cassie said, in a soothing voice.

Emma heard the threatening undertone. Apparently, Alissa only heard her grandmother's cooing, comforting words and quieted.

The van continued to bounce along the drive, past the first building to the second. Emma caught glimpses of large, rounded silver globes on its roof. Industrial exhaust fans like restaurants used. She wondered what this building had been, but her curiosity was overshadowed by fear. No matter what it had once been, was it to be the place where she, Cassie, and Alissa died?

The driver steered the van alongside the building and around the corner to what appeared to have been a parking lot. They jerked to a stop, and the motor fell silent.

Emma caught Cassie staring at her, an intensity in her dark eyes that Emma had never witnessed before. They didn't dare speak, but Emma understood. *Be ready.* She nodded.

If the driver exited the vehicle through his door, there would be a moment when they would be alone. Emma played an escape scenario through her mind. Alissa could lock the doors and help free Cassie.

Provided he left the keys inside and didn't shoot them through the windshield.

It didn't matter. He swung toward Alissa, grabbed her, eliciting a squeal of pain, and dragged her from her seat into the rear with Emma and Cassie.

"Get your hands off her," Cassie snarled.

His laugh sounded demonic. "How about I just shoot her right here?"

Cassie recoiled, but Emma could see her clenched jaw working.

"I'll take that as a no." He stood, bent over because of the low ceiling height, and kept one hand clamped on Alissa's shoulder.

She cradled her broken arm against her and bit her lip but managed to stay still.

"Now listen up. This is how it's gonna go. You ladies are gonna march yourselves into this building. I'll be right behind you." He withdrew his gun from his belt and held it up. "With this aimed at your little sweetheart. You try anything, she's dead. And if you feel like yelling for help, be my guest. There's no one around for over a mile to hear you." He smiled. "Otherwise, I'd have gagged you both. Do you understand?"

Cassie glared at him without a word. When his eyes shifted in Emma's direction, she gave a quick nod.

"All right then. Move." He gestured at the rear doors.

Emma struggled to climb to her feet without the use of her bound arms. Cassie did the same. Emma stumbled to the rear of the van, stopped, and looked at their captor. "How am I supposed to open these without my hands?"

"You have hands." He made a revolving motion with the barrel of the gun. "Use them."

His tone drove a wedge of terror into her throat. Crouching, she shuffled around, facing the front of the van. Her gaze settled on Cassie, who was bent over between Emma and the gunman. If only she could read Cassie's mind.

But Cassie's countenance offered no guidance.

Emma fingered the latch behind her and felt it click open.

Before she could figure out how to push the door open from this position, she caught a glimpse of an evil smile on the man's face as he released Alissa and lunged at Cassie, shoving her into Emma.

Suddenly, Emma was freefalling. Backward. Out through the doors. The cloudy sky above. The jarring halt, as she slammed to the ground, knocked the wind from her. A split second later, her head cracked against the pavement and sent an explosion of fireworks within her brain. She caught a brief glimpse of the shocked look on Cassie's face as she tumbled out after her. Then Emma's breath was further driven from her lungs as Cassie landed on top of her.

Emma didn't think she lost consciousness, but time had slipped a cog, like the antique mantle clock in her grandmother's bedroom when she was a kid. Wound too tightly at some point—probably by Emma or her sister—the spring would whir and release when someone twisted the key.

She hadn't thought about that in years.

"Get up."

Wincing, she opened her eyes and squinted into the gray sky above. She was still on the ground, but Cassie now stood over her, looking concerned. Emma's fuzzy gaze shifted to the source of the words. Their captor, who still gripped Alissa with one hand and a gun with the other.

"Get up," he repeated even more forcefully.

Cassie's concerned appearance reverted to furor as she turned on him. "She's hurt."

He took a step toward Emma. Not for the first time, she found herself looking down—or in this case *up*—the barrel of a gun, but her head throbbed so badly, she almost didn't care.

"I can just shoot her now, if you prefer," he said to Cassie.

"No," she replied sharply.

"Might be better anyway. Then I won't have an extra person to deal with. I never expected to have three of you to fuss with."

"Emma, get up." Cassie's tone was more imploring than demanding.

She inhaled deeply. The intake of fresh air revived her and helped her focus. "Okay." But it was easier said than accomplished. Her wrists were still bound. The effort to roll over made her feel like she was an upside-down turtle. On her third attempt, she managed to make it onto her side, press an elbow into the broken concrete, and roll up to her knees. From there, she wavered and swayed as she struggled to her feet. Cassie, she noticed, looked relieved.

"Good," he said. "I didn't care to waste a bullet on you. Ammo's too expensive these days." To Cassie, he added, "But don't get ideas. I have plenty." He used the muzzle of the handgun to tap his camo cargo pants' bulging pocket. Then he gestured to the building. "Inside."

Chapter Thirty-One

Matthias stopped at the evidence room on his way through the station and signed out Emma's memory card. The one with the photos of the sniper.

They hadn't had any luck identifying the shooter's face the first time. Maybe he'd have better luck this time. If not, he planned to take a closer look at whatever he *could* see.

If the sniper was Bethany Stone, the hands and arms would be thinner, more feminine. It wouldn't be a definitive identification, but it would narrow down his search.

Matthias's phone rang as he took a seat at his desk. Roth.

"What have you got?" Matthias demanded.

"We checked Cassie's security footage."

"And?"

"The cameras were blacked out, just like the one at Shawn's clinic, so nothing there."

Matthias swore.

"But while we were canvassing the neighborhood, a guy next door told us he saw a white transit van backed into Cassie's driveway about forty-five minutes ago. He didn't catch a plate number, but another neighbor did. When I ran it, the vehicle came up as reported stolen last night. I already put out a BOLO on it. Get this—we sent officers to question the van owner, and they spotted a silver 2018 Hyundai Accent parked a block away."

"Let me guess. Registered to Olivia Elkins."

"Yep. Our guy traded it in for the transit van. Anyway, we're still going house-to-house collecting footage from doorbell and security cameras." Roth paused. "We'll find them." The detective sounded as determined and angry as Matthias had ever heard him.

"Thanks. Keep me posted."

Matthias logged into his computer and inserted the memory card. He clicked on the folder from two days ago and watched the dozens of images populate the screen. Slowly, methodically, he pulled up those photos he already knew captured the gunman at the window. Enlarged them. Scrutinized every inch of what little was visible of the sniper.

With the intense pixelation, Matthias couldn't be one-hundred-percent positive, but close enough. There was no delicacy to the shooter's features. This was not a woman. The sniper was indeed a man.

He flopped back in his chair. Frustrated, he hit the computer mouse and closed the window with its thumbnail images. The screen returned to rows of tiny folders, labeled with dates.

His attention settled on a folder dated two days before Urban's murder. Saturday. The day they'd found Zimmerman's body. Emma had been there, too.

Matthias clicked on it.

She hadn't taken as many photos of the house on Cascade as she had of the sniper on 16th, but there were still several dozen. Matthias started with the first.

There were shots of the coroner's van, the house, a sobbing Misti with an i. None of him, Matthias noted. He smiled, knowing

Emma would protect his identity by keeping his face out of the news. Then he imagined where she was right now. What was being done to her. Was she still alive? His throat closed, leaving him glad there was no one else in Major Crimes at the moment. No one to see him battle to keep his composure.

Swallowing down his fear and rage, he continued through the images, shots of bystanders on the street, gawking at the police presence, curious about a violent death in their neighborhood. Finally, there was a series of photos of Hamilton and his deputy, wheeling a concealed body on a stretcher out to their van.

Matthias reversed through the photos, pausing at the shots of the lookie-loos. Men and women, kids, a few dogs.

And a man with a dog on a leash.

The building in front of them reminded Emma of her high school, except for the broken windows, glass strewn across the sidewalk, and the graffiti spray-painted across the three sets of wooden double doors. Two sets were chained and padlocked. The third stood open, the chain dangling from the handle.

"Inside," the man with the gun repeated.

Emma caught Cassie's gaze. This time, Emma spotted a glimpse of fear in Cassie's face. Somehow, as scared as Emma was —as badly as her head throbbed from smacking the concrete— she'd been able to draw courage from Cassie's toughness. Seeing the façade chip and peel away, much like the paint on the building's exterior, sent Emma's hope for survival plummeting.

She led the way into the dark cavernous interior, knowing Cassie was behind her, with their captor and Alissa bringing up the rear.

The vandalism didn't stop outside. Graffiti artists had tagged every possible spot on the tile floors and block walls of what Emma could now see had once been an indoor swimming pool.

The gunman guided Alissa to the edge of the shadowy crevasse. Cassie's raspy inhalation was audible in the silence. Emma knew what she was thinking. This crazy man was going to push the little girl into the dry pool. Shallow end or not, it was a huge drop for a little girl, especially one with a broken arm.

But instead, he used the weapon to direct them to line up along the pool's rim. Emma, then Cassie, and about six feet away, the gunman held Alissa in front of him.

"You're probably wondering why I brought you all here today," he said, sounding reasonable and sane—which he obviously was not.

Cassie didn't reply. Emma didn't either. She had a very good idea of what his plans were.

He directed his full attention to her. "You. You're the photographer, right?"

Emma's mouth went dry.

"You're the one who insisted on trying to get a picture of me on Monday."

The realization that she'd guessed right did nothing to buoy her spirits. "You were the sniper."

In Emma's peripheral vision, she saw Cassie's head snap around to look at her.

"That's right." His jaw clenched. "If I hadn't started taking fire from that damn cop, I'd have gotten rid of you then and there. I should've toughed it out and tried again, but I decided to let you go. I didn't think you were part of this at the time. Didn't realize you were friends with her." He repositioned the gun, aiming it at Cassie.

Alissa whimpered.

Cassie again faced the man. "What exactly is *this*?" she

demanded. "If you're after me, fine. Let's dance. But leave my granddaughter and my friend out of it."

"Do you know who I am?" he asked, venom oozing from his words.

"No. But I've seen your picture."

"The one she took?" He waved the gun at Emma.

"No. We couldn't make out a face from those photos. But you were at the clinic on Friday. I saw you on the security footage."

"Ah. Yes. I was there."

"John Boyd." Cassie's tone dropped to a lethal whisper. "You were in the exam room while my husband was gunned down."

"Yes, well, that didn't go as planned. Elkins claimed to be good with a firearm. He promised to get the job done. I was pissed off when I learned your beloved was still alive."

"Why? Clearly, you're after me. Why take it out on him?"

His grip on Alissa's shoulder tightened, and she yelped. But he didn't ease off or take his focus from Cassie. "Because I wanted you to suffer. I wanted you to know what it felt like to lose those you loved most. To have to go on living without them. For a while, at least."

Emma looked from the man—Boyd—to Cassie, who had angled her body toward him and away from Emma. To Alissa, who was sobbing with pain from his death grip on her small shoulder. Back to Cassie. Which was when Emma noticed Cassie's hands and bleeding wrists. She'd been trying to work the zip tie loose without Boyd noticing.

"You still don't know who I really am, do you?" he asked Cassie.

"Not a clue."

Emma shifted ever so slightly, like Cassie, concealing her back from Boyd's vigilant eyes. She twisted her own wrists. Compared to Cassie's plastic restraints, the strapping that bound Emma's arms had some give. She might be able to loosen it enough to slip her hands free.

"Do you remember Oakley and Tara O'Donovan?" he asked.

Cassie stiffened.

"Ah. I can see you do." His gaze slid to Emma and back. "I also can see that your photographer friend does not. Why don't you enlighten her?"

Cassie never took her eyes off the gunman. "Oakley O'Donovan was married to a madman by the name of Waylon O'Donovan. Tara was their daughter. Waylon walked into the auto repair shop from which he'd been terminated and opened fire with an assault rifle. Killed three. Sent five more to the hospital. One of them remains paralyzed from the waist down."

Boyd made a sour face. "Waylon was an ass. There's no denying that. But tell your friend about Oakley and Tara."

Cassie continued to focus on Boyd. "We were in pursuit of Waylon. He was driving at speeds of close to 100 miles per hour down 12th Street."

We, Emma noted, and wondered if she meant her and Matthias.

"He'd already blown through two roadblocks and crashed three police cruisers. He jumped the curb and severely injured a pedestrian to avoid our spike strips. We needed to stop him before he killed someone else. I took a chance and used a PIT maneuver."

Emma knew enough from Matthias to understand what a PIT maneuver was. Cassie would have tapped O'Donovan's rear fender with the front fender of her vehicle to send him into a spin.

"It didn't go as planned," Cassie said. "Instead of spinning out, his car flipped and ended up colliding with a pump at a gas station. It burst into flames. We tried but couldn't rescue him."

"Or the other occupants in the car," Boyd added, and Emma noticed the hand holding the gun was trembling.

Cassie lowered her face. "I—we—didn't know his wife and

daughter were in the backseat. They were crouched down, out of sight."

"You killed them." Boyd's voice dropped so low that Emma almost couldn't hear as he added, "You killed my daughter and granddaughter."

Cassie's face came up. "Your—" Her voice cracked. "Oakley was your daughter?"

"And Tara was the light of my life." He gave Alissa a shake that brought on another round of sobs. "Just like this little one is to you, I imagine."

Emma struggled harder against the straps binding her wrists.

"That's what this has all been about? You're getting back at me for something that happened five years ago?"

"Six. But I'm sure that anniversary isn't one that means anything to you."

In the dark space, Emma heard Cassie's inhale. "It's been five years and ten months. It happened on October twentieth."

Boyd seemed mildly impressed. "That's right. Five years and ten months since you took everything from me. Everyone who mattered."

"If you wanted payback, why wait so long?"

"Revenge is a dish best served cold, you know. I spent the first year grieving all I'd lost. All you'd taken from me. Grief festers inside a person. I decided the only way I could cleanse my soul was to get retribution. That decision gave my life purpose. But I needed a plan. I came here to Erie and surveilled you, your family, and your husband's clinic. Got to know his comings and goings. I came to realize the side entrance was the way in. I've always been good at sleight-of-hand, so it was easy to palm a piece of duct tape and press it over the latch mechanism. Plus, I did a lot of research into these vacant buildings as contingency plans." He turned his head and spat onto the filthy and cracked tile floor. "After all the time I dedicated to mapping it out, still it's come to this."

Emma bit her lip, ignoring the strap cutting into her flesh. Was it her imagination, or was it loosening?

If Cassie noticed, she gave no indication, her focus locked on their captor. "You tried to keep your hands clean by hiring Zimmerman, Urban, and Elkins."

He shrugged. "Keeping my hands clean had little to do with it. My role was to get them inside and then sit back and watch the show. My mistake was in choosing my team. Those three bums were crazy. Like Waylon was. I promised to pay them plus let them keep the spoils from the robbery. All they had to do was shoot and kill the veterinarian. They decided Elkins was the man for that task. He knew how to handle a gun better than the others. The damned idiot had one job. One. And he botched it."

"Yet he's the only one who's still alive," Cassie said.

Boyd scoffed. "Elkins? Hell, I killed him the first chance I got after hearing he botched killing your husband. Your friends with the police department just haven't found his body yet."

"And you killed the others to shut them up."

It wasn't Emma's imagination. All her efforts had created a miniscule amount of space ... almost enough through which to slip one hand free.

Boyd shrugged. "I hadn't intended to at first. But Zimmerman got stupid and took off his damn gloves. All because he was allergic to whatever they were made of. Big baby. He left a fingerprint on the door jamb. I knew the police would go straight to him and that he would spill his guts. So, I took my dog for a walk to his house. No one pays attention to a harmless old guy walking his dog. I told him I'd accidentally shorted his payout. Of course, the greedy bastard let me in. I asked him for a glass of water, and as soon as he turned his back, I used my dog's leash to choke the life out of him."

Emma stopped working her wrists. The strap Boyd used on

her looked like a dog leash. Was she tied with the same one he'd used to kill a man?

"And Urban?" Cassie asked.

"If he'd have kept quiet and left town like he was supposed to, it would've been fine. But he decided to go back to his drug dealing ways with the stuff he stole, and that got back to the cops."

"How did you know it got back to the cops?"

Boyd sneered. "Doesn't matter now, does it? None of this matters. And if you're trying to keep me talking to buy time for the cavalry to show up, you're only kidding yourself. Ain't no one coming to your rescue. And now that you know why I'm doing this, it's time to wrap up my mission."

Emma watched in horror as, with a flick of his wrist, he shoved Alissa over the lip of the pool. Cassie lunged for him, her enraged bellow merging with Alissa's shriek.

Boyd stepped back, dodging Cassie and throwing her off balance. Without the use of her hands and arms to catch herself, she dropped to her knees, somehow managing to not go all the way down. Below them, Alissa howled in pain.

Boyd raised the firearm, aiming at Alissa.

And hesitated.

Emma gave one last wrenching tug against the strap. One wrist jerked from its bindings.

Cassie lurched toward him in the same moment as Emma, hands freed, dived for the gun.

A shot reverberated inside the building, nearly drowning Cassie's scream. Emma's fingers closed on Boyd's arm before a second explosion deafened her. She was only vaguely aware of the heat searing her shoulder.

But she was deeply conscious of the sensation of once again falling.

And the impact of the sudden stop at the bottom of the pool.

Chapter Thirty-Two

A chill crept into Matthias's brain, rising from the base of his neck. Around him, the ambient sounds of the detective division stilled, drowned out by a loudening roar within his skull.

He zoomed in on the pair in the photo. The man's head was lowered, his face indiscernible because of a camo ball cap that hid all but a scraggly beard. The dog at his side had its head lowered as well, but not because it was trying to avoid being spotted. The shepherd mix appeared tired. Old.

Daisy. And John Boyd. His clothes were less rumpled than when Matthias had last seen him, but it was definitely Boyd. And Daisy's leash was red, just like the fibers found on Zimmerman's body.

There could only be one reason why Boyd would be outside the house on Cascade. The cliché about killers often being in the crowd when the police showed up to investigate was a cliché because it was true.

Matthias kept the image open while clicking back to the folder from Urban's shooting. He found the best image of the sniper in the window. While his face was hidden, he was wearing the same kind of camo ball cap.

Frazier strode into Major Crimes looking exhausted. "I heard about Cassie. Is there any news?"

Matthias met his gaze.

Frazier's eyes widened. "Oh, my God. What?"

Matthias realized he must've looked crazed. He shook his head, intentionally wiping the anger from his face. "No word yet. But I know who's behind all this."

"Who?" Frazier moved closer as Matthias pointed at his monitor and made room for the other detective. Frazier leaned in. "The dog walker?"

"That's John Boyd."

"The patient at the vet clinic when Shawn was shot?" Frazier let out a breath that sounded like he'd been punched in the gut. "I remember a couple of the neighbors on Cascade mentioned seeing a guy walking his dog the morning of Zimmerman's death. One said she'd never seen him before. But both described him as a sweet old guy with a sweet old dog."

Exactly as he'd seemed both times Matthias interviewed him. "What do we know about Boyd?"

"I ran a background check on him." Frazier strode to his desk. Matthias followed. Less than a minute later, Frazier found and read from his report. "Last known address is Cleveland, Ohio. Both his driver's license and his vehicle registration are expired. Have been for over a year. No criminal record." Frazier sucked a breath through his teeth and spit out a string of profanities.

"What?" Matthias asked.

Frazier didn't reply for a few long moments as he stared at the computer. "Son of a bitch. How the hell did I miss this before? Boyd had a daughter. Oakley O'Donovan."

The name sounded familiar, but it took a second before Matthias remembered why. The incident had happened before he'd been partnered with Cassie, but he knew it had demoralized the entire department. No one more than Cassie, who'd been the one driving the car.

"There's more." Frazier shook his head. "I didn't think anything of it before because his daughter's name hadn't jumped out at me."

"Just tell me."

"According to this, Boyd's an avid hunter. He's carried deer licenses for the last twenty years, including out-of-state licenses for Pennsylvania."

"Which means he can shoot and probably owns a high-powered rifle."

"Like the one that killed Urban."

And barely missed Emma. "You said he has an expired vehicle registration. What kind of car?"

Frazier huffed. "A 1989 Volvo station wagon. That's gotta be a dinosaur."

"And largely invisible. Not the kind of car that attracts attention." Just like an old man with an old dog. "Put out a BOLO on the Volvo and on Boyd." Matthias pulled out his notebook and flipped back to the page from his first interview with Boyd when he'd said where he could be reached. Matthias headed for the door, pocketing the notebook.

"Where are you going?" Frazier called after him.

But he was already halfway down the stairs.

Lake Erie Recycling was located on Tow Road, a stretch of two-lane pavement that ran between two sets of railroad tracks. Matthias slowed as he approached, his muscles tight, his brain vibrating, every nerve on high alert.

The property was bordered by industrial cyclone fencing, but the gate at the edge of the road stood wide open. As he pulled through, the crunch of his tires on gravel sounded deafening. He braked. Waited. Watched.

Matthias wanted stealth on his side. It's why he hadn't told Frazier where he was going. If Boyd did happen to be in there with Cassie, Emma, and Alissa, Matthias would call in the full resources of local and state law enforcement. But right now, he needed to reconnoiter the situation. Quietly.

A single-story metal building occupied the otherwise empty lot. Glass filled the top half of the door in the front of the structure with a CLOSED sign displayed. There was no movement. No activity that Matthias could discern.

He shifted gears and reversed out. The Malibu might not be marked with police emblems, but it screamed *cop*. If anyone was watching, they would think he'd changed his mind and was leaving.

He hoped.

A few hundred feet down the road, he pulled into another lot on the opposite side of the street, this one vacant and shielded by trees. He cut the engine, checked his service weapon and his phone—no messages—and stepped into the mid-morning heat. He thought of the abandoned garage with Elkins's body decomposing inside and hoped he wouldn't find anything like that inside the recycling center's building.

Matthias stood at the edge of the road. No traffic. He gazed toward his destination. Still no movement that he could see. He took a deep breath, then blew it out and sprinted across Tow Road, into the trees.

Undergrowth slowed his progress while keeping him hidden from searching eyes. The stand of trees ran along the train tracks, behind the recycling center. As he made his way through the brambles and vines growing in the shade, doubt began to settle. What were the odds Boyd would take the women to the one place he'd told Matthias to find him. Not good. He'd already left bodies at a deserted warehouse across town and inside a vacant manufacturing facility not far from downtown. He might be from out of state, but he clearly knew his way around Erie. Matthias almost changed his mind. Thought about returning to his car. But then what? Where else could he look?

He kept going. Even if Cassie and Emma weren't here, even if Boyd wasn't here now, he might have been recently. He might've left a clue as to where he'd taken them.

As Matthias drew closer, the rear of the business came into view. Unlike the front lot, four cars were parked near the back of the structure. The boxy profile of one of the vehicles sent a jolt of adrenaline through him.

A Volvo station wagon.

Matthias plowed on, ignoring the wild rose thorns that grabbed at his clothes and drew blood on his bare arms. Once he was directly behind the building, he paused, breathing hard. He swept an arm across his eyes to clear the sweat trickling into them and listened.

Birds chirped in the trees around him. Late summer cicadas buzzed. Somewhere in the distance, a car rumbled over one of the railroad crossings.

Nearer, he heard another sound. More plaintive. More pitiful. Whining. Then a soft yip.

Daisy.

Matthias stepped from the camouflage of the tree line. The cyclone fence blocked his way. He reached high, threaded his fingers through the chainmesh, and hauled himself up as far as he could. The toes of his thick-soled shoes were too wide to fit in the links, but a horizontal pipe midway up provided him with a solid foothold. Gritting his teeth, he muscled his way up. He swung one leg over, grateful whoever had the fence installed hadn't invested in a barbed wire extension on top. Using gravity and momentum, he swung his second leg over and dropped to the ground with a jarring thud. He blocked out the shooting pain in both knees, pivoted, and jogged toward the Volvo. He heard another yip, this one more excited, although still weak. Then he saw her.

The old dog belly-crawled from under the car, dragging a chain hooked to her collar. The other end of the chain was spiked to the ground near the recycling center's back door. Daisy stayed low but crept toward Matthias as far as the chain allowed.

"Hey, girl," he said, closing the distance between them. He kneeled and stroked the dog's head. Her tail thumped as she licked his hand.

He looked around. No water. No food. No empty bowls indicating there had been either. The only shelter on this sultry August day was under the car. The chain looked sufficient to restrain an elephant. Matthias unclipped it from Daisy's collar, and it clanked to the ground. She pressed against him as if he was a port in a storm.

He stroked her. The poor thing was all bones with a dry coarse coat stretched over them. He needed to get her water, food, and to a vet, in that order. Rising, he told her, "Stay." Whether she was well trained or merely too weak to do otherwise, she sat and waited.

Matthias circled the Volvo, noting the Ohio plates. He leaned close and cupped his hands over his eyes to block the glare as he looked inside. Blankets, a pillow, and a duffel bag filled the cargo area. Boyd had said he was sleeping in his car. It appeared that much was the truth. Matthias tried each of the doors. All locked.

He strode to the building's back door. It, too, was locked. A familiar stench filtered out. Decomp.

"Dammit."

Again, he shielded his eyes and peered inside. Bins of metals. A large floor scale. A desk with a phone and a laptop. And as far as he could see, no Emma, Cassie, or Alissa, alive or dead.

But something in there was deceased and had been for a while. Longer than the women and little girl had been missing.

Matthias turned back toward the car and spotted a blackened circle on the ground twenty or so feet away. He moved closer. At first glance, it appeared to be the remnants of a campfire. Logical, if Boyd was staying here. But Matthias dropped to his knees and touched the ashes. Cold. He unsheathed a knife he kept on his belt, opened it, and scraped it through the ashes. Nothing recognizable remained, but he suspected this was how the gloves and N95 masks had been discarded.

Matthias wiped and folded the blade and returned it to its case. Maybe the lab would be able to determine the makeup of the ash.

Back at Daisy's side, he pulled out his phone and called Armstrong.

"I found Boyd's car," Matthias told his lieutenant. He reported what else he'd found, including the stench, and gave him the address. "He left his dog chained here with no water. I need to get her over to Shawn's clinic. If she's microchipped, it might give us more information. Can you have Frazier or Roth get a warrant and take over here?"

"See to the dog. I'll take care of the car and the recycling center."

Matthias thanked him and pocketed the phone. He looked down at Daisy's sorrowful face. Could she make it all the way back to his car? He didn't think so. He briefly considered chaining her again, just long enough to retrieve the Malibu and come back for her, but he couldn't stand the idea of what she would be thinking.

Abandoned again.

He bent down and scooped the bony pooch into his arms before trudging around to the front of the building and across the lot to the road.

Matthias settled Daisy in the back seat of the Malibu before starting the engine. He cranked the AC onto high, then went to the rear of the car and popped the trunk.

He kept extra weapons, ammo, and equipment for just about every conceivable emergency in there. Doggie bowls, however, were lacking. He slammed the lid, returned to the front seat where he kept an insulated water bottle, and thumbed open the cap. "I don't have any food for you, but this should help you feel a little better," he told the dog as he slid into the backseat with her. Cupping a hand, he poured cool water into it. She lapped it up as fast as he could refill his palm.

His heart ached for this sad old girl. She had a crappy owner. And the same asshole who'd left her chained in the heat now had Emma, Cassie, and Alissa.

The bottle ran dry with Daisy still eagerly licking Matthias's hand. He snapped the cap shut, tossed the bottle on the floor, and stroked her head. "Hang in there, girl. I'll get you more."

He stepped out, shut the back door, and climbed behind the wheel.

Matthias phoned West Erie Veterinary Clinic as he drove, alerting them to his imminent arrival. He did not ask to be let in the side door. Something told him Daisy had no qualms about other animals.

He parked at the front and hoisted Daisy from the backseat, again carrying her in his arms. Sharon Long met them as he strode into the lobby, which was filled with owners and pets. Daisy looked around without reacting.

"In here," Sharon said, directing them into an exam room.

"I'll need one of those leashes you keep available," he said.

"No problem." She lifted one from a hook on the wall outside the room and set it on the exam table.

"She also needs water and some food, if you have any available."

Sharon gave him a smile. "Of course. I'll be right back."

Matthias set Daisy on the floor and studied her solemn brown eyes. "If only you could talk."

She wagged her tail.

"I guess maybe you can, in your own way." He dropped into one of the chairs.

A moment later, Sharon returned with two bowls—one of water, the other filled with a small serving of canned food. "We don't want her to eat too much too fast. From the looks of her, she hasn't been well cared for. If she gorges herself, her tummy will likely protest in a very messy way."

From the way Daisy dived into the food, Matthias knew the tech was right. "I understand."

"The doctor will be right with you."

No sooner had Sharon left than Dr. Nathaniel Campbell breezed in. He took one look at the dog and exhaled a sigh. "You know, I should've listened to my gut where that Boyd guy was concerned."

Matthias continued to pet the dog. "What did your gut tell you?"

"Nothing definite. I just had a feeling something was off about him. Daisy didn't seem all that attached to him, especially since he claimed to have owned her since she was a pup. I tried to blame it on her ailments." He gestured to her. "See how she's looking at you?"

Matthias looked down at her. Both bowls were empty, and her eyes were locked on his, her tail sweeping the floor.

"She knows you're trying to help her. She's looking at you the way a pet looks adoringly at their guardian. And you've only had her in your care … how long?"

"A half hour, give or take."

Campbell nodded sadly. "I never saw her look at Mr. Boyd that way." The vet lowered to the floor next to Daisy and began going over her, checking her teeth and gums, her coat, listening to her heart with his stethoscope, and taking her temperature. He shook his head as he checked the thermometer. "She's dehydrated and her temperature is elevated. It's been two days since she was last in here. Poor thing may not have been in great shape then, but if I was to venture an educated guess? I doubt he's fed her or given her water since then. I'll have one of our techs take her back and get her started on IV fluids." He reached into one of the pockets on his white lab coat and came up with a handheld scanner. "But first, let's see if she's chipped." Campbell moved the device over Daisy's shoulders, and it beeped. He looked at the screen. "Yep, she's been microchipped at least. I'll get you the information." He patted the old dog's head and climbed to his feet. "We'll make sure she gets the best care we can give her," he told Matthias and left the room.

Matthias scratched Daisy's ears, as much to calm himself as to soothe her. He felt like a coiled spring. Where had Boyd taken Emma, Cassie, and Alissa? Were they still alive? Here Matthias was, taking the time to care for this dog when he should be out on the street searching for them. But he couldn't just abandon Daisy.

And he didn't know where else to start. The recycling center and the Volvo station wagon were the only ties they had to Boyd. The car, the building, and the old dog.

The door to the exam room opened and Sharon entered holding a sheet of paper, which she handed to Matthias. "The information from the chip lists an animal rescue as owner of record. The address and phone number are on there, along with the chip number. They might be able to tell you more."

Like how they could turn over a sweet old dog to a killer.

Sharon picked up the leash and slipped it over Daisy's head. "I'll take her back now. We'll take good care of her."

"I know you will." He had a feeling he was more concerned for her than Boyd had ever been. As the tech started to lead Daisy out of the room, Matthias stopped her. "Excuse me. Do you have another one of those leashes? In red? It might help with the case."

———

A young woman with a long ponytail and a name badge identifying her as Sterling studied the note Matthias had given her and typed the information into the computer.

The rescue was bright and clean, although a faint smell of dogs and cats filled the air. Photos of happy pups and kittens covered the walls.

The woman straightened. "Okay. Daisy was adopted by a John Boyd two weeks ago."

"Two weeks?" No wonder she'd shown no sign of attachment to the man.

Sterling nodded. "According to our records, he came in and specifically requested an older, special needs dog."

So he would have a legitimate reason to take her to the vet clinic.

"And you just turn over pets to strangers without checking them out at all?"

She stiffened. "Of course not. We run a check on every adoption applicant. And we have them spend time with the animal here, to observe how they interact." She gestured to space off to one side, surrounded by pony walls.

"And how did they interact?"

"They seemed fine. Daisy was quite shy, as I recall, and Mr. Boyd seemed soft spoken and gentle with her."

An act, Matthias thought. Boyd was doing what it took to get what he wanted—revenge for his daughter's horrifying death.

Another memory from that incident rose to the surface. Not just Boyd's daughter. There had been a child in the car that went up in flames.

Matthias swore under his breath.

"Excuse me?" Sterling said.

He cleared his throat. "What about the background check you ran?"

She blushed. "It's not really a background check. Not the way you police do it. We checked to make sure adopters have solid living arrangements, whether they have other pets, that sort of thing. I can give you the form he filled out, if you like."

"Please."

She moved to a file cabinet and riffled through the contents of one drawer before coming up with a sheet of paper. "Here you go."

Matthias took it from her. The address was the same one they already had for him in Cleveland. There was a phone number with a 216 area code, correct for northeast Ohio. The rest were his scrawled answers to questions about his history as a pet owner. Everything looked satisfactory. Except it was all a sham. "Can I get a copy of this?"

"No problem." She scooped up the form and turned away, only to return to him. "Is Daisy all right? I remember she was such a sweet old girl."

"She's fine," Matthias said. "Now."

Chapter Thirty-Three

A shout jarred Emma back to consciousness. She opened her eyes and blinked up at the metal framework of the ceiling high overhead. The throbbing inside her skull and the scorching pain in her shoulder overwhelmed all other senses until Alissa's sobs filtered into Emma's brain. She turned her head to see Cassie's granddaughter curled into a fetal position, hugging her shattered cast.

"Hey!"

Emma recognized the harsh voice as the same one that had snapped her awake. And the same one that had brought them to this nightmare. She searched for the source until her gaze found him standing above them at the edge of the pool.

"You," Boyd said, glaring at her with his soulless eyes. "Is she alive?" He waved a hand but not at Alissa, whose whimpers were proof of life.

"I don't know," Emma mumbled. She took inventory of her own situation, lying flat on her back in the dry pool. She bent one knee, then the other, planting both feet on the ground. Her legs worked. Good. She could remove a broken back from her list of potential injuries. She brought her right hand, still wearing the dog leash as a bracelet, to her left shoulder and winced at the touch. Her hand came away bloody. But when she tried to wiggle her left fingers, they obeyed.

She rolled to her uninjured side and managed to push up to sit. That was when she spotted Cassie lying on her side, unmoving, facing the wall of the pool, her hands still zip tied.

"Grammie," Alissa called out plaintively through her tears.

"*Hey*," Boyd called again, even harsher than before.

Emma looked up at him and spotted the gun aimed at her.

He flicked the weapon's muzzle in Cassie's direction. "Go over there and check to see if she's alive."

"Why? So you can finish the job if she isn't?"

"Exactly."

Emma tried to focus. Tried to think. Weighed her options. Except right now, she didn't have any.

Other than fighting to protect Alissa.

Emma made it to her knees before the world around her started swirling. She planted her good hand on the floor and closed her eyes.

"Hurry up," Boyd growled.

When she opened her eyes and looked up at him again, the gun was aimed at Cassie's granddaughter.

"Like shootin' fish in a barrel," he said with a sneer.

"No. Wait. I'll check for a pulse." Taking deep breaths, hoping the dank air might clear her mind, Emma crawled to Cassie's side. Despite the mental fog, one thought filtered through. If Emma told Boyd that Cassie was alive, he would either correct the situation or kill Alissa.

Or kill all three of them.

But if she told him Cassie was dead, he would still finish off Alissa and Emma.

She reached over Cassie's shoulder and rested her fingers on Cassie's neck. There was no movement.

Emma had watched enough medical and crime TV shows to have seen actors checking for pulses, but she'd never attempted it herself. No matter how she positioned her fingertips, she felt nothing.

"Well?"

She sat back on her heels, her head and her heart so heavy, it was all she could do to not collapse. "There's no pulse."

Emma waited for the next shot, her gaze never leaving Cassie's back. But the only sound was the faint rush of wind from outside. She lifted her focus to Boyd.

He still had his gun trained on Alissa, but his expression, while angry, also seemed to be wavering. Then he heaved a sigh, turned and disappeared toward the entrance. A moment later, chains rattled, and Emma heard what she thought was the click of a padlock snapping shut.

Another wave of nausea struck her, but Alissa's sobs saved her from losing consciousness.

"Alissa," she whispered through the vertigo, "how badly are you hurt?"

"I don't know," she whimpered, then louder she cried, "Grammie!"

Emma blinked back tears as she looked at Cassie's motionless, lifeless form.

Except… Was Emma imagining a slight rising and falling of Cassie's ribcage? She gave her a gentle shake. *"Cassie."*

No reaction.

Emma gingerly rolled her toward her as far as possible with Cassie's wrists still bound … and saw the dark crimson hole in her abdomen as well as the puddle of blood oozing from it, ponding on the pool's floor.

"Oh, God," Emma whispered. She leaned over and pressed an

ear to Cassie's breastbone, listening. At first, she feared she only imagined it, but no. Cassie's heart still beat. "She's alive," Emma called over her shoulder to Alissa.

"Grammie." The little girl didn't sound as relieved as Emma felt.

"Cassie," Emma called sharply and pinched her arm.

Emma wasn't sure which worked, but Cassie groaned.

"That's it. Come on, Cassie. Wake up." Emma bent closer to her ear. "Alissa needs you."

Cassie's eyelids fluttered and parted. She blinked. Her focus cleared as she met Emma's gaze. Then she closed her eyes again, squeezing them shut. "Goddamn," she said, followed by a string of every top-tier curse that Emma had ever heard. She hoped Alissa wasn't taking notes. Finally, Cassie stopped swearing, moaned, and asked, "What the hell happened?"

"We ended up in the pool," Emma said. "And I'm happy to say it's empty, because none of us is in any condition to swim."

Alissa hiccupped. Emma wasn't sure if her sad excuse for humor had brought a laugh or a sob from the little one.

Cassie opened her eyes again, fully this time, and looked around, taking in the situation and settling on her granddaughter. "Baby, are you okay?"

"My arm hurts."

Cassie turned her fearful gaze on Emma. "He shot her?"

Had he? Emma closed her eyes and tried to make sense of what had transpired before they ended up in the pool. Boyd had aimed the gun at Alissa. But he hadn't pulled the trigger. He'd hesitated just long enough for both Cassie and Emma to lunge at him. She recalled two shots. Cassie's scream. Falling. "I don't think so. I know he shot *you*." She touched her own shoulder. "And me. But I'm okay." A lie.

"Go check on her." Cassie jerked her head in Alissa's direction.

Still afraid to attempt standing, Emma crawled on hands and

knees to Alissa's side and settled next to her. "Let me take a look at you. Can you sit up?"

Alissa wiggled upright. "Uh-huh."

Emma noticed a small goose egg—although it was more the size of a robin's egg—on the girl's forehead. "Look at me." As she did, Emma studied her dark eyes. Her pupils appeared to be the same size, which was as much as she knew about an impromptu neurological exam. Equal-sized pupils—good. Different-sized pupils—bad. She pointed at the bump. "Does that hurt?"

"I don't know." Alissa released her broken arm to reach for her forehead, but cried out and grabbed her cast, hugging it close. "My arm hurts."

"Let me see." Emma surveyed what she could without asking Alissa to release her hold on it. Even with a limited view, Emma could tell the cast had broken in the fall. There was no blood, but the shattered fiberglass no longer immobilized the broken arm.

"Is she all right?" Cassie asked.

"She's in the best shape of the three of us, I think." Emma glanced down at the red strap hanging from her wrist. "I have an idea."

After using the leash to create a makeshift sling for Alissa's arm, she guided her over to her grandmother.

"Grammie," Alissa cried out. "You're hurt."

"Yes, I am, baby."

Alissa snuggled in close, resting her head against Cassie's arm.

Cassie managed to bend over and touch her cheek to the top of Alissa's head. "But you know I'm tough, right?"

Alissa nodded.

"Good." Cassie straightened. Her gaze slid to Emma, appraising her with a clarity she'd lacked minutes earlier. "How about you? You took a nasty bump to your head outside. Now you've taken a bullet, too."

Emma fingered her shoulder, trying to ignore the burning pain.

"It's just a graze. The head though? Yeah. I'm pretty sure I have a concussion."

"First Denene, now you." Cassie swallowed hard. "Denene. She must be frantic. I was on the phone with her when Boyd came to the door."

"I remember. I should never have opened it without checking first."

"None of this is your fault. I've been so fixated on Shawn…" Cassie shook her head. "I missed so much. And I call myself a cop. I'm sorry you got dragged into this."

"None of it's your fault either. That guy—Boyd—is nuts."

Cassie barked a short laugh. "I think the proper term is bat-shit crazy." Her gaze swept the pool before settling back on Emma. "What happened? I remember—" She glanced down at Alissa snuggled against her and lowered her voice. "I thought he was going to shoot her. But he … didn't. I tried to get to him and the gun. The rest is a blur."

"I managed to get my hands free, and I grabbed for the gun, but it went off. Next thing I knew, I thought my shoulder was on fire. And I was falling."

Cassie grunted. "Thanks for trying. You probably did more to save my baby girl than I did."

Emma lifted her gaze to the rim of the pool. "I don't know about that. We aren't safe yet. He's gone for now, but he might come back."

Cassie shook her head. "I doubt it. Coming back here would be stupid. No. I think he left us here to die a slow death."

"I heard him chain the doors on his way out. We're locked in."

"There has to be more than one exit." Cassie took a long look at Alissa before coming back to Emma. "You have to go for help." Before Emma could argue, she added, "And you have to take Alissa with you."

"I'm not leaving you here."

"I'm not able to travel, and you know it. From what I could see when we were in the van, we aren't exactly close to civilization. It's gonna be a hike."

Emma had seen the same landscape through the windshield as Cassie. She was right about it being a hike. And about her not being able to walk that far. She was bleeding. Not a pulsing spurt, but her life was slowly seeping from her body. Emma looked around. At the far side of the pool, glass doors led to an even darker, more foreboding space. "This building looks like it used to be some sort of school or community center, although what community, I have no idea. There must be a first aid kit around somewhere."

"Even bandaged up, I can't make it as far as the road. You need to leave me here. I'll be fine until you get back."

"I'm not planning to bandage you up to make the trip. But I do want to try to stop the bleeding. Or at least slow it while I'm gone."

Cassie started to reply, but closed her lips, looking at Alissa and thinking. When she broke her silence, she said, "Alissa, baby, can you do something for your grammie?"

She looked up at Cassie and nodded.

"If Emma can help you get out of this hole in the ground, I need you to look around. Try to find a first aid kit."

Emma started to protest.

"Don't go too far. If you can't find one real close, you come right back. Okay?"

"Okay."

"She should stay here," Emma said. "I'll go."

"Let her," Cassie said, fixing Emma with a determined stare. "I have something else for you to do."

Emma knew there would be no arguing. She searched the pool's walls for a way out. There were no steps. The metal ladders had all been removed and sat, useless, on the walkway around the pool. Part of John Boyd's preparation, Emma bet. Boosting Alissa out with one injured arm would be a challenge. Hoisting herself out would be an even bigger one.

Resigned, Emma climbed gingerly to her feet and closed her eyes against the dizziness that swamped her. A couple of deep breaths later, she opened them again. The world around her settled, although she had a feeling it was only temporary. She reached out a hand to Alissa. "Let's get you out of here."

The little girl stood and took the hand. Emma led her to the shallowest part of the pool. Any other day, it would be an easy task to lift an eight-year-old three feet. Today, nothing was easy. Emma bent down and placed her hands around Alissa's tiny waist. "You're gonna have to help me by giving a big jump when I count to three. Can you do that?"

"I'm good at jumping. I take gymnastics."

"All right then." Emma counted with Alissa bending her knees for one and two. On three, she popped off the ground, allowing Emma to guide her over the edge.

And not drop her.

Alissa scrambled to her feet, while clutching her arm. "I'm okay," she assured Emma. Then louder, she said, "I'm okay, Grammie."

"Good," Cassie called out. "Now do what I told you. Go find a first aid kit."

Emma returned to Cassie's side and dropped to her knees. "I'm worried about her going too far. We don't know what else is in this building."

"That's why I need you to listen to me. You have to take her with you and get out of here. Find the nearest house or gas station or whatever and call for help."

"I can travel faster if I leave her with you."

Cassie's eyes suddenly brimmed with tears. "Do this for me. Take her." Her voice cracked. "I don't want her to watch me die."

"You're not—" The look on Cassie's face cut Emma off. Cassie had said she was tough. Emma knew this was true, but this could be her biggest battle … mortally wounded and fighting to keep it from her granddaughter. "Okay," Emma said.

"And don't worry about trying to bandage me up. That'd just be wasting time."

The sound of small footsteps pounding their way interrupted them. "I found one!" Alissa cried. "I found a first aid kit!"

"Well, I'll be damned," Cassie said with a soft chuckle. "That's my girl." Then she locked gazes with Emma. "But I told you—"

"I heard you." Emma stood and rested her elbows on the top edge of the pool. "Bring it here," she said to Alissa.

The little girl squatted and watched as Emma flipped open the ancient metal box's lid. She liked what she saw. "Good job. Stay right there."

Emma lowered the kit to Cassie's side, ignoring the virtual daggers shooting at her from Cassie's eyes. Emma pulled out a pair of scissors. "I'm going to cut you loose. Then you can take care of bandaging yourself. Okay?"

Cassie's expression softened. "You tell Matthias he's got a smart cookie for a girlfriend."

"You can tell him yourself when I bring him and the rest of the Erie PD back here." Emma meant it but could tell from the tears glistening in Cassie's eyes that she wasn't holding out any hope.

"One other thing," she said in a whisper. "Tell Shawn I will love him forever."

Chapter Thirty-Four

Matthias's phone vibrated before he could get to the lab to drop off the leash. Armstrong's name lit the screen.

"Where are you?" the lieutenant demanded.

"On my way to the lab."

"I need you to get back to the recycling center. Frazier's attending Elkins's autopsy and Roth is canvassing Cassie's neighborhood." Armstrong's voice sounded too tense to be merely redirecting resources.

"Do we have a warrant for the recycling center yet?"

"We're way past that. Patrol officers have already made entry." He paused before adding, "They found three bodies inside. All three are male."

He'd hoped the eau de decomp back there was from a dead raccoon. Or ten. Emma, Cassie, and Alissa hadn't been gone long enough to have started decomposing, but hearing the bodies weren't them was still a relief. "On my way."

Ten minutes later, Matthias pulled through the gates into Lake Erie Recycling. No longer empty, the lot buzzed with law enforcement. The officer at the front door logged Matthias in.

A trio of uniforms stood vigil at one dark corner of the building. Two more bent over a desk at the structure's other end. One of the uniforms near the corner waved to Matthias, gesturing him over. They parted as he approached, giving him a clear look at the decedents. All three were crumpled on the floor, two face up, one on his belly. The first had suffered a gunshot wound to his face, the second to his chest, and the prone man who must have turned to run, had been shot in the back. All three wore navy workpants and striped uniform shirts with their names embroidered above the breast pockets. At least, Matthias assumed the third man had his name on his shirt, the same as his coworkers.

"Is the coroner on his way?" he asked.

"Hamilton's in autopsy," one of the officers said. "They're sending a deputy."

Elkins's postmortem. "Right. Do we know anything about these guys?"

"Caleb and Bert, according to their shirts," the officer said flatly. He pointed across the space to the other uniforms. "You might want to talk to them."

Matthias nodded and crossed to the desk. "What have you got?"

The younger of the two stayed bent over a laptop. The older cop straightened and faced Matthias. "Inspector Gadget here used to work for some nerd squad, fixing computers, and he's damned good at hacking. Of course, you didn't hear it from me. Anyhow, he managed to get into this computer."

Without looking up, the young cop said, "It belongs to our suspect."

"Boyd?" Matthias asked.

"Yep. I thought it was the business's laptop at first. But it's definitely Boyd's."

Matthias looked over his shoulder. "Find anything? Like where he took Cassie?" And Emma. And Alissa.

"Not yet, but I'm working on it."

The rear door—the one Matthias had peered into earlier—swung open and Officer Kollman strode in, holding a paper evidence bag. When he spotted Matthias, he headed toward him. "Detective. Guess what we found in the Volvo."

Matthias met him halfway.

Kollman aimed a thumb over his shoulder. "Bolt action Remington .30-06 with a scope."

The rifle that killed Urban.

"Two Taurus .38 revolvers," Kollman continued.

"Two?" There had been three.

"Yeah." From Kollman's tone, he knew the ramifications of that missing handgun. "We also found Zimmerman's missing wallet with his ID. No cash or credit cards though." He held up the evidence bag. "And then there's this." He removed what at first appeared to be a walkie-talkie.

But Matthias realized it was much more than that. "A police scanner?"

Kollman's eyes were wide, his jaw tight. "With all of our frequencies programmed into it."

Roth had been right. That's how Boyd always stayed one step ahead of them. He knew where they were headed and managed to get there first. Zimmerman. Urban.

Elkins? He'd been dead for days.

But Urban?

Boyd had probably known they were moving in on Urban and followed the police chase on the scanner. He knew they'd lost their suspect in the vicinity of the old warehouse. During the hours they had searched for Urban, Boyd had slipped into the building and waited.

But how did he know his way in and around the warehouse? It was abandoned. Had been for decades.

"I don't know if this means anything or not," the young cop dubbed Inspector Gadget said from behind Matthias.

"What is it?" Matthias thanked Kollman and returned to the laptop.

"I checked his browser history. He's been spending a lot of time studying maps of Erie and surrounding areas, but this is what I find interesting." Inspector Gadget moved aside to give Matthias a clear view.

The website on Boyd's computer was titled *Haunted and Abandoned Buildings Near Erie*. "There's a website for this?" Matthias asked.

Gadget chuckled. "There's a website for *everything*." He grew serious. "Some people like to explore caverns. Others like to sneak into vacant structures. There are pages and pages of photos from inside old churches, old train stations, old—"

"Warehouses?"

"Absolutely. Look." The young cop clicked a link and images of the warehouse on 16th popped up. He continued clicking through a series of photos. "It's a virtual tour of the place, including hidden entrances, interior stairwells, and a few tunnels."

Matthias swore.

Inspector Gadget kept clicking. "Look at this."

Another series of photos came up, this time from the building where Elkins's body had been found.

"I didn't realize how many abandoned buildings we had around here," Gadget said. "According to Boyd's browser history, he spent hours viewing dozens of them."

Matthias stepped back and ran a hand through his hair. "Boyd has a thing for old buildings," he said, thinking out loud. "What if he's taken Emma, Cassie, and Alissa to one of these?" He looked across the room at the cops standing around the three dead bodies. What if that was the condition they would eventually find the women in? What if they already were too late? It had been hours. He'd had plenty of time to do God only knew what to them.

But if Boyd wanted them dead, he could've killed them at Cassie's house, Matthias reminded himself, trying to drown out the mental images of a murdered little girl, of his partner, and of the woman he loved. He needed to stay focused and tamp down his emotional ties to this case if he had any hope of finding them.

Matthias stepped closer to the laptop. "Can you tell which of these locations Boyd spent the most time viewing?"

Inspector Gadget clicked a few keys and grinned up at Matthias. "I can do one better. He actually bookmarked several of them. The warehouse and the place on West 19th were two. There are six more."

"Can you narrow it down a little?"

Gadget looked at him. "I'm good with a computer, sir. I'm not a mind reader."

Matthias's phone vibrated in his pocket. He yanked it out to see Roth on the screen.

"I thought you should know," the detective said, "we found a number of Cassie's neighbors with security video that caught the van as it was leaving. Combined with traffic cams, I was able to track it as far as Old French Road, northbound. We're checking footage for the van after that, but so far, nothing."

Northbound on Old French Road placed him headed for downtown. Or east or west on one of the major arteries. "Thanks, Roth." Matthias ended the call and looked at Inspector Gadget. "Eliminate locations south of the Malone residence. What's that leave us?"

He tapped the keyboard, squinting at the map on the screen. "Four."

Still too many, but better than six. "I need those addresses."

The young cop scribbled on a notepad and handed the page to Matthias, who thanked him and strode toward the door while placing a call to the lieutenant. "We have four possible addresses." Matthias punched through the door as he read them to Armstrong.

"I'm sending units to all four. Which one are you taking?"

Matthias paused outside his car and studied the list. Where would Boyd have taken them? All four were secluded. Matthias had a twenty-five-percent chance of guessing right.

He picked the closest one. "I'm headed to the old motel on Millfair."

Chapter Thirty-Five

With Cassie freed of the zip ties, Emma clambered out of the pool and held out a hand to Alissa, who took it. "We're going for help."

Alissa's chin quivered. "I wanna stay with Grammie."

"Go with Emma, baby," Cassie called out. "You find help and come back for me. You hear me?"

"Okay." But Alissa sounded as unsure as Emma felt.

"Come on." Emma hid her fear, intentionally coloring her voice with a perky inflection. "Let's go find a way out of here."

The obvious choice was the one Emma most doubted. The doors through which they'd entered were now closed. She pushed on one. It gave, but only a couple of inches, the padlocked chain holding firm. The windows contained no glass but were too small for Emma to climb through and too high for Alissa. The child had already almost been run down and thrown into an empty pool. The last thing she needed was another fall. Before giving up, Emma noted the dark clouds overhead and a distant rumble of thunder.

"Let's see where else we can get out," she told Alissa.

At the opposite end of the pool, a glass wall, mostly shattered, framed two sets of graffiti-tagged doors. Emma looked down at the glass shards while noting Alissa's sandals and bare toes. At least Emma was wearing thick-soled athletic shoes.

"I'm going to carry you, so you don't cut your feet, okay?"

Alissa nodded.

Emma hoisted her onto her hip, careful of their injured arms, and selected the opening that appeared least likely to slice and dice them. Once through and clear, she set Alissa down and took her hand.

The interior would've made a great setting for a Halloween haunted house. Plywood covered the windows. Even if it had been sunny out, not enough daylight seeped in to brighten the space. In the shadowy rafters, wings fluttered. Birds? Or bats? Emma didn't want to know. As long as they stayed up there, she wasn't going to think about them. The stale air reeked of excrement. Human or animal? Both, she suspected and filed the question away with the bird/bat one.

Hand-in-hand, they picked their way along a wide center hallway. Rooms, their doors hanging open, sometimes dangling on a single hinge, flanked both sides. After a few minutes, Emma's eyes adjusted, giving her a clearer view of their situation, which only meant she could read the often-vulgar graffiti and confirm the fluttering came from unhappily disturbed bats, not birds.

Alissa clung to her hand and pressed tightly to her side. "We're going to be fine," Emma said. "And so is your grandma."

Alissa made a soft noncommittal sound in her throat.

A few hundred feet into the belly of the brick beast, the hallway turned ninety degrees to the right. Straight ahead, another set of broken glass doors opened into a gymnasium, its wooden floor now a canvas for the graffiti artists. To the right, the hallway continued, and Emma drew a breath of hope. At the far end, an unlit exit sign hung over a set of wooden doors. She couldn't be sure due to the distance and deceptive shadows, but it appeared one of the doors stood ajar.

"Come on," Emma said and took off at a jog with Alissa alongside. The soles of their shoes slapped a beat that echoed into the bat-infested rafters. But three strides into the run, Emma's head rebelled. She stopped and squeezed her eyes tight against rising nausea.

"What's wrong?" Alissa asked.

"I just—I need a minute." Emma took a deep, slow breath. In through the nose, out through the lips. Her stomach settled. She opened her eyes. The world no longer tilted. "Okay. I'm fine now."

They continued at a walk.

She'd been right. One of the doors stood slightly open, and when she hit it, the door swung wide, letting in fresh air, and hazy gray light. They were free.

"Let's find help," Emma said.

Together, they skirted the exterior of the building, keeping close to the brick and battling the overgrown grass and brambles whose tendrils reached for them, snagging their clothes. They turned the corner. Ahead, through the nearly waist-high weeds, Emma spotted the driveway. She led the way, batting down the grass to make the going easier for Alissa. Once they reached the pavement, they turned their backs on the old building—and Cassie—and hiked toward the road.

They'd made it as far as an open pipe gate halfway down the drive when the clouds split, and rain pelted them. Emma's first instinct was to move faster, but the threat of vertigo and Alissa's short legs limited their pace. Besides, Emma realized, they had no shelter to run to. By the time they reached the two-lane road, they were soaked. "I guess you can only get so wet, and we've reached that point," she said with forced mirth. "Even my underwear is wet."

"Mine, too." Alissa looked up at her with a wrinkled nose and droplets dripping from her curls.

Emma glanced in both directions, evaluating their options. They'd made a left turn when Boyd drove them here. Heading back the way they'd come seemed like the obvious choice. But what if they were closer to civilization if they went the other way? "Do you have any idea where we are?" she asked.

"No."

"Me neither."

Alissa tugged on Emma's hand, drawing her to the right. "Come on. We have to get help for Grammie."

Right was as good a choice as any. "Yes, we do." Emma stayed between Alissa and the road on the narrow berm as they trudged the long straight stretch of road into the gloom. Yesterday, Emma had been sweating. Today, with her clothes saturated, the slight breeze chilled her to the bone. Poor Alissa had to be cold, too. Emma squinted through the gray misty rain, hoping to see headlights, hoping to hear the swish of tires on the pavement. All she needed was a good Samaritan to stop and make a phone call for her.

If the same good Samaritan wanted to let two dripping waifs shelter inside their car while they waited for the police, so much the better.

But all she saw was the haze of the rainfall, and all she heard was the spatter of rain on the leaves, the roadbed, and her head and shoulders.

They trod on for what felt like an eternity, before the gleam of headlights appeared in the distance, coming their way.

"Stay here," Emma told Alissa, placing both hands on her shoulders as if trying to plant her in place. Then Emma checked behind them to make sure a vehicle wasn't coming the other way and stepped out onto the road. She stopped on the yellow center line as the vehicle approached and waved her hands.

The car didn't show any signs of slowing. Emma contemplated stepping into its path and decided that was a really bad idea. Cassie hadn't wanted Alissa to watch her die. Likewise, Emma didn't want the little girl to witness her becoming roadkill.

"Hey!" Emma shouted as the car barreled toward her. "Stop! Help!"

With the heavy rain, the driver probably didn't see her until they were almost on top of her. Then the car swerved, dropping off the road before veering back on.

And speeding away.

Emma watched the red taillights fade into the mist and muttered a few words she would never say loud enough for Alissa to hear. With a sigh, she returned to the girl and held out her hand. "That's okay. The next one will stop."

"I hope so," she said, her voice almost swallowed by the downpour. Emma wasn't sure if the droplets streaming down Alissa's cheeks were tears or rain.

Probably both, she decided as they continued shambling along the road.

The sky in the distance seemed to lighten, or perhaps it was Emma's wishful thinking. But no, the driving downpour softened into a steady drizzle. "I bet the sun comes out pretty soon," she said, trying to cheer Alissa.

Through chattering teeth, the youngster managed to sing a few lines of the song from *Annie*.

"You've got a great voice," Emma told her.

"Thanks."

Ahead, another set of headlights pierced the gloomy mist.

"Look," Alissa said, pointing.

With better visibility, Emma hoped the driver would see them and stop. But as the headlights grew closer, she saw they were attached to a white van.

Her throat closed. She reminded herself that there were

hundreds of white vans in the area. Odds were slim this was the same one, driven by the same man. But her instincts screamed, *Run. Hide.* Slim odds or not, it wasn't worth the risk.

Emma took Alissa by the shoulders and directed her off the berm and into the thicket. "We have to hide."

"It's the bad man?"

"I don't know, but I don't want to find out."

Alissa didn't argue, and they both hunkered down in the wet weeds. Emma held her breath as the vehicle drew closer. Was Boyd returning? Had he seen them before they ducked into the undergrowth? Her heart hammered within her chest and pulsed in her ears.

They recoiled as the van rolled past. Through the rain and the streaked driver's window, Emma caught a clear view of the driver.

John Boyd.

Alissa saw, too. "That's him," she whispered.

"I know. Stay here." Crouching low, Emma stepped closer to the road's edge and peered out at the van, watching it roll away from them and toward the driveway to the building where they'd left Cassie. The van's turn signals came on, and, to Emma's horror, it turned in. What if Boyd discovered Cassie was still alive? And alone?

Alissa was clearly thinking the same thing. "Grammie," she cried, her voice trembling.

Emma couldn't breathe. They were miles from the nearest house or business. Traffic was almost nonexistent. Going for help now felt a lot like abandoning Cassie to certain death at the hands of a madman.

But taking Alissa back there wasn't an option either. Emma considered sending Alissa on alone while she returned to help Cassie, and quickly realized the absurdity of the idea. She couldn't leave an eight-year-old wandering out here by herself.

A steady soft whoosh filtered through the noise of her thoughts. Emma turned to see another set of headlights approaching. Another van, but not white this time. Potential roadkill or not, Emma stepped onto the pavement, waving both hands. The vehicle didn't slow.

"Stop, you son of a bitch," she whispered and took one more step, standing dead center in the oncoming lane, squarely in the headlight beams, and extended both arms, palms toward the van. "Stop!" she bellowed at the top of her lungs.

She knew the moment the driver spotted her. The vehicle's brakes locked up on the wet pavement. The van started to hydroplane, skidding to one side. She caught a glimpse of the driver's wide, panicked eyes—a woman, her hands battling the wheel. Emma heard Alissa's scream and struggled to unroot her feet as the broadside of the van screeched toward her.

Chapter Thirty-Six

Squinting through the blinding rain, Matthias circled the crumbling and rutted lot at the abandoned Millfair Travel Lodge before parking. Two marked units joined him to search the exterior of the building on foot. None of the boarded windows appeared to have been tampered with. Matthias ignored the downpour and personally checked every door of the single-story motel only to find all locked and secured with no signs of forced entry.

He battled away the mental images of Emma, held captive, alone, waiting for him to find her. No, not alone. She was with Cassie, and Cassie was as tough as they came. Cassie would keep Emma safe.

He hoped.

He phoned the lieutenant and reported in. "Nothing here. Have teams arrived at the other locations?"

"I've heard from Roth. His crew has cleared the old grocery store. Another team is currently searching the bowling alley. I'm waiting to hear if they find anything. Frazier's team is still en route. Wait. I've got another call."

Matthias returned to his car while Armstrong kept him on hold. The lieutenant came back on the line as Matthias slid behind the wheel. "The bowling alley is clear. Frazier's still five minutes out."

And then there was one. "Tell Frazier I'm on my way to his location." Matthias slipped his phone into the holder mounted on the dashboard, started the engine, and gunned it out of the parking lot. He was at least fifteen minutes away and sensed they would be the longest fifteen minutes of his life.

Rain pelted Emma's face. Every nerve in her body sizzled with jabs of electricity. Around her, screams of hysteria merged with the recognizable cries from Alissa. A terrified woman's face floated above her.

"Oh my God," the woman said. "I'm so sorry. Are you all right?"

"Yeah," she whispered.

"We didn't mean to hit you."

"You didn't." Emma replayed the past few moments. The van skidding toward her. She'd attempted to leap free and wasn't sure whether her vertigo or the rain-slicked pavement caused her to lose her footing. "I tripped trying to get out of the way."

Alissa was crying out to her. "Emma! Emma!"

She raised an arm and offered a gentle wave. "I'm okay." Barely.

"Can you get up?" the woman asked.

"I think so." Emma rolled to one side—the wrong side—and fell back. That was the arm the bullet had grazed. She tried the other side. Better. Not great, but at least she managed to curl her knees in and push up to a nearly seated position.

Her back burned from landing on the road. Her head and her

arm still throbbed from earlier. She was going to be one big bruise if she survived this day.

The woman offered a hand, which Emma grasped, and helped her to her feet. "I probably shouldn't have moved you—"

"That's okay," Emma said, willing the world around her to stop spinning.

When it did, everything else slammed into her. Alissa. Cassie. Boyd.

Boyd was heading back to Cassie. Was probably already inside the building.

"I need to use your phone to call the police."

"My sister has already called 911 about the accident."

"I still need to use your phone. Please." Emma looked at Alissa. The dripping, shivering child appeared ready to drop from the combination of cold, exhaustion, and fear.

"Sure," the woman said and guided Emma and Alissa to the van. "You two need to get inside to warm up."

It sounded good to Emma.

"I'm Suzanne, by the way." The woman slid open the side door revealing four youngsters from pre-teen to pre-toddler strapped in a car seat. "We were on our way home from the park when it started to rain. Then you stepped out in front of us. I'm so sorry. My sister's driving and did her best to stop."

"I know. And she did. Stop, I mean. Thank goodness." Emma watched as Suzanne helped Alissa inside, then put one foot on the step to join her.

But Alissa turned and blocked her. "You have to go back and help Grammie."

Emma's mind spiraled. She'd been thinking the same thing, but what could she do other than call for help? She was unarmed and had no training beyond the self-defense maneuvers Matthias had been trying to teach her.

Alissa's chin quivered. "Grammie told us to go for help and

then come back for her. We found help. Now you have to go back."

Emma noticed she'd said, *you*. Not *we*. Maybe Alissa was more attuned to the situation than Emma had given her credit for.

But Cassie had entrusted Alissa to Emma. Here she was, thinking about leaving Alissa with a van full of strangers. The women and the kids seemed harmless—normal—enough. Surely, they weren't part of Boyd's plan.

Emma shook her head—a mistake. She closed her eyes against the fireworks popping behind her eyes. Once they cleared, she realized Alissa was right. These women were moms. They would be the best caretakers for Alissa until the police arrived.

Emma opened her eyes and fixed her gaze on the little girl. "You call 911. Tell them where we are." Emma turned to Suzanne. "Where are we? I'm completely lost. There's an abandoned building down that way." Emma gestured.

"That's the old Gorge Community Center. It's been vacant for as long as I remember."

Emma turned again to Alissa. "Tell them who your grandma is and that she's being held at the old Gorge Community Center. And tell the dispatcher to get word to Matthias. Can you do all that?"

Alissa nodded determinedly.

"Good girl." Emma stepped back and faced Suzanne. "Take care of her. I have to go help her grandma."

"We can drive you," Suzanne said.

"No." The last thing Emma wanted was to put this family in jeopardy. "The best thing you can do is wait here for the police. I'll be fine." Emma gave her a smile she didn't feel.

Suzanne reached out to her. "Wait. You're hurt. You say her grandmother is being held against her will? You don't look like you're in any condition to help her."

Alissa choked a sob. "You have to. Please."

"She's right," Emma said. "I have to at least try."

Suzanne shook her head, but her sister leaned across the center console and popped open the glove box. "Here," she said, rummaging through the contents and coming up with a utility knife. "It's not much, but it's the closest thing to a weapon I keep in the van."

Emma gave her a weak smile and accepted the knife. "Thanks." To Alissa, she said, "I'll be back," before turning and breaking into a slow jog, back the way she'd come.

Matthias roared toward the fourth target location—the only one left that hadn't been cleared—when his phone buzzed, and Armstrong's name lit the screen.

"Frazier called in and gave the all-clear on the old scout camp."

Matthias eased off the pressure on the gas pedal as the weight within his chest doubled. "What do you mean?"

"Just what I said. They searched every cabin on the grounds. Nothing. No sign of anyone having been there in ages."

How could that be? They'd narrowed down Boyd's possible locations to those four vacant buildings. Now all four were a bust. They were no closer to finding Cassie, Emma, and Alissa than they'd been hours ago ... hours they'd wasted. Hours that Emma and the Malones might not have had.

"Come back to the office. We'll regroup. Maybe the crime scene techs will find something we missed at the garage."

"I'm not coming back without them." Matthias realized how amateurish he sounded and didn't care. "Call me if you get anything." He hit the red button and flung the phone onto the passenger seat.

Hands clenched, Matthias pulled off the road and jammed the shifter into park.

He needed to think. Where would Boyd go? Where would he take them? And what would he do to them? Matthias closed his eyes against images he'd encountered over the years. Brutalized victims. Unrecognizable bodies. Were the woman he loved and his partner and little Alissa destined to a similar fate? Matthias leaned forward, letting his forehead rest on the steering wheel. *Think.*

The phone buzzed, and once again, Armstrong's name appeared.

Matthias exhaled and answered it.

"Dispatch just alerted me to a phone call they received."

"From Cassie?" Matthias asked.

"From Alissa."

Emma kept to as brisk a pace as she could manage without feeling her brain bouncing against the inside of her skull. She made the turn into the driveway to the community center within a few minutes. The rain had all but stopped, and the heat generated by the exertion drove away the chill. At least for now.

She couldn't see the white van. Hadn't expected to. When Boyd brought them here, he'd pulled around the far end of the building. He'd likely done the same this time. Rather than risk him spotting her, she cut through the weeds to the far side of the structure, and eased along the exterior wall, the same way she'd led Alissa out. The same brambles grabbed for her, but she battled through, ignoring the thorns ripping her arms and clothes.

The door through which she'd escaped remained open. Before slipping inside, she hesitated and questioned what the hell she was doing. Boyd was armed and vicious. All she had was a utility knife jammed into one of her crew socks. What could she do to save Cassie from the killer? If Cassie wasn't already dead.

But Alissa would call 911. The dispatcher would alert Matthias. All Emma had to do was keep Boyd distracted—keep Cassie alive —long enough for help to arrive.

She could do this.

She had no choice.

Emma stepped inside and stopped to survey the hallway. During her previous trip through the building, her goal had been to get out as fast as possible. This time, she needed to be alert and aware of every sound, every shadow.

The building sure didn't smell any better. Ignoring the stench, she crept silently down the hallway, pausing to peer into each room. One open door led into what must have been a janitor's closet. Emma entered, giving her eyes time to adjust to an even deeper darkness than the hall. This room had no windows. She instinctively tried the light switch, but nothing happened, which, she realized, was a good thing. She needed to be smarter. Not give her presence away to Boyd.

Her eyes acclimated and she scanned what sparse supplies remained. Not much. Vandals had cleaned out most of what had been left behind.

An array of jugs and bottles lined one shelf in the back corner. Closer inspection revealed several contained caustic chemicals meant to cut through industrial strength grime. They would also do a number if splashed in someone's eyes.

She found a plastic spray bottle with about an inch of blue liquid in the bottom and unscrewed the lid. A quick sniff of ammonia told her it was glass cleaner. She dumped what was left into a galvanized bucket, grabbed a gallon of the nasty stuff bearing multiple warning labels, and carefully filled the spray bottle with it. The fumes choked her. Probably hazardous to her health, she thought, but no worse than facing an armed killer.

Sprayer in hand, Emma turned to leave, but another wave of dizziness threw her off balance. She grabbed for one of the shelves, caught herself, but kicked over the bucket with a clank.

Emma froze. Held her breath. Listened.

Nothing. Not even a flutter from the bats overhead.

Exhaling, she stepped out of the room and made her way down the hall.

As she approached the turn at the gymnasium, she listened for sounds coming from the direction of the pool. No voices. If Cassie was already dead, Boyd would have no one to talk to.

What if he found Cassie's body and left? Alissa and the family in the minivan could be in more danger than Emma was. The thought chilled her.

But no. She hadn't seen the van on her way in. Hadn't heard it drive past since she'd been inside. He had to still be here.

Above her head, she heard the rustle of restless bats. She looked up, willing them to be still.

From the corner of her eye, she caught a blur of movement. She sidestepped. Turned toward the source. But too late. Boyd leaped from the shadows. Grabbed her. And sent her spray bottle weapon flying across the floor.

Chapter Thirty-Seven

Matthias pressed the gas pedal into the Malibu's floorboards, careening southwest along a two-lane road. The rain-soaked greenery edging the route flashed past in a blur.

The Gorge Community Center had been one of the locations on Boyd's computer, but Matthias had ordered teams to the northern possibilities because the van had been spotted heading that direction. Now, he couldn't breathe. If anything happened to Emma, Cassie, or Alissa, it was all on him because he delayed the tactical response.

But Alissa had been the one to call 911. She was safe at least. So, what had happened to the other two? It couldn't be good. Otherwise, why have an eight-year-old place the emergency call?

Matthias replayed his brief conversation with Armstrong. Alissa had told the emergency dispatcher that her grandmother was seriously hurt, and Emma was going back to help her. Alissa had also said the bad man had returned.

Emma was going back to help Cassie. Against Boyd. Who'd already done something awful to Cassie and who had already killed six men that Matthias knew of.

He'd been seeking comfort in the knowledge that Emma was with Cassie, and Cassie would keep her safe.

Which was not the case.

After an unbearable length of time, he spotted a minivan at the side of the road. He knew he was getting close to the old community center and slowed, stopping across from the vehicle.

A woman lowered the driver's window, and he did likewise. A smaller face appeared next to the woman's.

"Uncle Matthias!" Alissa called out.

He identified himself to the woman before focusing on Cassie's granddaughter. "Where's your grandma, Alissa?"

She burst into tears and pointed down the road. "In the swimming pool. She's hurt. Bad."

For a fleeting moment, he pictured Cassie floating, face down, in water. "In the swimming pool?"

"There's no water in it. It's like a big hole. And she can't get out." Alissa's sobs overwhelmed her, turning her words into gasps between hiccups. "The bad man. Shot us. Left us. But came back. Emma—went to save Grammie."

Matthias gave her the best smile he could force. "Don't worry. I'm here now and more police are only a few minutes out." To the driver, he asked, "Do you know how much farther it is to the community center?"

"It's right up there." With a trembling hand, she gestured down the straight stretch of road. "No more than a quarter mile on the left."

He thought about asking if they'd heard gunshots, but decided, no, they would've mentioned it if they had, and he didn't want to send Alissa into a deeper meltdown. "Can you keep her a little while longer?"

"No problem."

"Thanks. One more thing. I want you to move your vehicle to a different location. There's a gas station a couple of miles west of here."

She gave an anxious nod. "We know it."

"Good. Go there and wait." The last thing he wanted was for Boyd to escape and spot them sitting here.

"Okay."

As soon as the minivan drove away, Matthias continued toward the community center, terrified of what he might find.

Once he made the left into the overgrown driveway, he assessed the property. A squat red-brick structure with broken windows perched among high weeds and a few pine trees. Beyond, he spotted the sprawling yellow-brick building. He'd come here once when he first moved to Erie. Some fellow cops belonged to a volleyball league that used the center for their games and had invited him to watch. Volleyball wasn't his thing, so he'd only attended once. But it was enough to give him the lay of the land. At least how it used to be.

He cruised to the pipe gate, which hung open, and stopped long enough to radio in his status. Three more units were en route but still ten minutes out.

Dammit. Ten minutes. So much could happen in ten minutes.

He remembered the parking lot at the far end of the building. The pool entrance. Alissa had told him Cassie was in the pool. That had to mean Boyd was back there.

Matthias knew he should wait for backup. Cassie would be the first one to tell him so. But no way was he giving Boyd ten more minutes with the two women he cared most about in the world. Since he didn't have backup, he hoped Boyd was still unaware of his presence so he could rely on the element of surprise.

He shut off the ignition, stepped out, and circled to the Malibu's trunk. Once geared up with additional firearms and ammunition, he started toward the building on foot.

For the fourth time in one day, Emma's bones ached from hitting the ground. For the second time, the ground was the concrete floor of the empty pool.

Boyd had used duct tape to bind her wrists behind her back, leaving none of the wiggle room the nylon strap had offered. Then he'd shoved her into the pool once more.

She looked over at Cassie's motionless body. She didn't so much as flinch when Emma landed next to her. This time, she feared Cassie really was dead.

Boyd glared down at them from the pool's edge. "Don't waste your time grieving your friend. You'll be dead, too, soon enough. Where's the kid?"

"Gone," Emma said.

"Bullshit. You've hidden her here somewhere."

Despite Emma's sodden clothes, Boyd thought Alissa was still in the building. Emma pressed her lips closed. Let him believe that.

"Where is she?" he demanded, each word a snarl.

Emma glared at him, refusing to answer.

He pulled his gun from the waistband of his pants and aimed it at her. "Tell me or I'll shoot you."

"You're going to kill me anyway."

"True. But I can make it quick and easy, or I can make it slow and painful."

She cringed at the thought. Cassie had tasked her with keeping Alissa safe, and it wasn't a task Emma took lightly. She'd succeeded in getting Alissa away from this killer and planned to keep it that way.

How long until the cops arrived?

"Why do you care where she is?" Emma asked. "I saw you. You had your chance to shoot her before and didn't."

"You're right." He lowered his gun. His eyes shifted, and he suddenly appeared old. Tired. "When I looked at that little girl, I saw my own granddaughter, and I couldn't..." He exhaled, his shoulders sagging. "Now her bitch of a grandmother's dead. I can't do anything else to make her suffer. I decided to walk away and let fate deal with you and the kid." His gaze slid toward the doors leading outside. "I went to get my car and my computer to get the hell out of here, but there were cops crawling all over the place."

Emma's heart surged with hope. Matthias was on Boyd's trail.

Boyd brought his focus back to her, all signs of contrition gone. "Now, all bets are off." He again raised the gun. "Last chance. Tell me where the girl is, and I'll kill you quick so you won't have to watch her die."

Emma raised her chin in defiance.

A demonic smile crossed Boyd's face. "Have it your way. Slow and painful it is."

"Wait," Emma cried out. She needed to stay alive until the police could get here. "Okay. But I don't know exactly where she is. I told her to hide while I went for help. I was trying to find her when you grabbed me. That's the God's honest truth." She silently apologized to her late mother for taking the Lord's name in vain. And during a lie, no less.

Boyd's lip curled in a snarl. "You went for help."

"And it's coming, too. The cops will be here any minute now."

He stuffed the gun into his waistband. "Not in time. I'll find her myself."

Emma opened her mouth to protest. Why not leave Alissa and get the hell out of here? Cassie was already dead. There was no reason for him to continue to make her pay by harming her family.

Except, he'd said all bets were off. He had no intention of running.

Emma closed her mouth and watched him storm away. From the pool, she could hear his boots crunch through the shattered glass doors and fade into the dark hallway.

She exhaled, half relief, half anguish.

"Is Alissa safe?"

Emma looked at Cassie, stunned. "You're alive."

"For now." She didn't move, her voice a weak whisper.

"Alissa is safe. A couple of moms with their kids in a minivan stopped for us. I left her with them to call 911."

"Help's coming?"

"Yeah. I just don't know how soon."

"Is Boyd gone?"

"For now. He's searching the building for Alissa."

"I heard." Cassie slowly rolled up to sit with her back to the side of the pool. She'd been curled around the first aid kit, concealing it from Boyd. Her shirt and a wad of gauze pads were soaked with blood, but her hands were still free. "When I heard him coming back, I kept playing dead, hoping he wouldn't shoot me again just to be sure."

"He still might when he doesn't find Alissa."

"Let's hope my brothers in blue get here first."

Emma knew the police would be closing in fast and soon. Cassie was one of them. But Boyd was already here.

"I know what you're thinking," Cassie whispered. "It's a crap shoot. And we're sitting ducks. Sorry for mixing my metaphors."

Except... "I think I have an idea," Emma said. "You keep on playing dead."

The agony on Cassie's face was replaced by a scowl. "And he'll shoot you instead."

"Only if he can find me." Emma scooted around, extending one leg toward Cassie. "In my sock."

Cassie reached for Emma's ankle and retrieved the utility knife. She smiled. "Smart girl. Matthias better hang onto you."

If I'm alive, Emma thought. She turned her back and her bound wrists to Cassie. "Cut me loose." Emma felt the pressure of the blade and then was free. "Thanks." She peeled the tape away and stuffed it in her pocket. She didn't want to leave it for Boyd to find and realize Cassie was still a threat.

"Now what?"

"I'm not sure."

"I am." Cassie held out the knife. "You get out of here."

"You should keep that. At least you'll be armed."

"That only works if he gets close enough. He'll shoot me again before he risks that. For now, he's written me off and will go looking for you, so you need to run like hell."

Emma decided Cassie was partly right. Emma needed to get out of there. Lure him away. He would search for her.

But she wasn't going to run, even if she could. She had another plan.

Or at least the start of one. She accepted and pocketed the knife before clambering out of the pool.

Unlike when Emma had previously checked the doors to the parking lot, one of them opened when she pushed on it. She stepped outside and made sure the door closed behind her. She looked at the dangling chain and open padlock. For a moment, she considered locking Boyd inside but realized she'd be locking him in with Cassie. No. Emma's intention was to draw him away from Cassie but not let him escape.

The white van was parked right where she'd last seen it after falling out and smacking her head. She pondered her options, opened the driver's door and popped the hood. Before closing the door, she checked the ignition. Empty. If Boyd had left the keys, taking them would be an even simpler solution, but he wasn't that stupid.

Emma circled to the front and heaved open the hood. She wished she'd paid more attention to her dad when he'd worked on the family's car when she was a kid. Swallowing, she reached in, closed her fingers around a handful of wires, and yanked.

After letting the hood drop shut with a clunk, she circled to the passenger side, pulled the utility knife from her pocket, bent over, and sunk the blade into the tire's sidewall. For good measure, she did the same on the back tire. Overkill? Maybe. But she wanted to make damn sure the only way Boyd was leaving here was in the back of a patrol car.

"I see you hiding back there." Boyd's voice curdled Emma's stomach. "Come on out."

She peered around the rear of the van. He stood just outside the community center's doors, his gun at his side.

Emma was certain he hadn't seen what she was doing. And she hadn't heard a gunshot, so she prayed Cassie was still *feigning* death. Concealing the utility knife, she crossed her wrists behind her back as if still bound and stepped clear.

"You really thought I was stupid enough to let you get away again?"

"No," Emma said, acting way cockier than she felt. "I think you're stupid enough to let me distract you so Alissa could escape."

Boyd's eye twitched. He believed her. The thought of being outsmarted enraged him. He stormed toward her, his fury driving her back a step. He brought his gun up, aimed at Emma's face. She retreated another step.

"Stop moving," he ordered.

"And give you an easy target? I don't think so."

Boyd lowered the gun slightly and laughed. "You've got sass, I'll give you that much."

She strained, listening for the sound of sirens that weren't there. "The police are gonna be here any second now."

"It doesn't matter. That bitch cop who killed my family is dead. I'll take that knowledge to my grave and be satisfied."

"So, why not cut your losses and take off?"

"Take off where? I got nothing. No one. Nope. I'm not going on the run, and I'm not going to jail."

Emma caught a glimpse of movement from the corner of her eye.

"Police," Matthias barked. "Drop your weapon."

Chapter Thirty-Eight

Matthias held his sidearm steady, braced against the brick corner of the community center. Boyd was aiming his gun at Emma. Matthias noted the blood soaking her arm and splotching her clothes but kept his concentration on the gunman. Emma was alive, and Matthias meant to keep her that way.

The moment he barked his orders for Boyd to lower his weapon, Emma turned her head in Matthias's direction. Instead of complying, Boyd lunged for her with the quickness of a snake, spun her around, and pulled her against him with one arm across her chest, the other pressing the muzzle of his handgun against her neck. She tensed, her pleading gaze on Matthias.

"Go ahead and shoot," Boyd said with a sneer. "This ain't the movies where you can pick me off at this distance with that pistol and not risk hitting her, too."

"I thought that's what you wanted," Emma said, her voice measured to be directed at Boyd but just loud enough that Matthias could hear. "Suicide by cop."

Boyd whispered something back to her that Matthias couldn't

make out. If what she said was true, Boyd was even more dangerous. He had nothing to lose and knew it.

Matthias grew hyper vigilant, hyper focused on Boyd, but not to the point of ignoring the rest of the scene. When he'd first arrived at the corner of the building, Emma's back was to him, her hands behind her. He'd assumed they were tied. But when Boyd grabbed her and spun her around, her hands had dropped to her sides and remained there, fists clenched. She was up to something, and Boyd was too intent on Matthias to notice.

Matthias and Emma had been in a similar set of circumstances once before. That time, she'd freed herself just long enough for the cops surrounding them to take the guy out. He met her gaze, and she dropped her chin in a miniscule nod of acknowledgment. She was thinking of that same incident. And he was ready.

"Now, Boyd," Matthias said, keeping his tone even, "you know I'm not going to risk shooting her. But I'm not letting you leave either. Put your gun down, let her go, and we can all live to see another day."

"Not gonna happen. I put my gun down and you're gonna blow me away. You're not gonna let me live. Not with that dead cop inside."

Cassie? Dead? Matthias had been afraid to wonder why Emma was out here alone with Boyd. Cassie would've done everything in her power to protect Emma, especially since Emma was the one who got Alissa to safety. He swallowed down the rage mixed with bile that rose into his throat.

Boyd pressed the gun harder against Emma's neck, and she winced. "I'll tell you what is gonna happen, though. She and I are gonna get in this van and drive away. You and your cop cronies are gonna stay clear. I'll let her go as soon as I'm well away and I know you aren't tailing me."

"Sorry. You're too savvy about police procedure to believe we won't follow you to the ends of the earth. You've killed too many people already. You'd never let her live."

"You're not going anywhere in that van anyway," Emma said. "Both tires on the other side are flat."

"What?" he snapped, shifting his full attention to her. "What did you do?"

She locked gazes with Matthias. "Now!"

Her right hand jerked as if punching Boyd in the thigh. He howled. Released her. And grabbed his leg. Emma twisted away but stumbled.

Cursing, Boyd wheeled toward her, raising his gun.

And Matthias squeezed off three shots.

Boyd flinched as the first one struck. His knees buckled after the second. At the third, he crashed face down, and his handgun skittered across the broken concrete.

Emma stood rigid, fists still clenched.

Matthias approached Boyd, keeping his sidearm aimed at the killer in case he still managed to move.

He didn't.

Matthias kicked the dropped weapon clear before squatting at Boyd's side. He slid his fingers to the groove in Boyd's neck. There was no pulse. "He's dead."

Rising, Matthias turned to Emma and surveyed her. Her wide eyes were locked onto Boyd's body, her face colorless. Her clothes were soaked from the earlier rain but also with blood. She clearly had an injury to one arm, but that couldn't account for all of it. Cassie's blood, he thought, fighting off the sickening weight of grief. Instead, he focused on her hand, also crimson.

She must've noticed him looking. Slowly she raised that arm, opened her palm, and let a utility knife with a bloody blade slip from her grasp.

She hadn't punched Boyd in the thigh. She'd stabbed him.

Matthias holstered his weapon and moved toward her,

reaching for her. But she backed away and looked toward the community center.

"Cassie's inside. You need to get an ambulance here."

It took a moment for her meaning to sink in. "An ambulance? For Cassie? She's...?" He let the question hang, afraid of the answer, afraid he'd misinterpreted Emma's words.

"She's alive." Emma broke away and staggered toward the doors, beckoning him to follow. "At least she was a few minutes ago."

Chapter Thirty-Nine

M atthias walked into Cassie's hospital room to be greeted by an assembly of walking—and *not* walking—wounded, all victims of John Boyd's vendetta. Cassie sat in her hospital bed, head raised, a smile on her face. Shawn, recovered enough to have been discharged from the ICU, sat in a wheelchair beside her. Denene perched near the foot of her mother's bed. Alissa sat in her lap, using the rolling bedside table as a desk to hold her art supplies.

Emma stood off to one side with a bandaged arm and—Matthias knew—a mild concussion. She looked his way as he entered and smiled. The most beautiful smile he'd ever seen.

Cassie's smile was a close second.

He'd come so close to losing both of them.

"Come in," Cassie called to him, "but only as long as you don't burst into tears."

"I don't burst into tears," he replied with as much indignation as he could muster. He crossed to Emma's side and slipped an arm around her waist.

"Aren't they cute?" Cassie asked Shawn.

"Adorable," he answered flatly, but with a twinkle in his eye.

"Stop," Matthias said with an unconvincing growl.

Cassie's gaze slid to Emma and a look passed between them.

"What?" he asked Emma.

She shook her head.

He looked to Cassie, who heaved an exaggerated sigh. "There was a moment back there when I didn't believe I was going to make it. Emma was injured but still managed to cut me free and set me up with a first aid kit—"

"I helped," Alissa protested.

"Yes, you did, baby. You absolutely did." Cassie brought her gaze back to Matthias. "Anyway, you, Detective Honeywell, have a smart cookie for a girlfriend. I wanted her to tell you I said that, but she insisted I do it myself." Cassie flipped one hand. "So there. I told you."

He pulled Emma closer. "No argument from me."

"Enough of that." Cassie lifted her chin at Matthias, looking smug. "Are you going to adopt that dog or not?"

"Daisy?" He squirmed. "I would love to, but my landlord doesn't allow pets. We need to find her a home, though."

Shawn chuckled. "Cassie's just giving you a rough time. Nathaniel's adopting her. He fell in love with the sweet old girl."

Matthias smiled his approval. With Dr. Nathaniel Campbell, Daisy would finally have the good life she deserved. "Good. I'm glad to hear it."

Cassie's gaze shifted to her daughter and granddaughter, and a vexed scowl crossed her face.

"What is it?" Matthias asked.

She shook her head. "I suppose with that son of a b—" She winced. "Son of a *gun*. With that son of a gun dead, we'll never know, but I sure am curious about how he knew the exact moment my girls were going to cross the street."

"I may have the answer to that," Matthias said. At her raised eyebrow, he explained. "The tech guys were able to pull GPS information off the car he was driving. Looks like he was surveilling the hospital for days. Apparently, knowing that Shawn was here, he decided to park on 3rd where he could keep an eye open for you or your family."

Denene snorted. "That would explain how he seemed to come out of nowhere."

Alissa slapped her marker down on the tray and shot a determined look at her grandmother. "Grammie, you haven't told me when we're going to Splash Lagoon. You promised we'd go before school starts."

Denene snickered.

Matthias remembered Cassie mentioning those plans last Friday. Nearly a week had passed since then. A week that felt like a decade.

Cassie looked at Shawn. "Uh…"

Denene gave her daughter a squeeze. "I think Grammie and Pappy aren't going to be riding the rollercoaster anytime soon. And how much fun are you going to be able to have with a broken arm?"

Alissa pouted. "But I still wanna go."

Denene sighed. "Tell you what. As soon as the doctor gives me the all-clear, I'll take you. We can go on the gentler rides and play the games."

Cassie cleared her throat. "And we'll take you again after we're all healed up."

"I get to go twice?" Alissa beamed. "Okay."

A nurse breezed into the room and came to a stop. "You do realize there's a limit of two visitors to a bedside, don't you?"

"I'm on police business," Matthias said, striking a stern pose.

Shawn raised his chin in defiance. "I'm not a visitor. I'm a fellow patient."

"I have no excuse." Denene pointed at the child on her lap. "But she's underaged and doesn't count, right?"

Emma raised both hands. "I have no excuse either."

Denene pointed at Emma while speaking to the nurse. "There you have it. The two of us are the only real visitors, so we're in compliance."

The nurse shook her head and snickered. "I'm sorry, but I still have to break up this party." She focused on Shawn. "I have to take you back to your room. Lunch will be coming soon and we're not bringing yours here."

"Blasted green Jell-o," he grumbled as the nurse wheeled him out, but he blew a kiss at his wife before they left the room. "I'll be back this afternoon."

"If you aren't, I'll come looking for you," Cassie called after him.

"Speaking of lunch," Denene said, setting Alissa on the floor and standing, "I'm going to get out of here and take my daughter to that taco place since we didn't make it last time."

"Drive," Cassie said. "Don't walk."

"Count on it."

Matthias removed his arm from around Emma's waist and took her hand instead. "Food sounds good. Since I'm on desk duty because of the officer-involved shooting, how about I take you out for a nice leisurely lunch."

"You're on," she said.

Cassie raised a hand. "Matthias, you go on. Emma can catch up to you. I need to talk to her for a minute. Alone."

He gave Emma a questioning look. She shrugged *I don't know.* He pressed a kiss to her cheek. "I'll wait for you in the lobby."

———

"Shut the door," Cassie told Emma once Matthias had exited.

Emma obeyed while wondering what the heck this was about. After they'd both been shot and left to die, there was darned little Cassie could say that would shock her.

Back at the bedside, Emma rested both hands on the side rail. "What's up?"

"At my house, before Boyd showed up, we were having a talk."

Emma thought back. "Before Boyd" felt like a decade ago.

"You were telling me about a story you'd found in the newspaper archives."

"Oh." Emma remembered. "Justin Wheeler's death."

Cassie nodded. "This has to stay just between us, okay?"

"Okay."

"That accident. I knew about it."

Not what Emma expected.

"The original report stated Shawn was driving," Cassie said.

"And subsequent reports listed Jerry Bain as the driver."

"Both reports were true."

"What?" Emma studied Cassie's passive face. "How can both kids have been driving?"

"Shawn started out behind the wheel, but realized he was too drunk. He wanted to call a cab, but his buddy Jerry insisted that they just switch. Jerry was better at holding his liquor than Shawn, but the fact is he was equally impaired. Maybe more so. Jerry was driving when they hit and killed Justin Wheeler, but Shawn wanted to save his friend by taking the blame. Thankfully, a good lawyer sorted out the mess. The whole thing has haunted Shawn since it happened."

"And you knew all this?"

"Yes. I've always known. And now so do you. I'm hoping you can keep it as quiet as I have."

Emma rolled it around in her mind. "Matthias?"

"Doesn't know. Doesn't need to know. It's ancient history and had nothing to do with any of what's happened in the last couple of weeks."

Except Matthias *did* know. She'd told him. She felt her cheeks flush. "So what harm would there be in telling Matthias?"

Cassie's gaze darkened. "Because I gave Shawn my word decades ago. You found out on your own. Okay. But I'm asking you…" She raised an eyebrow. "Don't let this go any further."

Emma lowered her gaze, debating whether she should confess.

"Oh, no." Cassie exhaled a raspy sigh. "You already told him."

Apparently, Cassie could read her as well as Matthias could. "I'm sorry," Emma said. "I was trying to help him find out who—"

Cassie dismissed her with a wave. "It doesn't matter, I suppose. I know you didn't mean any harm." She fixed Emma with a fierce stare. "What about that reporter you work with?"

"He was helping me dig through the archives. But I'll make sure Preston drops it. There's no story for him there anyway."

Cassie contemplated Emma's words, and her expression gradually grew calm. She nodded. "I … we … would appreciate that."

Chapter Forty

Matthias stood at his stove, sautéing onions and garlic in preparation of adding shrimp and a medley of vegetables. His shrimp curry was one of Emma's favorite dishes, and this evening, he planned to pamper her. The sauce was already made, the jasmine rice steaming. Unbeknownst to her, a slab of chocolate cheesecake from the Irish pub downstairs was stashed in his fridge.

She sat at the kitchen island, scrolling through her phone and sipping from a bottle of water. Usually, her refusal of wine or beer would mean she planned to drive back to the campground after dinner. Not tonight. He already knew she intended to stay. But due to the concussion, her doctor had strongly advised against all alcoholic beverages.

Matthias noticed she stopped scrolling and frowned. "What's wrong?" he asked when the frown deepened.

She didn't meet his gaze but drew a deep breath before exhaling long and slow. It took a few moments before she lifted her eyes to his. "Remember when I was here last?"

"When I fell asleep." It would take more than a shrimp curry dinner to live that one down.

"Do you remember anything about what I was telling you?"

He slid the shrimp into the pan and reached for the salt. "Something about a call from Eric and your property down in Washington County."

She nodded and lowered her gaze. "A land developer made an offer on the farm."

"What kind of offer?" Matthias wasn't sure he wanted to know.

"Over half a million dollars."

He whistled, keeping his focus on her face while battling to keep his own expression neutral. "Are you going to accept?"

"I don't know. It's ... complicated."

A word a lot of women used with regards to Matthias, but he didn't tell her that.

"Eric thinks he can negotiate more money. He thinks we could convince Sonny to let me keep a few acres and buy the rest."

"Sonny?"

"Sonny Jones. *Greyson* Jones, the developer in question."

Matthias's mind raced. He shifted his attention to the shrimp. The last thing he wanted was to burn dinner because he was wondering what Emma's future plans were. They'd never discussed anything beyond the present. Plans for the upcoming weekend were as far as they ever got.

Not that he hadn't ventured a few thoughts on the matter over the last few months. And at this moment, he wanted nothing as much as he wanted her to let go of her ties to her old home—sell the whole thing—and stay in Erie. With him.

Tempting fate, he asked, "What do you want to do?"

Another heavy sigh. "I don't know. Eric makes some good points."

Such as? He wanted to ask. But was suddenly terrified of her answer.

"It's a lot of money," she said. "But that property's all I have left of my family." Her voice grew softer. "After the fires ... the land is the only thing that wasn't taken from me."

Matthias knew what she meant. The fires. Plural. Two homes. Two arsons. One arsonist.

"And then there's the other part of it."

He looked at her. "What other part?" But the answer came to him before she spoke the name.

"Nell. Our parents left the farm to both of us. It's in both our names. I can't do anything without her."

And no one knew where Nell was. Matthias had been keeping feelers out to no avail. "Then it seems like a moot point. You can't sell."

"Exactly." She picked up her phone from the countertop and cradled it in both hands. "Eric knows that, yet he's still pushing. And over the last few days, he's left half a dozen messages. Both text and voicemail. I haven't looked at any of them. Haven't answered his calls."

Matthias dumped the prepared vegetables into the skillet, which erupted in a burst of steam and sizzle. "Why not?" he asked.

She raised one sexy-as-hell eyebrow at him. "I've been a little *tied up.*"

He bit back a grin. "Smart ass."

Her gaze slid back to the phone. "Besides that, though, I've had a feeling there's more to it. Something he knows but doesn't want to tell me."

"About Nell?"

Emma shrugged. "Maybe."

"Maybe," he echoed, giving her a raised eyebrow of his own, "you should check the messages he sent."

"Yeah..." She dragged the word out, took a breath, and thumbed the screen.

Matthias pretended to pay full attention to the skillet, giving the shrimp and vegetables a stir before pouring the curry sauce over the mixture. But through the steam, he furtively watched her expression as she read, clicked, and read some more.

Then she stopped and eyed the phone as if it had grown fangs.

"What is it?" he asked.

"A link." She swallowed.

"For what?"

"I don't know. He's just very insistent that I look at whatever it is. If it wasn't him, I'd be leery it was one of those spam links."

"Call him. Ask him what it's about."

"I'll listen to his voice messages first." She thumbed to another app and put the phone to her ear. "More of the same," she said as she listened. "Think about this offer. We can get him to go higher. That sort of thing." She palmed the phone, selected another message, and placed the phone back to her ear. This time, her expression changed to puzzlement. "The link is legit. He just ordered me to check it out and then call him."

Matthias gave the curry a stir, wiped his hands on his apron, and held one out. "Give it to me. I'll look at it for you."

"No. I'm good." She gave him a weak grin. "Thanks, though."

Emma scrolled and clicked. And read. The color drained from her cheeks and her lips parted.

"What is it?" Matthias asked.

She swallowed and handed the phone to him.

He shut off the burner before taking it.

The link had opened to a newspaper from Cleveland, Ohio. An obituary for one Ezekiel Allen Dyson. It only took a second for the name to register. Zeke. The man Nell had run off with.

The man Emma had been hoping would keep her on the straight and narrow. And safe.

Matthias met Emma's gaze, her eyes brimming. Then he went back to the obit, reading it in detail.

Ezekiel, better known to his friends and family as Zeke, had passed away three days earlier. Unexpectedly, according to the report, his death a result of a long battle with addiction, which finally was too much for him to endure.

Matthias skimmed through the names of those he'd left behind—his mother, a sister, two brothers, and a pair of nephews. His father was listed as deceased. Nell wasn't mentioned at all.

"Did you notice where he died?" Emma asked.

Matthias scrolled back to the top and read before meeting her gaze. "Washington Hospital, Washington, Pennsylvania?"

She nodded.

He understood. Zeke died where Emma and Nell had grown up. Where their family farm property was located. Matthias returned the phone.

Emma hit a button, put the phone to her ear, and stepped away from the island.

Matthias removed a pair of bowls from a cabinet and dished out rice, topping it with the shrimp curry. Emma spoke in a low voice, but not so low as to be secretive. She spent the first minute or so explaining to Eric why she hadn't responded sooner. Apparently, he grew apologetic when he learned she'd been kidnapped.

"It's okay. I know I should've been in touch sooner, but it's been an ordeal," Emma said. "What's going on? Zeke's dead?"

Only the clink of bowls and silverware against the quartz countertop filled the next long moments, along with an occasional "Uh-huh" from Emma. But then she inhaled sharply. "Where is she?" Silence. "You should've told me," she said, her tone icy. "Yes, I know… Of course… I'll be there tomorrow."

Emma stood facing away from the kitchen as she slid the

phone into her hip pocket. When she turned toward Matthias, she looked equal parts dumbstruck and determined.

He rounded the island and closed the distance between them. "What do you need me to do?"

Her gaze skirted the kitchen, the floor, the ceiling, before settling on him. "Nell's alive. Both she and Zeke are—were—using again. He... Well, you know what happened to him."

"Nell?"

"For the last few days, she's been staying with Eric. He's been in contact with her for a couple of weeks now, but she made him swear not to tell me."

"And now?"

"He's afraid of what she's going to do next." Emma swallowed. "I need to go there."

Matthias repeated his question. "What do you need me to do?"

She stepped into his arms and buried her face against his neck, her tears damp on his skin. "You're still on administrative leave, right?"

"Yep."

"Go with me?"

He pressed a kiss into her hair. "Absolutely. Before or after we eat?"

She choked a weepy laugh. "After. Definitely after."

Acknowledgments

While writing a novel is often a solitary endeavor, I'm grateful to have a wonderful team of experts on the email equivalent of speed dial: Adam Richardson of the Writers Detective Bureau and Sean Bogart of the Erie Bureau of Police help me with law enforcement issues; Holly Tonini guides me through the photography details; Chris Herndon provides answers to my autopsy questions; and Paul Sutton made sure I got the Army details right. If you find mistakes in any of these areas, I take full ownership.

Thanks to Sharon Long for lending her name to one of the characters and to the owners of Sara's Campground for granting me permission to use their business as Emma's home. However, if you visit Erie, PA, and try to find Emma's site, rest assured you won't. I created an entirely fictional area within the campground. All that's really there is a cliff.

For their eagle-eyes and valued opinions, I thank Donnell Ann Bell, my incredible beta reader and Jeff Boarts, Liz Milliron, and Peter W.J. Hayes, my fabulous critique buddies.

I'm ever so grateful to my agent, Paula Munier, for her support and guidance.

And finally, a big shout of thanks to the entire team at One More Chapter, especially my editor, Jennie Rothwell. You take my words and make them shine.

On the shore of Lake Erie, Pennsylvania, a body lays half hidden, the waves slowly moving it with the rising tide...

In the early morning mist, freelance photographer Emma Anderson takes pictures of the rocky coastline. She moved to Erie to escape a past that haunts her but the last thing she expects to capture is a dead body.

AVAILABLE IN EBOOK AND PAPERBACK NOW

When a badly decomposed body is found in the basement of an abandoned warehouse, Erie police detective, Matthias Honeywell, is called in to investigate.

Meanwhile, freelance photographer Emma Anderson is desperately trying to find her drug-addicted sister, Nell. Then a devastating piece of evidence found at Detective Honeywell's crime scene brings her world crashing down, a driver's license belonging to her missing sister.

In need of her assistance, Matthias asks Emma to help with the case, hoping to solve the mysterious disappearance of Nell Anderson. But in doing so, will the investigation uncover more questions than answers?

AVAILABLE IN EBOOK AND PAPERBACK NOW

When a murderous ghost from Erie City Police Detective Matthias Honeywell's past appears unexpectedly, his investigation into a double homicide in a quiet neighborhood gets complicated, and puts everything and everyone he cares about at risk.

Emma Anderson's first day as the crime beat photographer for ErieLIVE wasn't meant to see her photographing the scene of her predecessor's murder, and with ties to the victim as well as a deadly fire that follows in the wake of the crime, she fears she may also be in the killer's sightlines.

To solve the case and catch the killer, Matthias and Emma will have to face their own demons. But what happens when the devil himself comes calling?

AVAILABLE IN EBOOK AND PAPERBACK NOW

The author and One More Chapter would like to thank everyone who contributed to the publication of this story...

Analytics
Imogen Wolstencroft

Audio
Fionnuala Barrett
Ciara Briggs

Contracts
Laura Amos
Inigo Vyvyan

Design
Lucy Bennett
Fiona Greenway
Liane Payne
Dean Russell

Digital Sales
Laura Daley
Lydia Grainge
Hannah Lismore

eCommerce
Laura Carpenter
Madeline ODonovan
Charlotte Stevens
Christina Storey
Jo Surman
Rachel Ward

Editorial
Janet Marie Adkins
Rosie Best
Kara Daniel
Simon Fox
Charlotte Ledger
Jennie Rothwell
Sofia Salazar Studer
Helen Williams

Harper360
Emily Gerbner
Ariana Juarez
Jean Marie Kelly
emma sullivan
Sophia Wilhelm

International Sales
Peter Borcsok
Ruth Burrow
Bethan Moore
Colleen Simpson

Inventory
Sarah Callaghan
Kirsty Norman

Marketing & Publicity
Chloe Cummings
Grace Edwards
Katie Sadler

Operations
Melissa Okusanya
Hannah Stamp

Production
Denis Manson
Simon Moore
Francesca Tuzzeo

Rights
Ashton Mucha
Alisah Saghir
Zoe Shine
Aisling Smyth
Lucy Vanderbilt

Trade Marketing
Ben Hurd
Eleanor Slater

The HarperCollins Distribution Team

The HarperCollins Finance & Royalties Team

The HarperCollins Legal Team

The HarperCollins Technology Team

UK Sales
Isabel Coburn
Jay Cochrane
Sabina Lewis
Holly Martin
Harriet Williams
Leah Woods

And every other essential link in the chain from delivery drivers to booksellers to librarians and beyond!

One More Chapter is an
award-winning global
division of HarperCollins.

Subscribe to our newsletter to get our
latest eBook deals and stay up to date
with all our new releases!

signup.harpercollins.co.uk/
join/signup-omc

Meet the team at
www.onemorechapter.com

Follow us!

@onemorechapterhc

Do you write unputdownable fiction?
We love to hear from new voices.
Find out how to submit your novel at
www.onemorechapter.com/submissions